WE COULD FALL

WE COULD FALL

KATE MOSCHANDREAS

TABLE OF CONTENTS

Monday, September 23:
The milky paleness

There was the name again. His handwriting, black ball-point pen. He ran his finger across it. *Emmy Halperin.* Duncan had noticed the scrawled words on his script's back cover when practicing his lines in front of the mirror a month ago. And during the two weeks of table readings in L.A., the same name had stared up at him. He'd read the two words dozens, maybe hundreds, of times; yet, he had no idea who Emmy Halperin was.

There was no phone number, just the name, which was curious. *Why would he write the name of someone without any other information?* He wondered if it could be a journalist or the assistant of another actor he knew. He reviewed the people involved in this production – make-up crew, production assistants, wardrobe, and director's assistants. There was no Emmy. Up until now, he hadn't let this mystery bother him, figuring it would come to him eventually; he was usually so good with names. But this morning he couldn't let it go. *Who the fuck was Emmy Halperin?*

A heavy knock hit against his hotel room door. He opened it to a skinny young Four Seasons porter who wheeled in a cart full of coffee and covered dishes. The young, peach-fuzzed man poured the coffee, then handed Duncan a slip of paper; "Excuse me, Mr. Grier, I'm supposed to give you this note."

It was from Kallie: "Waiting for you downstairs in the car. Hurry if you can." There was a heart squiggled by her name. Duncan crumpled the note and grabbed cash for a tip.

It wasn't good to be late the first day of a shoot. But now that Kallie had asked him to hurry, he didn't want to. He carried his coffee mug into the dim bedroom that still smelled of his sleep. With a solid tug, he flung open the blackout drapes. *Holy crap, the world was bright.* The hotel windows were floor to ceiling, and Duncan searched for a latch to get some air; there was none. From behind the plate glass, he looked down on the Boston Public Gardens. A bike messenger zigged and zagged; a young couple kissed good-bye at a corner; suited people plodded toward their destinations. Peering at the Gardens from above, he couldn't help feeling the scene had a totality, that each person fit into the space like a piece of a jigsaw puzzle. Duncan wanted to fit. As soon as this simple thought articulated itself, he wished it hadn't. He moved away from the window's brightness.

It was nerves agitating him this morning, that's all. Undressing for the shower, he rolled his head and shook his arms, trying to wring the gloom out of his body. A lot was riding on his work over the next few weeks, and though he'd made it his business to assure everyone he "couldn't wait to begin," the truth was he didn't know what he was doing. He showered. He dressed. *Suppose Kallie was right?* This role could make him a joke. Throughout their fifteen years of working together, Kallie had never been as insistent as she was about *The Visiting Professor.* "This is not the movie to fix your career lull," she said. "The film's not your genre, and no matter how brilliant your acting, no one's going to accept the Grier as a nervous, nebbish-y guy having a mid-life crisis. It's not your type, and, sorry, it's too late to change that."

Duncan didn't tell Kallie he was sick of his type. He didn't explain he was, in fact, desperate to find a different type. No, that conversation would be too difficult to have.

Now, ready to leave, he grabbed his script and was just about to walk out the door. But there was the name again. *Emmy Halperin.* He had to believe if he applied himself he'd be able to remember how this woman's name came to be written on his script. Like scratching an itch in the middle of his back, he couldn't not try. He pulled out his cell phone and typed Emmy Halperin into the search engine. Nothing came up that made sense. Stuff about the Emmy awards. A journalist for *The Economist.* Then, on a whim, he typed in "Emmy Halperin + Boston, MA." And there it was: Dr. Emmy Halperin, with her Cambridge address, map and phone number.

A *doctor.* Now it came to him. The skinny dipper. With a wave of relief, he realized: Emmy Halperin could be part of his next five weeks in Boston. Before he let himself question the soundness of this idea, he touched the number to call her.

Emmy Halperin was trying to do two things: remember the dream and make coffee. To her surprise she found she couldn't do both at once. When she pressed the button on the coffee grinder, the abrasive *grrrr* from the small machine disrupted the dream's wispy euphoria, making it slip further away. She pushed the coffee machine's button to start and walked to the center of her big, white kitchen. Closing her eyes, she made her drowsy body stand pencil straight and held her arms open and outward, like a dancer about to take a spin. She wanted to will the dream's swirly happiness back into her being. The dream's joy had felt so very good.

"You doing yoga?" Jack walked into the kitchen. "Or is that your new way of making coffee?" Her husband's quips were usually phrased so that to the unpracticed ear they sounded like affectionate teases. But Emmy's ear was practiced; she heard no affection.

Lowering her arms, she muttered something about the coffee being almost ready, and turned to walk out of the kitchen, figuring she'd come back to get her cup when Jack wasn't there.

Jack called after her. "Emmy, there's actually something I'd like to… ask you about."

Emmy's walk stopped. There was a nervousness in her husband's voice, and having lived twenty-two of her forty-two years with Jack, she knew he was rarely nervous. Maybe this meant he was finally ready to talk about the plan. She'd turned back; she'd been waiting three weeks for this conversation. Her stomach tightened like a ribbon was being cinched around it.

"You know how Anthony Trippolli and I are working on those Weston library designs together. Last night, we were at the office pretty late, and the idea came up that we should have him and Francesca over for dinner sometime." He glanced up at Emmy, then back at his cup. "Anthony said October 12th would be good for them."

Emmy waited for him to continue, but that was it. Emmy stumbled over the pieces of this ordinary request. "Dinner on October 12th?"

"Yes, that's right."

"Three weeks from now?"

"More or less. What do you say?"

Emmy's shoulders were up at her ear lobes; she let them drop. Jack hadn't brought up their plan. Instead, he seemed to be modifying their plan. *What did that mean?* She ran her finger across her lips trying to figure it out.

"It's a pretty simple question. No need to complicate it. Anthony. Francesca. Dinner here. Yes? No?"

The return of Jack's irritability made it easy to formulate her response. "No."

"No?" He nodded to himself. "Why 'No'?"

"Because…" There were abundant reasons, but Emmy opted for the easiest to explain. "Because Francesca Trippolli talks incessantly about really boring things. Honestly, I'd prefer an evening folding socks."

Jack's lips twitched a relieved smile. "I'm not asking you to be her best friend. You can deal for one night, can't you? Talk to Francesca about your empty nest; I bet she'll listen if you chatter about that. And, you know, Anthony told me he loves your cooking."

Emmy studied her husband. *He wanted this.* Did that mean he didn't want to follow through with their plan? At the very least, he was postponing it by three weeks time.

"It's just a dinner," he mumbled.

Planning dinner parties was not what she and Jack were supposed to do this fall. Emmy thought of mentioning this point, but there was something incredibly relieving about forgetting it. "Could we make it a brunch instead?"

Jack's eyebrows shot up. "Brunch? Sure, that's fine."

She shrugged. "Then I guess we can."

Her husband's eyes widened as though he expected her to say something more, and likewise Emmy waited for Jack to offer an explanation for his request. The unfilled silence swelled, a balloon about to pop.

Abruptly, Jack picked up his coffee mug. "I'll go ahead and confirm it with Anthony today." He started to move toward the back door. "And tonight, for Celia's thing, we're meeting at the T stop, right?"

"Um, yes, that's what we worked out."

Four weeks ago, Emmy and Jack had tersely determined they'd both attend Jack's daughter's art gallery opening. These kinds of evenings had to be carefully planned. "Does *seven* still work for you?" She tried to emphasize the time.

Jack lifted his laptop strap onto his shoulder – "Sounds good" – and walked out the door. Emmy strode to the back-door and watched her husband, tall, lanky and business-suited, as he walked to the garage. In the morning sunlight, his hair looked shockingly gray – there was little brown left anymore. She called after him, "Remember, seven. Don't be late." He didn't turn to acknowledge her. She knew he'd be late.

Under her short nightgown, the morning air was brisk against her bare legs. She walked onto their backyard patio. Their almost-acre property had mature oaks, maples and walnut trees, and this setting was not unlike the one in which her dream took place. She wondered if she could bring the dream's sensations back. She closed her eyes, but that lovely inchoate intoxication wasn't there anymore.

Emmy returned to the house, nursing a disappointment disproportionate to the situation. *It shouldn't matter; it was only a dream.* Checking the clock, she saw she needed to hurry. She couldn't be late for her first appointment.

When Emmy opened the door to her office, the red light was blinking on her answering machine. She wasn't surprised, since her first client, Louisa Stanton, wasn't sitting in the waiting room. Louisa was always either extraordinarily early for her sessions or quite late, and in either case, liked to leave Emmy long, meandering messages detailing her anticipated arrival time. Emmy hit the play button, and Louisa's voice did indeed come on, though the message was brusquely short. "I can't come today. Sorry." That was it, no explanation offered. *Huh.* Emmy hung up her purse on her office's coat tree and resolved to call Louisa later to find out what was wrong.

A second message began. It was a man with a light Australian accent. "Hello, Dr. Halperin, I was given your name from a mutual friend, Kallie Stillingard." The name made Emmy spin back to the machine. The Australian voice continued, "I think you might be a good person for me to talk to. I'm only in town for a few weeks, and I'm guessing it could be more complicated seeing me than with your other clients. My name is Duncan Grier and I'm going to have someone call—"

Wait. Emmy paused the message and hit rewind. Had that man just said he was Duncan Grier? *That was a famous person, right?* Emmy rarely read more than the headlines of the *Vanity Fair* and *People* magazines that Maria, her practice partner, ordered for their office waiting room, but, still, she was pretty sure Duncan Grier was the actor in *Final Frontier.* Could that be the Duncan Grier calling her? No way!

Emmy hit the play button to begin the message from the beginning, but before the message re-started, the phone rang. Emmy started: *What if it was Duncan Grier again?* The phone rang again, and this time, she made herself pick up the receiver. "Hello?"

"Oh. My. *God!* Is this Emmy?"

Emmy knew the exuberant voice right away though she hadn't heard it in twenty-three years. "*Kallie?*"

"Yes, girlie, it's me. Let's not even think how long it's been! How are you?! How's your little bunchkin?"

"You mean Marc?"

"Is that what you ended up calling him? Don't even tell me how old he is. Is he like a teenager already?

"Marc's *twenty-two*. He's in law school already."

"Get out! Nooo, that can't be." Kallie sounded genuinely shocked. "Shit, I really am old."

"Actually, my youngest, Tess just started at Amherst last month. She's rooming in our old dorm."

"How can your kids be that *old?* Most of my friends just started having babies, but yours, yours are all grown up. I guess when you start as crazy early as you did, you never worry about the ol' biological clock ticking." She laughed, but abruptly stopped: "Are you and Jack still together?"

"I'm still with Jack." Emmy said the words as matter-of-factly as she could. She wondered what it would feel like to answer: *No, I'm not with Jack anymore.* She thought it would feel worse.

"Wow, I can't believe it! I mean, it's so great you guys have gone the long haul. You've got the husband, the grown kids. Wait, how many total?"

"Three total."

"Wow, that's… a lot that you have." There was a pause. "Of course, I wish we could gab more about your perfect, perfect life, but I'm calling with a very specific, time-sensitive purpose." Her voice curled with warmth, "You've heard, I'm sure, that I'm the manager for Duncan Grier."

"Uh, no, I hadn't heard that. That's wonderful. I mean, I would imagine that's wonderful. Congratulations." Emmy marveled that it had only taken seconds before she was again stroking Kallie's fragile ego.

"Oh, it's fantastic. He's like my brother, I love him so much. And, *he's* the reason I'm calling."

"I just heard his message."

"Oh, did you? Then I guess you know he's got quite the burr in his britches about doing some therapy while he's in town shooting this movie. And he feels..." Kallie paused as she seemed to momentarily lose then re-gain her enthusiasm, "he feels just insistent you are the therapist he wants to see."

This didn't make any sense to Emmy. "How does he even *know* about me?"

"Well, I think I mentioned you once, and now, bam!, you're the one. I've tried to suggest seeing a man might be better suited to him. I mean, doesn't that make more sense? But no, he wants to see you."

"Well, I'm flattered I guess."

"Listen, I don't have much time. Can you tell me what your pay rate is?"

Emmy didn't like the question's tone, but answered anyway.

"Great, we'll triple it."

"What? No, that's unnecessary; I wouldn't feel right doing that."

Kallie proceeded as though she hadn't heard Emmy's objections; "Duncan has plenty of special circumstances so it's only right we compensate for them. First, I'll need you to sign papers saying you'll never, ever disclose anything about Duncan and if you do, *hello!*, you have to give us, like, all your money, cars, kids – everything."

"Kallie, I would never disclose anything about any of my—"

"Great. Glad that one isn't an issue. Next thing is that Duncan wants to see you a lot, like every day."

"Every day! Oh, wow, is he okay?"

"He better be! He's got a movie to make." Kallie laughed cheerily, but Emmy didn't join in. "Oh, please, Duncan's fine. He's the Grier, right? It's just he's only in town five weeks, and actually he's only anywhere five weeks. He wants to max out his therapy experience, that's all." Emmy didn't say anything, so Kallie continued: "You know, a lot of therapists would feel honored to be chosen by a man like Duncan Grier."

Emmy brought out a soothing voice. "I'm sure that's true, Kallie, but the problem is I've never done daily therapy before. I'd need to consult with some colleagues before I would even know how to make that work."

"Now, now, now," Kallie's tone was sing-songy in its admonishment. "What was the first thing we talked about? No disclosure!" Before Emmy could respond, Kallie plowed ahead: "You know, we'll also pay you for all your time coming and going to the set."

"Coming to the set?"

"Well, there's no way we can have the Grier coming to a therapist's office every day. The paparazzi would be on it like gum to shoe; those wacko bastards are such slime."

Emmy realized she needed to be more direct. "Kallie, I don't want to disappoint you, but I can't do this. I've never seen a client outside my office. I've never seen anyone more than twice a week. I can't change everything about the way I do therapy for one client. Even for a friend like you. I'm sorry, but I just can't."

There was a long silence, then Kallie's voice resumed as chipper as ever. "Emmy, I just so totally love how you've become this consummate professional. Love it to pieces.

And you know, I already suggested to Duncan you might not go for this. I did try to tell him. But here's the thing: I'm a teensy bit worried if you don't at least meet with him, he'll think I didn't sincerely try to make this work. Which would be… problematic. What do you think, for your ol' freshman roommate, could you come to the set and meet with him? Just once? You can tell him about all your very, very legitimate concerns and see if you can work something out. And, if you can't – oh well, he'll just have to deal, right?"

This was a reasonable enough suggestion that it was difficult not to agree to it. "I suppose it does make more sense to have this conversation with him instead of you."

"Oh, very true. Good, good point." Kallie was noticeably relieved. "So, what are you doing now? Could you come by the set now? Because he's getting fittings and stuff, but he could squeeze you in now if you're free."

On her desk, Emmy nudged two envelopes so their corners matched up. "I did just have a cancellation."

"Excellent." Kallie began to give her directions from Emmy's Harvard Square office to the Allston set – it was just over the bridge, past the Business School – and she bantered on about the men with the walkie-talkies who would take her to Duncan's trailer. Emmy only half-listened until she heard Kallie's voice gleefully pitch upward, "See you in 15! Oh, I bet this is going to be such a thrill for you!" Kallie hung up.

Emmy looked at the receiver doubtfully. Telling a pampered person he wouldn't get his way was hardly Emmy's version of a thrill. In fact, she guessed it would be a pretty unpleasant interaction. *Oh well, it'd be nice to see Kallie. Kinda nice.* She grabbed her purse from the coat tree and checked to make sure her scarf was covering her sweater's plunging neckline. This sweater wasn't one she usually wore to therapy sessions, but there was Celia's gallery opening tonight and Celia's mother, Jessica, would be there. Emmy tried to look sexy whenever she had to see that woman.

As Emmy snapped her door shut and began walking down the stairs of the old Victorian house that was her office building, she made a mental list of the things she wouldn't think about during her walk to the set. Emmy used this trick regularly to keep moments of pleasure from being weighed down by heavy contemplation, and though Maria teased her that she'd never met a less introspective therapist, Emmy could laugh at this joke without wanting to change her ways. This morning her list of thoughts to avoid included: Jessica, Jack, brunch, divorce. With these considerations effectively cordoned off, Emmy guessed she could at least enjoy her walk across the Charles River bridge.

"Come in, " Kallie bellowed before he could say it himself.

Duncan was stuck. A stylist's assistant sat at his feet holding color cards up to his face as the hairdresser stood directly facing him, evaluating the cards' match against the three different temporary hair colors she'd applied earlier. Ling, his assistant, stood to the side and was telling him about various phone calls she needed to return for him. He couldn't move to greet Emmy, so he listened as Kallie did. With all the forced good cheer in his manager's voice, Duncan knew Kallie was hating every moment, and he felt a twinge of guilt. He hadn't called Emmy to make Kallie feel bad. Yet, he hadn't let Kallie's feelings stop him from calling Emmy either.

It was his manager, of course, who'd told Duncan about Emmy. The conversation had taken place months ago, over a dinner together, back in L.A. Duncan had come from an afternoon meeting with Gus, the director of *The Visiting Professor*, and still had the script in hand. In theory, Duncan and Kallie were meeting to discuss Kallie's plans for negotiating a gross-profit sharing payment contract for this small-budget film. When he reached Kallie's office, he offered to take her out to dinner. He knew she was upset he'd ignored her advice to pass on *The Visiting Professor*. The dinner was Duncan's attempt to smooth things out.

Duncan rarely allowed himself more than a beer, but he liked watching others drink. They became warmer, snarkier, more forthcoming, and Duncan happily took in all the revelations. That night, Kallie drank three martinis. She started the evening discussing Boston, the town where *The Visiting Professor* was to be filmed and a place Kallie had come to know during her summers off from Amherst College many years ago. But as the dinner progressed, Kallie's tongue loosened, her words slightly slurring.

"I think my old roommate Emmy Cruz still lives in Boston. I heard she was a psychologist." Kallie gave a sarcastic snicker. "I'm sure all her patients end up in love with her. Of course." Kallie took another substantial sip of her martini. "I remember this one hot spring night when a bunch of us drove to this swimming hole. We were drinking beers and after awhile, everyone slipped off their clothes, all of us skinny-dipping in the dark." She paused, and when she began again she looked to be reliving the night. "There was this moment when I was in the water, and Emmy was standing on the shore. Her long hair and her body, they were wet, and the moonlight shone off her, glimmering really, and she was…" Kallie stopped herself and looked down at her martini glass. Her voice was suddenly thick with an interplay of admiration, envy, and disappointment, "I remember thinking I'd never seen a more beautiful woman in my life." It sounded like Kallie was going to cry.

Duncan didn't know what to say. He'd seen Kallie catty with envy before, but never teary. He knew she worked hard on her appearance; she trained, dieted, highlighted, whitened. Yet, resolutely, she was not an attractive woman. This unalterable reality was something most would have moved on from to find more meaningful life rewards, but Duncan was pretty sure it remained the greatest disappointment of Kallie's life. She seemed to blame every other disappointment – and there were several – on this big one. Duncan had grown to understand these aspects of his manager's personality over their seventeen years working together; yet, he'd never seen Kallie's toughness so fully falter as in this moment talking about Emmy.

After an awkward pause, she tried to cap the story, "Emmy married this preppy rich guy, Jack Halperin, so I guess she's Emmy Halperin now. I should probably call her when we're in town, right?" Kallie looked up at Duncan, forced a smile. Her self-consciousness was painful, and he tried to say something funny to put her at ease. Kallie excused herself to go to the ladies' room.

While she was gone, Duncan couldn't help but consider the image that Kallie evoked of this wet young woman standing naked in the moonlight. *How beautiful could she have been?* A pen sat beside the check on the table and he used it to jot Emmy's name on his script. For years, Duncan had made a habit of noting therapists' names – people whom he'd read about it in articles or names that friends mentioned casually in conversations. So far, he'd never called any of these collected names. The thought of sitting across from a mental health professional who asked endless questions about his past – ah, just thinking about it made him sweat. *Yet, if the therapist was the most beautiful woman Kallie had ever seen?* Maybe the experience would be less awful. It was a fleeting notion, and he didn't think about it again. Until that morning.

When Duncan met Kallie in the waiting town car for their drive to the set, Duncan realized he needed to tell his manager about his therapy plans. Kallie organized all aspects of his life, including matters like this, so it was natural she'd make the arrangements for his therapy sessions too. Still, he was reluctant. She wouldn't be pleased. In the backseat of the car, Kallie sat in her corner, he in his. He began talking about the challenge of playing Benjamin B and brought up the notion that his portrayal could benefit from doing some therapy. "Don't you agree?" he'd asked amiably. Kallie nodded as she drained the coffee from her paper cup. "That's why this morning I called that friend of yours, that Emmy Halperin, so I could start seeing her, you know, as my therapist." He purposefully didn't wait for Kallie's reaction but instead launched into detailing how he'd like Kallie to arrange it so Dr. Halperin came to his trailer daily during the mid-day breaks. He was using the same monotone he always employed when asking Kallie to arrange his life when Kallie's indignant voice interrupted him.

"Emmy Halperin? Duncan, are you kidding me? Of all the therapists in the world, you want to see Emmy Halperin?" She didn't wait for his response. "Good grief, it's because I told you she was pretty." Her head was shaking, her voice revving. "Leaving aside what a pubescent way that would be to pick a therapist, it's been twenty years. And she's not going to sleep with you. You do realize that, right?"

Duncan hated hearing Kallie's patronizing tone. It was especially irritating that she had a point. *Why did Kallie always have a point?* Usually, in these situations, he would make a joke and later seek a less confrontational way to pursue what he wanted. But just then, he didn't want to back down. "I didn't ask your opinion." In the car, he pivoted to face her. "You do realize *that*, right?"

The way he'd snidely mimicked her own question made her eyes go blank and her cheeks dot red. He leaned his head against the car's window and prepared to say what he knew would be even more upsetting. "Kal, it's fine. I don't need you to make those arrangements for me. I'll do it myself." The car had just pulled past the set's barricades and was coming to a stop in front of his trailer. Duncan began to open his car door, when Kallie reached out to grab his shoulder. Her voice was apologetic and take-charge all at once. "I'll call Emmy. Don't worry; if that's what you want, I'll get it for you."

By the time Kallie had cleared the hair stylist, colorist and the assistant out of the trailer, Duncan and Emmy's first impressions were already formed.

Duncan looked different than Emmy'd expected. He was tall and lean and, yes, good-looking. Still, he wasn't quite as dazzling as the movies made him out to be. He had smile lines around his eyes and creases in his cheeks. He was older. Tired. What made as big an impression on Emmy were the women literally at his feet and in his hair. It was too much. *He must be a piece of work*, she thought and then tried to un-think it because, really, that wasn't very therapist-like of her.

Duncan got it right away that Emmy wasn't impressed by him. Most people were, so the absence of her starstruck appreciation stood out. Physically speaking, she wasn't what he'd anticipated. He'd expected fair-haired, and she was dark. *Was she as beautiful as Kallie said?* With her pencil skirt and stacked heels, she cut a nice figure, sure, but he wasn't about to start crying over it. Which was fine, because despite Kallie's insinuations, all he wanted was a therapist. Someone to talk to about why things felt so lousy lately.

"Would you like us to sit over here Dr. Halperin?" He stepped back to let Emmy proceed first to the trailers' built-in corner couches. Kallie had already mentioned that Emmy had reservations about doing therapy with him, and he'd decided to make it a personal challenge to remove those reservations. He liked those kinds of challenges.

"You can call me Emmy," she said as she sat on one of the thin-cushioned, brown sofas. She tried to make the phrase sound casually comfortable, but she was nervous. The first time meeting with a new client was always awkward, but in most situations, she at least felt she controlled the interaction. Here, as she situated herself kitty-corner to this famous man in the tight space of his narrow trailer, she felt more cornered than in control.

"Well, *Emmy*, thank you for coming to the set. I realize therapy doesn't usually work this way."

His tone was ingratiating – like he was welcoming her to a job interview – and she noticed he sounded altogether different than he had in *Last Frontier*. She gestured to her mouth. "I didn't realize you're Australian. From your astronaut movie, I'd never have known."

Duncan smiled. "That's good you didn't know. That means you probably don't know much about me."

Emmy could tell he meant his response to be light-hearted. *But geez, did he think most people knew about his life?* "I don't follow movie stuff much." She tried to find something friendlier to say. "It's interesting to be on a movie set though; I've never been on one before."

"We're shooting *The Visiting Professor.* You ever read that book?" He leaned back, resting his arms on the sofa back.

"*The Visiting Professor?* Oh, I did read that actually. For a book club, years ago." It was a novel that had worked its way under her skin. It was a perplexing story – about marriage and choices – with an ending she wasn't sure she'd understood.

He watched her reactions. "Did you like the story?"

She smiled, "I liked it a lot until the end. Then I wasn't as sure. The line that Benjamin says at the end—"

Duncan interrupted, "'We would be the envy of the neighborhood'?'"

"Yes, that's it. I couldn't stand that last line."

"That's incredible." Duncan was at the edge of his couch cushion.

Emmy thought she'd been too blunt. "I'm sorry, that was rude of me, here you are making this movie and I've just insulted—"

"No, I hated that line too. It was the last line of the script, and in table readings, I asked the screenwriters to change it. I never do stuff like that." He examined her more carefully: "Huh."

Emmy thought the coincidence was remarkable, too remarkable. *Was he lying?* Her eyes squinted, "Is that really true? You really asked to have the line changed?"

"Yeah," he laughed, shaking his head. "I couldn't make that one up. The writers thought I was being a dick, but I got my way."

"That is... uncanny, that we both had such a reaction to that line." Emmy was trying to pick her words carefully since this was, potentially at least, a therapeutic setting. *But how could she not remark on this coincidence?*

Duncan leaned back again, trying to build on their rapport. "So, why did you dislike the line?"

Emmy wasn't sure that this should be their conversation topic, but she didn't see how she could leave this question dangling. "I don't know, to be envied... Why is that a happy ending? Envy feels empty. Lonely."

"Lonely?" He looked at her more closely.

The way Duncan said the one word made her wonder if she'd just confessed to being lonely. She hadn't meant to do that. In fact, she needed to stop answering questions and start asking them. "And, what's the reason you don't like envy?"

"The same as yours," he said it quickly, and then began his next thought. "You know, Kallie envies you a great deal. She says you married the big man on campus."

Her eyes shot wider. *It was ridiculous that Kallie would have put it like that.* "The circumstances were hardly enviable."

His eyebrow arched. "They weren't?"

Emmy froze. She kept meaning to stop answering his questions, to get this meeting under her control; yet, she kept saying too much. *She had to stop.* She straightened herself in her seat and brought out the soothing, authoritative voice she usually used in therapy, "So, Duncan, I know from your call that you want to start therapy. Have you ever been in therapy before?"

Duncan watched Emmy's reasoning take place on her face. He scratched his cheek. "Nope, never."

"Are there reasons you want to do it now?"

"I don't actually *want* to do it."

"Oh?"

"I *should* do it."

She waited for him to continue, but he said nothing more. "Have you been feeling upset or sad lately?"

"Not sad exactly."

He was much more subdued answering questions than he'd been asking them. "But not happy?"

He looked at his hands. "No, not happy either."

With his face at rest, his smile's absence was made more pronounced by the fine lines that lay slack. "Do you have thoughts about what might be keeping you from being happy?"

He took a deep breath. "There are a lot of thoughts. A good number of possibilities to choose from. But, it could be as simple as…" he shrugged, "I work too much."

Given his evasiveness, Emmy sensed there was more stress here than she would have expected. She treaded lightly. "Have you had any breaks lately? When was the last time you went back to Australia?"

"I've never been back."

"Never?"

"No. There's no reason for me to go back. I don't even do press there. It's in my contracts." He crossed his arms in front of him.

This was interesting. "When did you leave?"

"When I was 19." His brows tensed. "So, that makes it about 19 years ago. I've been away as long as I was ever there to begin with." He tried to make it sound like this calculation was trivial, even amusing. But he'd never worked that ratio before.

"That's a long time. Have you seen your parents since then?"

These were the sorts of questions Duncan usually dodged. He was finding it uncomfortable to answer them directly now. "My mum, she comes out to L.A. every now and again. She's a pain, but I still see her."

"And your dad?" Emmy asked this hesitatingly. She already sensed Duncan was bracing for the question.

Duncan didn't say anything for a while. Then he leaned back, jutting his feet out so close they almost hit Emmy's heels. "Emmy, you are good at this. I get interviewed a lot. All sorts of asinine questions. 'Why did you become an actor?' 'Who's your hero?' 'If you could be an animal, which would you be?' But you, you've zeroed in."

Emmy looked for further confirmation, "I've zeroed in on your father?"

"Yes." His eyes flashed angry, but quickly he sought to cover up the disclosure. He made himself smile. "Let's talk about something else. I know, let's figure out if you're going to keep seeing me or not. Kallie told me you had all sorts of objections. Let's talk about those."

This was the opening Emmy had been waiting for, her opportunity to explain why she wasn't able to do therapy with him. But now she wasn't so sure. She could tell this man was carrying a lot of hurt around. From Duncan's discomfort in discussing his father, she gathered his dad was the source of emotional injury. And given that Duncan refused to even return to Australia, she believed the trauma was likely substantial. Maybe she'd agree to see him a couple times of week. She leaned forward, seeking a more caring pose.

"Duncan," her voice was measured, "therapy requires a lot of attention and energy. It can be exhausting. I'm not sure that you'll want—" Emmy saw Duncan's eyes drift toward her chest, then abruptly back to her face. She looked down. *Oh crap.* Her scarf had come untied. The deep rectangular slice from her sweater was now uncovered, and the way she was sitting put her cleavage abundantly on display.

"Oh, sorry," Emmy rushed to tie the scarf back.

"No, don't be," he said. "It's, ah, it's good."

Emmy looked over at Duncan. His eyes were playful, not leering, as though he was inviting her to see the humor in the situation.

She let herself smile. Duncan grinned back, relaxed and welcoming. He *did* have a nice smile.

Duncan sat forward. "Emmy, you tell me how you want to do this therapy stuff, and I'll make sure I do it that way. I can't come to your office, but if we can agree on times you come here, I promise I'll be serious and ready to go, whatever you want." He looked earnestly at her; he thought he had her.

And he did. She couldn't say no at this point. She was going to be the trailer-visiting therapist to Duncan Grier. *Oh well.* She did want to help this man. In fact, she was confident she could. Checking to make sure her scarf was where it needed to be, she made her voice crisp. "Okay, if we're going to see each other, there are some ground rules we should set up." Using her most authoritative tone, she began to explain the conditions that must be met if their therapy sessions were to proceed.

Duncan had an urge to smile at Emmy's quick sternness, but he didn't. Instead, when Emmy met his eyes square-on, Duncan's face wore just the seriousness Emmy was telling him she required.

It was 7:29 p.m. when Emmy and Jack finally walked into Celia's gallery opening. Jack had been late, just as Emmy had known he'd be. Yet, by the time he held the heavy glass door open for Emmy to walk through, she realized she wasn't annoyed with him anymore. Instead, having her husband put his hand on the small of her back as he followed her in the door was pleasurable. *They must look like a normal, married couple.* She and Jack didn't walk into many public spaces together these days, and maybe tonight would be the last time Jack stood by her side and introduced himself to strangers as her husband. She glanced at him. He had on his dove gray suit, the one she'd helped him pick out at Nordstrom's a few years ago, back when they were still "trying." Emmy always thought he looked handsome in this suit, and as she leaned into his tallness and studied the deep brown eyes that sat on his thin face, a surge of something – was it affection or melancholy? – clamped her chest. *She wished they were a normal, married couple.*

The gallery space echoed a cacophony of sounds, and Emmy could feel the room's vibrations on her fingertips. There were dozens of scantily-clad college-age people standing in the open space, chatting and laughing as they tried to look more sophisticated than they were. *God, they looked like kids.* The room was large and the ceilings high, yet Celia's canvases were at home with the gallery's scale. Her paintings were huge – many were ten feet by ten feet – and what they showcased in intricate, almost photographic detail were body parts. In each of her oil paintings, Celia had taken one small part of a body – something that on a real scale was no more than a few inches wide – and blown it up enormously so the images felt both hyper-realistic and otherworldly. As Emmy glanced around the room, she saw canvases of ankles and hands. And there was a nipple. And, *there you go,* that one looked like a pubic bush. Emmy was not surprised to see these intimate images; she knew Celia relished the genital close-up.

It was an enormous honor for Celia to have her work shown at this gallery and that's why Emmy made herself come tonight. Emmy's own father had been an artist, though most of the money he made, and it was never much, came from being a cabbie. Emmy thought her dad's works were beautiful, but his many canvases had mostly sat in neat stacks against the wall of the Cruz's small two-bedroom apartment; no gallery ever asked to put them on their walls. Yet, here at age nineteen, Celia had already accomplished what Gabriel Cruz had not. Her precocity was impressive – *or was it her fearlessness?* Either way, Emmy supposed she was proud of her stepdaughter.

Jack and she stood in the middle of the loosely crowded space and turned around and around looking at the canvases. "There are a lot of naked people here," she said it lightly since she was aware her husband might be uncomfortable viewing the uncontestable evidence of his 19-year-old daughter's affinity for nakedness.

Jack ran his hand across his chin. "I can't get over how many *men* there are. I'd assumed 'nude' meant female nude."

"Is that a close-up of... balls?" Emmy took a few slow steps toward a canvas that was across from them. Jack moved closer too; they agreed: it was.

Jack pointed to another canvas at the far end of the room. "Is that what I think it is?"

It took a few seconds before Emmy got it. "No, no. It's a bellybutton. Just a bellybutton."

Just then Celia descended on them. "Hel-lo-o!!!" Emmy had always thought Celia tended to sing her words, and tonight was no different. Like her mom, Celia was loud and assertive, with shoulder-length blonde hair and a body with many rounded curves. Her little black dress showcased her ample chest, and the small diamond in her nose sparkled as she leaned in to kiss her dad.

"Cece, maybe I shouldn't ask this, but where'd you find all these naked people?"

"Mostly they're friends. Some professional models," Celia explained cheerily. "Ben's canvas is over there." She pointed toward the other end of the gallery.

Jack's face contorted: "Eeeew."

"Ben posed for you?" Emmy was also alarmed. Her son and Celia were about the same age and half-siblings; Ben shouldn't be naked in front of Celia.

"Yup. Such a blast. I wanted Marc too, but he refused. It's not his kind of thing, is it?" Noticing her father's shocked face, Celia put her hand on her hip: "Now, guys, don't go all prudish on me!" Her abundant breasts jiggled as she held her hands out with exasperation, "There's nothing to be scared of with bodies. Please. They're sacred after all."

Emmy couldn't help herself. She pointed to the nearby canvas, "Is that a sacred scrotum?"

Celia never answered the question because just then her mother came in from behind her. "Oh, sweetheart, you've done such incredible work!" After bestowing a kiss on her daughter's cheek, Jessica nodded: "Jack." Emmy noticed Jessica held her husband's name in her mouth too long, and when Emmy glanced Jack's way, he was still holding Jessica's gaze. Jessica and Jack had fought for decades over money and dividing parenting responsibilities, but tonight Emmy felt her stomach turn as she saw the live wire between their eyes.

Jessica, of course, hadn't said "Hello" to Emmy; she hadn't even looked at her. The sweater Emmy picked so she'd look sexily sophisticated, it'd never registered. Quietly, Emmy stepped back from the family huddle. Grabbing a white wine from the tray of a passing waiter, Emmy began to wander the gallery. Evaluating each of the canvases, she asked herself: Could that close-up of a butt cheek be Ben's butt cheek? That clavicle bone? Nah. Finally, she recognized her son in a canvas that was a huge blow-up of a man's armpit; Ben's mole gave it away. Maybe he'd only been shirtless during his sitting for Celia. At any rate, that's how she was going to think of it.

She was a good decade or two older than most of the crowd in the room. The young people moved in tight when they spoke to one another; they laughed mouths wide open, eyes sparkling, energy cackling. Desire drifted through the room enough that Emmy imagined she could grab at it like snow in the air. She was rapt. She'd never experienced that part of her youth.

The summer night twenty-three years ago when Emmy saw the pale blue plus-sign on her pregnancy stick, she'd known right away she was at a crossroads. The choice was remarkably clear-cut: she could have an abortion and stay on her college path or she could get off that path completely. Most of the girls Emmy knew would have quickly made the appointment at the abortion clinic. This choice would not have been cavalierly made; there would have been anguish and tears. Emmy understood this approach; she contemplated it.

The difference for Emmy was that she wasn't so attached to her path to begin with. School was fine, sure, but she woke up nights in cold sweats thinking about the debt she was amassing. Even with her scholarship award, there was still a stack of loans she worried she'd never pay off. Picking another path had appeal. Having a baby, getting married, starting a family. She'd yearned for a more traditional family her whole life, with a father who came home every night and a mother who futzed over mittens when it was cold and who cared if she did her homework. Maybe, she thought, she could be that mother. If she had a baby of her own, her loneliness might be displaced with love. And Jack, maybe Jack and she would be a great couple together. They'd only been together such a short time, but he was nice, right?

The next morning she borrowed her mother's friend's ancient Subaru and drove from New York's East Village to Wellesley, Massachusetts where Jack then lived with his parents. Her plan was to tell him she was pregnant with his child and see what he would say. Finding his address, Emmy was shocked at how enormous the Halperin property was. It felt like a park to her, with tall leafy trees and a creek that ran through the back of it. The day was hot and humid, and Jack took her to the stream in their backyard so they could be close to the shaded water. As Emmy poked a stick in the shallow creek bed, she knew Jack was observing her closely. Shyly, she began to tell him her story. She wanted it to be his story too.

On the drive up from New York, she'd cautioned herself not to have particular expectations. She knew Jack was starting at the Harvard Graduate School of Design in the fall. He wouldn't want to have a baby to worry over, and even if he would support the child, there was no reason to think he'd offer to marry her. It wasn't what twenty-two year old Harvard boys wanted, was it?

That sticky, hot day by the water, Jack heard Emmy's news quietly, solemnly, and at first he said nothing. He sat there and studied her so carefully, so unusually. Then – it was a moment that long ago Emmy liked to replay in her head – he grasped her hand and kissed it. As she gazed at him incredulously, he kissed her tear-wet lips and told her not to worry, that he would take care of her. "I'll do the right thing Emmy; I'll marry you." He sounded certain and noble. In that afternoon by the stream, Emmy's heart brimmed with such gratitude it felt like love.

Before the summer turned completely to fall, she and Jack married. His family bought them a little row house off Inman Square, so Jack could continue to go to graduate school as planned. Emmy quit Amherst and tried to ready their new home to have a baby. In a blink, she'd assumed the life of a woman much older than the nineteen year-old she was. She had a baby, a husband, a home, and she loved all of it. For a long while, she thought everything was perfect.

As Emmy looked around the gallery now, she wondered why it wasn't that way anymore. Probably Jessica was the pithiest reply. But Emmy didn't want to think about her, no. She watched the way the young people flirted some more. *God, they were having such fun.*

Suddenly, Jack was standing right beside her. From the way he glanced dismissively at the armpit canvas, she could tell he had no clue it was his son's portrait. He touched her arm lightly; "Celia wants us to meet a friend of hers. Some guy named *Rocco.*" Jack muttered: "What kind of parent names their kid Rocco?"

He made a gesture to indicate the direction they should walk, but Emmy hesitated. Perhaps it was the two glasses of white wine or maybe just the memories. She tipped her head to look at her husband. They'd been through so much together. Maybe they shouldn't give up. Maybe they should just... She leaned in close. She touched her lips to Jack's and let them linger in a light kiss. Jack stilled himself as Emmy slowly pulled back. She opened her eyes and noticed his eyebrows were raised skeptically. "Was that for Jessica's benefit?"

Emmy took a step back. "No. No, that was not." And she walked toward Celia without waiting for Jack to join her.

❧ ❧ ❧

"Mrs. Robinson..." Duncan hit pause and played the scene again. It was 9 pm; he was in his hotel room, in bed, watching *The Graduate* on his laptop. The scene he was re-watching was the one where Benjamin Braddock and Mrs. Robinson are in the hotel room trying to decide whether to continue or end their affair. Duncan wondered if anyone had watched this scene as many times as he had. It didn't seem possible. For his portrayal of Benjamin B, Duncan had watched *The Graduate* in its entirety a dozen times, but this scene in particular, he'd watched fifty or more times. It was his favorite scene in the movie, the one where a lot of the irony was stripped back to reveal two lonely people who wanted so badly to be connected – to anyone – that they ignore all sorts of reasons they shouldn't be connected to each other.

Despite Duncan's deliberate nature, it was the recklessness portrayed in *The Graduate* that appealed to him – in fact, the very same desperation that drew him to *The Visiting Professor*. Of course, some people thought *The Visiting Professor* and *The Graduate* were completely unrelated stories. Before his death, Percy Hildenmessen, the author of *The Visiting Professor*, had done interview after interview in which he insisted his book had no connection to the 1967 Dustin Hoffman movie. A lot of people seemed to buy it. Duncan didn't. *The Visiting Professor* was about a man, 'Benjamin B,' who, in 1984, was a 40-year old plastics executive living in Southern California with his wife El. The story opened with Benjamin receiving an offer to guest-teach at Harvard Business School for a semester. Benjamin accepted this offer and left El behind in California to head to Cambridge, MA. While there, he began an affair with his colleague's twenty-year-old daughter. It was Benjamin B's mother-in-law, a Mrs. Robins, who saved him. Or destroyed him. The book was deliberately unclear about how to read the ending – was it redemptive or dooming? Whichever it was, *The Visiting Professor* and *The Graduate* shared too many unusual narrative congruencies to be accidental.

The Visiting Professor's similarity to *The Graduate* was, in fact, the reason Kallie didn't want Duncan to take the role. "A beloved character like Benjamin Braddock, you're never going to fill those shoes. You're too tall for one. And for two, you'd be playing an insecure, nervous guy. I'm not saying you can't *act* that part. But that's not what the audience expects from you, and you'll be held accountable for their expectations. Think about it; the whole tension of *Visiting Professor* is about whether Benjamin B will sleep with the young Maggie. But with you, *poof!* bye-bye goes that tension. You're the Grier; *of course* you'll sleep with her! No, I'm sorry; I know you want to do this, but, really, you should not. Benjamin B will only give you more career trouble, and you don't need that trouble now." Kallie's arguments were sound; Duncan had to acknowledge that. Still, he ignored them. He wanted to take this role. He couldn't explain why. All he knew was that *The Visiting Professor* was a good story, and it spoke to him. He wanted to be part of making it speak to other people. More than any role he'd been offered in years, he wanted to be Benjamin B.

These last few days, they'd rehearsed the Cambridge-based scenes on set, a lot of the apartment stuff. And to everyone's surprise, a lot went well. Duncan was a good mimic, and he replicated the mannerisms Dustin Hoffman had given Benjamin Braddock forty-five years ago. Duncan could perfectly imitate the slight shuffle in his walk, his whiney nasal voice and particular brand of nervousness. He also was happy with the way in which he'd aged the character. For *The Visiting Professor*, Duncan's middle-aged

Benjamin B was a man who occupied a leadership role but nevertheless felt a fraud.

Even with all that was going right, still, the portrayal hadn't completely gelled, and Duncan knew that too. Earlier that night Duncan went to dinner with Gus Kremlin, his director on the film. "You're too fucking charming, my friend," Gus said while he sipped down his glass of expensive red wine.

Duncan knew he hadn't been Gus' first choice for the role. Indeed, he knew Gus only relented in offering him the role because it was the singular way to move the movie's production forward. The Grier's involvement had allowed everything to fall into place. A second production company came in, final financing was secured; other actors became eager to join the production. When Duncan signed on, Gus told him he was pleased with his enthusiasm for the role, but he was also unusually frank in discussing the public's likely predisposition to criticize his performance. "People have strong feelings about Benjamin B, and there can be no trace of 'Grier-ness' in this role. We'll have to strip it out of you." The fierceness with which Gus intoned the word "strip" worried Duncan. Gus had a reputation in the industry for going to unusual lengths to extract the performance he wanted from his actors, and Duncan couldn't help wondering what the "stripping" of his Grierness would entail.

That night, at dinner, Duncan had asked Gus to tell him frankly what he thought wasn't working yet. "My friend," Gus smiled, "you're used to 'bang-bang, run-run, kiss-kiss,' and don't get me wrong I don't think anyone does that better than you. But this character, he's defined by his *pathos*. He's befuddled, confused, lost, desperate. Look," Gus cut his steak bite, "your characterization of Benjamin is dynamite. The voice, the walk." Gus took a bite and talked with his mouth slightly full. "That stuff, you got. Couldn't be better. But your Benjamin, he doesn't yet feel like I could know him, like I can see his pain as my pain." Gus paused to swallow. "You know, you can't hide from Benjamin B's bleakness. Can't sugarcoat that." He leaned in close, "Duncan, you're so, so close to having it be brilliant. You have to decide: how much of *yourself* will you bring to this portrayal? It comes down to that. How bare will you let yourself be?"

Gus was forthright; Duncan appreciated that. Most directors would have cheerleaded Duncan this close to filming, and he was glad Gus respected him enough to be direct. He decided to be direct back.

"You should know something." Duncan used the earnest look he always employed when he wanted to get something. He leaned into Gus, as though to convey a secret. "I'm working with someone, a therapist. She's going to come to the set every day at the mid-day break." Duncan sat back again. "I know you want me to bring more emotion to this role, and I know it needs it too, and I think she – this therapist – is going to help me."

Gus chewed his steak; he looked slightly perplexed. "A daily therapist?" He chewed and chewed. "Duncan Grier, you are a constant surprise." Gus swallowed. "No one can say you aren't committed to this, can they?" He poured another glass of wine, "Well, you've got my full backing, of course. Whatever you need to make it happen." He almost chuckled, putting his hand on Duncan's shoulder. "Remember, go deep. Feelings are where you find the truth. Not to go all Obi-Wan on you, but for story-telling and for life, it's what you feel that makes it."

As Duncan reflected on the dinner from his hotel room, he realized it accomplished what he wanted. Gus, like everyone, saw him as a lightweight, so it behooved him to continuously remind his director how seriously he took his commitment to the film. And he was glad Gus knew about the therapy for practical reasons too; now it wouldn't be as complicated to meet with Emmy each day. If Gus hadn't sanctioned the sessions, Duncan doubted he could pull them off. Now that he'd cleared the hurdle of contacting a therapist, he was surprisingly concerned that it work.

At the end of today's session, Emmy had laid down the law about what she expected. She said in no uncertain terms she would see him daily if he was serious, but not if he was not. Serious to her meant that they would meet when they planned; there would be no interruptions – no cell phone calls, no knocks on the door – and their sessions would last a solid fifty minutes. Not fifteen minutes here or there; that wasn't therapy. She also said, with a pointedness that amused him, that there could be no eating or drinking; this wasn't a lunch date. If they had a standing appointment and he couldn't make it, he had to let her know as soon as possible. She looked serious and commanding, but it wasn't difficult for Duncan to see she wasn't a drill sergeant. Quite to the contrary, she was all emotion. He guessed she was someone naturally vulnerable who taught herself to be tough. He understood this dynamic; it was one he knew well.

Thinking about this therapy stuff now, there was a rush of agitation. He stood up from his bed; he had to get out of his hotel room. Now. He was in his running clothes in under a minute and out the door. The film's insurance carrier wouldn't approve of its star running late at night through the streets of a busy city without a bodyguard. But Duncan did it all the time. He found if he left quickly, wore a base-ball cap, and ran *fast*, no one noticed him. Not running wasn't an option. His chances of keeping his shit together were zero if he didn't run.

Tonight, as his feet rhythmically hit the ground and his skin tingled with the rushing air, the tightness in his body's muscles loosened and the murk of his agitation receded. He ran for an hour. When he was close again to the Four Seasons, he saw a Barnes and Noble bookstore. Perfect. They closed at 11, so Duncan was speedy. He went to the self-help section, the titles of which were familiar to him, and bought every book about therapy they had, eight total. If Chris, his publicist, knew he'd made these purchases from a store, he'd have given him grief. *Dude, that's what Amazon's for.* But no one in the store paid Duncan attention. And having the books made him feel more prepared.

It was midnight when he walked back in his hotel room. He pulled out his eight new books and decided to start with a biography of Freud. Duncan was used to reading a lot, random, crazy titles, anything he could get his hands on. It was the only way he fell asleep. He needed another person's story in his head, not his own, before giving into the night.

Tonight, he wasn't drowsy in the slightest. He took a sleeping pill, but he wasn't expecting it to work. Sometimes when he was unsettled like now, even drugs couldn't bring the sleep to him. He called room service, ordered a milk shake. A pretty girl came with it; he noticed her shirt was unbuttoned so low it showed most of her bra. He drank the shake and sat in bed planning to read until he fell asleep.

When he was about halfway through the book, he put it down. Psychoanalysis seemed a hell of a lot different from what he expected to do with Emmy. Freud's concern with his clients was merely as expositions for his theories, and his approach offered judgment over comfort. Emmy, he already knew, would not be like that. He thought of her expression when her scarf slipped, when he'd seen the sweater's cut show the milky paleness of her round breasts.

In that instant, he realized: he would tell her everything. All of it. Expecting this thought to panic him, he was surprised instead to feel relieved. Someone would know.

He put down the Freud book, turned off the light and let his thoughts drift. In seconds, his memories of the day shape-shifted into dreamy, ethereal images. The image in his head at 4:13 a.m. when he finally fell asleep was of a nineteen-year-old Emmy, standing on the rocks above the pond, naked in the moonlight.

TUESDAY, SEPTEMBER 24:
SALTY SMELL

There'd been no answer, so Emmy knocked again. Still, no one came to the trailer door. *It was the time they'd agreed on, right?* 11:30 a.m., Tuesday. Ling, Duncan's assistant, had called to confirm. She opened the door slightly. "Duncan?" Still nothing. "Duncan, it's Emmy."

Duncan bolted awake. *Oh shit.* He'd fallen asleep. Wobbly, he stood from the sofa and rushed to the door. "Emmy, hi."

She looked at him. He wasn't wearing a shirt.

Duncan didn't even look down; he saw Emmy's expression. "Here; come in." He walked to the back of the trailer to grab a T-shirt. *Damn, what was it with them?* Yesterday, Emmy bared her chest and today him. *What would Freud say?* T-shirt on, he came back to where Emmy sat on her brown couch and plopped down on the couch perpendicular to hers.

"Sorry about that," he rubbed his face as he spoke. "I didn't sleep much last night. I was planning to take a short doze; I thought I'd be up before you got here, but..." He stopped rubbing to look at her. Her cheeks were flushed crimson. He'd embarrassed her.

Emmy was trying hard to look composed, but she wasn't yet. When Duncan opened the door to her, his bare chest was there, beautiful and close. This visual was unexpected, but it was his smell that made her catch her breath. His body's natural odors were earthy and sweaty and smelled like sleep. And sex. She hadn't meant to make that association, but her senses caught the connection before she stopped herself.

Duncan continued, "I know you'd said yesterday how important it was to keep to the schedule we set up, and I talked with the director…" He stopped because Emmy was looking at him quizzically. "Is something wrong?"

"I'm sorry. I was just noticing – Didn't you have brown hair yesterday?"

Duncan laughed. "That was hair dye, temporary. This—" he grabbed the wavy sandy blonde hair mopping his eyes, "this is my real hair. It's going to be permanently colored later today."

"Oh." She paused, feeling foolish for even bringing up the matter. "See, you were right; I don't know much about you."

"You were pissed when I said that yesterday."

"I was not."

Duncan laughed. "You were too."

Emmy didn't know what to say. He was right.

"Emmy, you have a very easy face to read."

There was a tease in his voice and warmth in his eyes. He'd called her Emmy when he hadn't needed to use her name. Yesterday, he'd been controlled and purposefully charming. Now, fresh from his nap, his attention was sleepy and unprotected. *Sexy*. She swallowed; she wasn't supposed to think that. "You were having trouble sleeping last night?"

"I get insomnia from time to time. Do you ever have trouble sleeping?"

She'd never had a client ask her so many questions. She smiled, but tried to make it a therapist smile, which, like a teacher's smile, was caring but established distance. "Sometimes I do. Especially when something's on my mind." She leaned in slightly, trying to make her next question launch their session. "Was anything on your mind last night?

Duncan paused for a second. *How much did he want to tell her?* He took a deep breath and leaned back, stretching his legs out in front of him. "Starting therapy with you was a fairly impulsive decision for me. I'm not an impulsive person."

"No?"

"No. I like being thorough and deliberate about what I do."

"Then, how are you feeling about therapy today, after a night thinking about it?"

Duncan rubbed the back of his neck. "Still pretty fucking uncomfortable. I don't like talking about myself. But," he paused, "I know I have to do this."

She nodded and took her time with her next question. "Why do you feel you have to?"

"It's time. I'm 38. That has something to do with it, though it's hard to say exactly what. I guess if I don't take care of my problems now, I never will."

She hadn't expected him to be so forthcoming. "What are the problems you want to take care of?"

"Well." He looked around the dim trailer as he thought about the best way to put it. "I want too much."

This was not the answer she expected. She was ready for him to talk about his father or his career or something having to do with relationships. Nonetheless, she nodded. "Is there something in particular you want?"

He chuckled, like the joke was on himself. "No. What I want is definitely vague. I want... to want. But wanting, it's not a good idea for me. I've made myself successful by letting that go."

Emmy was confused. "Usually people say they are successful when they've achieved what they want. But you feel you're successful because you don't want?"

"It does sound absurd when you put it that way."

"I don't think it sounds absurd. It sounds... intriguing."

"Well, trust me, it's not intriguing. It's boring and practical. It's what I've had to do because..." he looked at her warily and shrugged, "my destiny is failure."

Emmy tried not to let her face show its surprise. *He was so different than she'd expected.* She kept her voice soothing, "Tell me why you think your destiny is failure."

"It really doesn't matter now. I don't want to talk about it now."

"Then," Emmy tried to think of a way to re-direct the question, "tell me more about what you want to want."

Duncan leaned back again. He noticed her cheeks wore a pretty flush. They were a nice color, like the ruddy pink you found in a ripe peach. He cleared his throat. "Last fall, my dog died, and I broke up with my girlfriend of a year and a half."

She was aware his response didn't exactly answer her question, but she nodded anyway. "That sounds like a tough fall."

"It was. It sucked. But I was more upset about my dog than about Alison. By a lot."

Somehow, despite the therapeutic appropriateness of their conversation, this conversation still didn't feel like a therapy session to Emmy. Maybe it was because the two couches were nestled in a tight corner of the trailer, making the physical space between her and Duncan quite close. Or, maybe it was because she was a visitor to his space. Whatever it was, the therapeutic distance she normally took for granted wasn't comfortably in place. She swallowed. "Did you love Alison?"

"I thought I did. But not enough." He paused, evaluating what he perceived to be Emmy's discomfort. "I never told her some of the stuff I will tell you."

"Oh." This remark surprised her, and something else too. *Was she pleased?*

Duncan continued, "It was odd the way it became clear it wasn't right. My publicist Chris called me to tell me that Alison—" He stopped, mid-sentence, "Do you know Alison Lockyer? She was Tess in *Tess of the D'Ubervilles?*"

"Oh, yeah, I know her. She's British, right? She has a great, dry wit."

"So you read Alison's interviews, but not mine?"

Emmy laughed; "I just read whatever magazines are at the dentist office."

Duncan smiled; he was sure Emmy enjoyed Alison's costume dramas more than his own brand of movie, but he liked that she wouldn't simply say that. He continued his story. "Chris called to tell me he'd received this advance copy of an interview with Alison where she'd said I was *the love of her life.* It was strange she'd made this announcement in a magazine since Alison and I'd agreed we wouldn't talk too much about each other publicly. And she'd never told me I was her life's love when we were alone." He paused to think. "When I asked her about it, that's when everything became clear."

"What became clear?"

He paused before he answered. "Alison liked being publicly in love with me more than privately in love with me."

"Did you want Alison to be the love of your life?"

"Maybe at one point I did. By the time of her interview, no, I guess by then I did not."

"Why didn't you?" She worked to make her voice sound therapeutically gentle and discerning, not merely curious.

"I guess the simplest way to put it is that we didn't take good care of each other."

That's an interesting answer. "And you feel like that is important to you?"

"Well, what good is a love of your life if you don't take good care of each other?"

From the way he posed this question, it seemed he expected Emmy to answer it. Since she didn't want that, she posed another question fast. "Have you had a love of your life?"

He smiled. "It's a weird expression, isn't it? At one point, a lifetime ago, I thought I did. But I don't have one now, so I guess I was wrong." He looked down for a moment, then back up. "What about you?"

Emmy's eyes bulged. "What about me? This isn't supposed to be about me."

Her apprehension with this question interested him. "Okay, then what if I put it a different way. A more general way. Do you think you can be happy without love? How important is love to your happiness?"

Emmy met Duncan's direct look. "How important is it to you?"

"You're not going to answer the question?"

"No, because I'm more interested in hearing what you think." And there was the issue she didn't know how to answer it.

"I think…" He looked down at his hands for a second. "I think it's everything. I think it's the reason I'm so fucked

41

up. Because it's been easier for me to love my dog than any of the people in my life."

"Why was it easier to love your dog?"

He laughed. "Because I didn't have to tell him anything."

"And you want that to change?"

He thought the answer was obvious. "That's why I'm here with you."

Before Emmy could figure out what to say, a knock hit the trailer door. *Tap, tap, tap.* They both startled at the noise and looked in the direction of the sound. Ling cracked the door open; "Duncan, I'm sorry, but they need you in make-up now."

Duncan went to the door to speak with Ling, and when he came back, Emmy could tell he was annoyed. "They changed the schedule, and I guess they've decided I have to get my hair colored now instead of later. I'm sorry."

She stood up. "Tomorrow you'll be brown again?"

"Actually, tomorrow I'll look exactly like Dustin Hoffman."

"Except you're a foot taller."

"Not a foot! Just how tall do you think I am?"

Emmy laughed, though she wondered if this was the sort of joke she was supposed to make with a client. Technically speaking, she'd said nothing inappropriate. She joked around with several of her clients, especially the teenagers she saw. This was, possibly, no different.

"You know, they've rigged parts of the set to make me appear shorter." Duncan looked carefully at Emmy. "If you'd like, I can show you around sometime."

"Uh, maybe." She knew she wouldn't let herself take a set tour with a client.

Duncan saw her reluctance; he decided to bring out his most earnest voice. "I know that today we started late and ended early, but tomorrow I'll make sure it goes without a hitch."

She realized she could use this opportunity to re-establish her therapeutic authority by emphasizing the importance of keeping their fifty minutes uninterrupted – except she didn't want to be reprimanding right then. "Sounds good," she smiled.

Duncan had watched her deliberate over what to say and was happy with what she chose. "Thanks for understanding," he said as he headed out the trailer.

When the door clicked shut, Emmy realized she was smiling at the space he'd left behind.

Emmy's body jumped. She screamed.

A Bibio song had been playing loudly while Emmy was scrubbing the kitchen countertops and dancing like a maniac. Then, like that, the loud music cut.

She turned to see Jack standing there, an amused expression on his face.

"You scared the shit out of me!" Emmy's heart was still pounding. She hadn't heard him come in at all. It was nine at night. "Why'd you *do* that? God, I feel like I jumped out of my skin."

"You looked like you were doing that even before I turned the music off."

Jack was smiling, which was unusual.

She pointed to the now-quiet speakers. "That's the song I'm going to use for, you know, the Hourglass performance. The piece I'm choreographing." She was still breathing heavily. "Isn't that song great? It's different than the usual, right?"

"It's different alright." Jack walked to the refrigerator and opened it wide.

She'd thought all evening about whether she should ask this question. "Would you like to come to the recital?"

Emmy saw his back stiffen at the question, though he kept his head buried among the refrigerator shelves. "Oh, you guys are performing soon?"

"Yeah, that's why there've been so many rehearsals lately." As she said this, she realized how unlikely it was Jack would have noticed. Emmy was in a small modern dance group, and in three and a half week's time, they were performing at the Cambridge Multicultural Arts Center. That afternoon, during a rehearsal, one of her fellow dancers, Kurt, had come to each of the troupe members and asked how many tickets they wanted reserved. Most of the dancers reserved large blocks, but as Kurt approached Emmy with his clipboard, she realized that since her kids were away at school, Maria was the only person who might come. "One ticket is all I'll need," she offered. Kurt wrote this information down cheerfully; "One for the hubby."

Kurt's easy presumption made her consider for the first time whether she should ask Jack to come. Jack didn't like her dances; he hated the music, or at least that's the reason he always given when he begged off in the past. But, if they were going to be married in three weeks to host a brunch, they would likely be married in three and a half. Maybe he should come this time.

Jack pulled a beer from the refrigerator door and turned to face Emmy. "When is the dance thing?"

"October 16th," Emmy twisted her lips.

"The 16th? Like a month from now?"

"Uh-huh." Emmy recognized his interest in the timeline was the same as hers had been about the brunch. "It's a Wednesday night; that's the only time we could get the space."

Jack took a swig from his beer bottle. "I'll come."

"Really?"

"Yeah, sure." Jack made it sound like this was no big deal. "You know," he changed the subject, gesturing to the refrigerator, "there's enough food in there to feed five hungry families."

Emmy smiled at Jack's agreeability. "I know. I haven't adjusted to cooking for..." she was about to say "one" but stopped herself. She changed the subject; "So, what do you eat for dinner when you stay out so late?"

For twenty-two years Jack had come home promptly at six thirty, and their family of five had eaten an Emmy-prepared dinner together. Friends of the Halperins joked they were like Ozzie and Harriet, and Jack and Emmy always protested, "Not at all," though, in truth, they enjoyed this joke. A strong family structure was a value both Jack and Emmy worked hard to create, and their nightly dinners were a big part of that effort. It was Jack who'd first insisted on the dinners since it had been his tradition growing up. In the beginning, Emmy had found the cooking to be pure drudgery, but over time, she grew to relish it. Cooking was the one area of the household where Jack ceded all authority to Emmy, and the practical creativity that cooking required came to be a project she enjoyed at the end of the day. As the kids grew, work meetings and sports practices and play rehearsals made it so they didn't eat dinner together every night. Even those evenings they were together, the kids still talked over each other, the conversations were bickery and chaotic, and Jack was always reminding his sons not to slurp or burp or chew so disgustingly. Yet for all their dinners' challenges, Emmy hadn't realized how much they anchored her days until they stopped. Since Tess left for school a month ago, there hadn't been a single sit-down dinner. Emmy continued to cook, but no one joined her. She'd thought Jack might show up some nights, but so far, no, he hadn't returned home before 8 p.m., and most nights even later.

"I grab a sandwich at my desk," Jack said casually. "It's not as good as your cooking though."

This was a surprise compliment; her face brightened.

Jack smiled back as he started to un-button his shirt. "I'm going to head upstairs. You want to come or do you have more dancing to do?"

Emmy studied Jack; his delivery had the slightest twinge of affection. "I don't need to dance anymore."

She followed Jack up the stairs to their master bedroom suite, trying to remember the last time they'd been so nice to each other. Maybe the kiss last night had created a delicate appeasement. She considered asking Jack some of the questions she'd been thinking about while she ate her leftovers alone. Her conversation with Duncan had percolated in her brain all afternoon. All the stuff about love. She knew, no way, was she going to ask Jack if she was the love of his life. She had no desire to hear his answer. Which was disconcerting because if the question were to be posed to her – "Is Jack the love of your life?" – her answer, however equivocated, would have to be "Yes." Jack was the only man she'd ever loved; he won the title by default.

This silly designation, however, wasn't what Emmy thought about most. Instead, she'd mulled over whether her happiness required love. Duncan seemed so certain his did, that the lack of love was why he was miserable. *Was it the same for her?* She knew her kids loved her, but that wasn't quite the love she thought Duncan was talking about. She sat at the edge of their king-size bed, and called loudly so Jack could hear her from the walk-in closet where he was changing from his work clothes: "Jack?"

"Mmmm?"

"Do you think you need love to be happy?"

Jack emerged from the closet in his boxers and looked at her quizzically, "What?"

"Do you think you need—"

"No, I got the question. I just don't understand where this is coming from." His voice tightened, "Are you trying to get into—"

"No." Emmy rushed to clarify. "No, it's nothing about us." As she heard her own protest, she realized how preposterous it was. *Of course, this question was about them.* She tried to find an explanation that would deflect his irritation. "It's just I was talking with someone today, and it came up. It's an interesting question, don't you think?"

"If you don't say so yourself."

"I didn't mean it that way."

"Well, if you want my answer to that question..." he paused as he tied his pajama bottoms. "My answer is that happiness is the wrong goal. It might be nice if it happened, sure." He buttoned his pajama top. "But as a goal, happiness is useless. Trying to live according to principles, doing your best, that's all anyone can do."

Emmy stared at Jack. It seemed he'd had his answer ready, as though he'd posed this very question to himself before. "You think happiness is a useless goal? But why? I mean, what's a useful goal then? Just principles?"

Jack was ignoring her questions. "Do you know where the remote is?" He was looking under the couch pillows.

"It's in the basket," Emmy pointed to where it was. "Don't you want to know what I think?"

Jack grabbed the remote out of the basket. "Okay, what do you think?" He did not try to disguise how contrived he found the situation, and his voice became snide as he parroted the question. "Emmy, do you think *you* could be happy without love?" He looked at her, and his eyes flashed an accusation.

Immediately, Emmy guessed at what he was accusing her. She *had* asked Jack to be happy without love. Without Jessica. She felt her face flush. *Why had she thought they could have a conversation about this?* A rare moment of agreeability was ruined. She sat there for a second looking at Jack, whose eyes were fierce on her.

"Shit, it's been like ten goddamn minutes since I walked in the door. You can't leave this stuff alone, can you? Should I set my stopwatch for the tears? How long before that begins? Five seconds? Ten?"

"No." Emmy shouted, willing to meet his anger with her own, "No, I won't be crying because I won't be staying. Turn on the TV. Watch your stupid, stupid TV!"

"That's exactly what I'll do, thanks." He hit the remote, and the TV popped on. As Emmy stormed out of the room, the volume grew and grew until it became unbearably loud.

WEDNESDAY, SEPTEMBER 25: THE SOLID, UTTERLY STATIONARY BED

Once Emmy walked past the guards at the set's parking lot entrance, she followed the narrow corridors that ran between the many trucks and vans. Duncan's trailer was all the way in the back. She turned a corner created by a large truck and was beginning to walk the long straightaway to his trailer when she noticed Duncan standing at his open door. He called out to her: "I like your leaves."

Emmy looked down at the bouquet of leaves she held in her hand: "They're good colors, aren't they?" Though most of Cambridge's trees were still hardy with green leaves, a few had started to turn to fall colors. In walking the nine blocks from her office to the set, Emmy stopped occasionally to pick up bright yellow walnut and flaming red sugar maple leaves from the ground.

Duncan studied Emmy as she neared the trailer. She moved gracefully. Her cheeks were ablaze and her shoulder-length brown hair blew behind her. Duncan realized Kallie had been right: she was really pretty.

Now that he saw her attractiveness, he was puzzled he hadn't been more impressed with it from the beginning.

Was it because Emmy was older than most of the women he found attractive? He studied her coming closer to him. She had broad cheekbones with an open face, and the way she side-parted her hair, it swept across her forehead with a school-girl quality. No, Duncan realized, the reason he hadn't been more aware of her beauty had nothing to do with her age. It was because Emmy hadn't asked him to be aware of it. Duncan was used to women who announced their beauty with their ego first, daring those around them not to be impressed. But, there was nothing boastful with how Emmy carried herself.

"You're brown again," Emmy said as she walked up the stairs.

Duncan touched the top of his head. "Did you mistake me for Dustin Hoffman?"

"Completely," she smiled.

They walked inside the narrow trailer, and each went to the places where they sat the day before, Emmy on one brown couch and Duncan on the other. There was the awkward moment that Emmy knew well. It was never easy to begin a conversation with a relative stranger about heartfelt matters, and even in her own office setting, Emmy sometimes had to will herself to express an ease with this intimacy she didn't always feel. Here, it was even harder to get right. Yesterday, she'd been pleased Duncan had shared as much as he had, but was aware the communication style was … off. Too comfortable, actually. Today, Emmy had considered bringing a pen and notepad to the session, but at the last moment took them out of her purse. Their seating arrangement was such that anything she wrote down, Duncan could read. That would be awkward. No, she'd have to make her authority clear with her voice and manner. She'd already prepared how she would start. She propped her elbow on the couch's armrest and rested her head in her hand. "So, today I thought we could talk about your dog."

"Abner? You want to talk about Abner?"

"Oh, that's a nice dog name. I think a dog name should be one you wouldn't pick for your kids." She added, "But maybe I shouldn't say that. Maybe one day you'll want to name your son Abner too?" Her question was a purposeful lead.

Duncan laughed: "No." He leaned back on the couch, his legs outstretched; he was surprised at how comfortable he was to begin this conversation. "No, I'm not going to have kids for one, and if I did, I definitely wouldn't go with Abner."

"You don't want to have children?"

"No, I have no interest in becoming a father. Zero appeal." Duncan put his hands on his knees. "It's nothing against parenthood though. I mean, I'm sure being a mom has worked out great for you."

This threw her. "You know I'm a mom?"

He nodded; he'd prepared for the session too. "I asked Kallie to tell me about the *un-envious situation* under which you married your husband... and she told me what happened. Do you mind that I know?" Duncan was examining her closely.

She *did* mind, though she wasn't sure why. She worked to keep her voice cool and professional. "I guess it was obvious from what I said."

"But your marriage worked out in the end?"

There was such curiosity on his face that, again, she had to focus on not being ruffled. "I... I suppose so."

He smiled. "You don't sound sure."

She tried to think how best to respond – *"Well, I am sure"* or *"Actually, I'm not sure"* – then realized she shouldn't respond at all. "I think... we should talk about you now."

"Whatever you want." He smiled and leaned back in his chair, satisfied with what he'd learned from the exchange.

"Do you want to tell me why being a father holds zero appeal for you?"

Duncan shrugged. "You know why."

"Because of your father?"

"Yes. And I really don't want to talk about him yet." He wasn't angry, just adamant.

"Okay, that's fine." She tried to reestablish the comforting tone she'd meant today's conversation to have. "So, let's talk about Abner. Tell me about him."

"Okay, but…" he sat forward, "before I start going all gushy on my dog, I have to know if you've ever had a dog yourself."

Emmy nodded: "Yes. We had Sissy."

"*Sissy?*" Duncan grimaced.

Emmy laughed at his obvious distaste for the name. "My kids named her. They wanted to express she was like a sister for them. So: Sissy."

"Maybe it's okay then." He was readying to answer Emmy's question when a thought occurred to him. "What if the dog had been a boy?"

"Oh, it probably would have been much worse. Bro? Broey? Low-Bro?"

"Low-Bro!" He laughed, "Sissy is a hell of a lot better than Low-Bro."

Emmy laughed too. "I think anything is." She made herself stop laughing. She sat up straighter. "You were going to tell me about Abner?"

"Yes, that's right. Abner." He leaned back again, stretching his arms out in front of him. "What can I say? I got him from the pound right after coming to L.A, when everything in my life had just gone to hell. And I don't know what

would have happened to me without that dog in my life."
He looked at Emmy, "He... uh, he saved me."

This was an unusual way to put it. "How'd he save you?"

"Well, he loved me." Duncan said the answer like it was
obvious. "He was my family. He came with me everywhere
and did everything with me. There were a lot of 5-star experiences I missed because I always travelled with Abner. I
didn't give a shit. I liked taking care of him – I liked spoiling
him. I liked sleeping with him. Even the way he smelled –
that natty doggy breath, I liked that too. He wasn't a pretty
dog like those fucking ritzy L.A. dogs, but he was whip smart
and a good mate, and the day I had to put him down, that
was a bad, bad day."

Emmy let the silence sit before she spoke, "So, this might
seem like a funny question at first, but what do you think
worked with Abner that didn't work with Alison?"

Duncan laughed outright. "Okay, interesting question."
He put his hands palm down on his knees. "Well, with Alison,
she is, like you said yourself, very funny. She's smart and—"

"And beautiful."

Duncan looked at Emmy curiously. "She is that too."

"Sorry, I didn't mean to interrupt you."

Duncan noticed that Emmy's cheeks matched the color
of her lips when she blushed; it was a good color. He kept
his eyes on her cheeks. "Well, with Alison, her humor could
be harsh. She could cut someone to pieces, then leave them
there disassembled. It cracked her up. She wasn't mean
exactly, but she valued wit above compassion. And," he
paused and rubbed his hand against the back of his neck,
"that's probably why I never told her anything about my
past. The stuff I think I'm going to tell you. She wouldn't
have known what to do with it. She wanted me to be... *fun*."
He squinted his eyes. "The odd thing about her saying this

stuff about me being the love of her life was it made me see how superficially we knew each other. I didn't want that anymore. I wanted real."

"And 'real' is different than what you usually wanted?"

"You could say that. For most of my adult life I've not been..." he paused to figure out how to say what he meant, "very relationship-oriented."

"No?"

He shook his head; "No."

"What were you oriented toward?" She tried to ask the question seriously, but a hint of teasing found its way in.

Duncan sat up straighter. "Now, wait. You're getting the wrong idea."

"I don't think I have a wrong idea. You are a single man with a lot of options. That's fine. I understand."

"You make it sound like..."

"Like?"

"Like I'm a... *slut.*"

Emmy's eyes popped: "I didn't say that at all!"

Duncan ignored her protest and leaned forward. "Just so you know, I don't sleep with women under the age of 25. I don't have one-night stands," he rubbed his cheek; then added, "anymore. And I would bet every woman I've slept with in the last few years, they've thought of me as a notch on their belt way more than I've thought of them that way. Besides, most of these women with whom I've had..." he searched for the word.

"Flings," Emmy offered.

"Yes, flings. They're biding their time too. After awhile, neither of us wants to stick around. That's when I run. I'm pretty good at running. Every month, a sprint."

"Well, then. You have an arrangement that works well for you."

His eyes darted up. "Is that what you think I'm saying?"

The edge in his voice took her by surprise. "It's not what you're saying?"

"Not at all." He sat back. "Huh. It's interesting you heard it that way. Why would you think I was saying that?"

There he was again asking her another question. She shook her head. "What *are* you saying?"

"That it *doesn't* work for me. That it sucks. That it's very... *tiring*." His voice angled on this word. He sat silently, as though he was reflecting on what he'd said.

Emmy let the silence grow. "What makes it tiring?"

He didn't say anything. Duncan knew the precise answer to the question but when he looked up at Emmy he realized he couldn't say those words now. "I'm tired of being alone" should be the kind of thing you could say to your therapist, but deliberately he chose to say something else. "It would be nice to take care of someone."

"Take care? That's interesting. Most people would say it's nice to be taken care of."

"Well, I guess that's good too." He paused and took a deep breath. "Can I tell you about something?"

Emmy smiled gently. "That's why I'm here."

It was a trivial story in most ways, but he'd thought about it a lot. He leaned forward, his knees only a foot from Emmy's knees. "Before this shoot, I was back in L.A for around five days, and this thing happened there with my publicist Chris."

"A publicist is different from a manager?"

"Yeah, Chris manages different things than Kallie, media things. And Chris – unlike Kallie – is someone if you'd asked me two weeks ago, was he my friend, I'd have said, yeah, of course he is. I talk to him multiple times a week, he knows every aspect of my personal life, we shoot the breeze, yeah, we're good mates.

"Well, on Thursday, Chris mentions he's going away for the weekend and his regular dog sitter is away. So I told him I'd be happy to take the dog for the weekend. He knows I love dogs; he knows I was upset when Abner died. But he says no thanks, he has a plan already in place. I figured he'd have a neighbor keep the dog, something like that. Well, the next time we talk, Chris mentions in passing his dog had been in a kennel for the weekend. I couldn't believe it. I asked him why hadn't he just bloody fucking given me the dog. And he said ..." Duncan imitated Chris' Californian cool delivery – "Man, I would never ask you to do *anything* for me." He said it like he was trying to do right by me, like he was upholding some kind of professional code or something. So, there it was."

Emmy asked: "There what was?"

"For Chris, I'm a *client*. Not a friend."

"You feel like you aren't real friends unless he—"

Duncan interrupted: "Unless he's willing to ask me for help. But he won't." Duncan leaned back; he put his hands behind his head, looked up at the ceiling. "It shouldn't surprise me. I know why it happened; I know what I created."

"What did you create?"

It was hard to explain it, he realized. His voice grew grim. "I keep myself pretty fucking self-contained."

Emmy nodded. She knew exactly what he meant; she did this too.

He looked at her for a moment and looked away again. "My cell phone has around 300 peoples' numbers in it, but no one on that contact list would call me for *help*. And there's no one there I'd call to say the stuff I'm going to say to you. If there was that one person, I probably... I probably wouldn't be talking to you." Quickly, his eyes furrowed, and he looked over at Emmy, who sat so close he could have touched her. "I'm sorry, I don't think that came across the way I meant it."

"Don't worry," she smiled back, "I'm not offended."

"I like talking to you." He said it simply, without trying to be earnest.

"Well..." Emmy stalled. *Should she return the compliment?* "Thank you."

Duncan continued, "Everyone I do talk to regularly, they are mostly people I pay to be there. There are literally teams of people who make money taking care of my life. But these relationships, they're clean-cut. They are business; transactions." A thought occurred to him; he winced. "Of course the irony here is I'm paying you to tell you this."

Emmy saw his discomfort. "But it's different here."

He cocked an eyebrow. "Is it? You tell me how."

"It is, because ..."

Duncan interrupted: "Would you let me take care of your dog?"

"I don't have a dog."

"Sissy?"

"Dead."

"Anyway, it doesn't matter. I know you're not supposed to—"

Emmy interrupted, "But if I had a dog now, I'd let you take care of her."

Duncan stopped, examining her more closely. "You would?"

Emmy nodded. She wasn't sure she was telling the truth, but right now it didn't matter. "I think you'd be great for my dog."

"Your dog would like me?"

"No question."

He looked at her for a long moment. "Well, that's good to know." He grinned. "Thank you."

Emmy smiled back. "It's me who should be thanking you. You know, for all your great dog help."

There was a knock on the door; Ling stuck her head in. "Duncan, you're supposed to be in wardrobe in five."

Duncan looked at his phone. "I should probably go. Can I walk you out?"

Emmy gathered her purse and sweater, and together they walked out the trailer's narrow door and down its tiny steps. As they began to cross the parking lot that was crowded with trailers and trucks, Emmy grew aware that everyone they passed stopped to watch them.

She leaned toward Duncan. "What are people going to say if you have a woman come to your trailer every day at 11:30?"

"They'll *say* a lot. But I don't give a shit. Do you mind?"

She considered it for a moment. "No, I guess not."

"Good." He found her response relieved him more than he expected it to. They were standing where Emmy needed to turn to head out. Duncan stood close enough so he had to look down to her. "I'll see you tomorrow then?"

"Yes, right, tomorrow." She briefly took in the nearness of his broad shoulders, the ease of the smile in his gray-blue eyes and realized she needed to make herself turn now. She did, making her stride purposeful.

As soon as Emmy left his side, Ling approached him, eager to have his attention. She had an iPad that included an apparent list, and as they walked toward the set, Ling posed questions and typed in his responses. With Ling tapping at her screen, he peered behind. Emmy was just in the process of picking up a bright red leaf from the ground. Duncan watched her walk away, holding the leaf like a flower.

Maria wanted to give Emmy the utility bills for the month. Honestly, she couldn't believe how pricey August's electricity bill was. The old Victorian house that held their offices had no insulation, and during that hot spell, both she and Emmy had their window air conditioning units running the whole time, and now, holy moly, they were paying the price for it. Maria knocked on Emmy's slightly ajar door. "Emmy, I've got the electri—" Maria stopped short; she stared at the content on her friend's laptop screen, then at Emmy, who whipped around when she heard Maria enter. "Honey, are you looking at pictures of… Duncan Grier?"

Emmy spun around in her seat. "Yes. He's making a movie nearby. Did you know that? I was out walking the other day, and went right by the set. It made me curious. That's the reason I looked him up."

Maria couldn't help smiling. "That's a lot of explanation. It's not *porn*." Maria laid the bills on Emmy's desk and leaned in close to the laptop to look at the picture of Duncan Grier. She pointed to the photo on the screen, "That's a nice one of him and Alison." Leaning over Emmy's shoulder, Maria used the keypad to click through to the photos in the library. "Oh, that shot is right after their break-up. Doesn't he look relieved it's over?"

Emmy leaned in to look at the photograph. "He looks like he's walking through an airport."

"Oh, honey, it's right there, clear as day: Immense relief."

"Mmm, don't see it. How can you be so certain?"

Maria stood up, hand on hip. "I simply resist uncertainty. It's a great way to propel life forward. That way you don't… *stall*. I think you should try it." Maria couldn't keep herself from hinting sometimes. She didn't want her friend to divorce necessarily, but she did want her to *decide*. Shit or get off the pot. A crude expression, but didn't it apply here? Yes, it did. Her husband, Nathan, was frequently reminding Maria that she needed to "seriously self-edit." He said, "She's not your daughter and she doesn't need hen-pecking."

The narrow eyes that Emmy cast on Maria now made it clear Maria had probably overstepped. Again. "Honey, I just mean you should try to have more fun. That's all. You see, having opinions is fun. Being certain about little things like Duncan Grier and Alison Lockyer were a lousy couple – fun!"

Emmy seemed to pounce on this comment. "But why are you certain about that?"

"Well…" Maria loved celebrity gossip. "Alison Lockyer: *such* a prickly pear, all about herself. And the Grier, ah, there's a man with hidden vulnerability. If you ask me, it's the secret of his smile; he's got that a trace of fragility in it. Women eat that stuff up."

"Hmm. I guess they do." Emmy clicked through a few more photos in the website's library, then abruptly turned around. "Maria, would you ever ask a client to take care of your dog?"

Maria snorted, "I thought you were going to ask me something about Duncan Grier."

"No, no, not about him. I'm just trying to figure out if maybe I crossed a line in a therapy session today. I told this client I would let him take care of my dog."

"You don't have a dog."

"I know; it was a pretend dog, a hypothetical dog."

Maria shook her head, "You've got to stop this hemming and hawing! Go boldly; ask for help with your pretend dog. No one should worry as much as you do!"

Jack's car was not in the garage; there were no lights on in the house, even though it was almost 10 p.m. Opening the front door, the sound of Emmy's heels against the floorboards echoed against the house's bigness. She shivered as she heard it.

Tonight, she'd taken herself out to dinner at Henrietta's Table, then walked aimlessly around Harvard Square. She wanted to delay her time at home. Ever since Tess left for school, the house was like a shoe two sizes too big; its emptiness chafed. When Marc and Ben had gone off, she'd felt their absences too – there was less clutter, laughter, laundry, bickering. But the emptiness didn't feel as stark as it did now. Without Tess there – without any of her children there at all – the house was dead. There were multiple rooms for dining where no one dined, a library where no one read, a TV room that was always quiet. Emmy decided to go to each of her kids' rooms. She climbed the stairs. Marc's room. Ben's room. Tess's. She sat in them, smelled them, looked at the odd collections of things they'd left behind.

Something about the stillness reminded her of the small Manhattan apartment that had been her home growing up. That apartment had been such a tiny one – Emmy imagined its whole 720 square feet could fit inside their current kitchen – but even in its crowded clutter, that apartment was a lonely place. Her mother usually worked two jobs, as a dance teacher at a small studio, and then sometimes as an evening receptionist or occasionally, a waitress – whatever paid most. And her dad drove his Yellow Cab most evenings, or at least that's what he said he was doing. This meant Emmy returned alone to that apartment every day after school or dance class. She hated the lonely feeling of that place, but her parents insisted she stay in and do her homework. They always reminded her how much they were sacrificing to live in an area where she could get a good Manhattan education. And even though Emmy's parents weren't terribly responsible themselves – Gabriel sometimes went on drinking binges for days and Rose had trouble keeping food in the fridge or the electricity bill paid – they counted on her to be careful and conscientious.

Now, Emmy undressed, pulled back the comforter and plopped up the pillows on her bed to make herself cozy. She was eager to begin re-reading *The Visiting Professor*, which she'd just bought that night at the Harvard Coop bookstore. The last time she'd read the novel, she hadn't been able to decide whether the story ended happily or not, and walking around Harvard Square tonight, it struck her as quite important to figure that out. It would be nice too to tell Duncan she was reading it again. He'd like that.

Emmy was only five pages in when she heard Jack's car pull into the driveway, then the back door open and close, and eventually Jack's even plodding coming up the stairs. She was relieved not to be the only one in the house anymore, though when Jack walked into the room, he walked past her without even a "Hi." Seeing his mood, Emmy stayed quiet too. She guessed he was still pissy about last night. That was fine. It was easier for them not to talk; it was what they did best. Once Jack was in his pajamas, he sank into the loveseat in front of the TV and clicked it on, loud noise filling the space between them.

Emmy thought about all the empty rooms in their house and how peculiar it was that they still regularly chose to ignore each other in this one. Maria often marveled that she and Jack still slept in the same bedroom, but Emmy knew why they'd never deviated from the arrangement.

For one, the whole reason she and Jack had waited two years to divorce was to preserve the perception of family unity for their children, and this objective was obviously better affected with one bedroom than two. The second reason was one Emmy chose not to share with Maria: she and Jack still slept together. Not just shared a bed; they had sex.

Emmy knew this was unusual in couples as estranged as she and Jack. But to Emmy it made sense. She liked sex, and her sex with Jack had always been the best part of their relationship. Two years ago, when they'd made the decision to divorce after Tess left for college, it never occurred to Emmy they'd forego sex while they remained married. Their sex wasn't loving per se, but Emmy preferred their purely carnal connection to no connection at all. Sure, sometimes the emotions of their intimacy created confusion, but erecting dams to compartmentalize unwieldy floods of feelings was something Emmy did instinctually, and she'd trained herself to enjoy the sex itself without hoping to give or get more.

She looked at Jack sitting on the love seat, the TV's lights shifting across his still face. She wondered: once they divorced, would she still miss sex with Jack? Probably. It wasn't a reason not to divorce of course. Divorce was what was best for them – she convinced herself of this over and over again multiple times most days. Last night was proof they couldn't even maintain a simple conversation without shouting. *There was a reason they'd made their plan. They should move forward with the plan.* It occurred to her: They were in the same room now. There was no reason not to announce that to Jack this moment.

The TV shut off. She opened her mouth, but as Jack walked toward her rubbing his eyes, she shut it again.

"Ems, I'm nodding off already. Mind if I turn off the light?" He sleepily gestured to her book, "Can you use your reading lamp?"

Emmy wondered why he'd decided to speak now. And he'd called her "Ems." *That was nice.* "It's okay; I think I'll just go to sleep too."

With the light off, Emmy lay on her side of the bed. Only two feet away, Jack's body became more relaxed and his breathing more measured. Soon, he would be asleep. Emmy looked at her husband, at his closed, peaceful eyes, his expressionless face, his lips quiet and full. She knew what she wanted. With a quiet motion, she moved to Jack's side and brought her body close enough so her breasts grazed his chest; she slid her hands down the inside of his pajama leg and cradled his balls in her hand. Jack's body startled at the contact, then relaxed again. He opened his eyes; Emmy looked into them. Without saying anything, he groggily pulled her into his body.

This was the way their sex life worked. They didn't talk about it, they didn't kiss or caress each other much; they just had sex. And as sex went, it wasn't bad. Emmy usually came. Jack slept soundly afterward. But the prominent emotion of their intimacy was anger. There was passion to this anger, which made the sex itself still work. And sadness too. They didn't like needing each other in this most bodily way when they tried so hard not to need each other at all. When Emmy and Jack would lie next to each other afterward, their breathing heavier, their bodies warm, their smells so near, Emmy would sometimes find tears streaming her cheeks. She doubted Jack knew this. It was dark after all. And Emmy herself rarely realized the tears were coming. They were just there.

When they were first married, their sex had been different. Then, they'd made love three or four times a day. Jack adored Emmy's pregnant body, her super swollen breasts, her belly so curved. And Emmy relished the act of their bodies working in sync, Jack's nakedness beside her afterward, the languorous exhaustion that came from their over-indulgence in each other.

Actually, when her young body wasn't having sex with Jack, she sometimes still felt awkward in his presence. They were married and about to have a child together, but for all that bound them together, they were still getting to know each other too. The more Emmy learned about Jack, the more she recognized how different they were from each other. Jack liked precision, clean lines, neat spaces. Order, he liked to remind Emmy, was his aesthetic as an architect. When Emmy left dishes piled on the kitchen counters or dirty underwear on the bathroom floor, Jack would get angry, not just because she didn't keep things neat but because she didn't care about space in the same deep way he did.

Jack also couldn't stand Emmy's tears. All her life, Emmy had cried easily. Her tears were not loud or dramatic tears, just her body's way of leaking the built-up emotionalism she tried to ignore. But when the tears appeared, Jack would respond as though they were an insult to him, to all his efforts. At first, he told Emmy that she had to be crying so much because of the pregnancy. But after Marc's birth, the tears didn't stop. In fact, they came more frequently. "Why can't you just control it?" he stormed at her. She couldn't, and eventually Jack began to ignore her when he saw her crying. That's at least how it felt to Emmy.

It made Emmy unhappy that Jack sometimes found her annoying, but it didn't alarm her. She reasoned that annoyance was part of marriage. Her parents had driven each other crazy –a running fight was always going between them – and not having many other models of marriage, she assumed her husband's frustrations were part and parcel of matrimony. Still, as Jack's irritation with her became a backdrop to their interactions, Emmy began to realize that one of the things she liked best about her husband was no longer true. He used to adore her; now he didn't. She began to consider, maybe she wasn't so keen on him either. He was a man who didn't like to dance. A man who rattled on and on about preposterously pompous design theory. A man who frequently made her feel silly or unsophisticated or weak.

Still, it never occurred to her – and she didn't think it occurred to Jack either – that they should separate. Marc was born five months after their wedding. And right away, Jack said he'd hate anyone to think Marc was the mistake that brought them together. Their family shouldn't be anything short of enviable. Emmy liked it when Jack talked about building their family; he wanted at least four kids, close together in age. So, Ben was born fifteen months after Marc. And then Tess another sixteen months after Ben. Everyone thought they were crazy. Emmy's mother sent a gift-wrapped package of condoms. Their friends teasingly reminded them they were twentysomethings, not thirtysomethings. But Emmy knew they were trying to do their best with what they'd been given, and she enjoyed how united she and Jack were in their fervent determination not to fail.

They'd been so young. Every time Emmy looked back on those years, this was the thought that hit her like a revelation. At the time, neither Emmy nor Jack considered their age to be a particular challenge. Parenting was hard, yes, but they didn't consider it harder for being youthful themselves. Marc was a colicky baby, then a huge tantrum-thrower as a toddler; Ben was a trouble-seeker who landed in the emergency room first with a marble stuck up his nose at eighteen months and then with a broken arm at three; and Tess was Emmy's sensitive child, so clingy she never wanted to be put down. Jack would return from his days at school and then later from the Boston firm where he'd taken a position, and Emmy would tell him about her days and he would listen and try to help. He was an involved dad; he'd play ball or chase while Emmy made dinner and handle bath time and read bedtime stories. Emmy was so impressed with Jack's commitment to his parenting, she'd always assumed he was just as committed to her. They'd worry and exult over and adore their children so much, it was easy to forget there was little else they wanted to share with each other.

On the winter day Jessica knocked on the Halperin door, everything Emmy understood about her marriage changed. It was a Thursday, and Jack was at work. Emmy held Tess, then only four months old, tightly to her chest as she held the door back. The blonde pregnant woman who stood there was no one Emmy had ever seen before, and she guessed she must be a friend of Jack's from work or Harvard. "I'm sorry, Jack's at work," she explained.

"I know. May I come in anyway?" Jessica asked the question but didn't wait for its answer. She walked right in and arranged herself on the living room couch. Emmy didn't know what to do. Her house was a mess; her sons, Marc and Ben, then just toddlers, were playing at throwing wet paper towels around the room, and Emmy had been hoping to nurse Tess to sleep. She didn't appreciate this woman's sudden intrusion and didn't like her manner either. "What can I help you with?" she asked curtly. Jessica set her eyes directly on Emmy; "Oh, I'm here to help *you.*" Jessica rubbed her pregnant belly and then put a most unusual smile on her face. "This…" she waited, "is your husband's child."

Years later, Emmy overheard her sons – by then teenagers – discussing how clearly they remembered their mother's reaction in that moment. Ben said, "I remember it like a storm." And Marc agreed: "Yeah, Mom became a tornado." Until overhearing this conversation, Emmy assumed her two sons had no memory of the incident. They were barely verbal then. But somehow the scene must have imprinted on their memories, for their description was apt.

With Jessica's announcement thick in the air, Emmy stood staring at her sitting on the couch for one second, maybe two. A lot of questions and confusion slapped her brain, but she clung to two quick conclusions: one, Jessica was trying to ruin her life; two, she wouldn't let her. When Emmy found her voice, it was loud, throaty and furious: "You will leave our home now!" She shouted this statement over and over again, and though she held Tess close with one arm, she used the other to violently yank Jessica to the door and push her out of it. Jessica tried to resist, but Emmy overwhelmed her. She didn't care that Jessica was pregnant; she didn't care that her response lacked control or that her children saw her act violently. No, those things didn't matter then.

Right away, Emmy called Jack and ordered him home. When he walked in, Emmy met him at the door, holding Tess tight to her chest, rocking her up and down as the baby wailed. Amidst the din of the infant cries, Emmy said coldly: "I know about Jessica. She's been here; she's shown us what you've done." Jack's face drained of color; he opened his mouth. But Emmy's eyes darted at him, and his lips closed tight. She kept her voice level, restraining all its desire to pitch into anger, to melt into sadness. She bopped Tess up and down like the action was as necessary to her as to the baby. "You'll have to choose, Jack. Our family. Or hers. You can't have both." Jack's expression did not move from its frozen state of shock, and this was when her voice began to tremble: "You should leave now, and..." her voice finally cracked, "...not come back until you've decided."

Jack began to mumble an apology, but Emmy went into Tess' room and shut the door. When she emerged, Jack was gone. The rest of that day, it was though a siren was going off in Emmy's body that wouldn't turn off. She'd done a quick survey of her life as soon as the door had closed on Jessica, and it hadn't taken long for her to see: Without Jack, she was utterly alone. Her mom had died just months before. Her father had been gone for years. She had no siblings, few close friends, no money of her own, barely any education. She was twenty-three years old with three children under the age of four. If Jack left her, she couldn't fathom how she'd make it. And it wasn't just money she worried about; it was the thought of living without Jack. She needed him. To feed the boys at breakfast time, to read them stories when he came home, to share one of the several wake-ups that happened each and every night. In that moment, losing her children's father felt far, far worse than accepting his affair. She didn't care whom he loved. She wanted him – badly – to stay.

When he came home again it was 2 a.m., but Emmy was up, waiting in their bed. "I did what you wanted," he said tersely. "It's over." His face looked drained, his eyes haunted, as though he'd seen too much that day. He started to get undressed, and Emmy sat silently, watching him. When he finished putting his pajamas on, Jack slumped on his side of the bed, sinking his head in his hands. "I love her; it wouldn't have happened if I didn't love her." His hands covered his eyes, his voice cracked. The statement offered explanation, apology and accusation all at once. Emmy sat, taking everything in. Right then, it didn't sting that her husband was professing his love for another woman. She was too relieved he'd chosen her. What she did feel was enormously sad – for him, for her, for them as a couple. When he reached out to grab her hand, she gave it to him. He bowed his head and wept, and that night, Jack didn't mind that Emmy cried too.

Despite their closeness that night, the light of day cast a different shadow. In the daytime, Jack's emotions no longer spilled; they were tightly buttoned up. He didn't seem sad or angry, only blank. For Emmy, all the hurt she'd postponed feeling the day before came crashing into her. She was excruciatingly humiliated to find she needed a man who loved someone else. Everything was changed, and because Emmy was unclear about what to say or how to say it, she decided to say little. It became a stony silence that formed the foundation of their new relationship.

Over the years since, there were periods when this silence was interrupted by overt hostility and other times when Jack and Emmy got along reasonably well. There was even a period when they tried hard – really hard – to make their relationship work again. Overall, they were never so far off the mark. They respected each other; they worked well with each other. Tasks like cleaning the kitchen or loading the car for a trip, they did these well together. When Marc screamed and threw things or when Ben stayed out all night when he was 16, they easily agreed what the consequences would be. They voted the same Democratic ticket and read the New York Times cover to cover each weekend, albeit in separate corners of the house. Their lives had a full schedule, and all the elements in it were ones they'd chosen together. From the alarm ring in the morning until their kids were settled in their beds, there was such a rush of meals and carpools and business trips and soccer games that when they sat together on the bedroom's loveseat at the end of their days, their lack of affection wasn't hugely apparent. There were still plenty of logistics to discuss. They kept their emotional worlds separate from each other, yes. But they were still tied together tight with the intricate type of knot used to fasten boats to their anchors. Emmy thought that if the knot were untied, she'd drift and bob endlessly on open water.

Now, in the dark bedroom, Jack returned to his side of the bed to get sex-sated sleep. Emmy turned over too, closing her eyes, trying to be restful under the covers. The sex hadn't made her feel closer to Jack, nor less close. It just was, as they just were. Two naked bodies next to each other in their big bed, in their big house, together and alone. They'd now spent the better part of their lives falling asleep beside each other. In their solid, utterly stationary bed, they'd travelled through so much time together.

Should they have?

As Emmy was finally dozing off to sleep, she realized it wasn't even the right question to ask.

THURSDAY, SEPTEMBER 26:
BUTTERFLIES

Emmy had just fastened her seat belt when she heard her cell phone ring from deep within her purse. She scrambled to find it in time.

"Hello?"

"Emmy, hey, it's me; Duncan."

"Oh... hello." She put the phone on her shoulder and started to slowly back her car out of the driveway. "You're calling me today instead of Ling?" They had an arrangement that Ling, Duncan's assistant, would call Emmy every morning to confirm that nothing had come up to derail their 11:30 a.m. meeting.

"Actually, that's why I'm calling. Ling screwed up. She should have called you last night. I don't think I can meet today."

"Oh." She stopped the car's reverse. Her spirits plummeted. "Why not?"

On the other end of the phone, Duncan's face brightened. He'd wanted to place the call himself to hear firsthand how she'd respond to the cancellation. Emmy's disappointment couldn't have been clearer had she announced it. "We're shooting over at Harvard Business School today and tomorrow," he said. "I don't think I'm going to have the regular mid-day break; there's a tight shooting schedule because we only have this spot for two days."

"So, then you won't be able to meet tomorrow either?" This time Emmy controlled her voice.

"No, I'll find a way so I can see you tomorrow. Can I call you later to work it out?"

There was no reason to say "No." So, she said, "Yes," and quickly got off the phone.

Rearranging clients' appointments was part of her job; she did it all the time. *So, why did she have butterflies in her stomach?* She hit the accelerator and reversed far too quickly out of her driveway.

FRIDAY, SEPTEMBER 27:
PROMISES

Ling pointed Emmy to the top of the stadium stairs where Duncan was sitting. It was Friday, 11:30 a.m., and since Duncan had no trailer at the Business School, he'd asked Emmy to do their therapy session in the bleachers of the Harvard Stadium. Emmy's feet hitting the concrete steps kept an even rhythm as she climbed the stairs to meet him.

When Duncan had called the night before, Emmy just happened to have her cell phone close at hand. Jack wasn't home yet, so ostensibly, she was waiting for Jack's call, but she wasn't sure for whom she was preparing this alibi; she knew it was Duncan's call she anticipated. After seeing him these three days, a day without him was noticeably less interesting. This worried her. She didn't mean to be thinking about him; she tried not to. It wasn't working. Reviewing each of their three therapy sessions, she could isolate no one remark that was flirtatious in and of itself; yet, she was aware the overall tenor of their conversations swayed toward a familiar comfort rather than a therapeutic comfort. She wasn't sure how this kept happening, so it was difficult to know how to stop it. But, *she would, she would.*

When Duncan eventually called, however, she found it hard to keep this resolution. He asked about her day, inquired jokingly about what she'd done with the extra time he'd given her, told her about the scenes he filmed. She tried to clip the chatty conversation, returning again to the matter of rescheduling, but Duncan refused to take the hint. When he laid out his plan for how they could meet at the Harvard Stadium the next day, it had been her plan to say "No." Travelling to different locations wasn't inherently *un*professional, but it was unusual. She was just about to suggest they wait to see each other in his trailer on Monday when Jack walked in. Her husband examined her quizzically, and Emmy realized she had a loopy grin on her face. Suddenly, it felt altogether easier to agree to Duncan's location suggestion than to have Jack overhear a longer, more delicate conversation about why she could not.

"Have you ever done a therapy session in a football stadium before?" Duncan called out to her as he trotted down the stairs to meet her.

"Only baseball stadiums." She smiled, then waved an arm outward to indicate the big open space: "Don't you worry photographers will find you here?"

"I'm not very interesting to the paps these days. Too old."

Emmy reached Duncan's level. "Kallie made it sound like they *hound* you."

Duncan quipped, "Kallie wishes they hounded me." He studied Emmy curiously, "You're not even winded? When Ling climbed up here, she just about had a coronary."

Emmy was happy he noticed. "I run a lot. I did a marathon a few years ago."

"You're a marathon runner?" He was impressed. "I've run a few too. What's your time?"

Emmy laughed. "I can't tell you my time! I'm sure you ran it twice as fast as I did!"

Duncan liked the sound of her laugh. He wanted to make her laugh more. The air was warmish, in the mid-sixties, but her cheeks were still ruddy, and the breeze blew lightly so that her hair wisped across her lips. Duncan had to restrain himself from brushing it away. He found he wanted an excuse to touch her.

Emmy had flitted through Duncan's mind over the last two days too. And yet, for all her time in his head, he wasn't sure what, exactly, he was thinking about her. He liked the way they talked together. He liked looking at her, watching emotion transpire on her face, looking at her lips, her eyes. That was all he knew. The thought had occurred to him that he was playing a game with her. Trying to draw out her desire for him when he knew damn well she wasn't supposed to feel that. He wasn't meaning to be careless right now; in fact, he meant to be on his absolute best behavior.

They sat beside each other, on a top bleacher, and the gray sky was so low with its clouds, it felt like they were in them. The stadium was deserted save for some grounds-keepers who were moving football equipment on the field far below them. It was a huge empty space they had to themselves.

The concrete benches were hard and it wasn't easy to face forward and look at each other. Emmy had to pivot at her waist as she spoke. "I thought today maybe we could pick up on some of the things we were talking about last time. You had said you wanted people to seek your help and rely on you. But then you also described that in your... flings you frequently found yourself running away when your... girlfriends, or the women you're with, wanted more."

Duncan enjoyed seeing how Emmy navigated around the phrasings she found awkward. "Mmm-hmm." He tried to remind himself not to joke.

"Do you have any thoughts on that dynamic?"

He looked out at the green turf field below him. "I'm not sure it reflects well on me, but with most women, I don't want them to stick around. The relationship issues, all that figuring out where 'things stand,' – ah, it's a pain in the arse."

"Arse?"

"Arse, ass. What, you're making fun of my accent now?"

"No, no, it's just you sounded more Australian with that one word. Sorry. I shouldn't have interrupted you."

His eyes danced. "Do you think there's something psychologically meaningful that I prefer 'arse' to 'ass.' Something Freudian?" He leaned back so he could watch her better. "You know, ass just doesn't sound as nice. Doesn't arse sound nicer?"

"Hmm," she considered it. "Arse. Ass. I guess it does. Rounder somehow."

"Precisely. *Rounder.* I'm glad you agree."

Emmy realized this exchange might have crossed the line into flirtation – *in and of itself* and otherwise. *She would be more careful.* She sat up taller. "So, you were saying," she smiled, "that women feel like pains."

He laughed. "Is that what I said? Well, let me rephrase. Women are not pains. They are wonderful. I like them a lot." He looked out at the empty rows of stadium benches. "I think my problem with relationships is I have a low tolerance for effort. If it starts to feel like too much work, I run." He pivoted himself to face her, and his voice grew playful. "So, Emmy, you'll have to teach me how not to run."

Emmy let a smile escape before she locked it down. "I don't know if *not running* can be taught. And besides, I doubt you'd want to stay only for the sake of staying." As the words left her mouth, she couldn't help noticing how they applied to her own life.

77

"But if I never want to stay, isn't that also a problem?"

Emmy observed his tone had lost its jokiness. "Let me ask you this: if I were to teach you…" A breeze blew a strand of Emmy's hair across her face; she pulled it away, "Rather, if *one* were to teach you to stay, what do you think should be taught?"

He smiled at her correction. "I guess *one* would have to teach me about what is good about staying. What I could get out of it. Why it can be better in the end than running."

Emmy saw Duncan was looking right into her eyes, and she chose to return his gaze. "What do *you* think would be good about staying?"

He laughed, and ran his hand across the back of his neck. "Abstractly, everything. You have love, you have company, you have someone to take care of, someone who is taking care of you. As a concept, it's brilliant. It's just not anything I've found myself wanting to do in reality." He leaned toward her. "Have I convinced you yet I'm fucked up?"

She smiled. "You're not fucked up."

"We'll see if you still think that later," Duncan said doubtfully, but he was grinning again. He leaned back stretching his legs out in front of him.

"You haven't always wanted to run. You said you once had a love of your life."

"I did." Duncan nodded. "But that was ages ago. I was a kid really."

"Did she know everything about your father?" Emmy asked, as that seemed to be the linchpin for him.

Duncan raised his eyebrows; "She knew."

"Did you want to run from her?"

"From Sarah? No. Not at all. I wanted her too much." He stopped. "That's… that's what ruined it."

Emmy could tell that talking about Sarah would provide helpful insights for their therapy. *Wasn't it just as a therapist that she was curious? Yes, yes.* Emmy shifted her position on the hard concrete seats, turning toward Duncan. "Could you tell me what happened with Sarah?"

Duncan grimaced. "I could, but it feels pretty fucking ridiculous as a 38-year old telling you about my teenage girlfriend. You really want to know about this?"

Emmy nodded.

"What do you want to know?"

"Whatever you want to tell me."

He studied how comfortably Emmy sat watching him. Most people looked at him expectantly, as though they were trying to guess what he'd want them to say next. Emmy had a comfort about her that was... serene. Yes, serene. He took a big breath and let himself think about that time long ago. "Well, when I first met Sarah, we couldn't have been more different. She was smart and studious and good and pretty in this quiet way. And I" – his eyes squinted with the recollection – "I was probably a minute away from juvenile delinquency. I was surfing a lot and hanging with these guys who skipped school, and we'd go to Maroubra beach and get drunk and high. But when Sarah and I started dating," he half-smiled with the memory, "well, I decided I needed to become like her.

"Sarah liked to do her homework right after school, and as we started to hang out more, I started to do homework with her too. I began paying attention in school and since I knew Sarah was going to go to college, I worked to save money for college too." He turned to Emmy, "That's how I got started with acting. I was just trying to make the most money possible; I did some modeling and then a couple commercials here and there."

He sat for a moment thinking, looking out at the stadium below him. Duncan's accent was usually only barely detectable, but Emmy noticed it grew stronger, his voice deeper, as he talked about Sarah. "It's strange to remember now because I haven't been like this in a long time, but all I wanted was to be with her. We were inseparable those last two years of high school. And she turned me around. My grades and scores were suddenly great, and the teachers and guidance counselors," he snickered, "they all thought I was the living embodiment of the comeback kid, Albert Einstein from the hood. So through some sort of miracle I ended up getting into the University of Sydney just like Sarah did. Considering what a fuck-up I'd been, it was unexpected; my mother near about jumped out of her skin when I told her. And when we went off to school, everything felt perfect; Sarah and I were there together; her mates were my mates. We even took some classes together. "He didn't say anything for a while."

Emmy purposefully stayed silent, waiting for his story to resume.

"But mid-way through our first year, I realized I wasn't going to have enough money for my sophomore year. It worried me because I didn't want anything to change. Then like a gift, this director on a commercial I'd done suggested I put together an audition tape for this horror flick. He knew the director and he passed the tape along, and I ended up getting the part. "*In Nancy's Room*." Duncan turned to Emmy with a cocked eyebrow; "Ever seen that one?"

Emmy smiled back: "Nope, missed it."

Duncan half-laughed. "It was miss-able. I got paid a lot – or at least what I thought was a lot then – but I had to go to L.A. for the summer. Which I did." Duncan stopped again, this time for several seconds. "That's when it ended."

"What was it that made it end?"

Duncan didn't turn toward her; he stayed facing forward as he answered the question. "Well, it was pre-cellphone, pre-caller i.d., I don't even think Sarah had an answering machine. But there was a week when I probably called her twenty times a day, and she was never there and she was never calling me. I was going crazy. And then finally, she picked up the phone, and she told me she had started seeing this guy, Brian. A guy I knew. Really if there hadn't been an ocean separating us, I would have tried to kill him. But..." Duncan paused for a very long time.

"But?" Emmy repeated.

"I didn't kill him." He looked up at Emmy, who was watching him quietly. "Instead, I decided I'd never go back to Australia. And I would try hard not to fail, even without her in my life." He turned back to the football field below. The clouds were settling lower in the sky, foggy and humid. "Sometimes I wonder what Sarah thinks about the person I've become. I mean, I'm sure she's aware of me."

"Definitely," Emmy said softly.

"I think she'd be puzzled by me now."

"Why do you say that?"

"Well, I'm pretty fucking different than I was then."

"How are you different?"

"It'd take less time to say how I'm the same." He started to smile, then stopped, his face left to an expression that was undeniably sad. For the first time, Emmy thought Duncan looked vulnerable.

"Do you feel more comfortable with the person you were then or the person you are now?" Emmy asked.

Duncan saw her eyes were on him full of concern. It was nice to be looked at like that. He spoke slowly, "I know why I am who I am. And I know what I could have become.

I'm okay with how it turned out." He admired her for a moment longer. "Emmy, can I ask you a question?"

Emmy guessed from his tone that the question was not one that belonged in a therapy session. "Well, you can ask."

He wasn't sure how to phrase what he wanted to know. He was barely sure what he wanted to know. "Are you... are you happy?"

She didn't know what she'd expected, but this question wasn't it. It took her so by surprise she couldn't think what to do but answer honestly. "I'm, I'm not sure," she said, her voice suddenly wobbly. Without being able to stop it, tears filled her eyes. Quickly, she turned her head away.

Duncan saw the tears; he felt responsible for provoking them. He reached out to touch her arm; "I'm sorry; I shouldn't have asked that."

Emmy shook her head lightly and wiped the tears from her face. "No, no. I cry really easily. It's pretty pathetic actually."

"It's not pathetic. It's nice, the tears."

"They're nice?" She laughed; "No one thinks they're nice." She ran her hand across her wet cheeks.

"I do," he said.

That night Duncan knew he had to go for a run. Gus had asked if he wanted to have dinner together after they'd watched the dailies, but Duncan begged off. He was too agitated to be anyone's company. He arrived back at his hotel room at 10 p.m. and only minutes later, jogged out the service entrance. It was colder than he expected; he needed a fast pace to stay warm, but that was fine. Duncan enjoyed it when he had to run farther or faster or push more, because he would make himself overcome the challenge. He thought this aspect of exercise – where he had to use his mind to control his impulses – was what he liked best.

As he ran, he could feel the layers of confusion in his body. He couldn't believe that when he should be laser-focused on keeping in his character's head, he instead felt loose and scattered. Usually, when he was working, he went to great efforts to avoid distractions. He was getting paid ridiculous amounts of money, and hundreds of people's work couldn't look good unless he delivered his best. It seemed a basic responsibility to cordon off personal problems until filming was done. Location shoots rarely lasted more than five or six weeks at a time. It was do-able.

This time, however, he was finding it hard to put up the blockades. He thought back to Emmy's tears. He liked that she let him see her sadness. He wanted to know more about why it was there. When she said good-bye to him at the stadium, he'd only walked a block before he began to think he had to see her again before Monday; he couldn't wait two full days.

With most women, the time between the inception of his attraction and consummation was quite short. With Emmy, he wasn't sure consummation was even an option. He felt certain Emmy was unhappily married, but still she was *married*. There was this therapist-client thing too. Perhaps this connection he felt to her, maybe she didn't even feel it. She might think of him only as a client. In fact, she probably did.

Thinking about Emmy as he ran, especially in the context of all his stirred-up memories about Sarah, he felt something akin to insecurity. It was a long time since he'd felt insecure about a woman. Actually, it probably hadn't been since Sarah.

When he talked to Emmy about Sarah, he made it seem that Sarah was important because she showed him his greater potential, and it was true: Sarah helped him this way. However, when his thoughts drifted to Sarah, this is not what he thought about. His memories lingered on their sex and how perfect it still seemed to him. During their summers together, they would spend day after lazy day holed up in his bedroom while his mother was away at work. They would run to get fish 'n chips or head to the beach for an hour, then come back to get naked again. Even now, he doubted there was a woman with whom he'd had more sex. Occasionally, he'd still have dreams – rich, detailed dreams – in which they were making love, and he'd wake up with the sensation of her skin against his. He could still recall her body with photographic precision, moving from her small breasts to her slender waist to the hips he liked to grip. He'd adored her.

A week after the telephone call that ended their relationship, an airmailed letter from Sydney arrived at his Culver City apartment. It was near twenty pages, written on see-through thin, aeropostale sheets. In her loose scrawl, Sarah wrote about her conflicting emotions. The letter opened with her description of how desperately she loved him. "You are my beautiful, beautiful boy." She said that all she'd wanted for the last few years was to soothe him and take care of him and love his body and his heart. This had been Duncan's favorite part. And though he never let himself read the letter in parts, if he did, this would have been where he stopped. From there, Sarah described that though she adored being held by him, she "sometimes found his grip too tight." Her friends did lots of fun, carefree things, and she wanted to do those things too. "But I know you don't like it when I do." Shortly afterward, she confessed: "Since you've been away, I've been out with my mates more, and it's been quite good fun." Then she described how she'd come to hang out with Brian. He'd come along one night with Sarah's friends to play pool. Sarah said they'd had a nice time and had gone to play pool again the next day too, just the two of them. "I hadn't meant for anything to happen," Sarah said. But it had. Sarah tried to reassure Duncan that what she felt for Brian was "nothing like what I feel for you, though it does feel good too. Lighter and fun and free."

Duncan never wrote back. Sometimes he felt guilty about this. He wondered if it wouldn't have been the stronger response, to succinctly write back that he understood. Probably it would have been better. But by the time the letter arrived, too much had changed.

A half hour after his telephone call with Sarah, Duncan was sitting on his living room floor in front of the phone, when Brad Follower, another actor from the horror movie, knocked at the door of Duncan's studio apartment. "Come drinking with us, man," Brad said, and Duncan agreed to go, never letting on to what had just happened, to how his world had just turned upside down. At the bar, Duncan drank. He drank a lot. By midnight, he was barely able to see straight. Then a guy bumped into him, the kind of bump that happens many times an hour inside a crowded bar. "Fuck off!" Duncan had shouted; and the guy shouted back in Duncan's face. Duncan punched him. Hard. Then again. And again. Until Duncan was pummeling the guy so intensely he sank to the ground, losing consciousness. Brad pulled Duncan away; "What the fuck is your problem, man?!" Duncan ran from the bar in order to be gone before the police came.

The morning after that horrible night, Duncan awoke with a start. He was still in his clothes from the night before. He knew right away he was going to be sick. He rushed to his apartment's toilet, but he was too late. He threw up every-where – on the sink, the floor, himself. His clothes covered in vomit, he sat on the bathroom floor and started to cry. He never cried. But in that moment, he recalled the expression on the face of the guy he punched. The expression was one he knew well, though he'd never actually seen it on his own face. *Why*, the expression asked, *why are you doing this to me?*

Duncan stepped in the shower and stayed there for half an hour, making resolutions that would impact the rest of his life. He decided he'd never allow himself to drink – really drink – ever again. He'd never return to Australia; there was nothing there for him anymore. He'd do everything possible to be a success, to avoid being like his father. His last decision: He'd get himself a dog.

These were all promises he kept.

Here, on this fall night, nineteen years later, Duncan came back to the hotel, sweaty, slightly cold, breathing heavily. His run had helped him get clear on what he needed to do now. He'd quit therapy. It's what made most sense, both professionally and personally. It was a stupid idea to begin with. He was risking too much. The possibility he'd be disappointed: great. So, that was it. He'd call Emmy tomorrow and tell her.

SATURDAY, SEPTEMBER 28:
PUMMELING

"**D**on't we pay people lots of money to do that?"
Emmy was raking leaves in the Halperin backyard, and at Jack's shouted comment, she looked up and saw her husband walking toward her big leaf piles. It was Saturday afternoon, and the sun overhead provided a distinctly autumnal light. Straight and sharp against the blue sky, the light's clarity revealed a duller, harder palate of colors. Summer's lush saturation was already fading.

As Jack approached, Emmy could see her husband waiting for her explanation as to why she was raking. It was true the Halperins paid someone to come weekly to take care of their yard. "I'm bored," Emmy offered as she leaned against her rake. "With Tess gone, I feel like there's nothing to do."

Jack stopped a few feet from where Emmy stood, the leaf pile between them. "I miss Tess too. It wasn't as big a change when Marc and Ben went to school, was it?"

This was the most Jack had offered conversationally in days, and Emmy was surprised at how relieving it was to hear his voice. "No, everything's different now." There was silence. As they stood across the leaf pile from each other Emmy, realized Jack was carrying his overnight bag. She pointed to it, "What's that for?"

"You remember, right? Charlie and I are going to the cabin tonight."

Emmy blinked as she processed this information. Charlie was Jack's brother, and twice a year, a big production was made over the two brothers having a weekend at the cabin together. None of the usual preparation, however, had been made for this weekend. "No, I don't *remember*. Did you tell me?"

"I know I'd meant to tell you because actually…" he cleared his throat; "Charlie called me a few days ago. He said he and Jenny have decided to file for divorce."

Emmy looked at her husband. He'd said the word, the word that had been lurking in their own shadowy corners for weeks. "A divorce?" Emmy repeated the word.

"Yes." Jack looked down. "They're going ahead with it."

Emmy stood for a moment, taking in the gravity with which Jack spoke. Charlie and Jenny had been living apart for the last year, and news of their divorce did not surprise Emmy in the slightest. In fact, she'd thought the divorce filing had already begun. Jack probably expected her to continue talking about Charlie and Jenny, but this was not the matter that held her attention then. "So, you're going to meet Charlie at the cabin to talk to him about his divorce?"

Jack bristled, as though he knew exactly where this was going. "Yes, that's right."

"You'll talk with Charlie about his divorce, but you won't talk with me about ours."

Jack took a step back. "That's quite the compassionate response there. I'll be sure to tell Charlie just how concerned you are."

Emmy knew Jack had a point; she didn't care. "You're still deflecting my point."

"Good grief;" Jack looked upward to the sky. "Why do we have to talk about this now? Why can't you just let this be?"

"Let what be, Jack?" Now that she'd finally broached the subject, she found herself determined to see it through. "What are we letting be? What are we doing? We had a plan. Now we don't have a plan. You keep avoiding me, and I don't know what... I don't know what we're doing anymore." Emmy could feel the sting behind her eyes, but she willed herself to hold the tears back.

"I'm not avoiding you."

"Please."

"Can't I just go to the cabin, and when I get back—"

Emmy shook her head, taking a step forward. "No, you can't. I keep waiting and waiting for us to talk about this, and we have to just do it. Are we going to get a divorce?"

Jack's face flinched at the question. "God, Emmy. You want to know why I'm avoiding you? I don't want to talk about this!"

"Just answer the question."

Jack looked down at his shoes, and there was a long silence.

The wind blew, and the leaves rustled on their limbs; a bird squawked as it flew overhead. Emmy waited. She watched her husband. She saw him adjust his bag on his shoulder and look briefly around at their yard. Then, to her surprise, he stepped around the leaves to come to where she stood with her rake. He put his free arm around her; he leaned into her. "I don't know," he whispered, "I don't know what we should do." He held her close for a second. Emmy wanted to lean into him; she thought about it but – quickly, abruptly – he pulled back again. "I'm going to go to the cabin, okay?"

Emmy nodded. She understood: she'd received as much information from her husband as he could offer just then. He didn't know. He was confused too. *Was it strange that his confusion felt soothing?* It did. So very comforting.

❧ ❧ ❧

Emmy poured herself a glass of water and drank it down in one long gulp. She didn't want to rake anymore, but she couldn't think of anything else to do. *Was there a project she could begin? A place to head?* She needed activity; she didn't want to think about Jack or divorce. She sat at the large island amidst their enormous kitchen. This room was one that Jack had spent months designing, deciding in the end to completely reconfigure the old house so that a full third of the first floor's square footage could be used as kitchen space. She hadn't bothered to turn on the lights, and the room, which usually felt so expansive and warm, was now drab and shadowy. Her insides felt the same. *She had to get out of here.*

Rooms away, her cell phone began ringing. She followed the ring and caught it just in time. "Hello?"

"Hey."

"Duncan?"

"Yeah, it's me."

"Are you okay?" She didn't understand why he'd be calling her on a Saturday.

Duncan thought for moment. An idea came to him and he turned it over in his head. Quickly, he decided to go with the idea. "No, actually, I'm not."

"Oh, what's wrong? Did something happen?"

"Is there any way I could see you?" His voice now sounded considerably more downcast, with a panicky edge.

"Now? You want to see each other now? What's happened?"

"I feel awful. Really awful." Formulating these words felt strange since this was the kind of self-consciously unhappy remark he rarely let himself make.

"Are you on set?"

"No, I'm at my hotel."

"Oh," she paused before continuing. "Where would I see you then?"

"Could you come here?" He added more dreariness to his voice. "If it's easier for you, I could come to you."

This was awkward. "Well, I'm not set up to see clients here," she said, and realized she was just saying something to fill space as she thought. *She wasn't going to his hotel room; was she?*

"If you could come here, it would mean a lot." He could tell she was reluctant. "It's no different than the trailer."

"Um" She was thinking and wishing she knew what was right.

"I wouldn't ask if I didn't think it was serious."

Emmy regularly told her clients they could call her any time the need arose. Few called her, and when they did, they arranged an in-office meeting the next day. However, she knew several therapists who visited their clients at home. It wasn't out of the question she should see Duncan now if he was in a crisis. *Was it?* He did sound dreadful. "Well, I guess I can come by," she said. "Where are you staying?"

"The Four Seasons, the State Suite. I'll call down and let them know you're coming so they'll let you up."

"Okay, I'll try to be there in half an hour." She'd take the T.

"Thank you Emmy." Duncan hung up. Well, that had gone differently than planned. He'd called to tell her he couldn't see her anymore. Instead, Emmy was going to be in his hotel room in half an hour. *Not bad. Not bad at all.*

⚜ ⚜ ⚜

God, he's handsome. That was Emmy's first thought when Duncan opened the door to his hotel suite. She'd been trying hard the whole week to stay steadfastly focused on him as a person, not as a heartthrob. Occasionally, sure, she'd been aware he quickened her heart rate – like when he'd come to the door shirtless. But, given he was a man people paid $12 to sit in the dark watching, she thought she'd done well ignoring his physical assets. Except now she wasn't. When he came to the door, Duncan was barefoot; he was wearing a green t-shirt and jeans, and his body was strong and easeful. His hair, which had been slicked back the last few days for his business school professor costume was now wavy and some locks brushed across his forehead. When he smiled at Emmy, his eyes and cheeks creased with smile lines that amplified the magnitude of his famous grin.

"You look like a lumberjack," Duncan said to her teasingly. Emmy hadn't changed out of her yard work clothes; she was wearing an oversized red and grey plaid flannel shirt.

"I was raking leaves," Emmy said, trying to sound calm, though in truth her palms were starting to sweat.

"I can see that," and his hand went to Emmy's hair. At this unexpected contact, Emmy froze. Duncan felt it. He held out the small piece of leaf he'd pulled from her hair. "See, I was just getting this."

Emmy looked at him; he back at her. She quickly assessed he was not in the throes of desperate depression. Just as fast, he determined she was very uncomfortable, being here in his hotel room with him. For the last thirty minutes he'd indulged a fantasy that maybe he could seduce her that night, and he realized: no, that would not happen.

"You're not really in crisis, are you?" Emmy asked.

"I wanted to see you." He turned to walk from her since he didn't like to see the rebuke in her eyes. "Do you want something to drink? A water? A beer?"

"No, I don't want something to *drink!*" She did not try to hide her irritation. "Duncan, I came here because you made it sound like you were really, really upset."

"Well, who says I'm not? Just because I offer you a drink? You know, Freud served snacks."

"He did not."

"He did!" Duncan pointed to the eight therapy-related books he'd bought a few nights before; on the top was the Freud biography. "Tea and cakes. Apparently, he had a good baker."

Emmy saw the pile of books, and she couldn't help but go to them. "You're reading all these?" She picked up the Freud biography, then the next book in the pile and the next. "Wow, some of these are quite academic."

"What, you think I'm too lightweight to be reading these titles?"

Emmy picked up another book in the stack and read the back cover. "No one could think you're a lightweight."

Duncan laughed outright. "Emmy, *everyone* thinks I'm a lightweight! I'm the Grier."

Emmy looked up from the books. "Well, everyone's wrong."

Duncan liked how protective she sounded. He grabbed the beer he'd been drinking and walked to where she stood.

Emmy put the book back on the pile. "We should see each other Monday. Duncan, I only came because "She looked around his hotel suite; there were French doors to his bedroom and a made-up king size bed. *God, she shouldn't be here.* As someone who prided herself on being careful, she was embarrassed to realize how imprudent she'd been. She was in a client's hotel room. *What the hell was she doing?*

Duncan watched Emmy's thoughts on her face, and he especially noticed how apprehensively she looked at the open doors to his bedroom. "Here, we can close the doors." He walked to the bedroom's doors and cinched them shut, but when he turned to face her again, he realized it had been the wrong thing to do.

For Emmy, the gesture presumed the very dynamic she wanted to deny existed. She struggled to keep her voice level. "I know a lot of people rush to do what you want so they can stay in your good graces. But I can't be like that. Therapy is not like that. I'm not a groupie. I'm not here to be your..." she tried to find the right words, "drinking buddy."

Duncan raised his hands up like a criminal caught by the police. "I'm putting the beer down." He saw Emmy was not slightly amused. He needed to change tactics. His voice grew deep, his tone earnest. "Emmy, that's not why I called you; I asked you to come this afternoon because I wanted to talk with you."

"We can talk to each other on Monday." Her tone was curt. She walked toward the door.

He called after her. "I want to tell you about my father."

Emmy turned to look at him.

"That's why I phoned you," Duncan said. "I would like to talk about... him."

"You didn't say that on the phone."

"That's because I knew you would tell me we could talk on Monday." He waited.

Emmy's face twitched with its confusion. "And what's wrong with talking on Monday?"

"There's no way I could tell you about my father during the midday break." Duncan walked to pick up the beer bottle he'd put down. "It's just not something I can recount, then return to the set."

From across the room, Emmy tried to study his face to evaluate his truth-telling. "Are you saying this stuff about your father now only to get yourself off the hook?"

"No." He shook his head. "I'm not doing that."

She was pretty sure he was. *But what if he wasn't?* She was uncertain about the therapeutic protocol in such a situation. Breakthroughs in therapy frequently occurred in windows of opportunity, when the right combination of factors precipitated a client's willingness to discuss a delicate subject. The windows didn't stay open indefinitely. Emmy looked around the hotel room; the space was elegantly decorated but still sterile and cold. The neutral-toned, thickly filled armchairs and loveseats reminded her of a furniture warehouse. "You shouldn't tell me something you're not ready to discuss just to make me stay. I'm not leaving because I'm *mad* at you."

"Well," he smiled, "you are mad at me. But that's okay. That's not why I want to tell you."

She considered what she should do; this was all so different from what she was used to. The trouble was she needed an answer fast; she didn't want to appear indecisive. *Should she go because Duncan had been dishonest? Or, should she stay to make a breakthrough with his therapy?* Finally, she gestured toward the two loveseats behind the desk. "Should we sit over there?"

Duncan looked at her to assess her decision. He nodded, "Sure, that's a good spot." He was relieved she was going to stay. Dutifully, he walked to the couch that Emmy had indicated, and silently, Emmy walked to sit on the couch kitty-corner to him.

Do you want your beer? It was Emmy s peace offering. She was unused to being sharp with her clients.

"I thought you said no eating or drinking during therapy?"

"Well, there are around seventeen exceptions to my rules happening right now. If you want your beer, I think that's fine."

"No, I honestly don't know why I opened it. I don't really drink."

"You don't?"

"No, not really."

"Does that have to do with your father?" she asked gently. She was trying to create a different energy to their interaction so that it would feel more like therapy.

"Yes, my father is probably the reason I don t drink. He realized his heart was beating faster. "You know, I bet this is going to be anticlimactic. You probably have it all figured out."

"No, I don't think I do. But I have wondered," she paused, trying to get the tone right for what she wanted to ask. "I have wondered if your father hurt you. Did he? She wanted to convey she was ready to hear only what he wanted to say.

Duncan wiped his sweaty palms on his pants before he responded. "Uh, you could say that, yeah. He was realizing he was actually going to talk about this. Five minutes ago that had not been his plan. Now, here he was. He tried to remember he'd already promised himself he would tell her. Besides, he didn't have to say much now. He leaned forward, resting his elbows on his knees. He looked quickly up at Emmy, then just as quickly, down again. He took a deep breath; he'd just say it. "My father, hmm ... well, he beat the shit out of me. Pretty regularly. He briefly assessed Emmy's reaction. She didn't seem surprised; instead, her forehead was creased with sympathy.

He returned to staring at his hands. "I think my first memory of anything at all is of my father smacking me across the face, over and over again. I think I could have only been about two and a half. His voice sounded loud in his head. "As I grew up, he'd sometimes use his belt or once he clobbered me with a beer bottle, knocked me unconscious that time. But mostly," he paused as he remembered, "mostly, he just hit me a lot or punched me. Pummeling me, really. Duncan could tell his face was flushed; his torso had broken out in a light sweat.

He didn't say anything for quite some time. "I'm not sure what else to really say about it. I don't want to give you a blow by blow so to speak. He laughed an empty laugh. As little as he'd said, he knew he couldn't say much more. He felt sick to his stomach. "That's it, that's the big secret of my father. I guess it's probably what you guessed."

Emmy swallowed as she assessed how much more she should probe this topic when he was clearly reluctant to discuss it. "Did your father ever sexually abuse you?" she asked gently.

"No;" Duncan shook his head. "No, he never did that. He was just a very angry man, and I was the person he would take his anger out on."

"What did your mother do when he got angry with you?"

"She didn't do shit until—" He stopped himself. "She didn't do much. My mother is a weak woman, and my father – he couldn't stand her." Duncan began to run his finger along the ribbing of the armrest. "My father liked to think of himself as this misunderstood genius, holding court with his big important ideas. Then my mum would come along, and you could watch it happen – she would do something to interrupt my father's pontificating bullshit, and he would have to stop and see again how stupid and ridiculous she was. How that was his life, not the grand stuff he wanted to think was his life. It would send him over the edge."

"Would he hit your mother too?"

Duncan waited a long time to respond. "No. Only once really."

"But your mother and father separated, didn't they?"

There was another long pause. "I guess you could call it that. When I was around twelve."

"Did you ever see your father for weekends or holidays after they separated?"

"No. No, I haven't seen my father since I was twelve. For all I know he's dead now." He thought for a few seconds; his voice contorted. "I don't think he is. But he could be." He looked directly at Emmy. "I think a lot about whether he's dead."

"He's in your thoughts a lot?"

"Yeah, he..." his voice trailed and when he spoke again the words were soft, "he haunts me. Like a ghost." He didn't say anything for a few seconds. "If he's still alive, I wonder what he thinks about me. You know, as much as he tried to run me into the ground, he's the reason I could become what I've become. He's how I learned how to act."

"Is that right?" Emmy thought it interesting that Duncan wanted to credit his father with his success. "How did he teach you to act?"

"Well, no, he didn't *teach* me." Duncan's voice was tense. "My dad was no drama club coach. There was no instruction. But I was always on high alert with my father; I had to monitor his face, his moods – to see what was coming. And I could tell: he had a twitch that would happen in his eyebrow. It was pretty fucking subtle. I doubt that most people, even if they were looking straight at him, would have noticed it. But I saw it. I always saw it."

He looked off into the distance for a few seconds, then, abruptly, sat up. Emmy knew right away that Duncan was done with his revelations for the night. His voice was now more assured and easy-going. "It was actually from watching my father so much that I became interested in watching emotion generally. I began to see how his small facial gestures come together to telegraph an expression. You know, it's easy for me to tell the difference between, say, worried and afraid. I wouldn't say I'm good at many things, but reading people, that's something I can do. And so, in terms of acting, I can reproduce a lot of the expressions. I know what micro-expressions produce the emotion that's called for."

Emmy considered this. "But from watching your dad, it would seem you'd know the expressions for angry, hurtful people. And though I haven't seen a lot of your movies, that's not what you're known for, is it?"Duncan's face relaxed into his question; "Emmy, have you seen *any* of my movies?"

"I have," she said fast.

"Which ones?"

"Well, I saw *Final Frontier*."

"That hardly counts."

"Why?" She smiled. "Because you can't turn on the TV without it being on?"

"Precisely. That would be the reason. That's how you saw it, isn't it?"

"Uh-huh." She was sheepish. "But you know, I really liked it."

He half-chuckled; she looked so sincere he was amused. "Well, even though you haven't seen them, you guessed right. I'm about the most typecast actor out there, and though I've played bad guys before, it's been a long time. Lately, I'm like the—"

"Hero guy?"

"Yeah, I frequently play a kind of wisecracking hero guy."

"And you learned how to play that by watching people?"

"Yeah, watching became my way. Observing. Listening. My home was such a shit hole, so when I went to school I made it my mission to extract maximum approval from the people I could. Every teacher, every kid, every fucking hall monitor – I had to have them like me. It was the way I saved myself. If I knew everyone at school thought I was funny or cool, then I had this alter-ego my dad or mum couldn't deflate."

Emmy smiled. "So, that's how you got your charm?"

"Yeah, I guess." He looked at her. "And thank you."

Emmy tried to regain her therapeutic voice. "How do you feel now that you've started to tell me about some of what happened with your father?"

"Started to…?"

Emmy made her face gentle; she didn't want Duncan to worry she was going to ask him to tell more now. "I know this isn't easy to share."

He thought about it before he responded. Actually, he didn't feel as awful as he'd thought he would. He hadn't told her about the big stuff yet, but perhaps that wouldn't be so bad either. "I'm glad you know," he said.

"I'm glad you're glad." From a therapeutic perspective, they'd taken a huge step forward. It felt good to her too. She wanted to leave it at that, yet the circumstances under which they'd begun this conversation still nagged at her. "Duncan, I have to ask you," she looked at him directly, "did you really call me over tonight to tell me about your father?"

He saw immediately: he was caught. She'd know now if he lied again. "No," he said. "No, I called you to tell you I was going to quit therapy."

"*Really?*" She was hurt. "Why?"

He gave a slight grimace. "I was feeling an itching to run."

"You were?" Emmy considered what that meant: it could mean so many different things. "But you didn't say anything like that on the phone?"

"No, because when I heard your voice, I decided I wanted to... not run."

"Oh." Emmy wasn't sure what that meant either. Probably he was having a hard time with all the emotional complexities of therapy. *Or, did he mean something altogether different?*

"Emmy, I want to ask you a question."

"Are you going to make me cry again?" she asked jauntily, trying to bring levity to the exchange.

"I hope not, but I can't promise."

"Ah, okay." *What could he want to know?*

He watched her, realizing he would learn more from her face than from what she said. "Do you... do you love your husband?"

Her eyes flared surprise, and there were waves of it. First there was Duncan's expression; he was undeniably apprehensive asking the question. Then came the shock of the question itself. And in the next heartbeat, its answer, which arrived fast and stark, a one-word response. It was not the answer she expected. She blinked. "Duncan, I cannot answer that question for you." She looked down, then almost right away stood up. Her voice was weak; "I think I should go."

Duncan stood up with her. "I'm sorry I upset you." It was a meager apology; he'd known the question might be upsetting.

She started to walk toward the door but in the middle of the hotel room, she turned back. "I don't understand; why... why would you ask me that question?" She was confused about a lot in that moment, but especially she didn't understand Duncan's motivation. *Why would he care if she loved her husband or not?*

Duncan considered and rejected several responses. "I had to know" is what he said.

She looked at him, confused, hurt, slightly angry. But there was something else in her consideration of him as she walked out the door, and Duncan saw that too.

Sunday, September 29:
The hard, hard ground

Jack stood watching his wife. It seemed she hadn't moved from that spot in their backyard since yesterday. Now, instead of raking the leaves she was trying to bag them. It wasn't going well. The tall brown gardening bag kept collapsing inward just as she tried to drop her handful of leaves into it. Leaves were scattering everywhere.

He watched. Once the bag was fuller, it would lie more rigidly and the work would proceed more quickly. He saw this, but he had no inclination to help. Renaldo would be by to rake the leaves in a few days. If the project weren't so stupid, he would have helped.

He'd spent the entire drive back from the cabin reflecting on his marriage, and one of the observations he made – he was trying to take an honest assessment – was that he did *try* to do the right thing. Of course, there was the big mistake. Other than that though, he tried to be good. He thought even Emmy would agree with that.

Hearing his brother go on and on about his divorce plans was like watching an implosion. Charlie was usually an upbeat guy, but that weekend he sat in front of Jack and cried. He kept asking him if he thought Jenny had cheated on him. It was pretty damn obvious she had. But

Jack didn't say that. Overnight, his brother had become a pathetic, simpering wreck; it gave him a sour taste in his mouth, just watching it. Jack was supposed to have stayed at the cabin with Charlie through the afternoon, but this morning over breakfast, he explained that Emmy had called to say she needed him home. Emmy would never have used those words, but Charlie couldn't know that, and Jack had an excuse for leaving early.

On the drive from the cabin, Jack thought about the questions Emmy asked before he left for the cabin. It was true: they had held this plan to separate for a long time. He had fully expected it to move forward this fall. In fact, he'd already met with a divorce attorney a couple of times. Yet, when he and Emmy had driven home after dropping Tess off at school, he'd panicked. Sitting in the passenger seat, Emmy broached the topic. She'd said the word "divorce;" she'd asked what they would do next. He hadn't been able to respond. He refused to say a single word. It wasn't that he'd reconsidered his feelings for Emmy; no, she wasn't going to change; he wasn't going to either. But on that car drive, it had become clear: they were taking a wrecking ball to their lives.

Was what they had bad enough that they should ruin it and start over? This was the question Jack had asked himself over and over again the last few weeks. He could not decide. He liked a lot about his life, and right there in the middle of that life was Emmy. If he took her out of that middle slot, maybe his life wouldn't feel so nice anymore. Maybe – though he didn't like to form these words – he needed her. Not a lot, but some. And even if Emmy would never say she needed him, he thought she had to. She used to, very much.

That morning, he let his thoughts drift to those times when Emmy needed him. Those were easier times to think about than now. The very first night he talked to Emmy was at Puffer's Pond. She looked so breathtaking, swimming naked in the moonlit water. Then, when he swam to her, the warmth of her smile and the sound of her laugh – she'd transfixed him. There were only four weeks left to school then; it made no sense to begin a relationship. Usually he was a practical person, but at the swimming hole, he convinced himself: maybe he didn't have to make sense. In the days following, he persuaded Emmy of the same idea. He wanted badly to sleep with her and, eventually, she wanted that too. Those last three weeks of school they met each afternoon in Emmy's dorm room to have hushed and sweaty sex on her squeaky twin bed.

At the school year's end, they said goodbye. It was only supposed to be a fling after all. Yet, as the summer went on, and he had no other distractions, Jack frequently returned to his thoughts of Emmy. The way he remembered their sex, it seemed nothing would ever be as good. Emmy gave him her virginity; she was delicate and he, in turn, so very strong. That summer, the memories of their sex were the wallpaper lining his mind.

When, on that blistering July day, Emmy drove up his parents' driveway, she looked so exquisitely pretty, he didn't try to hide how genuinely happy he was to see her. When she sat there at the stream, her big brown eyes full with tears and her cheeks flushed with heat and emotion, it felt obvious: It was his destiny to be with her forever. She was going to have his child. If he married her, she would be his, this beautiful woman. He would be able to have sex with her *all* the time. And so after thinking about it for only a few minutes, he told her he would like her to become his wife. He felt like he was acting in a play, reading the lines for doing the "right thing." There was something thrilling about it. He felt heroic.

At first, married life was everything he wanted it to be. Every day, coming home from graduate school, he had a gift waiting for him, a pleasure ready for him to savor. Even after Marc was born, it still felt good. Only after Emmy became pregnant again with Ben did things start to feel harder. With that pregnancy, Emmy became tired a lot and wanted Jack to do a lot more. He always tried to be as helpful as he could, but there never stopped being more to do. After Ben was born, Emmy grew even less adoring and started to seem downright needy. When she became pregnant again so quickly – maybe it had been too fast. Her mother had died right before Tess was born... *God, Emmy cried so much.* It's not that he didn't sympathize with what she was going through – yes, he knew it was hard to be pregnant and breastfeeding and sleep-deprived and then with her mother. Yes, he tried hard to understand. He was always loading the dishwasher, unloading the dishwasher. Sleeping in Ben's bed most nights so he wouldn't get nightmares. Picking up all the fucking plastic toys that lay around their house. When Emmy talked about how sad she was that her mother would never see Tess, he listened as well as he could. But it was an unpleasant time. *Who would not have thought it unpleasant?* He was initially considered heroic for his helpfulness; now no matter what he did, nothing could be made better.

He went off to graduate school each day, and each day he saw Jessica there. Here was a woman so fierce in her independence, so razor sharp with her intelligence, so utterly self-posssessed; nothing could make Jessica cry, no way. Without meaning to, he fell for her. To this day, he couldn't understand how she became pregnant – he'd been so goddamn careful. He never meant for the situation to become complicated, but once it was, he had no idea how to fix it either. He loved Jessica. It was a different kind of love, but it was real, and he didn't want to hurt her either. He remembered how he would go back and forth between the two Cambridge houses, back and forth between the two women, and he'd try to figure out – rationally, reasonably – what was the right thing to do? But the answer never came. It was only when Emmy called him home from work that wretched day that his decision grew clear. Watching Emmy lay out his choice so clearly, he was horrified. All the guilt he'd tried to sequester came rushing over him. He'd done a dishonorable thing. He'd betrayed his wife and family. It was shameful. He tried to undo the damage. It didn't work. Perhaps he could not un-do it. Or, at least, Emmy never let him feel he could.

Emmy was so quiet after that. She never rushed to kiss him hello or goodbye anymore. When she told him about her day, she made sure it only included a narrative about the children. Their conversations became information exchanges, very practical and plan-oriented. Their sex, which had always been loud and lusty, lost its tenderness and became almost athletic in its objectives. After awhile, it started to piss him off. He was doing what Emmy wanted. He'd given up a lot. But still, the shame never went away. Emmy never let it go away. She held onto it like a shield.

He tried not to let this disappointment bog him down. He tried to be mature; that's in fact what motivated a lot of his life: acting older than his age. He supposed Emmy did the same. They managed; it was what people did with life, right? Emmy went back to school. First to finish her B.A., then to do her PsyD. *That school stuff went on for fucking ever.* But he was there, supporting her every step of the way, wasn't he? It was never like his work wasn't demanding too, with the pressures to make partner at the firm and then the challenges that came once he did. Everything was always busy, busy, busy, with no time to navel-gaze about the state of their marriage. There were after-school activities and weekend games and business trips and scheduling nightmares. It wasn't only with Emmy and the kids that he had these obligations; there was always Celia to take care of too. When they remodeled the Brookline house nine years ago, that was the worst time, a complete living hell. Emmy let him make all the decisions, which was good since she had no idea what she was doing, but for a year and a half there was constant disorder and dust and chaos. Even in the last few years, when the efforts with the house and work stabilized, there was still always something. Marc ran into some trouble in college, and he and Emmy had to meet frequently with his therapists and psychiatrists to discuss their son's anger management issues. They had a fancy name for it, oppositional something-something. And there was the situation with Tess and those mean girls who bullied her; he wanted to kill those bitchy girls. Yes, life churned and whirled and spun so quickly. And in the center of the spinning, there was Emmy, beside him.

There had been happy times too. At the cabin, he and Emmy made nice memories there – they hiked well as a family and the boat rides on the lake were always fun. And at dinner each night, hearing the kids tell about their days around the dinner table. God, he hadn't realized how much that ritual meant to him until now, when it wasn't there anymore.

He would never try to deny he and Emmy had troubles. Probably not talking about their troubles was the biggest trouble of all. They practiced their particular type of quiet too much. And she did irritate him too. There was no point denying it. But find him a couple married for over twenty years that wasn't irritated by each other? *By most measures, hadn't they done pretty well?* Their kids were great. Their house was beautiful. Didn't they have the life people envied?

Maybe they shouldn't take that life apart.

As Jack drove back from the cabin, he was shedding his confusion on this question. Having Emmy ask him so directly about the divorce yesterday and then seeing his brother such a god-awful wreck, what he didn't want grew clearer and, in fact, urgent. It was true that the divorce had been a plan for a long time now, but maybe they were planning a mistake all along. He decided he would tell Emmy that. She would probably be relieved. *Wouldn't she?* Yes, she would. She probably didn't want her life to fall apart any more than he did.

He called out to her now. "Have you moved since I left?"

At the sound of his voice, Emmy jumped. When she saw it was only him, she laughed at her own fluster. "Yesterday I never finished bagging the leaves, so I thought I'd try that now."

"I guess there's nothing like the thrill of completing unnecessary work, right?" Jack tried to make the tease sound affectionate rather than sarcastic; he thought it had worked.

Emmy walked closer to him too. "How was it with Charlie?"

"Fine, I guess. He's a wreck." He paused. "I told him that you were heartbroken about their news."

"That's nice that you—"

"Made that up?"

Emmy's chin lifted. "I am heartbroken for them, actually."

His toes scuffed the ground. "Yeah, me too."

"But, you know, they've been unhappy for so long, and it's not like they have kids. Maybe it's for the—"

"We have kids," he interrupted her.

Emmy looked at him; her eyebrows rose. "I know that Jack." She started to smile as though it was funny to say something so obvious: "I know we have kids."

He didn't think it was funny, not at all. He cleared his throat. "Emmy, I don't want *us* to fail."

Her eyes darted across his face. "You don't?"

"No."

"Do you want us to *succeed?*"

The question irritated him. "Are you being flip?" He shook his head. "Jesus, I'm trying to finally have this conversation, and you're cracking jokes."

"No, no, I'm not cracking jokes." She walked closer to him, and her voice grew slow and deliberate. "I'm trying to understand what you mean. What does not failing mean? Do we try to be married, or do we just not get a divorce?"

He didn't like how starkly Emmy put their options. "We do as we do. We are as we are. I don't want us to break up our lives, to turn everything into a mess. You *know* we can do better than that."

"But it's been our plan, our plan for so long to—"

He interrupted her: "Well, I've changed my mind." He tried to make his words short and certain, but there was an unpleasant vulnerability he heard too.

Emmy's mouth opened, but no words came out. Jack worried she was about to say her mind had *not* been changed. Panic prickled his skin. Abruptly, he picked up his overnight bag, "I'm going in. Are you going to keep doing your little leaf project?" This time, the tease definitely came off wrong.

"I'll stay out here." She said these words distractedly like she was having a conversation in her head. She stood looking at the leaves.

Jack walked to the house, but before he went inside, he glanced back at his wife. She was raising a cumbersome armload of brown and yellow leaves to slide into the tall bag, but as before, the flimsy bag wouldn't stay still. Some leaves made it in, but others drifted back down to the hard, hard ground.

MONDAY, SEPTEMBER 30:
JUST TALK

I *bet Emmy's breasts look like this.* Duncan was waiting for Emmy in the European Impressionist room of Boston's Museum of Fine Art, standing in front of a Dante Rossetti statue of a woman's torso. The statue's breasts were round and high, not huge, but bigger than medium, and from what Duncan had seen when Emmy's scarf slipped, these breasts were like Emmy's. He pivoted away from the statue and began to nervously pace around the big, high-ceilinged, skylight-lit room.

Duncan had asked Ling to call Emmy the night before to explain that since there was a location shoot today, they'd have to reschedule their usual 11:30 a.m. therapy session. Duncan had instructed Ling to give Emmy the option of either postponing their session until Tuesday or changing their appointment time to meet Duncan later, at 5:30 p.m., at the MFA. It was a good sign that Emmy agreed to meet him at the museum. He'd worried she might still be angry with him for asking whether she loved her husband.

All day Sunday, Duncan thought about that last interaction between him and Emmy. At first he reasoned that if she loved her husband, she would have said: "Yes, I do." Since she hadn't said that, it must mean, no, she did not love him. Yet, upon further consideration, he realized it was only clear the question upset her. It could very well be that she was upset because she *did* love her husband. Her marriage wasn't happy, of that he felt sure. But he wanted it to be *very* unhappy. He wanted her to be unhappy enough she wouldn't hesitate to betray her husband to be with him.

Duncan saw how absurd it was to be fixated on a woman he couldn't easily have. There were few of these women. He questioned again whether it was the challenge of the chase he found compelling, but, honestly, no, that wasn't it. He recognized he knew little about Emmy – she had a home, friends, a husband, kids, a complete world he knew nothing about. Regardless, he felt he understood her better than he understood most people. Moreover, he felt like she understood him. He wanted her to understand him more. This was a new sensation. Usually, he kept an awareness of himself as a person who maintained his separateness from others. With her, he wanted to sink in. He thought a lot about what it would be like to sleep with her. He envisioned holding her naked body, being inside her, having her looking up at him. He could picture it wellA security guard walked into the large, empty open room and Emmy followed behind him. Duncan hadn't been outside since 6 a.m.; still he had an awareness that it was a summer-y warm day. Seeing Emmy confirmed it. She was wearing a flowered, loosely guaze-y dress, sheer enough to see the camisole slip underneath. The dress stopped well above her knee and her legs were long and lean in stacked heels. Her hair was down except for a delicate barrette that pulled a few strands back. Warm from walking, her cheeks glowed.

"I've always loved this room," she said to Duncan as she walked up to him.

"That's good because I've arranged for them to give it to us for our..." he leaned in to whisper, "appointment."

"They're giving us the room? You can do that?" Emmy's eyes grew round.

"Ah, if you're impressed by that..." Duncan grinned. "Yeah, that's an easy thing to do."

Emmy smiled big, almost a laugh. She had a funny tease ready to spring from her lips as a response, but, fast, she stopped herself. It wasn't the sort of thing a therapist should say to a client. She reminded herself: *She had to think like a therapist.*

Emmy had thought a lot about Duncan on Sunday too. Once she finished bagging all the unruly leaves, she still had not wanted to join Jack in the house. *Had he just unilaterally taken their divorce off the table? Had she just let him?* She needed to be able to articulate what she wanted before she could face Jack again. So, instead of staying inside, she changed and went for an eight-mile run, starting at the Brookline Reservoir just outside their house and then over to Jamaica Pond and up to the Arnold Arboreteum and back down and around again. As she ran, she tried to let her body's rhythmic movement organize her thoughts. She decided there were two major categories of confusion, loosely titled Jack and Duncan. Of the two, the former had much more impact on every aspect of her life and future. Yet, she barely thought of Jack. Her entire run, her mind was full of Duncan. *Why had he asked whether she loved her husband?* And all that talk of wanting to run but then hearing her voice and deciding to stay.

Over the past week, she had worked hard to keep her thoughts about Duncan on the right side of therapeutically appropriate. But as her feet hit the pavement and her body moved swiftly through the cool fall air, her thoughts jostled and moved too, no longer remaining neatly on any one side. She thought of Duncan's hard history with his father and how much closer she felt to him for his wanting to share this side of himself with her. This closeness was not the usual sort of sympathy she had with her clients. It was a different closeness, thicker, tighter. She replayed moments from their conversations that week – arse v. ass, the way he asked her if she was happy and liked her tears. These memories gave off a glow, like tiny Christmas tree bulbs, and as she held them in her mind's eye, her whole world became brighter. She ran and thought and did not want to stop.

That night, she and Jack deftly avoided each other, separately snacking on leftovers so as to avoid any expectation they would sit at a table together. He stayed upstairs while Emmy tried to find tasks to busy herself with downstairs. She read more of *The Visiting Professor* and left phone messages for each of her kids. The more she tried to distract herself, the more she was aware that the wistfulness she'd drawn up during her run was not subsiding. Despite the pleasure of this ache, she saw the problem it posed. Therapists should not be attracted to their clients. She went to bed that night contemplating whether she should tell Duncan she could not be his therapist anymore. As she drifted off, she decided that would be best.

By the time Emmy checked her phone the next morning, Ling's text had already arrived. The long message was mostly about the logistics of scheduling and the possibility of meeting at the MFA, but it closed with these two lines: "Duncan says he needs the 'follow-up' today, if possible. I'm assuming you will know what he means." As she showered, Emmy considered the progress Duncan had made in terms of opening up about his father. Certainly, it would be a shame to see all that therapeutic growth come to a standstill. *In fact, maybe it was therapeutically ill-advised to abruptly end their sessions now.* Yes, it could be very bad for Duncan's healing. Perhaps, Emmy considered, she could keep seeing Duncan if she worked hard to compartmentalize her feelings and keep the sessions strictly professional. It was only four more weeks. *She could do that. Definitely.* She texted Ling back, arranging to meet Duncan at the MFA.

"Impressionism isn't really my favorite. Do you like it?" Duncan asked, as they wandered around the room.

"Well, it's very pretty, but almost *too* pretty if that makes any sense."

He smiled; that was what he thought too. "Can I show you the one painting in here I do like a lot?"

Duncan led Emmy to a corner of the room where he showed her a Monet oil painting of a single Cypress tree. The tree was weathered and stood on a craggy hill.

Emmy tilted her head, "Oh, I like this one too. Alone. But strong."

"Yes," Duncan evaluated Emmy's response. "I guess that's what I like about it too." Without saying more, they ambled over to a large backless bench that was in the middle of the airy, sun-soaked room.

Once they were sitting next to each other, Emmy decided to bring up what had happened Saturday night. "Duncan, I'm sorry I left abruptly the other night. Especially after you had shared all those things about your father. I..." she realized, actually, she didn't want to make this about her. She started again, "How did you feel yesterday after telling me?"

He studied her. "You know there's more, don't you?"

"Is there?" she asked delicately.

He chuckled, shaking his head. "Is there some professional code that says you have to respond to my questions with your own?"

Emmy smiled. "In a way, there is. I want you to be the one to answer your questions."

"But I *know* you could tell there was more. You even called my bluff on the reason I asked you over. I like to think of myself as a pretty good liar…"

"You were good."

"But you were better?"

"I didn't say that," she laughed, then looked at Duncan more thoughtfully. "Do you want to tell me the rest? About your father?"

"Here?" The idea was absurd to him. "There's no way I could tell you here. Not now, no way." Duncan's tone lost its easiness.

"That makes sense," Emmy purposefully made her words soothing. "This isn't the best place. You should tell me only when the time and place feel right."

"Yeah, well, this is definitely neither."

Emmy looked around. "Maybe I shouldn't have agreed to do our session here. Probably the American Psychological Association wouldn't approve."

"They're anti-art?"

"No," she tried not to laugh. "They wouldn't approve because, as a therapist, I'm supposed to provide a comfortable environment where the setting and I are a blank slate. So my clients are at ease, not emotionally compromised."

"Emmy, you're *so* not a blank slate."

This assessment worried her. "I'm not?"

"No."

"Do you feel… emotionally compromised?"

He ran his hand across his chin. "I'm not sure how to answer that." He didn't say anything for a second. Then: "I respond to you."

Their eyes locked. Emmy realized she shouldn't dance around this subject anymore. She should talk openly about it. However, her throat had no words; her hands went clammy. "So, how was filming today?"

"You're changing the subject."

"Maybe, but it's not a bad question."

He rearranged himself on the bench, pushing himself to its furthest point and straddling the sides, so he was facing Emmy directly, taking her fully in. "Well, it went well today. Since you read the book, you probably know the scene we filmed."

"The scene where Maggie tempts Benjamin?"

"Yes, where she *tempts* him." He liked the way she phrased it.

Emmy remembered the scene well from the book. She'd just re-read the chapter the night before. In it, Benjamin B waits in the museum for Maggie, the 22-year old with whom he's contemplating beginning an affair. When Maggie arrives, Benjamin tells her he cannot see her anymore. Before Maggie tearfully leaves, she surprises Benjamin with a delicate kiss on the lips. In the book, the kiss is described at some length.

"How many takes did you have to do?"

Duncan's eyes danced as he examined Emmy's expression. "I think there were seven takes."

"Seven!" That's a lot of kissing, Emmy thought. "Who plays Maggie?"

"Sasha Lerner; you might not know her—"

"No, I do; she was in *Ridiculous Fun*."

"You haven't seen my movies but you've seen *Ridiculous Fun*?" He was astonished.

She laughed. "My daughter, Tess, she made me watch it with her. Sasha Lerner, she's stunning."

"Well, she's also, like, twenty. It's awkward."

"Oh, I'm sure it was a hardship, having to be kissed by her so many times."

Duncan looked at Emmy disbelievingly. She was being so jokey. He loved it. "Well, actually, it *was* weird. I'm old enough to be her father."

"I thought you dated lots of young women."

"Not so much, actually. Why would you think that?" Right away, he saw the answer on her face. "You've been reading gossip crap about me, haven't you?"

"I googled you," Emmy admitted.

He nodded; this was good, he thought. "And, what'd you find out?"

"I mostly saw pictures of you."

"And from the pictures you think I date lots of young women?"

"Uh-huh."

"Does that really ring true to your perception of me, that I'd want to be in relationships with girl-like women?"

"The women did look quite young."

Duncan examined Emmy's expression. "You're jealous." This was pleasing.

"I'm not jealous," she scoffed.

"You are." He was certain.

"Maybe you're mistaking womanly envy for jealousy. It'd be nice to look as good as those women."

"Ha! You shouldn't want to look like those women." Duncan replaced his smile with seriousness. "Emmy, you're very beautiful."

Emmy had been grinning ear to ear, but, abruptly, she stopped. *What the hell was she doing?* This was just the flirtatious behavior she'd promised herself not to engage in. *She was really screwing up. Crap, crap, crap.* "Duncan, I shouldn't have..." She stopped; she wanted to proceed carefully. "Sometimes when we talk, I think there's a flirtation to our conversations."

Duncan sat back; he waited. He both wanted and didn't want to have this talk.

Emmy continued, measuring her words. "As your therapist, I want you to know that you don't have to flirt with me for me to care about you." She was trying to sound calm, authoritative. "There are lots of ways of having relationships – close, caring relationships – that don't have to be about desire."

"I don't think you get to choose if desire is there or not."

His eyes were earnest, but she wasn't going to let herself be affected by that. "It's possible you're so used to people responding to you desirously that you look for that as your angle. You've said it yourself that it's your way to charm."

"Do you think that when I'm talking – *flirting* – with you I'm somehow being insincere?"

Emmy shifted on the bench. "No, not insincere. It's more that I think flirtation is how you make our interactions more comfortable for you."

"You make it sound like my motivations are devious." He looked at her directly, "They're not. You know that."

She couldn't think how to respond.

Duncan continued, "I feel like you're saying this now only to check a box, to do your therapist duty."

"Well, that's what I'm supposed to do. I *am* your therapist."

"It's a convenient shield for you, isn't it?"

Emmy blinked at the question. It was the intensity of his tone that took her off guard; there was nothing jokey or flirty about it. She tried to keep herself composed. "Since you're unhappy with how I've described our interactions, how would you describe them? Why is there a charge to our therapy sessions? I mean, first, do you think there is a charge?"

He raised his chin. "Yes, obviously there's a charge. But, that's not a bad thing. At least I don't think so."

Emmy tried not to be impacted by his seriousness, by how open he was about expressing himself. She made herself continue her point. "But it makes it more complicated, don't you think? Therapy is supposed to be contained – a separate, safe place for you to explore feelings so that, when you're ready, you can take them back to your real world."

"Are you saying therapy isn't in a real world too?"

"No, therapy is real." She thought for a second. "But the relationship between therapist and client, it's supposed to be contained within therapy. It doesn't really exist outside of therapy."

"Well, don't be offended, but I think that's screwed up." He stood up from the bench and walked the few feet to the bronze statue of the woman's torso, then turned to face the bench where Emmy sat. "Actors engage in a contained space too – a set. But if two actors decide their emotions feel real, then they go ahead and make them real. Therapists – you're supposed to care and support, nurture. But only in a *contained* way? I mean – and again, no offense – but what the fuck does that mean? It's like you start with real emotions and then act to create this false barrier."

Emmy was trying to piece together what he was saying. *Did he want there to be real feelings between them?* She went back to playing her role. "But there's a good reason for the barrier to be there. It's so the risk in disclosing hard, deep stuff feels more comfortable." She stood up to walk to where Duncan was standing. "I mean, don't you think the charge between us is because you're telling me personal things? You told me about your father. It makes sense that this disclosure would make you want more closeness in our relationship."

He looked straight into her eyes. "You think that's all it is?" He didn't try to disguise that the insinuation pissed him off.

"What do you think?" Emmy tried to sound assured, but the intensity of his gaze was making her heart beat faster.

"I asked first." He waited.

She shrugged. "I think that's what it is."

"You're lying."

She took a step back. "You think I'm *lying?*"

"I do. And I think it's strange that I'm in therapy because I want to learn how to stop running, and here I am with every reason to hike out of here but I'm the one trying to get you to stay."

"You think I'm trying to run? But I'm not saying I'm going anywhere."

"No, but you're making this… distance, with the rules and terms you're forcing in place." He was surprising himself with the things he was saying, but it didn't feel wrong; he didn't want to stop. "Just because we're not supposed to feel something doesn't mean we don't."

Emmy quickly considered: maybe this conversation was merely an actor-ly way of making drama. Duncan didn't look insincere, but creating emotional moments was what he did for a living. She turned away from him; she needed to think. She walked back to the bench and sat down. "Duncan, I don't want to do you a disservice. You deserve to see a therapist where there aren't the complicating factors that are here between us."

He followed her to the bench. "I like the complicating factors."

"But I think another therapist would help you more. I really do."

Duncan sat down on the bench beside her. "I really don't. Emmy, I'm certain you're the only person I want to do therapy with. You're helping me." He could see the confusion crossing back and forth across her face. He leaned toward her. "Why is it bad to talk like we want to talk? It's just talk. That's all. Why can't we do that?"

Emmy looked sideways to Duncan's close face. His eyes were caring; they were kind. There were reasons to object, but she didn't want to. "Just talk?

He nodded.

"Okay," she smiled. "I guess we can talk."

"Where've you been?" Jack hit the remote to turn off the TV.

Emmy turned to the loveseat where Jack was sitting; he was in his boxers and t-shirt, a bowl of pasta beside him. Jack hadn't returned home before her in weeks, but, tonight, when she would have preferred to be alone with her thoughts, there he was.

Jack pivoted to face her: "I came home to have dinner with you and you weren't here."

"You were home for dinner? *Really?*"

"Yeah, for all the good it did. Where were you?"

"I was seeing a client."

"Since when have you started seeing clients in the evenings?"

"I haven't exactly had to rush home for dinner lately, have I?"

"True enough. How was your day?"

Emmy had been walking toward her dresser, but this question stopped her in her tracks. *Jack asking about her day?* "It was... good. Thanks for asking. How was your's?"

"Fine, I guess. I had this weird lunch with Anthony Trippolli and the Weston library woman."

"Oh?" Emmy was puzzled by Jack's desire for conversation. "Why was it weird?" She pulled a tank top from the dresser.

"They were *giggling*," Jack said the word like it disgusted him. "I swear, I think Anthony was flirting with her."

"Anthony? I can't imagine him being too adept at flirting!" She pulled her dress up over her shoulders and stood before him in bra and panties. "Do you think Anthony would ever cheat on Francesca? It can't be easy being married to her."

"Emmy, that's not nice."

Jack's admonishment again took Emmy by surprise; there was something almost affectionate in his tone. He walked over to the side of the bed where Emmy was changing; he sat down on the bed's edge. "You know, on the drive back from Weston, Anthony mentioned he and Francesca had done this tour of Italy last summer; it was this three-week guided architecture tour."

"Mmm-hmm." Emmy unsnapped her bra and took it off.

"I thought we could do that next summer. What do you think?"

Emmy froze. She looked at Jack. "Next summer?" Immediately, it made sense. She now understood why Jack was being so normal and chatty: he was making sure the divorce plans were off.

"Yes, in the summer. That's when people take these kinds of vacations. Summertime."

"Oh." She pulled her tank top over her shoulders. She needed to think. Part of her was touched that Jack was making this effort to do something nice. It was unexpected and relieving – yes, very relieving – that he wanted to stay together. Yet, right beside these welcome feelings were others that gnawed at her too; they whispered and prodded: *There was a reason for the divorce plan; don't go back on the divorce plan.* She sat down next to her husband on the bed, "Italy sounds lovely Jack, but I'm not sure—"

Jack interrupted her: "We could get the kids to come too. I can call them this week and see if their summer schedules would allow it. They probably wouldn't set aside three weeks for coming back home to Brookline, but don't you think they'll make time for Italy?"

"That's probably right," she smiled uneasily. "But—"

He interrupted again: "This architecture tour is supposed to be amazing. You have a guide who takes you to a new destination daily, and each morning begins with this in-depth tutorial about the way the building was built. You learn about the structural engineering, the heating and plumbing systems, the materials used in the walls and foundations. In some cases, you even get to look at the architectural drawings. It's supposed to be fascinating."

Emmy worked so her face did not betray how miserable she thought the tour sounded. "But Jack..." she reached her hand out to touch his arm; she tried to make her words sound caring. " It's a nice plan, but summer is a long time from now. I think maybe we should wait, wait before we make those kinds of plans." Emmy watched as Jack's face twisted.

He stood up. "Okay. That's fine. You think we should *wait.*"

Emmy wished she knew how to have this conversation. If she knew what she wanted, it would be easier, but she only knew how confused she was. "We've had our plan to separate for so long and there are... so many reasons we made that plan. I'm not sure we're going to do any better for ignoring that."

Jack's stance grew wide. "Is that what you call what I'm doing? *Ignoring?*" He shook his head. "Jesus, here I'm doing something I thought you would appreciate. But you've found a way to be dissatisfied." His voice grew louder, "You've actually made Italy sound onerous. How do you do that?" He stormed across the room back to the loveseat.

Emmy followed behind him. "Italy doesn't sound onerous, I didn't say that. I think it's nice you came up with the idea. Maybe we should even take the trip. But I think we should talk some before we start pretending we're a happy couple."

She could tell Jack had barely registered what she was saying. "What do you want to say? What haven't we said so many *goddamn times* before?" He glared at her, "No. No, don't even tell me. I don't want to hear it right now." Jack began furiously looking for the remote control in the loveseat's cushions.

For a moment, Emmy felt guilty. *Maybe she should have just said yes to the Italy trip; maybe she hadn't been very nice. Maybe if Jack was trying, she should too.* And then, quickly – like a wave it came – she knew she couldn't stand to be in the same room with him anymore. She mumbled an explanation. "It looks like you want to watch TV, so I'll go downstairs." She didn't wait for a response; she knew there wouldn't be one.

Tuesday, October 1:

Trafficking Desire

Ling pointed across the warehouse, "Duncan's over there, just off stage of Benjamin's apartment. Go closer so he knows you're here, but, you know, don't go too close. And remember: you have to be very, very quiet." With these adamant instructions, Ling turned quickly – *did she do anything slowly?* – and walked through the heavy curtains and out the warehouse door she and Emmy had just come in.

Emmy wished she could have stayed in the trailer. Moments ago, she'd been sitting on the top of the trailer steps, waiting for Duncan to arrive, when Ling pounced on her, explaining that Emmy needed to come to the set today. Ling talked as they speed-walked: "Duncan forgot he had to do this short interview for the DVD extras. It won't take too long, but he worried you'd be bored waiting for him."

Now, Emmy looked around the warehouse's huge, open space. It was both darker and quieter than she'd expected it to be. Temporary walls sectioned off the space into three distinct sets, but only one of them was visible from where she stood. It was a living room space that appeared directly transported from 1984. Emmy wouldn't have considered the '80s such a long time ago, but the living room was clearly other-era. The furniture was boxy but small, the fabric too bold, the TV thick and tiny.

Emmy scanned the bigger warehouse space. Duncan was sitting in a tall director's chair a hundred feet away. There were lights surrounding him and a video camera pointed at his chair. A woman was dabbing make-up on his chin and smoothing out his hair. Emmy edged closer just as the videographer began to film. She was too far to hear the interviewer's questions, but as she watched Duncan answer them, she could tell he was being funny. The interviewer laughed; the make-up woman tried to suppress giggles. He's charming them, Emmy thought, and she found herself proud, as though she had a proprietary connection to his talents. As the exchange grew noticeably more serious, Emmy tiptoed a few feet closer to hear what he was saying.

To her surprise, Duncan sounded remarkably actor-ly. "Gus is such a master of his craft. As much as I think I know this character, he's always pushing me to see it differently, do it differently. Sometimes I'm not sure we're telling the same story I signed up for," Duncan purposefully laughed, "but I'm willing to go wherever Gus wants to take me." That was the last question. The interviewer came up to Duncan, and the make-up woman took the lapel mike off him.

Duncan stood and looked around. He wondered if Emmy was there yet, and when he saw her standing off set, right away his body became more alert, like a shot of adrenaline whipped through him.

The afternoon before, in the museum's airy room, after Emmy agreed they could talk without constraint, they did. First about a painting, then about Paris, where they'd both visited. Duncan told Emmy a few funny travel stories about Abner; she teased him and they both laughed a lot. It was only forty minutes or so before a security guard came to tell them the museum was closing. It had been a great forty minutes. She was comfortable in the exact way he thought she would be. Still, on his drive home, he laughed out loud when he realized how he'd pleaded with her for that time. Pleaded so they could do what? Talk? Flirt? It was absurdly chaste.

Duncan was not used to chaste. He had a reputation that preceded him, and though it wasn't a reputation he'd sought to earn, he'd be the first to admit, it came in handy. Being in the public eye for almost two decades, the women who dated him now had few expectations he'd ever want something serious. Instead, "fun" was what he was supposed to want. He gathered this because women reassured him over and over again not to worry; "I just want to have fun with you." These assumptions allowed for his "relationships" to rev to roaring starts and end with minimal emotional fallout.

Those possibilities didn't exist with Emmy, did they? He wasn't cavalier about what she had at stake; he didn't want to hurt her. *But what then did he want?* He didn't know, and usually he would have worked hard to dissect what was tempting him and develop a deliberate understanding of how best to proceed. He wasn't doing that now. He was letting himself feel whatever the fuck he wanted. The decision felt defiant, and it was. He was bucking a self-management code he'd faithfully followed for over eighteen years.

For Duncan, it was always funny that he was well known, even celebrated, for being laid back. He would have described himself as a driven man, though not in the usual way. He wasn't trying to go somewhere; he was rushing away. Failure was trying to track him down. And success? Success was just a vehicle to elude it.

When he signed with Kallie that second year in L.A., he diligently did all she suggested. He went to every audition she lined up, attended the parties for which she secured his invitations, schmoozed and flirted as appropriate. He saved to have the best headshots taken, won a role in a play at the Mark Taper Forum, asked the right people to see him in it. He approached everything about his acting career with the zeal of an A student who does the extra credit for kicks.

Yet, the project that most preoccupied him was not about movies or his career. His bigger concern was to make sure he didn't end up like his father. Acting success might assure he didn't end up a disgruntled paper pusher like his dad, but that vocational distinction was meaningless. He didn't want to act like his father. And sometimes he did. His head would storm with anger, his reason disappear, his blood pulse like it couldn't be contained a second longer.

These episodes of fury petrified him. He knew what they could do. And had done once. Twice, if he counted that bar fight. So, the year he lived alone in his small Culver City studio apartment, he used the same resolution he applied to disavowing drinking and Australia and Sarah to exorcise his father's rageful legacy. He approached the project as if it were a scientific experiment. First, he formulated his objective: how could he be immune to rage? Then he gathered his data, watching for the situations that triggered the stormy reactions. Slowly, he pieced together the patterns: When he wanted something too greatly – desperately – he risked a frustration that seized his body and vanquished his control. The key, it seemed, was to avoid this type of frustration. Following logically from there, Duncan deduced that to avoid rage, he should give up desire.

Even with this logical conclusion, Duncan was unsure how to proceed. How could he make himself stop wanting? He read a lot of self-help books that year, though they didn't do much good. Theoretically, sure, he understood the value of being mindful and present and so on – but as a twenty-one-year-old guy working in the entertainment industry, these principles were too abstract to be useful. From a purely practical perspective, what worked best was when he cultivated passivity. He took to repeating to himself: *nothing really matters; nothing really matters.* These reminders gave him the permission not to care if he won a part or if the girl at the gym called him back or if traffic made him late. Not caring was hard at first. But eventually it took. And, immediately, he saw: his new easy-going ways leant him an appeal he'd never had before. People wanted him more if he wanted them less, it was that simple. Listening instead of yakking on, he was considered thoughtful. Laughing instead of joking, people found him funnier. By selectively choosing when to charm, his magnetism grew. It was only a year he ran the audition circuit; then the parts came to him.

As his success skyrocketed, Duncan tried to maintain an un-opinionated stance about the shaping of his career. Kallie would line up movies she thought were good for his talents and bank account; he would agree to them. His very passivity became the trademark of his celebrity. He was known for his easy grin, his good-natured charm, his relaxed manner. He had a reputation in the industry for not taking himself too seriously, and people liked working with him because he wasn't a prima donna.

Dan the Man was his first big hit. It was a small-budget movie about a stoned college student running from the mafia. The movie had a far bigger afterlife on video, and over the years, half a dozen lines became popular catchphrases. It was then that he picked up his moniker "the Grier," since everyone assumed Duncan, like Dan the Man, was the easy-going California guy who rode the waves. Duncan never bothered to clarify. Maybe there had been an odd reassurance in thinking he was what people thought. His career went along happily, with B action flicks, buddy movies, a couple of rom-coms. *Final Frontier,* the eleventh highest grossing movie ever, was his biggest film. He was – for then at least – a star.

He knew he was ridiculously lucky. Given who he was and what he'd done, he couldn't believe what people perceived him to be. He was a fraud, sure, but what a lucky bastard of a fraud he was. Knowing how much work went into the construction of his new self, he was always careful not to ruin it. He did what people asked him to do, went where people told him to go. He didn't party; he steered clear of the entourages that tried to leech off him. Overall, he liked his work; it wasn't hard, and he appreciated the perks that came with it. Women happily crawled into his bed; people rushed to do him favors; his life was flush with money, opportunity, fun. His smile, people joked it was worth millions. So, he smiled all the fucking time. How hard was that? All he had had to do was let it ride. Submit.

His plan had worked, and not just because he was successful. He was calmer too. Most of the time, he really was the easy-going, laid back guy he was known to be; it wasn't an act. Occasionally, a familiar agitation would come over him, and he would know he needed a run. Or sometimes he wouldn't be able to sleep because his body coursed. These were things he could live with. He kept the rage away – that's what the goal was after all – and for years, that was satisfaction enough.

But not recently. In the last year, the passivity had begun to drag on him. Being agreeable to stupid people's stupid opinions felt more of a chore. Beginning nothing relationships, he found them draining. Even with work, he was frustrated. The scripts sent to him were no longer as big or as interesting as they once were. Most were dumb. And his patience for the celebrity aspects of his job was disappearing. The last photo spread he'd shot, the design gimmick was that he was motor biking in the desert, a setting, he thought obvious, was dry. An hour into the shoot, he was sweaty and dusty but not sweaty and muddy which was apparently the look the photographer was trying to achieve. So, the stylists concocted a special mud-like paste made up of everything except real mud; they applied it carefully to his chest and legs, splashing him in some parts and dotting him with Q-tips in others. This shouldn't have bothered him; artifice was his medium, and he was usually good-humored about these kinds of things. But that day and others since, he felt like a dog being groomed for best in show. Everyone and everything around him began to feel unbearably fake and unworthy, including himself. He didn't want to contrive his actions anymore. He wanted to feel authentic. He wanted to want.

That was why he'd ignored Kallie's advice to decline *The Visiting Professor*. He wanted to try to steer his choices on the basis of his own tastes, just give it a try. Kallie accused him of sabotaging his career, and he didn't deny this possibility, if only to himself. There were few good reasons to do *The Visiting Professor*, only foolish ones. The story was a midlife redemption story, so for obvious reasons, that felt apt. And there was a line in the script that resonated with him. It was probably a corny line, but that didn't keep him from turning it over in his head. In a scene where Benjamin explains his doubts about returning to his wife, his mother-in-law, Mrs. Robins counsels him. She tells Benjamin he is about to ruin his life, and she urges him to go back to her daughter. "She has been a good wife to you Benjamin; she is your home." That was the line: *she is your home.* That sounded so good to him, a person who was his home. That line was the reason he'd wanted to make the movie. It was nonsensical, he knew that, but nothing else made more sense.

Now, here, on the sound stage, he continued to fake interest in the interviewer's never-ending banter, and he kept stealing glances at Emmy. Occasionally, she would meet his eyes and smile, seeing how stuck he was. But most of the time when Duncan looked over, Emmy was engrossed in her own thoughts; her eyes fixed on a distant point, her head tilted. She looked as though she were trying to solve a tough math problem. Even from across the set, Duncan could sense her befuddlement, and he was relieved to see it. He hoped he was part of it.

Finally, when the interviewer stopped blabbering, Duncan made his way to where she stood. "I'm sorry you had to wait through this. I completely forgot about the interview..." and before she responded, he put his arms around her in a hug. There wasn't anything sexual or even romantic about the move, but it was more of an embrace than a therapist and a client would typically share. Emmy pulled back to look up at him questioningly.

Still holding her, he winked. "We're on set. Everyone hugs here."

"Oh, I wouldn't want to look out of place." She meant to sound assured and slightly sarcastic, but her breathing staggered as she spoke.

"Especially since everyone's watching you," Duncan said, enjoying the situation.

Emmy turned to see that, indeed, several crewmembers had stopped what they were doing to watch this interaction.

"Come on, let's go back to the trailer," Duncan said, and he put his arm to her back to indicate the way to go.

When they opened the warehouse door, the brightness of the outdoors came as a shock, and Emmy was glad the light gave her an excuse to keep her head down. For the last week, she had, of course, been aware her client was a movie star, and she'd worked hard not to care about his "celebrity." Yet, in this moment, she felt uncomfortably starstruck. Duncan was clearly a king on that set, people watching his every move, laughing at all his half-jokes, eagerly seeking his attention. Even now, as Duncan said "Hi" to some of the crewmembers they passed, there was a reverence afforded him that was something to see. With him so aggrandized, she felt small.

"That's a big bag there. Do you want me to carry it for you?" Duncan asked. He was trying to assess her sudden quietness.

"Do I look that feeble?" She pulled her exercise bag tighter onto her shoulder.

They were at the trailer, and he walked up and held the door open for her. "Can you tell me what's in there, or is it a secret?"

Emmy walked through the door. "It's my dance stuff. I have a rehearsal today after I leave you."

"So, you're a performer too?"

She laughed at this label. "I wouldn't say that! My performance, it's in a community hall. It's very small potatoes."

He sat down on his couch, facing Emmy on her couch. She was all closed up right now, and he wanted to open her again. "I still want to hear about it."

"But we're supposed to be—"

Duncan interrupted, holding up his hands. "Oh, no, no. Don't even think of protesting. Yesterday, you agreed to *talk*. You can't renege now."

Emmy was surprised at the authority with which he was mandating the situation. "Okay," she smiled. She'd agreed to talk; she wanted to talk. However, now that they were back in their "therapy spot," she recognized how far this arrangement strayed from her professional purpose. *Did she have a professional purpose anymore?* She fiddled with her necklace. "We still have to mostly talk about you. This is still therapy."

Duncan started to object – he didn't give a shit about therapy at this point – but he stopped himself. He put on his most earnest voice, his half-grin. "Let's work out something where you give me ten minutes to ask you questions. No therapy for ten minutes. Would that be okay?"

"And then after ten minutes we'll talk about you?"

"Then we'll talk about me."

It was hard to remember the last time anyone wanted her to talk about herself. *When could it have been?* Emmy smiled. "Okay."

"Since you're giving me so little time, I'll have to make this a speed round." Duncan looked at his watch, then leaned forward like his question could pounce. "Are you ready?"

Emmy's elbow was on the armrest, her face resting on her palm. She nodded.

"What's Emmy short for?"

The way he threw the question at her, Emmy couldn't help laughing. "Amelia. My Irish grandmother's name. No one's ever, ever called me that."

"Where'd you grow up?"

"Manhattan, Lower East Side."

"No way!" His head flew back. "You're not at all Manhattan-y."

"I know. It surprises people. I'm a slow talker, but I can be pushy when I need to be."

His right eyebrow cocked dubiously.

"Really; you'd be surprised."

"Do you have brothers and sisters?"

"Nope. Only child."

"So, you're like me?"

"Yup, like you. And that's not the only similarity."

"Is your father... Did he—"

"No. My father didn't hurt me. But my home was volatile. Like yours. My parents fought *a lot*. Sometimes physical fights."

"What'd they fight about?"

She sighed. "What didn't they fight about? My parents were artists, or at least that's how they would have self-identified. They definitely had artistic temperaments. Emotional, super sensitive, tunnel-visioned. My dad was a painter. His canvases were beautiful – abstract and dreamy, with these great rich colors. But no one bought them. He'd come from Spain when he was 18 thinking he would live a grand New York arty life. He had no real art education or connections, but he always hoped his big break was just around the corner. It never was. He drove a cab, and he was extremely frustrated to feel he had a talent that was unappreciated. He always told me, 'You have to be good to be happy,' but I doubt he was ever happy."

"And your mom wished he would be more successful?"

"My mom wished he would be less moody. She didn't have a lot of toughness to her, and with my father as her partner, she was tasked with being the responsible one. She was *not* suited for that job." Emmy stopped, and Duncan saw that her eyes were reliving her memories. "They would have these big, loud, mean fights in our tiny, tiny apartment. And afterward, they would both confide in me about how wronged they felt by the other." She looked over to him and smiled. "So, you see, I was a therapist before I ever had any training." "You're talking about your parents in the past tense. Did they die?"

"Uh-huh."

"Both of them?"

"Uh-huh."

"Shit, Emmy, I'm so sorry."

"It's a long time ago now." She paused for a few seconds. "My dad died when I was seventeen. A car hit him late at night. Every few months he would disappear for two or three nights at a time, and then this last time, when he was on one of these benders, we got the call in the middle of the night. He was already dead by then."

"He was on a bender? Did he drink?"

Emmy's eyes squinted. "Oh, he did it all – booze, drugs, probably cheated on my mom a ton too."

"Damn; this is not the childhood I would have thought you'd had."

"Really? What'd you expect?"

"Something serene and lovely."

Emmy laughed. "No, that was the kind of childhood I desperately wanted. Didn't you?"

Duncan nodded. "Yeah, of course. I yearned for it."

"Yes, that's it. Yearning." She liked that he understood.

"What about your mum? When did she die?"

"She died when I was 22, right before... right before some other stuff." Emmy paused. "She and I were very close. After my dad died, I had to take care of her a lot. Even though she'd always been so frustrated with my father, she was very fragile without him. When I was at Amherst, I'd take the Greyhound back every other weekend to check in on her, and then when I left school, we would pay for her to come up and visit. When she died, I was... devastated."

"How'd she die?"

"She had an aortic dissection; it's like a heart attack, but it came out of the blue. She was a dance teacher and always so fit; she had no idea she had a bad heart. She died in minutes, before she even made it to the hospital." Emmy twisted her lips. "I didn't get to say goodbye." She realized her eyes were about to fill with tears. "Sorry, here I go again."

"You don't need to apologize." Duncan could tell Emmy was uncomfortable with her tears; he tried to find another question to distract her. "So, your mum at least was a good mother to you?"

Emmy wiped one cheek, then the other. "She tried. She really loved dance; it was her passion. But she wasn't the best with practical things; she couldn't make much more than toast and didn't care if my shoes were two sizes too small. I doubt she knew a single name of my schoolteachers – it wasn't her thing to care about things like that. We got by, and she had a happy spirit; she taught me to dance, and..." She furrowed her brow; "I had to take care of her a lot, but that was mostly okay. I knew she adored me." Emmy was suddenly aware of how intently Duncan was watching her. "So, I guess we must be close to the end of the ten minutes."

Duncan checked his watch and lied. "Actually I have some time left." He changed the subject to end on a lighter note. "Tell me more about the dancing."

She shifted in her seat. "It's nothing serious, but I do love it. When I move to music, I can feel my body making emotion, and that's such a fantastic feeling." Her description, she realized, sounded unexpectedly sexual. She added more words to cover up the impression. "I only started up again in the last few years, and it's just a tiny troupe I dance with."

"What's it called, your group?"

"Hourglass. The Hourglass Dance and Go."

"Hourglass? What, are you guys trying to brag about your figures?"

"Isn't that name awful?" Emmy tugged on her necklace. "I hate there's that implication. I think it's supposed to be a reference to the passage of time, sand through an hourglass. We're all older in the group, over 35."

"And you're performing soon? When?"

"Why do you want to know that?" She looked at him warily.

He smiled, shaking his head. "This is my turn to ask questions. Your turn will come."

"But how is it not my turn now?" She leaned forward to try to see the time on his watch. "What kind of watch are you using?"

"Hey;" he moved his wrist away from her sight. "Don't wiggle out of the deal!"

She sat back in her spot, happy to give in. "Yes, we are performing soon. In around two weeks."

"Are you the star?"

"No! There are no stars. I'm not like you." Suddenly a thought flashed into her mind, and she got excited, waving her hands. "I can't believe I haven't told you yet!"

"What? You sound like a teenager."

"I saw *Drawback Drive* last night."

"You did?" Finally she'd checked out one of his movies.

"Yup, I downloaded it and stayed up until one watching it."

"What'd you think?" He was concerned; *Drawback Drive* was no work of art.

"I loved it!" Her face lit with enthusiasm.

"Really?"

"Completely. I've discovered a whole new genre of movies."

"You're going to become an action lover?"

"I think I already am!"

"Okay, not to sound ego-maniacal, but what did you like about it?"

"Well, you of course." She beamed, happy to give him the answer he wanted. "You were so funny. And you moved really well, and you were like this great good guy."

He grinned. "I moved really well?"

She laughed. "Maybe that was a strange way to put it." She could be embarrassed, but she wasn't, only happy.

Duncan leaned in: "What'd you think of the kiss at the end?" It was a steamy kiss that had been nominated for MTV's Best Kiss award.

Emmy's eyes danced as much as Duncan's. "Hmm. I'd love to answer that question, but look at that" – she raised her wrist, pointing to where a watch might have been – "your ten minutes are all used up. You'll have to start answering my questions, Mr. Grier."

"Em-meeee!"

Emmy recognized the voice right away. "I'm in here," she called back. She snapped green beans and waited.

Celia bounced into the room and rushed to kiss first one of Emmy's cheeks and then the other. "Mmm, that looks good," Celia eyed the Salad Nicoise Emmy was preparing, "Would you feed me, sweet, most marvelous Em-ster?"

Emmy was relieved to have the company. Jack wouldn't be home until late, and after their conversation last night about Italy, he probably wouldn't talk with her anyway. "Of course," she smiled.

Emmy's relationship with Celia defied categorization, though if it had to be given any designation it would fall more neatly into a "friendship" category than a "motherly" one. After Jessica gave birth to Celia, Jack came home from the hospital and reported to Emmy he planned to be an active and present father to this daughter too. At the time, Emmy said she supported this decision. It was, after all, appropriate for Jack to honor and take care of this child too. *How could she not support that principled position?* The truth was she hated that Celia existed as a constant reminder of all that had gone wrong for her family, of all that could never be set right again.

It didn't help that Jessica complicated the situation even more. From the outset, Jessica made it a condition of Jack's relationship with Celia that Emmy had to be kept away from the new baby at all times. This meant that when Jack visited baby Celia, it had to be at Jessica's house, and when Jack took Celia out for an activity, Emmy couldn't join them. Jessica's stipulations enraged Emmy, and eventually they enraged Jack too. The Halperins consulted lawyers to see if there was a way Jack's parenting could be carried out more on his terms. But since Celia's birth was the result of an extra-marital affair, he was advised he would not be looked on kindly by judges, and any legal action might only worsen his fairly generous access to Celia. So, as a result of Jessica's rules, Celia never visited Jack and Emmy's house, and each weekend and holiday, Jack disappeared for a few hours, sometimes taking Marc and Ben and Tess with him to spend time with their other sister. Emmy understood Celia was blameless in the games Jessica played; yet, this recognition didn't keep her from resenting Celia's presence in their lives. Celia was the phantom child who pulled her family from her.

Emmy of course recognized – as did Jack – that it was Jessica's pettiness that made everything more difficult than it needed to be. In fact, a benefit of Jessica's stipulations was they made Jack furious with Jessica too. In the first weeks after Jack and Jessica's "breakup," Emmy suspected Jack's promised fidelity had again strayed. Yet, once Celia was born, the loud, angry telephone conversations Emmy overheard made her sure her husband was beginning to despise his ex-mistress. Jessica would call the house daily to demand Jack do something to make her parenting challenges easier. It didn't take long before Jessica's demands centered on money. Though Jack had already arranged for generous monthly payments to provide for Celia's care, Jessica wanted more. First, she asked for a full-time nanny, then followed requests for baby gear and furniture and clothes. A year later: A new car. Eventually, a house. Once Celia grew to school age, Jessica insisted Celia attend the expensive Shady Hill School in Cambridge. This demand in particular irritated Emmy since Marc, Ben and Tess all went to public schools.

Only when Celia was fifteen did Jessica abruptly decide the whole arrangement should change. Jessica provided some ennobled explanation for her about-face, but Emmy knew – everyone did – that her decision was born from self-interest. Jessica had begun to date a man she wanted to marry, and suddenly it was quite handy to have another household where she could leave her rebellious teenage daughter for the weekend. Without much ceremony to mark Celia's official birthing into the family, Celia came to live at the Halperin house two weekends a month. It was awkward at first. Emmy didn't know how to handle this wild teenage girl who was suddenly a family member. Celia had not been raised the way that Emmy and Jack had raised their three children – with manners and chores and curfews. Celia knew no boundaries, and as a teenager, was intent on vocalizing the most outrageous opinions. Her confidence so intense, it was hard to distinguish from arrogance. Emmy wasn't sure she would ever like her.

It was only one Saturday night when she and Celia both found themselves up late that they began an uneasy but increasingly confiding conversation. When they began to make hot chocolate together, Celia stirred the warm drink and tearily confessed, "Emmy, I know I'm supposed to hate you, but lately even when I try I can't." The statement's sad honesty made Emmy realize: she couldn't hate her either.

Yet, the structure for their burgeoning relationship was by no means easy to set. Emmy had no desire to act motherly, since she didn't particularly want to think of Celia as a daughter. She tried to be her friend, though this was also an awkward fit. One day, when Celia was sixteen but did not yet have her driver's license, Emmy offered to drive her to a far-away birthday party. On the way there, as they drove past the Chestnut Hill Mall, Celia suggested a different plan: they should blow off the party and instead spend the afternoon shopping, just the two of them. Hours of lingerie shopping ensued; and when they were done, Celia and Emmy had tried on and bought dozens of panties, bras, camisoles, and sexy nightgowns together. It was an entirely different type of outing than Emmy would have had with Tess, where their conversations would have been about fit and functionality, and the tone of Emmy's advice maternal and helpful. But with Celia, the expedition had an almost raucous quality, as though both women were indulging a secret desire to be girlfriend-y with each other. Celia, even at sixteen, had a throaty laugh and ample chest, and was proud of cultivating a mystique. If Emmy were honest, she found Celia's amped sensuality intimidating.

Now, in the kitchen together, Emmy turned to her sorta-stepdaughter, "So, what brings you here tonight?" Celia frequently had a habit of showing up unannounced, and the therapist in Emmy theorized there must be something about the impromptu drop-bys that comforted her, a reassurance that she was genuinely part of the family if she could stop in unannounced.

Celia grabbed a green bean from the cutting board and began to chomp on it. "I came to get the keys to the cabin. I've got to head up there to look at that bridge that goes over the creek bed near the Duncy's property." She chewed. "Would you say that bridge counts as architecture that's integrated into its environment?"

Emmy envisioned the spot. "Oh, that bridge is lovely. Yes, it definitely feels integrated to me. But what do I know? Ask your dad, he's the architecture expert."

"No way. That would mean hours of blah-blah-blah. About bridges. About environment. About integration. Life's too short to ask Dad a question."

Emmy suppressed a smile.

"Anyway, I'm pretty sure I'm going to use that bridge for the project. I have to sketch it and write an essay about..." Celia began to use a highbrow voice, "*the architectural elements that contribute to making it integrated rather than conspicuous in its environment.*" Celia grabbed another green bean and took another bite.

As Emmy cut a tomato, she decided it would be harmless to ask the question that felt top-most in her mind: "What do you think of Duncan Grier?"

Celia's mouth fell open, exposing the green bean within. "Wow, what do I think of non-sequitur?" She started to giggle. "Emmy, are you chopping vegetables and fantasizing about Duncan Grier?" Celia leaned in closer. "I've heard 40-year old women have *major* sexual fantasies. You are at your sexual peak, right? What's a girl to do?"

"Give me a break;" Emmy threw a green bean at Celia. "I'm only asking because Duncan Grier is filming a movie down the street from my office. I'm not up on celebrities, and I guessed you would have an opinion."

"Hmm." Celia continued to eye Emmy before she cleared her throat. "Well, then, for whatever it's worth, I think Duncan Grier is a grey goat. Way past his prime."

"Past his prime? But he's only 38!"

"Now, now, don't get all indignant! You're not past your prime." Celia rushed to quell what she assumed to be the source of Emmy's indignation. "With what you do for a living, you get older, you get wiser; better. But *Duncan Grier...*" Celia's face contorted in an exaggerated grimace, "God, I mean, he's an illegal trafficker in the only real currency that exists. He can't do that forever."

Emmy stopped chopping and let her face show its amused befuddlement. "*An illegal trafficker?* ... Celia, just what is he trafficking? Movie tickets?"

"Please. It's obvious. He's trafficking *de-si-re.*" She enunciated the word like she was reading it for a spelling bee. "That's what all those shallow Hollywood types do. They manufacture desire. But of course it's fake desire. That's why I get so pissed off about it. Those stupid celebrities cheapen the purity of the concept."

"I guess I didn't realize desire was so pure to begin with."

Celia looked at Emmy with horror. "What is more real and primal than desire?"

"I don't know." Emmy held out a green bean, "Love?"

"Emmy, please tell me you're not serious. Love, it's not primal; it's not bodily. Love is all about *lasting*. All about continuing. What a drag, right? I get tired just thinking about it."

Emmy considered this unusual opinion. "You don't want love. Only lust?"

"Oh, I love it when I hear your maternal concern. With a twinge of the mental health professional thrown in too." She chuckled. "No, of course, love rocks. I'm not anti-love. I'm just way pro-lust."

Celia took a handful of green beans and began to lay them out in a star design on the countertop as she continued, "Very few give lust its proper due. Celebrities definitely don't help, parading their abs and shiny hair like lust is about winning a friggin' beauty contest. But every body – good, bad, or ugly – wants. Body joining body – that's succor for the soul." Celia looked up from finishing her star design. She sought Emmy's approval: of her star, her profundity, her appropriate use of the word "succor."

Emmy let her face shine admiration on Celia. This young woman was so certain she had every explanation. *Was it naiveté that allowed for that? Or courage?* She couldn't decide.

Breaking the moment, Celia grabbed a whole cucumber from the cutting board and took a bite right off the top. Mouth full, she joked, "But, hey, if Duncan Grier gets you all hot and bothered, I say, who cares if he's your guilty google search? Who cares if he's a grey goat? Fantasize away!"

WEDNESDAY, OCTOBER 2:
SOMETHING DIFFERENT

"Starting... *now!*" Duncan pressed, "begin" on his phone's stopwatch. He'd already reminded Emmy she had to start today's meeting with the agreed ten minutes of his questions for her. The time he set on his phone stopwatch was not, however, for ten minutes but twenty-five.

Emmy sat on her spot on the trailer's muddy brown couch. It was raining outside, and when she'd arrived at the trailer five minutes before, she'd been chilled in her bones. Now, as she looked across at Duncan, she wasn't even slightly cold. She let her eyes linger on Duncan's broad shoulders, the pleasing shape of his strong torso. She saw a few strands of his chest hair from where he'd unbuttoned the top buttons of his shirt. Seeing his hair – just those few curls – made her aware of the nakedness his body held beneath his clothes, the intimacy that lay under that broadcloth shirt. It was so close, really. Just a few buttons...

Duncan took in Emmy too. She sat across from him, her eyes eager, her broad cheekbones flushed. He found himself having to restrain himself from leaning over and kissing her. It was what he wanted, and in other circumstances might have been what he did. Here, he knew, it would ruin everything. He could feel Emmy starting to soften toward him, and he didn't want to risk doing something that would have her walk away. Not now.

He'd never been attracted to a married woman before. He was surprised and perhaps disappointed in himself for how minimally Emmy's marriage impacted his attraction to her. She didn't seem married. She seemed alone. He guessed Emmy tried to minimize her marriage's impact in her life, working to contain the spill of its unhappiness. This was the story he told himself, knowing it accommodated what he wanted to believe. Today, he wanted to find out if this story was true.

He cleared his throat. "Are you nervous to find out about today's line of questioning?"

"Nope. I'm ready for it," she said, laughing.

Duncan cleared his throat, "Today, I want to know about you being a mother."

A mother? It seemed like a funny question, since for once, she was feeling very un-motherly.

"Kallie told me you have three kids, right?"

"Mmm-hmm. There's Marc, who's 22. Ben, who's 20, and Tess is 19."

Duncan sat a second. "Marc. Ben. Tess." He was surprised at how heir names pulled them from abstractness into reality. He put his hands behind his neck and stretched, looking at her. "So, ah, do you like being a mother?"

"Well, of course! I would be in big trouble if I didn't. The answer has to be yes."

"Come on, you have to give me more than that. What do you like about it? Not like about it?"

"Hmmm." She was flummoxed at how to describe the complexity of motherhood in a speed round. "It's a lot of work. Anyone who says otherwise is doing a crap job. And it's hard. Kids are needy. They need you, need you, need you, and then one day, poof! they don't. They're gone." She felt her face go flat.

"They still need you," he said reassuringly.

"You think?"

"I'm sure of it."

"That's a nice thing to say." She tilted her head, looking at him. "I know you said you don't want to be a father, but you might be surprised. I think you'd be wonderful at it."

"Naah." Duncan shook his head. "I'd be a shitty father."

"I don't think so. I think years from now I'll be at my dentist's office reading *People* magazine and you'll be in there with a spread about your new baby, saying something about how it's changed your life so much, and your wife—"

Duncan interrupted. "Why are you saying this?"

Emmy's face stiffened as she assessed the edge in his voice. "I was just trying to imagine your future."

"But that's not what I want my future to look like."

"Oh." Her lips twisted. "I'm sorry."

He shook his head, trying to resume the easier tone they had between them. "We're supposed to be talking about your kids. Let's get back to talking about them."

Emmy studied Duncan for a moment. Distractedly, she began. "Marc just started law school in New York. He's very serious, very certain about everything, just like his—" She stopped.

"Father," Duncan finished for her. His eyebrows shot up at her hesitation to use the word.

"Yes." Emmy wished she'd simply said the word and kept going.

Duncan kept his eyes on her. "Your husband is very certain?"

"He is."

"Do you want to tell me more about him?"

"Not really."

Duncan hadn't expected that answer. "Will you tell me his name?"

She took a second. "Jack."

Duncan expected Emmy to say more, but the only sound was the *patter, patter* of raindrops against the trailer's roof.

"I should keep telling you about my kids," she said to break the quiet. She tried to make her voice upbeat, but it was noticeably tinny. "My son, Ben, is the diplomat of the family, super funny and eager to please. And Tess, my youngest, is very gentle and observant and smart. I could go on, but you get the idea. I love my children." She was aware this last statement had an odd defensiveness to it, and looking at Duncan's reaction, she could tell he heard it too.

"Of course. You love them." He searched for a question to distract from the dullness in his voice. "So, do you do carpools and sit on soccer fields?"

"Not anymore. I used to. Swim meets, birthday parties, theater camp, college trips. That was my life for years. Not very glamorous."

"Why do you say it like that?"

"Like what?" She asked, though she knew what he meant. She'd sounded like she was embarrassed by her life.

"Do you think I care about *glamor*?" His face contorted as he said the word.

The tension was growing greater in Emmy's stomach. "I'm just saying my life is very different from yours."

"We're very different?"

"Well, at least our lives are." Everything she said wasn't working.

He took a deep breath inward. "I could give a shit about glamor." He looked at his hands, trying to synthesize the information she'd given him. "You and your husband have raised three great kids. That's a lot. You must be proud and happy."

Emmy listened to Duncan's summary of her life, knowing he was asking her if it was accurate. Her stomach turned over again. "I sort of have a fourth."

"You *sort of* have a fourth? A fourth kid?"

"A stepdaughter," Emmy offered.

"Ah, okay." His brows furrowed. "But you got married so young; did your husband already—?"

Emmy shook her head. She realized she wanted to tell Duncan. Their conversation had veered so far from what she'd expected it to be. Yesterday, everything had been so easy and smooth between them, and, today, they kept bumping into false impressions of each other. She wanted him to have the right impression. She lightly cleared her throat, "Jack had an affair. For a year. Early in our marriage. And a baby was born from that affair. Celia. I didn't get to know Celia until the last few years, but now she... she is also a part of our family. I'm not her mother; I'm not even quite a stepmother, but we joke about how every other term is too awkward." Emmy stopped; she could see Duncan was still piecing together the implications of this information.

"Did you only find out about the affair a few years ago, once you met Celia?"

"No. I knew about the affair before Celia was born. Celia's mother, she came to tell me about her affair with Jack when she was seven months pregnant. So," Emmy swallowed hard, "I knew."

"You didn't leave Jack?"

"I did not." This decision was one she'd reflected on endlessly. Not because she regretted the choice; she didn't. Nonetheless, she felt a sense of shame for staying with a man who'd cuckolded her. Over the years, Emmy had wondered if the reason she kept so few close friends was due to the awkwardness of sharing this part of her life. Most people, she assumed, would regard her as spineless for failing to walk out on Jack. She hoped Duncan wouldn't. She leaned toward him. "I was very young when it happened. I had no one else in the world who'd help me. No family – my mother had just died six months before; no money; no education; nowhere to go. I was 23, with three children under the age of four; Tess was only four months old then."

"He cheated on you when you were pregnant?" Duncan's face contorted.

"He did."

"You forgave him?" The question was sharp.

"Well, I'm not sure, actually. He never asked for my forgiveness; I don't know he would have wanted it." Emmy looked at her lap. "We just continued. We both wanted to be good parents to our kids. And I worked very, very hard to become self-sufficient."

"That defeats the point of staying married, doesn't it?"

"Maybe. After his affair, it made me sick – constantly sick to my stomach – to need him. I didn't want to."

"Do you now? Need him?" Duncan asked the question and realized it was the pivotal one. He waited for her response.

Emmy chose her words carefully: "I try hard not to."

"But you do?"

Her eyes moved to the window; the rain had stopped. "I honestly don't know if I need him or need to be away from him."

"Then, you do think about ending your marriage?"

Her eyes stayed on the window. "All the time."

Duncan noticed that Emmy was dry-eyed, her expression more tired than sad. He leaned back in his seat, watching.

Emmy felt his surveillance of her. "I've been talking to you like you're the therapist."

Duncan smiled. "Not therapist, friend. That's okay, right?"

She smiled back. "Technically the APA wouldn't approve of that either."

"Fuck the APA."

He was being glib, but Emmy knew the matter wasn't simple. Sitting here in this cozy corner of the trailer, with the afterglow of their intense conversation, it was impossible not to notice how far she'd strayed from conducting a therapeutic session. She'd meant to take only the smallest wiggles from the therapeutic constraints. *Just talk.* It had seemed so innocent. *Wasn't therapy just talk anyway?* But now she saw how seriously she'd fooled herself. She was being irresponsible, negligent. *Unprofessional. Bad.* Her hands went to her cheeks. "I'm sorry Duncan. I haven't handled this well. As your therapist, I never should have—"

His brows creased in confusion. "Why are you apologizing? I don't want you as my therapist."

"You don't?"

"I like it better when we're two people talking in a trailer. Honestly," he grinned, "I bloody well wanted to fire you days ago."

"Fire me?" she laughed, surprised by the word. "When did you want to fire me?"

Duncan didn't answer the question because a buzzer sound came from Duncan's pocket. It was the stopwatch on his phone. Emmy's hands popped up. "That was so much longer than ten minutes!"

"Was it? It must have been a technical malfunction."

"We should talk about you now."

He groaned. "Oh, let's not. Let me buy you a cup of coffee instead."

"You can do that? Leave the set?"

He stood up, stretching his back. "Ah, no, can't leave. Just using the expression; I meant a crafts services cup of coffee." He grimaced. "It's not as bad as it sounds."

"Mmm..." Emmy laughed; "Your expression says otherwise."

"Well, okay, it's awful, but it'll get us out of the trailer."

"Okay." She wanted to get out of the trailer too. She gathered her stuff, and as they walked to the door, Duncan watched Emmy's hips as she walked. The slope from her waist to her hip formed a pleasing curve; his hand wanted to rest there and he had to consciously remind himself not to touch her.

When they reached the trailer door, Duncan held it open for her by pushing it and extending his arm to hold it back. As Emmy squeezed past him, their bodies brushed against each other. Emmy froze and looked up at Duncan to find he was looking right back at her. For a second, she thought he might kiss her. But he didn't. He stopped himself; his eyes scanned her face, trying to read what she wanted.

Emmy broke into a nervous smile. "You really can't do that!" And she turned and bounded down the trailer's outdoor stairs.

"What?" He said with mock obliviousness, following quickly to catch up with her. "What can't I do?"

People in the parking lot stopped to watch the two of them walk down the puddle-strewn alley. Emmy walked ahead of Duncan; she turned back to say, "Look at me like that." She tried to sound stern but her face radiated happiness.

"Why not?" He rushed to catch up to her.

"Because ... because it will undo me."

Now beside her, Duncan leaned in close to her ear. "Would that be bad?"

Emmy assessed Duncan walking beside her; his whole expression anticipated her response. "No." She looked ahead as she considered it more. "No, maybe it wouldn't be."

Duncan liked this answer. They walked lockstep to craft services, their combined quiet comfortably full.

Emmy was naked. She'd rushed home from work, eager to get in a run while it was still light, but once out of her dress, bra and panties, she found she didn't want to put on running clothes. Instead, she stood before the full-length mirror, examining her body. Her inner self was so altered from the day, it didn't seem possible her body wouldn't look different too. But, no, there she was: knobby knees, slightly saggy breasts and nothing – really nothing – to show that inside she was, for the first time in ages, ablaze with happiness. She lay on her and Jack's big bed and stretched, feeling the coolness of the comforter under her skin. A good man cared about what she thought. He wanted to know her. She replayed moments from the afternoon again and again. Her whole being felt opened up, like a flower whose tight petals were bursting outward.

From the bed, she rolled to look out the window. The yellow walnut treetops were saturated with the evening's sunset. Pinkish-purple clouds streaked against a mostly azure sky, giving off a rich, almost velvety lushness to the evening. Her memories of her afternoon with Duncan danced through her head. The effort he took, the way he went out of his way to make her feel good. It was like he'd given her a box of sunshine. All the grayness in her life, he'd replaced with brightness and warmth. *How could she be so lucky?* He was Duncan Grier, for crying out loud.

She pulled a pillow into her tummy. She'd thought a lot about her lack of professionalism in this situation, and now she made herself think about it some more. *Was she manipulating his interest in her?* This explanation didn't seem to reflect the dynamics of their relationship, but she made herself seriously evaluate the question nonetheless, as though there was virtue in asking the right question. Maybe, she made herself consider, she'd unconsciously signaled her desire for Duncan and, as his therapist, made him feel obligated to reciprocate. She stretched her neck toward the window. *Nah.*

That afternoon, after she'd returned to her office, she'd received an email from Kallie requesting she forward the first week of Duncan's therapy bills. Emmy responded right away explaining that, as it turned out, her therapy with Duncan "hadn't quite worked out." Kallie wrote again, asking for the invoice for those sessions when they'd seen each other, and Emmy replied that there was no bill. After this e-mail exchange, a panicky nausea swept through Emmy. She searched online for the rules set up by the Massachusetts licensing board. On the website, there it was in black and white: therapists weren't allowed to begin a relationship with their clients until two years had passed from the termination of their therapeutic relationship. A grace period of either four weeks or eight sessions existed in which a therapist could terminate a therapy relationship without invoking this two-year prohibition. Today had been their eighth session, though Emmy thought their true termination date was likely at the museum. Regardless, Emmy squeaked by. Barely.

Even if she wasn't technically afoul, she wasn't oblivious to the fact that therapy had influenced their attraction. What worried her was the possibility that Duncan's interest was only transference. This was the term therapists used to describe how patients developed feelings of attachment toward their therapists after they'd shared intimate details. Transference was a natural, even normal, response to the act of sharing, and a dynamic that existed routinely in therapy. However, what worried Emmy – unnerved her, actually – was the possibility that Duncan's romantic interest in her was *only* transference, nothing more.

She thought about why she liked Duncan. Because he was smart and funny and sexy. Couldn't that the same reason he was attracted to her? *Couldn't it be?* She badly wanted him to want her too. She stretched, and her body had the most wonderful ache, as though a serum had been shot through her bloodstream, making every cell tingle. She let herself think of what it would be like to taste Duncan's kiss, feel his skin against hers, have his smile so close. She pulled the pillows closer; it seemed unbearable how fantastic he'd feel.

Would having a short affair really be so bad? Jack would never know. Duncan was leaving in three weeks – 22 days to be precise – and after he left, Emmy would never see him again. On this point, she made herself be brutally realistic. Duncan might be charming her now with his attention, but there was no chance for a sustained relationship. At the end of his shoot, he'd return to L.A., continue to live under his bright lights, and she'd stay in her cloudier world. That would be the end. She'd be heartbroken when Duncan left, she knew that. But wouldn't it be better to experience a short-lived happiness than to never experience it at all?

The brilliant sky had drained to sepia, and inky shadows were now moving slowly across her bedroom floor. With the room's growing chill, Emmy grabbed the throw blanket that lay at the foot of the bed and wrapped it around her. As the blanket unfolded, the smell of Jack – soapy and sweaty-sweet – wafted upward and around her. It was perhaps strange, but the question of whether to have an affair with Duncan and whether to stay with Jack existed in her mind as two wholly discrete questions. Whether to have an affair with Duncan was about the next three weeks, but the question of her marriage would perpetuate long after Duncan left. With his offer of the Italy trip, it was clear Jack wanted to try again. *Did she?*

Once before, she and Jack had tried to make their marriage work. It started the day she'd gone lingerie shopping with Celia. Emmy came home in the late afternoon to an empty house and took her six shopping bags of lacy, sultry bras, thongs and nighties upstairs. She undressed and began trying on her new purchases in front of her bedroom's full-length mirror. She was taking off one satiny red bra to try on another when she saw Jack behind her.

Emmy didn't know how long her husband had leaned against the door jam watching her twist and turn in the mirror, but when she saw him, she jumped, instinctually covering her bare breasts with her arms. Jack's voice was low and gravely. "I'm your husband, Emmy. You don't have to cover yourself from me." He came to where she stood in front of the mirror and stood behind her, so close. As Emmy watched their reflected selves, Jack put his hands around her waist, kissing her neck, holding her breasts. There was pleasure watching these two people's reflections; they were bodies – only bodies – in the mirror, detached from their emotional complications. When Emmy turned to face her husband, she kissed him, a swell of pent-up need overwhelming her. They made love three times that night before collapsing in a deep sleep wrapped around each other.

The next morning, Emmy rose with the sun but remained motionless in the bed, scared that if she moved, she and Jack would resume their old roles and lose the night's closeness. When Jack awoke, to Emmy's surprise, he pulled her to him and began kissing her neck, her cheeks, her arms. Emmy happily snuggled into him and let herself feel safe with his body enveloping hers. "Let's try Ems, let's try to be good to each other," Jack said to the top of her head as she nuzzled closer into his chest.

They did try. They wanted it to work, but all those years of not trying with each other made them clumsy at knowing how to share themselves now. Emmy took Jack to one of her dance rehearsals, but he couldn't stand the music. Jack asked Emmy to go fishing with him at the cabin, but she found the whole thing hopelessly boring. Conversationally, they tried to tell more about their days and show interest in the other's, but here the weight of their previous patterns made it especially hard. For years, they'd used the intonations to their word-appropriate conversations to passively convey their disinterest and hostility toward one another. Now, a disinterested "oh" needed to be replaced by an interested one, and they found themselves monitoring their simplest exchanges to affect an interest that wasn't always there.

Since it was sex that prompted their reconciliation, they tried to have a lot of it, and Emmy happily adorned all her new lingerie to encourage the return of that night's passion. But they'd shared a bed for nearly twenty years at this point, and their sex was usually comfortable, not passionate. The tenderness of that night did not return, and its absence was apparent.

What they worked hardest at was not fighting. The first time Jack snapped at Emmy, he stopped himself, walked across the kitchen, kissed her hand and apologized. Ben was in the kitchen at the time, and he yelled out to his brother and sister who were in the family room, "You aren't going to *believe* what just happened in here!" Yet, with time, Jack and Emmy found it harder to stem their irritation with each other. Their natural tendencies were so dissimilar that they were constantly irked by the other's choices. Minor annoyances built on top of others until, gradually, they returned to familiar territory, with frustrations quipped, potent silences lingering, and blowouts ready to ignite.

The final collapse came on a day when Jack returned home and found a handyman had replaced a stair floorboard tread with the wrong type of wood. He was furious that Emmy had paid the worker without noticing the error. Emmy, Ben and Tess were already at the dinner table trying to ignore Jack's cursing and kicking of the stairs. When Jack stormed into the kitchen, Emmy saw right away he was ready to explode. "How could you not see that? Huh? The woods are completely different colors. How is it even *possible* you didn't see that? Did you look?" Emmy refused to answer; she knew that whether she said "yes" or "no," Jack would be equally condemning. His voice seared with its loudness and anger. "I work so fucking hard on this house. But you don't give a shit. Do you care about anything, *anything*, that's important to me? No. No, you don't. And I have to live with it. Live with you. That's what I get. You're all I get. I keep hoping you'll get better. But," he shook his head, "you never do."

Jack frequently made nasty jabs, but this time, Emmy knew his words weren't an exaggerated expression of his anger. His voice wasn't merely cutting; it was sad; his posture wasn't only angry; it was resigned.

She stood from the table. "Jack, we shouldn't be together anymore." The words came out as a declaration, as though she'd reached a conclusion she couldn't contain herself from reporting. Yet, in twenty-one years of marriage, Emmy had never said anything like this.

Immediately, Jack's expression went slack. She'd said it. What they'd both worked so carefully not to say all this time, now it was said, done.

Tess and Ben watched with horror as their father's confusion transformed into rage. His whole body tensed, and his eyes on Emmy became so piercing Emmy's heart quickened. He looked like a bull ready to charge. He stormed toward her, "How dare you say something like that in front of our children!" Emmy felt his encroaching presence, and for the first time in her marriage, she wondered if he would hurt her. She rushed to their back door, and Jack moved just as quickly to prevent her from leaving.

She opened the door before he could stop her and shouted loud and sad and shrill, "Because it's true! It's true! *It's true!*" Without looking back, she slammed the door behind her.

That night, she walked in the dark for hours. It was late October, and the air was chilly and dank. Since there was no place to go, she had to return home eventually. She walked into their bedroom near 11 p.m., and Jack was waiting up for her. He seemed calmer sitting on the loveseat in front of the TV, but Emmy could tell he was seething. He turned off the TV, and pivoted to her, apparently having prepared what he would say. "It seems…" he cleared his throat, "that once Tess goes to school, we should get a divorce." There was an angry edge to his words, but they were posed as a question more than a statement.

Emmy knew he was challenging her to rescind her earlier outburst. But she wouldn't. She was sick of how he made

her feel. "I agree; that should be our plan," she said as matter-of-factly as her trembling body would allow.

Her response surprised Jack, though he tried not to
show it. "Well, then, it's decided."

"Yes, it is." She left the room to take a long, hot shower.
Once she'd emerged, Jack was in bed with the lights off.
Their "trying" was over.

Over the last two years, they rarely spoke of their agree-
ment to divorce, but it was an understanding from which
they never reneged. They obliquely discussed separating
their finances; they followed the sales of houses in their
neighborhood with an unspoken understanding that theirs
must ultimately be sold too; and from a few of Jack's passing
remarks, she gathered he'd already consulted with a divorce
attorney. As Tess's departure for school neared, they both
became even quieter around the other, as though they were
scared to speak. Emmy thought they'd return from driving
Tess to college, and that would be that. Their divorce pro-
ceedings would begin immediately.

She'd dreaded it. Its inevitability she accepted because
their discontent was obvious; it was rational to take action to
respond to the situation. And yet, she knew she'd miss Jack
too. He was the only person who'd ever taken care of her.
He hadn't done it well, she knew, but no one else had done
it better. He held her hand when her mother was lowered
into the ground, carried her up the stairs after she'd given
birth, orchestrated elaborate Mother's Day banners every
year with the kids. He was the only man she'd ever slept
with, the only man who knew her vulnerabilities and hurts.
She saw his face in all her children's, and together they'd
made a family with a structure and history and tradition that
now would be torn apart. It was a lot to lose, and what she
gained in return seemed paltry. The freedom to pursue her

own kind of happiness. Ah, it didn't even sound appealing; it sounded lonely and hard.

The day they dropped off Tess at Amherst, the route they drove home took them past the swimming hole where they'd first met. From the passenger side, Emmy looked sideways to see if Jack registered the sign to Puffer's Pond; he had. She waited for him to say something, to discuss how they would proceed with their plans. But Jack was quiet. Twice, she put out an opening to start the conversation she'd expected he'd want to have. But Jack ignored her, building a silence that would not be broken. He stayed that way for weeks.

When Duncan asked Emmy that night in his hotel room if she loved her husband, the answer that came was: "Yes." It had been a shock to hear the word in her head. Emmy hadn't said the words, "I love you" to Jack in a long time – years. And with their abundant frustrations, she didn't think of him lovingly either. But the answer had no ambivalence attached to it. She did love Jack. Her heart wasn't full with this love. He didn't make her happy; she didn't want to open herself to him; she didn't even enjoy his presence. Nevertheless he was part of her and she of him. That couldn't be denied.

"Emmy?" She groggily turned around. Jack was standing at the bed's edge, looking at her lying on their bed.

"Oh." Emmy looked out the window; now, it was very dark. *Had she fallen asleep?* She felt like she'd been thinking, but she couldn't possibly have been thinking for hours, could she have? "What time is it?"

Jack sat down next to her on the bed. "It's 8," he answered brusquely. "Why are you lying here naked?"

"Uh…" She realized she didn't know the answer to that question herself.

"Are you okay?" Jack was trying to figure out why Emmy looked so dazed.

She looked at Jack; even in the dim light, she realized she knew every speck of his face, so familiar and solid.

Jack leaned in. "You smell good."

This was a remark Jack would only make if he wanted to have sex. Emmy sat up. It was all happening again. A chill ran through her body; she shivered.

"Are you cold?" Jack asked, but Emmy still didn't say anything. *They were going to start the loop all over again, weren't they?* "Ems, would you please say something." Jack was losing his patience.

Emmy shook her head to come out of her daze. "Sorry, sorry." She looked around the room. It was the same setting. It would play out the same way. *Was this what she wanted?* She whispered to herself, "I want..." but she couldn't finish the sentence.

Jack was perplexed. "What? What do you want?"

Emmy took in the room, the setting, how close Jack was sitting, the goosebumps on her skin. She tried to figure it out. It was hard, like catching a shadow in the dark. "Something... different."

His face clouded; his eyes squinted his annoyance. "What does *that* mean?"

Emmy saw she couldn't convey what she meant without hurting him. "I'm confused, Jack," she said. "Horribly, horribly confused." And before Jack's face could register his further irritation with this answer, she leaned into him and kissed his lips. She knew this was what Jack wanted. He kissed her back, fully there, and his arms wrapped around her hips to pull her body to his lap.

Jack kissed her neck, her breasts. He wanted her now in a way he usually did not.

Emmy went along. She knew his desire was not for her. Not even for the sex itself. Or not exactly. His desire was for sameness. This he wanted fervently. To stop him would have been unpleasant. To change, hard. She let him have what he wanted.

It was easiest.

Duncan thought they'd be sleeping together by Saturday. If he asked Emmy to come to his hotel room again, she'd come. He thought so at least. He was doing sit-ups on his hotel room floor, still sweaty from his nightly run. As he ran his five miles through Boston's downtown, he thought a lot about what Emmy had told him that day. Jack was a jerk. This bit relieved him. And Emmy, she was undeniably a mother. This bit perplexed him.

Once when Duncan was in his mid-twenties, he'd dated a nice woman, Anita, who had a five-year-old son. One Sunday, she'd suggested they take her son to a park before having dinner together. During that day together, Duncan liked the boy a lot, and it was hard not to crack up at the hilarious things he said. But after Anita and her son left that night, Duncan found himself growing tenser as he thought about this goddamn kid. *If it was so fucking easy to enjoy children, why had his father hated him so much? Why hadn't his mother protected him?* That night, Duncan paced his house with mounting anxiety until in an impulse both desperate and determined he slammed his hand against a large mirror. His palm's impact tightly crumpled the epicenter and the glass cracks rippled outward toward the edges. When he heard the blood's drips hitting the wood floor, he realized his middle and index finger were sliced. The blood streamed outward, and Duncan watched it, stunned. The red thickness oozing from him confirmed: there was pain. It was something he usually tried to deny. That night, he held his hand in a towel and stayed up, dazed. At daybreak, he left a message for Anita, breaking it off. He never spoke to her or the kid again.

From then on, he made it a point to never date women who were mothers. In fact, it was his intention to date only women who would never want to *become* mothers. This quality wasn't one he could necessarily identify – he hadn't yet met a woman comfortable broadcasting she was anti-motherhood on a first date. So, he used proxies. Typically, his girlfriends were career-oriented or pleasure-driven and shared little in common with, say, your typical nursery school teacher. He chose not to examine why these types worked for him. They simply felt safer.

Yet, here was Emmy. She was nurturing. She was a mom. She said her world had been centered around her kids. *How was he going to reconcile that one?* Duncan wasn't oblivious to how hard he was working to carry Emmy's heavy load of obstacles. Everything that would usually make him turn away he ignored, and he did wonder why he was acting this way. Why was it that when he should run – *he really should* – he wasn't? If anything, the more he knew about her, the more thoughts of her filled his head. He liked the self-containment she had about her, and he wanted to crack through it, to be on the inside of her shield.

Beside him on the ground, his cellphone rang. He saw it was Kallie; he didn't want to talk with her, but he picked it up anyway. "You've been avoiding me!" Kallie sang her words like a teacher in front of a classroom.

Duncan stood up. "Never Kallie." He wanted to be off the phone as quickly as possible. "What can I do for you?"

"Well, I've e-mailed you half a dozen questions you haven't answered. I had lunch with Chris today and he told me you weren't responding to him either."

Duncan ran his hands through his hair. "Yeah, I guess I haven't been terribly good about that stuff lately."

"No, you haven't been. Chris and I were saying we can't recall a time when you've fallen so completely off the map. It's strange."

"Yeah, well, trying to stay in character." He walked back and forth between the couches and the desk. "What do we need to discuss so urgently anyway? Give me the drop-dead items."

"I need to find out if you want me in Boston for your breakfast meeting with Ned Reddux on Sunday."

"I'm meeting with Ned Reddux on Sunday?"

"Wow. Are you saying that as a joke? Yes, you're meeting Ned Reddux on Sunday! Remember: *Black Attack*. Ned is flying in just to see you."

Duncan was usually careful with his schedule, but in this instance he'd completely forgotten. "Oh, *that* meeting. No, you don't have to fly in for that. I re-skimmed that script a few nights ago; it's dumb."

"Well, it's smart dumb."

"No, it's dumb dumb."

"I think you should try to stay open to it."

"Kallie, it's more of the same. I don't want the same."

"You don't?" There was exasperation in her voice.

"No."

"Duncan," she took a second before she continued, "sweetheart. Your horse – your beautiful horse – has left the barn. Galloped away. It's a horse that people love. A horse that wins races. Please, please don't let your newfound interest in artistry ruin your beautiful horse."

"What if I don't like my horse?'

Over the phone, Duncan heard Kallie let out a long exasperated breath. "You know, a lot of young actors would die to take your place. You've got the life a lot of people want."

He knew she was right; that's what made him feel even worse. He started to say something, then realized, no, he didn't want to get into this again with Kallie. He sighed, "Fine, I'm meeting alone with Ned on Sunday for breakfast, and I'm staying open to the idea of *Black Attack*. What else do you need from me?"

"I'm not sure there's anything else that's pressing. Oh, wait, your therapist friend – our mutual buddy – I got her bill today, and it seems she's got your head for business." Kallie's voice grew gossipy. "I'd told her to charge three times her rate, and did she do that? No. Said there was no bill. Like you need the freebie."

Duncan smiled to himself. It was a good sign that Emmy wouldn't charge for their sessions.

"So, I guess that didn't work out so well after all?" Kallie prodded.

"What do you mean?"

"Um, in her e-mail she said that after seeing each other for a few sessions, you'd both 'agreed that the therapeutic relationship hadn't quite worked out.'" Even over the phone, Duncan could hear the air-quotes Kallie was using.

"When'd she say our last session was? Saturday or Monday?"

"Saturday? You saw her Saturday?"

Duncan winced; he shouldn't have said that.

"Wait. Oh, shit." Kallie's voice lowered an octave. "Duncan, are you getting it on with Emmy Cruz?"

"Halperin."

"Whatever. *Are you?*" She sounded horrified, hurt.

Duncan didn't want to answer her question, so he decided to ask a different one. "You lived with Emmy in college, right?"

There was a hesitation. "Yes."

"Were you friends?"

There was silence before Kallie eventually responded. "We got along okay, yes."

Duncan knew Kallie well enough to realize that if he sat quiet a second, Kallie would expound on that thought.

"In truth, I didn't like her much at first. I mean, who wants to live with the girl who all the boys come to see? But Emmy made such a point to say they were stopping by to see both of us – which they *so* weren't. And she was... protective of me. She walked me home when I'd had too much to drink and helped me with my econ problem sets, so, um, I came to like her, yes." Kallie sighed.

Duncan could tell she didn't want to talk about this subject, but he posed his next question anyway. "Was Jack one of the boys who came by?"

"Jack? No, not Jack. He wasn't one for fawning. You know, he and Emmy only dated a few weeks before he graduated. Though..." she gave a bitter chuckle, "I suppose that was enough time for him to plant his seed."

"Did you like Jack?" He'd pitched the question to convey the answer he wanted to hear.

There was an uncomfortable second before Kallie responded. "Jack knew how to send out the invitations." This was a phrase Kallie used frequently. "Everyone was cordially invited to be impressed with Jack Halperin. He was rich. Smart. Not a disagreeable package by any means. Just not someone you wanted to hang out with."

"But Emmy liked him a lot?"

Kallie blew air into the phone. "God, I can't believe we're having this conversation. Um, yeah, I guess she liked him a lot. I heard her lose her virginity to him. Our thin dorm-room wall couldn't block that one out. She liked him enough for that. But would I have put the two of them together? No. Never. Emmy was so sad that year. Her dad had just died; her mom was a wreck. But even with all that yuck, she had this – I don't know how to put it – wistfulness. And Jack, ugh, he was so literal and serious in a way that always made me feel like crap."

"Huh." Duncan sat with this information and let it sink in. There was a long silence.

Kallie was the one who finally broke it, her voice noticeably gentler: "You know they've been married like twenty-something years."

"I know." He said it fast.

There was another long silence, and Duncan let it play out. For all their recent bickering, he valued Kallie's advice; he realized he was waiting to hear it now.

"Duncan, I know you're frustrated with me lately, but I think you'd be surprised by how much I think about your happiness. I want you to be happy."

"That's nice Kallie, thank you—"

"Well, wait, let me finish. Because what I want to say is: Be careful. Okay? Marriage, it's more sacred than those of us who aren't married realize. I mean, I know I'm talking to the Grier here, and your powers of persuasion are legendary but, in my experience, marriages don't die easily."

There was a hard knock on his hotel room door. It gave him an excuse not to respond. "Sorry, Kallie, someone's at the door."

Duncan walked across the suite to look through the peephole. It was the milkshake girl. He opened the door and noticed right away her blouse was again barely buttoned; tonight, her bra was bright pink. *What color had it been the other night?* He couldn't remember.

"Hi," the young, blonde, pony-tailed woman looked at Duncan expectantly. She held a tall glass of chocolate milkshake out to him. A big red cherry rested prominently on the milkshake's frothy top.

"You brought me a milkshake?" Duncan said, and he gave a reluctant smile. "But I didn't order a milkshake tonight."

"I thought you might want one anyway." And she took the cherry from the top of the milkshake and slowly placed it in her mouth, pulling it from her lips with a slow, suggestive suck. "Sometimes it's nice to have a surprise, right?"

Wow. Duncan's body immediately registered how nice her surprise was. A milkshake *and* sex. God, that was hard to turn down. "That does look like a really good milkshake," he said trying to stall for time. He had to decide now if he was going to take her up on the offer. *Quick, quick, quick, what did he want? what did he want?*

"But I couldn't tonight." He saw her face register the disappointment. He felt his body register the same. "Usually I like milkshakes. Maybe another night." After a few more exchanges, he thanked the milkshake girl – Stella was her name – and closed the door, feeling conflicted about the self-restraint he'd just exercised. *Why had he said no?* She was old enough, pretty enough, clearly eager enough. No harm would have been done. *Was it because of Emmy?* He ran his fingers through his hair, making it stand up on end. God, for all he knew she could be screwing her husband right now. He half-laughed at the idea: No, he was sure *that* wasn't happening.

He picked up his cell. "Sorry Kallie; what were you saying again?"

THURSDAY, OCTOBER 3:
DOING THIS

That morning, when Emmy walked across Harvard's Great Bridge, students elbowed her for sidewalk space. The traffic was loud: one car honked and another revved its engine to swerve around it, coming close to hitting her. These irritations didn't annoy her as they usually would. The trees in the distance wore pumpkin-y orange and brilliant gold in their topmost branches. Geese were flying overhead, and the midday sun made the river sparkle like it was coated with diamonds. Emmy's booted feet click-clacked against the pavement; she couldn't wait to get to Duncan.

In the beginning of her walk, she'd tried to fight the anticipatory excitement that floated inside her. Very purposefully, she made herself think about Jack. The night before was fine, she supposed. Jack might have wanted sex, but he hadn't lingered long afterward. After he came, he breathily explained there were e-mails he needed to send and roused himself right away from the bed. For a while, Emmy pulled the sheets around her and watched her husband as he sat naked on the loveseat tapping on his laptop. His concentration on his screen was complete, his mind so focused on what he needed to accomplish next. She put on a nightgown and wordlessly left their bedroom. Grabbing leftovers from the fridge, she cozied under the ugly afghan in the TV room, reading *The Visiting Professor* until she fell asleep there.

Now, as Emmy began to walk into the set's parking lot, her eagerness made her stomach flitter. This restiveness was amusing to her. *It's like they say in the songs.* When she turned the corner of the last row of trucks, she finally had a visual on the trailer, and to her surprise Duncan was there, sitting on his trailer stairs. He wasn't wearing his usual Benjamin B costume, but was instead in jeans and a jacket. When he saw her walking toward him, he stood up. When he reached her, he put his arms out to hug her, and Emmy didn't hesitate to hug him back.

She lightly tapped his running shoes with the toe of her boot. "You don't look much like Benjamin B today."

He smiled at her shy flirtiness, "I thought we'd go for a walk today."

"But you said yesterday you can never leave the set."

"I got to thinking about it;" Duncan touched her arm to indicate they should walk toward the set barricades. "Ling has checked, and there are no paps around today. Actually, none have come around for awhile; they tend to have a herd mentality. So if I'm back by one, it should be cool." "But won't other people recognize you?"

"Not if I keep my eyes on you."

She laughed. "That's not really a disguise."

"It'll work; you'll see."

They began to walk toward the exit. As the two passed through the alleys that the trucks and trailers made, the crewmembers who stood idly near made no disguise of surveying Emmy and Duncan's progress through the parking lot. Emmy asked, "Have people started to talk about why I come around so much?"

"Well, they *started* to talk the first day you showed up. Now they're *debating.*"

"Debating? Are they trying to guess what we do every morning at 11:30?"

He laughed. "Given that Ling and Gus know you were my therapist, I think everyone must know."

"Oh. Then what's left to debate?"

He tried to decide if he should say it or not. "Whether we're sleeping together."

"Huh." Emmy walked a couple paces before she responded. "What's the consensus?"

Duncan grinned at her manufactured unflappability. "Well, no one's exactly filling me in, but given the looks we're getting," Duncan scanned the parking lot and leaned toward Emmy, "I'd say they think we are."

Emmy spent time evaluating the scene. "I'd say you're right."

The rest of the walk, their conversation skipped and hopped. Emmy told Duncan that she was re-reading *The Visiting Professor,* and they debated whether Benjamin's mid-life crisis was redemptive or ruinous. Duncan found it redemptive; Emmy thought otherwise.

"He dodges a bullet," Duncan said. "If Benjamin were to have left El, he would have ruined everything good in his life."

"I don't know," Emmy countered, leaning into his sauntering walk. "Living with El wasn't such a picnic." They went back and forth discussing this fictional married couple until they agreed the book's meaning hinged on a single conversation. It's one where Mrs. Robins meets with Benjamin to ask him to return to California – the very scene, in fact, where Mrs. Robins says that her daughter, El, is Benjamin's home. "Whether the book has a happy ending or not, it all comes down to how you read that scene," Duncan said. Discussing novels is not something he did – ever. Yet, as he strolled beside Emmy, it came naturally to share the ideas he'd mulled over but never discussed.

As they walked, Duncan picked up orange and red leaves from the ground and handed them to Emmy to compose a leaf bouquet. Their steps kept the same even pace, their arms grazing each other. Duncan kept his chin down and directed toward Emmy the whole time, and no one gave him much attention. When they turned onto the quiet street of Emmy's office, she pointed out her office building.

"My office is on the second floor," she pointed to the windows of the old Victorian house that had now been converted to three separate office suites.

"So, that's where you meet your regular clients?"

"Mmm-hmm."

"Do they lie on a couch while you talk to them?"

She laughed. "Usually, they *sit* on the couch." Tipping her head, she asked, "Do you want to sit on my couch?"

His eyes widened. "Excuse me?"

"I mean, do you want to come upstairs?" She pointed to the stairs leading to the front door.

His smile was playful. "That's *not* what I thought you meant."

Emmy caught the tease; her face flushed. She wished she had a witty comeback, but nothing came to mind. She pointed to the door. "Want to come with me?"

He grinned. "Ah, now you're just doing it on purpose."

She looked at him curiously, saw how his eyes sparkled, and then got his meaning. The laughter spilled out of her lips, joyful, snorting. She tugged on his arm and ran up the stairs, "Come on."

He followed her and it felt like a game of chase, climbing the two sets of stairs, following the narrow hallway to her office space. She opened up the door to the waiting room and then quickly went to her own office door and unlocked it. She strode in and Duncan followed.

"Here," she quietly announced, "is my office."

Duncan ambled slowly in the space, examining it. He wasn't sure what he'd expected to find, but now that he was there, he realized he was looking for something. The room was pleasant; there was a red couch and a wooden rocking chair settled on a nice Persian rug. An abstract collage hung between two sets of packed bookcases. "Did your dad do that?" Duncan asked.

Emmy nodded.

Duncan admired it. "You're right; he was really good."

He kept scanning the room, when suddenly he understood what he was looking for: photos. Emmy with her kids. Emmy with Jack. He wanted to see the people to whom she was attached. But there were no photos anywhere. Instead, he saw a clock; it said 12:50. "Is the time on that accurate?"

"Five minutes fast," Emmy said reassuringly.

"Still, shit, I should go."

"I'll walk you downstairs," Emmy walked out to the waiting room and Duncan followed her, admiring her silhouette from behind: her long tight-clad legs in her short skirt and, now with her jacket off, her sheer pale blue blouse that flowed over a low-cut camisole.

"So, Emmy, don't take this the wrong way, but aren't you – as a therapist – supposed to dress more, " he searched for the right word, "demurely?"

She looked down at what she was wearing. "What isn't demure?"

She said it with such conviction that he considered maybe he was the one being too sensitive. He walked closer to her, "Well, leaving aside all the leg you're showing, this… this is not demure." He lightly pulled on a thin gold chain that fell from her neck and anchored itself within the cleavage of her breasts. As he pulled up the chain, he saw it was a locket that weighed it there.

"It's a locket. A very demure locket." Emmy was trying to be jaunty, though the nearness of his body made her swoony. She looked up at him. "Do you want to see what's inside?"

"Your kids?" He kept his eyes right on hers.

She undid the clasp and held out the opened locket. She realized she was inviting him to stand even closer. "My parents."

He took a small step in toward her and their bodies were facing each other, a breath from touching. He looked at the locket's pictures, bending slightly at his knees to keep his eyes at the level of the locket. "You look exactly like your mother, but … with your father's coloring." He looked back at her eyes, and he was happy to see both a nervousness and a will to steady that nervousness. He could hear her breathing, smell the shampoo on her hair. His eyes moved to her lips, how close they were, how full. He leaned in and tipped his head to bring his lips—

Squeaak. The door of Maria's office suddenly let out a high piercing squeak as it swung inward. The door stopped before it was fully open, but anticipating someone to come through it, they each took a step back from their intimate position and looked at the half-open door.

No one came out, but Maria's voice was now a close presence. *"Does the same time next week work for you both?"* She was finishing up a session with a couple.

Emmy whispered to Duncan, "You have to go. Maria's going to come out."

"Who's Maria?" Duncan whispered back, not moving. They could still hear Maria just inside the door's threshold.

"Would it help to see if I have an opening next Tuesday afternoon?"

Emmy whispered to Duncan, "Maria's my practice partner. My best friend." She started to push on his chest with both her hands to convey how much she needed him to leave.

"Your best friend? Then I want to meet her," Duncan whispered back, amused with Emmy's ineffective attempts to push him out the door.

"Unfortunately," Maria chattered on in the next room, *"Tuesday afternoon is all full. But I can check to see about Wednesday. Could Wednesday maybe work for you?"*

"You can't meet her," Emmy tried to be as adamant as a whisper would allow.

"Why not?" Duncan suddenly looked grave. "Because of Jack?"

"Because I was your *therapist.* I'm not supposed to be doing this." She continued to try to push him out the door.

"And Wednesday is full too. I guess we're best just sticking with the same time, next week. That'll still work, right? Oh, Cheryl, isn't that your scarf? Over there by the couch."

"But *are* you? Are you doing this?" Duncan whispered, looking at Emmy.

She dropped her hands from his chest. "I don't know what you mean."

"Yes you do!" He leaned in to her, still whispering: "Just tell me and I'll leave: Are you doing this?" He was smiling, but his eyes were tight on her, waiting for her answer.

The door creaked as it began to open more. She jumped: "Okay, okay, I'm doing this. Now, *go.*"

As Maria sauntered into the waiting room, she chatted with Cheryl about her scarf, *what pretty colors, was it homemade?* Duncan was by then already at the waiting room door, opening it and moving into the hallway. As he pulled the door to close behind him, he glanced back to Emmy; she was watching him, her whole face beaming.

FRIDAY, OCTOBER 4:
Y-E-S

It was pouring. The weather had transformed overnight, and sheets of rain streamed down, sometimes blowing in howling gusts against Emmy's office window. She leaned her head against the glass and watched the sky, so low and dark and angry. She was trying to imagine what her daughter would think of Duncan.

It was a peculiar contemplation. Surely there was no situation under which Tess would meet Duncan, and of course she wouldn't confide in her daughter what was going on right now. But she did wonder. If Tess were to have a conversation with Duncan, would she like him? Would she find him interesting? Kind? Smart? No one's opinion mattered more to Emmy than Tess'.

A loud burst of lightening lit up the outdoors: so bright and brilliant. Emmy waited for the thunder and when it came, terrifically loud and sharp and craggly, Emmy couldn't help but laugh. It was all very dramatic. Life could be so quiet and then, unexpectedly, a lightening bolt.

The day she and Jack had dropped Tess off at Amherst, Emmy had worked hard to not cry in front of her daughter. She busied herself with unpacking a few of her daughter's essentials, making her bed, and asking friendly questions of her daughter's new roommate. Then, when there was nothing left to do but say goodbye, she steeled herself. She wanted to make sure not to cry. Tess was comfortable and ready to begin something new, exactly what a mother would want as she launched her daughter into the world. Emmy's grief was coming on fast – *how alone she would be without her dearest friend, her youngest baby* – but she was determined Tess wouldn't see it. After Jack gave his good-bye kisses, he waited in the hallway, and Emmy knew she had to make her departure speedy if she had a shot at being tear-free. She went to give her daughter a fast hug, but Tess clung to this embrace, and even when Emmy pulled back, her daughter drew her close again. She whispered in her ear, "Mom, don't worry, it'll work out. We'll all be okay with it."

Emmy thought at first: Tess only meant the remark to be generally encouraging. But as Emmy searched her daughter's expression, she saw precisely: Tess knew. She knew her parents were going to separate. Emmy and Jack had tried so hard to keep their divorce plan a secret, but as Emmy studied her daughter's sympathetic eyes, she realized their clumsy subterfuge was no match for their her daughter's sensitivities. *No, of course, Tess would know. How could she have thought she wouldn't know?*

Now, from across her office room, Emmy heard her cell phone *dhwip* in a way that meant a voicemail was just left. She walked to where her phone sat on her desk; her ringer, she realized, was off, and the message from Duncan. She played it: "Emmy, it's me. I'm sorry, but I don't think I can see you today. We couldn't film earlier this morning because of thunder, and now we're not going to break after all. I hope you get this in time. It's like bloody Noah's Ark out there." There was a long quiet, and Emmy thought the message was over, but then Duncan continued: "I want to see you still. Tomorrow, it's Saturday, I know. But can we get together? Could you text me and let me know. Actually, no matter what, text me to let me know you got this message. I'm worried you're getting drenched in the rain."

Emmy sat down and texted him: "Got your message. Not drenched. Have dance rehearsals all day tomorrow until 5."

She went back to the window and looked out at the rain. She couldn't help feeling Duncan and Tess were similar to each other. They were not at all alike on the surface – Duncan so good at charming people and Tess so shy – but she believed each of them shared a quality in their core. It was the way they were aware of people; both had a sensitive sensibility they had to cloak as they interacted in the world. Tess unwrapped herself to precious few people, perhaps only fully to Emmy. *Could that be true with Duncan too?*

As soon as the thought formed, she realized she shouldn't let herself think it. This thing with Duncan – whatever it was or would be – had to be short-lived. Ephemeral. Then: over. She had to keep reminding herself of that.

She watched the rain drive down: hard, dark, dreary. Despite the storm's hammering, she heard her phone make its announcement of a new text message. She walked to her desk and read Duncan's text: "Can you come by tomorrow at 6?"

She read the sentence several times. She knew what it was asking. Her heart started to beat faster. She knew she didn't have to answer now. But, she typed "y" "e" "s" and hit send.

SATURDAY, OCTOBER 5:
THE PURPLE LEOPARD PRINT BRA

Duncan stretched a long sleepy stretch and looked out on his dim hotel room. He thought he'd been dreaming of Emmy before he woke. His body was warm, with a twisting sensation in his chest. The wispy images were now drifting off him like steam, impossible to hold. Rolling over, he got out of bed to open the dark drapes. The thick windowpane was dotted with raindrops. It was still pouring heavily, and across Boston Garden were dark umbrellas.

The rain reminded him of the soggy 38th birthday party he'd held for himself eight months ago in L.A. *Damn, it had poured.* It hadn't been his idea to throw the party. Kallie convinced him to do it, saying he needed to remind everyone why they liked him so much. It was obvious she was worried about his waning stardom, and to placate her concerns, he agreed to do exactly as she liked. Kallie found the people to plan it, and the orchestrations were wedding-like: a deejay, a bar, flowers, catering. He invited 150 people; 200 came.

It took place on a Saturday night in February, and it rained the whole night – driving, piercing lines of rain. Heated tents were set up around the swimming pool, but no one went to them; instead the revelers crowded inside, and his swanky bash took on the hot, crowded feeling of a frat party. No one minded; people became outrageously drunk and rowdy, though he, of course, did not. He made sure to switch the drink he wasn't drinking – martini, beer, champagne – so no one would notice he was stone sober.

If anything, his clear-eyed view of the evening allowed him to take in too much. He floated about the party, mingling as he was supposed to, but becoming increasingly aware: he had no particular spot that drew him back, no group or girlfriend that anchored him as he moved through all these acquaintances and casual friends. Throughout the evening, people kept asking him about his several floor-to-cciling bookcases: "Where'd your decorator find all the used books?" and other such remarks. The questions were wholly serious; no one could imagine the Grier was the reader of these thousands of books. "She picked them for the color scheme," Duncan deadpanned before changing the subject.

He was ribbed a lot. As was expected for a 38-year old bachelor, jokes were frequently made about his perpetual single-ness, his "male biological clock." He played along, laughed, made the expected self-deprecating remarks. However, a couple hours into it, his affability was stretched. A constant refrain of the night was that Dan the Man was now middle-aged, and the notion that this perpetual stoner was facing maturity became the night's great hilarity. As Duncan tried to laugh at the constant references to Dan the Man, he thought about the character he'd created sixteen years before. Admittedly, Duncan had never worked hard to divorce himself from the role. Yet, as he watched his so-called friends chuckle over his apparent lack of maturity, his perpetual man-childness, he realized they really thought he was Dan. They believed he slacked his way through life. It rather pissed him off. *He hadn't done that, had he?*

The last guests left around 3:30 a.m., but the catering crew stayed to clean up, and Duncan hadn't felt like sleeping. He sat alone in his living room opening some of the many presents he'd received. A few friends had apologized when they had handed him their wrapped boxes, saying it was hard to find a gift for the "man who has everything." The phrase had been said enough times that it began to buzz in Duncan's head, taunting him to review what he had – *was it everything?* He refused to answer. He stayed focused on unwrapping the bowed boxes, but when he'd opened about a dozen, he saw something remarkable: he'd already received four bottles of single malt scotch. It was uncanny. *Really, what were the odds?* He could have felt proud that no one guessed he didn't drink. But he hadn't felt that.

Then he opened the gift from Bill.

Bill was Duncan's financial manager – he managed all of Duncan's money, his investments, his properties, his payrolls – and Duncan and he met regularly and talked weekly. Duncan gave a lot of money away, and Bill managed that too. The bulk of Duncan's charitable gifts were to organizations that helped battered women and children, and these gifts were all made anonymously. Bill was always careful not to pry into Duncan's motivations for choosing these charities, and likewise, Duncan offered no explanations. The obvious was never discussed, which was how Duncan wanted it. Yet, when Duncan opened Bill's gift, he saw, of course, Bill had known all along. The gift was a book about grown-up survivors of abuse, and Bill inscribed it: "I was beat up too." Duncan sat looking at the inscription for a long time.

In his pile of presents, the book stood out sharply. People couldn't give you meaningful gifts unless they knew you. Duncan contemplated: maybe no one did. With that acknowledgement, he considered that maybe he'd made a mess. Not of everything. But of some things. Important things. He'd not let anyone know who he really was. He'd been passive; he'd kept people at bay. *That wasn't normal behavior, was it?* It was, he had to admit, a problem.

Usually when Duncan recognized a problem he would deliberately set out a course of action to correct it. Yet, as the party receded weeks and then months away, he still couldn't settle on a solution to fix this thing. It was too big. It was him. And he was the way he was because he needed to feel in control of himself. His passivity was what made him safe.

Now, he looked out his hotel room's window to the rainy world outside. Despite the dark skies and hanging gloom, he didn't feel downcast. He was, instead, hopeful. He set out to find the source of this unexpected lightness; he got it fast. He couldn't wait for Emmy to come.

Oh crap. Jack was there. Emmy was outside the back door, looking into the house through the door's window; she was about to go inside; her key was in the lock. But, with Jack there, she hesitated. She hadn't seen her husband in two days, and she'd hoped to avoid him tonight too. She planned that she would leave before he came home, return to the TV room couch after he was asleep. But, no, now she would have to talk with him. He seemed angry too, opening drawers, rummaging through them, slamming them shut.

She'd worked all day to ignore her pending betrayal of Jack. It required some effort. In rehearsals, she purposefully turned her dance music very loud, hoping its blare would drown out any nagging guilt about her evening plans.Now, she was becoming soaked. She took a big inhale of air and made herself open the back door and walk into the kitchen.

"Hey," she said blandly, putting down her wet dance bag and closing her umbrella.

Jack didn't turn to greet her. "Hey." He closed one drawer and opened another. "Listen, have you seen a small key anywhere?"

"A small key?"

"Yeah, it's to the wine cellar at the cabin."

"Uh, no, I haven't seen that key."

"Don't get pissy, but I'm going up there tonight."

"I'm not *pissy*."

He opened another drawer. "Shit. I know I put the spare in one of these drawers. Where the *fuck* is that key?"

Emmy knew enough not to try to answer that question. She let him slam another drawer before asking, "Why are you going to the cabin *tonight*? It's horrible outside."

Jack kept his eyes on his search. "Fishing. My dad wants to go fishing tomorrow morning."

That didn't make any sense. "He wants to go fishing in a *hurricane?!*"

"It's a tropical storm, not a hurricane. " His eyes stayed sifting through the drawer. "They say it will clear overnight. And the fish, they bite well after a storm."

"Oh." *Who knew?*

"A-ha." He proudly held out a small key. "Got it." Finally, he turned to face his wife. "Wow, you're drenched. Why didn't you use an umbrella?" Before Emmy could answer he leaned against the countertop, raised his eyebrow, and changed the subject altogether. "So, Dad found out about Charlie and Jenny getting a divorce."

Emmy raised her eyebrows too. "Not happy?"

Jack smirked, "Uh, no, not too happy. He's..." his face briefly flinched, "*angry* at Charlie. He told me on the phone he thinks the divorce is 'wrong' – not just like a mistake wrong, like *morally* wrong. And he thinks it's his duty to tell him so. He wants me to tell Charlie he's making a mistake too." Jack turned the key over in his hand. "But I won't." He looked up at Emmy. "Obviously." His eyes returned to the key. "My father's such a piece of work."

Emmy took a hesitant step toward her husband. "Have you ever told your dad that, you know, we've talked about separating too?"

Jack's face contorted with disdain. "No! Why the hell would I do that?"

"You don't have to get angry about it. I just thought maybe you'd have shared that piece of information with him over the years."

"And since when do I *share* with my dad?" His question started snide, but ended sad. Disappointment washed his face, and his bluster disappeared. "This is my *dad*, right?" He looked to Emmy to have her confirm the hurt his dad caused.

"Right." Emmy saw the sad in her husband's eyes. "You're right. Hank: not a sharer."

"No, not a sharer." He gave Emmy a brief smile: "You know. More than anyone in the world, you know."

Emmy nodded. "I do." Jack's father was a stern man whom Emmy had never seen effusive or affectionate. Over the years, she'd watched Hank search and select remarks with the purpose of most unsettling Jack, and she'd watched her husband's equilibrium sheer and swerve when those remarks hit.

Jack walked to his overnight bag and pulled it over his shoulder. Emmy now noticed that Jack already had his rain jacket on. "You don't *have* to go, Jack." It seemed so obvious to Emmy.

"No, I do." He adjusted the shoulder strap over his jacket. "I'm the dutiful son, right?" He face went bleak. "I'll see you tomorrow."

Without another glance, Jack walked out the door. No goodbye. No interest in Emmy's day or questions about her evening ahead. Jack was focused on his experience, bracing himself for his challenges, and he saw nothing else.

Yet, when the door closed shut with a thud, a knowledge came with it. *She couldn't cheat on him.* In that small exchange, it was baldly apparent that Jack still trusted her. He expected her to be on his side – against his father, against the world if need be. To cheat on him would dishonor that trust. Perhaps this trust was the last bit of their marriage that still had merit, the nub where her latent love for Jack resided. She thought it could be nowhere else.

She stood looking at the closed door. She slowly ran her hand across her chin, back and forth, thinking, thinking. She didn't particularly want to be thinking; she saw these thoughts were ruining everything. But it was too late, she'd already met her reasoning's irksome conclusion: She shouldn't betray the one good and honorable thing about her marriage for a night's worth of pleasure. Her time with Duncan was fleeting. Her marriage had lasted most of her life. It wasn't right to disrespect all that time together; it wasn't right to breach Jack's trust. She shouldn't do it.

Her anticipation of her night ahead – of the fun she was going to have – evaporated. Her body sagged. She looked around at the kitchen, seeing how dreary it looked in the stormy twilight, how alone she was in it. She pulled her cell phone from her purse; it made most sense to call Duncan to tell him. There was no point going all the way to the hotel, was there? No.

As she was about to touch Duncan's number to dial, she considered: *Then again, maybe it was inconsiderate to tell him something like this over the phone.* Perhaps it was, in fact, more thoughtful to tell him in person. She could leave the dark, empty house and visit him quickly in his hotel room to explain her thinking. Now that she thought more, it really did seem the more appropriate approach. *Yes, yes.* She put down her phone and ran upstairs. She could get ready fast if she tried.

Duncan opened his hotel room door. Emmy stood there. She was wet. Soaked.

"Wow. That rain really got you."

Emmy walked in, dripping. "I thought the Four Seasons would have its own parking lot." She started taking off her soaked jacket. "I mean, that seems reasonable, right? But they don't. I had to park at the Commons. It was only a few blocks, but it's so windy, and my umbrella is—"

"Still in my trailer. That's my bloody fault. I saw it there yesterday. Sorry. Here, you should take off your boots." Duncan walked to the bedroom, and when he came back, he was carrying a t-shirt and some sweat shorts.

"Huh, you're a shrimp." Duncan said looking at her in shoe-less state. "You're always wearing your look-at-my-legs shoes. I've never noticed how small you are."

Emmy protested, "I'm five foot five."

Duncan smiled at her indignation. "Like I said, shrimpy. Here."

Emmy looked at the clothes Duncan was handing her.

"They're clean," Duncan offered, pushing her to take them.

She still didn't take the clothes. "Duncan." Emmy wiggled with discomfort.

He smiled at her nervousness and waited to see what she was going to say.

Her voice quivered, whether from nerves or cold she wasn't sure. "I can't..." she looked down, "I can't sleep with you."

He tried to manage the surprise on his face. And the disappointment. *What had changed since her "yes"?* He took a second. "Okay." He tried to laugh; "Ah, okay."

Emmy wanted to find words that would ease her awkwardness and explain why she had been so blunt. "I'm sorry, I realize this is..." she furrowed her brows: *What was it?* She felt so stupid. The blood was rushing to her face; she put her hands over her cheeks. "I shouldn't have come."

Duncan had never seen Emmy this flustered. "You know, you're making a puddle." He laughed, but it sounded thin. "Why don't we talk about this after you change out of your wet clothes?" Again, he held out his clothes.

She thought about protesting further because, really, once she was wearing his sweats, wouldn't her attempts to explain her decision only grow more preposterous? She thought so. Yet, in that moment she was so mortified, there was an appeal to disappearing into the bathroom, collecting herself, letting her face's flush cool off. "Okay," she said and went to the bathroom to change.

Once she'd peeled her wet clothes off her body, she stood in the bathroom looking at her bedraggled reflection. *I should not have come; I am so stupid; I should not have come.* She had to make herself open the door to walk back to the sitting room.

Duncan watched her timid re-emergence, thinking she looked both shy and sexy at once. Her black bra was showing through his white t-shirt and his too-big sweat shorts seemed to want to slip off her hips. He considered walking to her and kissing her. If he just kissed her, this would all become considerably simpler.

As though anticipating his thoughts, she looked at him warily. *Fine, he wouldn't kiss her.* She stopped a few feet from him and leaned against one of the couch's backs; she tried to affect easefulness, but she doubted it was working. She felt incredibly, horribly awkward.

Duncan noticed how resolutely she stood so far from him. "How was your rehearsal?"

"Good."

He walked closer. "When is the performance again?"

"In a week and a half," Emmy said simply.

He stood next to her. "So, you don't want to sleep with me?"

Her face tilted into a smile. "I didn't say I don't *want* to."

"So you *do* want to?"

She laughed; "I didn't say that either."

Duncan had already reasoned that if Emmy had no intention of sleeping with him, she would have cancelled. She was here, he was persuasive; he would appeal to her sympathies – he knew how to open her up – and they would, he felt confident, be together. *How could they not?*

"So are you going to tell me your new objections?" Duncan asked teasingly.

Emmy shrugged; she was disinclined to explain. "This is simple for you; there are no repercussions. But for me, it's not as simple."

Her cynicism surprised him. "Why is it simple for me? Who says I want no repercussions?"

"You don't have to say that. I know."

"You do? I don't." He was adamant. "How can you know? We have to see. Don't you want to see?"

His look turned playful, and Emmy found it hard not to mirror his expression. Duncan reached out to touch her still-sopping hair. "You're still pretty wet."

Emmy saw the tease in his gaze, and she hated to balk at it. "I am…" she was about to say *wet* but stopped herself. She laughed; her words would have a double meaning. *Again.*

Duncan laughed too, his eyes still directly on her. "Are you cold?"

Duncan was experienced with this type of persuasion, she could tell. "I…" she tilted her head, "I run warm."

Duncan grinned. "I bet… I bet you do." He took a step closer toward her.

And Emmy knew: this was it. She quickly looked down at her bare feet, at the shorts that were slipping off her hip. She understood that as compromised as her commitment to her marriage was in this moment, it would only get worse. She had to decide right then: *Was she going to stay faithful to her marriage, or betray it?* "I should go." The words were anguished; she hated saying them.

Duncan realized she was serious. "Come on, Emmy, don't."

"No, I'm sorry, I feel ridiculous, but this, it's not what I should do." And she realized if she was going to go, she had to actually move. She walked to the door and started to put on her wet boots.

Duncan followed her to the door, where she'd come in only minutes before. He couldn't believe she was going to leave. "You can stay, and we'll just talk."

Emmy laughed. "No, we *won't!*"

Duncan saw Emmy already had one boot on; she really was about to walk out the door. He knew what would get her to stay. "You said you would hear the other stuff about my father. You said you would. And I want you to know."

"I'm not your therapist anymore." She slipped her foot into her second boot. "You don't have to tell me—"

"But that's it, I want you to know." He stepped toward her as she yanked up the boot. His voice grew slower, deeper. "I've only told one other person this story, and she ... she was the person I thought I was going to be with forever. I've never told another living soul. And I want to tell you. Will you let me tell you?"

Emmy looked up at him. "Are you trying to seduce me with painful self-disclosure?"

"It's probably a bad idea. Letting you see I'm a monster."

She stood upright. "Nothing will make me think you're a monster."

"Why not? Maybe I've done something really bad."

"Doesn't matter. I know you, and you're not a monster." She tried to find his eyes, but he kept his gaze on the ground.

"Maybe that's why I want you to know. To see if you'll still think well of me, even when you know what I did."

"Like a challenge?"

"Like a fear." His words clipped.

She saw his face was stonily set. "You don't have to worry." She touched Duncan's arm. "*I'm* not worried. Actually, I want you to tell me."

"You say that now—"

"I mean it." And to show him she did, she turned to walk to the sitting area where they had talked last weekend. She didn't feel foolish anymore. No, now she felt quite comfortable. She sat down on the couch. She had not wanted to leave. And if they were going to merely talk, well, then, she didn't have to. Talking was not a betrayal. Everything felt less compromising. Much safer.

Duncan watched Emmy cross the room to the couch. He didn't move. What had begun as a tactic to get Emmy to stay – something begun as overt flirtatious scheming – now was turning into something altogether different, something that wasn't flirty, that wasn't fun. His knees were weak; he couldn't swallow.

"We're back to where we were last week," Emmy couldn't believe how much had happened in the last week; she looked to Duncan to see if he would share her astonishment. What she saw instead was that Duncan was still planted at his spot by the door. His expression was grave; the color had drained from his face. He looked like a different man. For the first time, she worried: *What did he do?*

Duncan walked slowly to sit next to her on the couch. He had wanted to tell her; he remembered that. But now that the moment was upon him, he questioned why he'd ever thought it a good idea. Here was something good – something that made him happy – why should he ruin it? It was hard to breathe. *He should not tell her.*

Duncan's face grew paler by the second; she put her hand on top of his. "Duncan…"

He flinched at the touch. "Have you guessed what I did?" His tone was gruff, his eyes darting and anxious. He was – Emmy saw it – angry.

Emmy's skin prickled. Their dynamic had shifted so swiftly she was trying to get her bearings. "I've had some guesses." She realized she was using her therapist voice.

"Can you tell me your guesses?"

"No. They're just guesses." But then, seeing the penetrating, fearful way he looked at her, she knew. The knowledge came instantly, as though Duncan had telepathically placed it in her mind. This possibility, she had not contemplated it before. It was ... *awful.* She looked down, trying to hide her shock. A shiver ran through her.

"You know." He was sure, and noticeably relieved. "I'm certain you know. Say it; I know you know."

She didn't want to say the words. She looked around as she tried to think what to do. She couldn't say it.

"Just say it," he was pleading with her.

She whispered, but still her voice cracked, "Did you, did you *hurt* your father?"

"Come on, you know it's worse than that." He looked right at her, waiting.

"Did you kill him?"

His eyes flinched at the word, but he was otherwise still. "I did." He assessed her reaction; she looked back at him, eyes wide. "I think, however, he came alive again." He waited for her to react, but she did not. "I think he did, but I'm not certain."

Even though what he said made no sense, Emmy didn't say anything. She didn't think anything either. Her head was full of heartbeat.

Duncan had worried Emmy would flee or in some other way register her revulsion; her stillness was assuring. He looked at his hands, "I was twelve." He cleared his voice, "And I... I strangled my father. His body – I felt the life leave it. He was gone. Dead." He heard the word hanging in the air; it sounded maudlin and ridiculous.

"My mother, she was screaming and hysterical and she left ... she left me with the body." Duncan's body went stiff. "I was terrified. I couldn't stand looking at him ... so I ran away. It was dark and it was night and I walked and I ran and I don't know how long I was gone, but when I came back, hours later, my father's body wasn't there." Duncan didn't say anything for several seconds. "My mother thought I'd hid his body, buried him or something. But I didn't. I definitely don't think I did. But he was gone." He realized his voice was somewhat shaky. He leaned forward, his elbows resting on his legs. He did not look at Emmy.

Emmy wasn't sure what to think. She'd never actually contemplated that Duncan had done something like this. All along he'd told her he had a secret. *Why hadn't she listened?* As she ran over the pieces of his fractured story, it didn't make sense: *How does a person die, then disappear?* She thought she should be appalled or scared, and though she wasn't sure yet what she felt, it wasn't those things. Duncan's hands were shaking. She moved in closer to him on the couch and put her hand on his back. She said what she wasn't sure was true, "I want to hear about it, all the things about it."

He looked sideways at her sitting there with him, but then turned away again. If he was going to tell this story, he couldn't see her face while he spoke. He had to feel detached, like he was telling someone else's story or playing a role. He began slowly. "I've told you my father beat me up a lot, but ... in all those years, he'd never hurt my mother. It'd never happened. She was always off to the side, crying and telling him to stop, but he never hit her."

He stopped a few seconds, and Emmy could see from his face's moment-to-moment twitches that he was remembering. "Then there was this day." He stopped again and blinked several times. "My mother was cooking in the kitchen, and my father came home. He'd been drinking. He stunk of it. At first, he was making stupid jokes, and my mom made jokes back, and they were laughing together. It was fine. Even nice. But then my mom, she said something – I'm not even sure what it was – but he disagreed with her, and she – god, sometimes she was so dumb – she talked back. I think it was meant to be a joke. My dad didn't think it was funny. He got angry, and he was over at the stove fast, shouting into her face, standing over her, spitting his anger. She was so shocked at how fast everything shifted that she started to cry."

Duncan stopped for a moment; his eyes squinted with the memory. "The tears enraged my father even more. He started slapping her, and as he did, his own actions seemed to fuel his anger. He slapped her again and again, hard. Her mouth was cut; she was begging him to stop. *Wailing.* And I just stood there at first. It was terrifying, but strange too. It was always me he'd hurt, and as I saw him flailing at my mom, I was seeing what it must have looked like when he hurt me.

"At some point, my mum dropped to the ground in a crouch – I think she was trying to protect her face – and she was saying over and over that she was sorry. But my dad didn't quit. I think he might have been scared to stop, like he would have had to see what he'd already done. With her on the floor, it was harder to slap her, so he started to kick her. With the first kick, I heard his foot hit her body so hard. It was…" he took a big breath in, "awful. She screamed out." He was quiet for a few seconds. "That's when I, I attacked him.

"My dad was hunched over my mother, and he had his back to me. I came from behind him and reached my arm around his neck and I … I pulled back tight. He was *much* stronger than me – I was just a string bean then – but I was tall and I had this leverage on him. My heart was going a mile a minute the entire time because I knew if I let him go, he was going to beat the crap out of me. And so I pulled on his neck, my arm tight around him – I pulled *hard.*" He stopped for a few seconds.

"Then my mum started screaming at me. 'Let go, let go,' she kept saying. 'You're killing him.' I did feel that his body wasn't resisting anymore. I didn't want to let go but—" Duncan thought for a second, "eventually I did. I did let go eventually."

He thought before continuing. "When my grip loosened from around his neck, his body went slack. He fell to the ground. He lay there, on the floor, in a slumped fetal position. He didn't move. Not at all. My mother was in hysterics. 'You killed him. You killed him,' she said it over and over. Shrieking and screaming. I had no idea what to do. I was *twelve*. I just stood there, looking at his body, at how still it was. I didn't move either. It felt as though my body wasn't mine anymore, like I could watch myself. Nothing seemed real. My mother was leaning over my father's body. She kept asking me "How could you? How could you?" It felt like she asked me that a hundred times. I just stood there, wanting to cry but not crying. Not knowing what the hell to do.

"And then ... my mother, she left." Duncan's voice grew edgier. "She became hysterical, throwing her head and arms back, crying, moaning and she walked out the door. She didn't say where she was going; she didn't say anything to me." His face contorted with confusion as he replayed the scene in his mind. "I didn't know what to do. Was she going to go get the police? Was I going to go to jail? I kept looking at my father on the ground, at his face. It wasn't peaceful like they say dead faces are; it still looked angry. It scared me. I thought he might leap out of his dead body somehow and beat me 'til I ... 'til I died too. So I ran out of the house. Ran into the night. I ran and ran. I tried not to think. God, I was scared."

Duncan stopped for a long time and when he resumed his voice quivered: "I remember hiding in an alley to sob.

I wanted my mum. I wanted her to understand. To forgive me." He waited for a time to strengthen his voice.

"Eventually I went home, because I didn't know where else to go. When I got there, it was probably three or four in the morning, and my mother, she rushed to the door. She had been waiting for me. She hugged me. She was calmer now. Her face was fully black and blue, and one of her eyes was swollen shut and her mouth cut. Her voice was shaky and sad; she said, 'Luv, what'd you do with him?' I had no idea what she was talking about at first, but I looked around and my father wasn't there on the floor anymore. I asked if they'd taken him away, had police come and taken him away. And my mother just looked at me. 'You can tell me what you did with him. You can tell me.' And I realized my mum thought I buried him or hid him or something. It made no sense. I was half my father's weight; how could I have dragged a dead body out of our Maroubra house without detection? What would I have done with him? But he wasn't there, and no one had taken him. My mum didn't believe my claims of ignorance. 'A dead body don't bloody disappear,' was the way she put it."

Duncan sighed. "There really weren't too many options. Either my father hadn't actually died, and he'd walked out of the house himself or I'd moved his dead body and hid it. I could tell what my mum believed; she thought it was me. Me, the killer; me, the concealer. But unlike earlier, she wanted to protect me now, I could tell that too. She decided we should wait to see if he came home or turned up at work the next day, and if he didn't, we'd make up a story to explain his absence. She said she wouldn't let anyone take me away.

"So we waited. And," Duncan stopped and he looked hard at his hands, "he never showed up. Not at work the next day. Or the day after. We'd assumed if he were still alive he'd eventually come back. But he didn't. I started to think maybe he was dead. And yet, things were missing. Things of his. His favorite leather jacket, missing. All the cash my dad kept in a dresser – around a couple thousand dollars, that was gone. His pocket knife, not there." Duncan sighed. "So that would seem to say he was alive. Those things couldn't have disappeared unless he took them. Yet other things it would have been natural for him to take, they were still there. The car, his clothes, his favorite books – they all remained. If he'd really moved away, he left so much behind. And no one ever said they saw him; no one from work or the neighborhood, not even my grandma – his mother – she always maintained he never contacted her. He was gone. My father had never done anything well. How could he have disappeared so completely? How could he have pulled it off? It was inconceivable. So maybe..." Duncan let his voice trail off. He shifted in his seat.

"When I can't sleep, I think a lot about whether I've blocked the memory of removing my father's body from the kitchen. I know it's possible. People create stories around traumatic events to convince themselves the trauma didn't happen; I know that. But I feel like that night – everything about it, I remember and replay; I can see, hear, smell it. I know I strangled him. I know that. But..." Duncan wiped his hands on his jeans, "I don't think I hid him. I don't think I did. I can't really be certain though. Maybe I wanted to create a story where I made his death less certain, made it less likely I'd done something that horrible."

He turned his hands over, looking at his palms. "My mother thought I hid him. After that first night, she never said it again, but I knew. I swear she thought I took the money too. It was this strange dynamic between us. She hated my father was gone, hated she had to go to work now to take care of us, hated that everything about her life had become so much harder. And she resented me. She felt all the badness was my fault. From her perspective, she was being this great protective mother by concocting this story of my father's disappearance. What we told people was that he'd left us, gone out for the proverbial pack of smokes, never come back. There was the issue of my mum's face that gave away it hadn't all happened that smoothly, but her face wasn't entirely inconsistent with the story. So that was what we said; we told it to the detectives who eventually came knocking. We told it to the neighbors and my school. I believed the story was true. She didn't." Duncan sighed, "She thought he was dead, that I'd done it. And she never forgave me for it."

"But you were trying to *save* her." Emmy finally spoke.

Duncan shrugged. He turned sideways, only now looking at Emmy for the first time since he'd started the story.

He saw her eyes were full of tears. "Are you crying?"

She nodded, wiping the tears at her eyes' edges.

"But why?"

"Because it was wrong..."

He faced her, bracing for her judgment.

"You were so young." Emmy's voice wobbled. "You needed someone to take care of you, to console you. To believe you. You were just a *boy*." Her face stretched with sadness, and she put her arms around him, hugging him tight.

Duncan didn't hug her back. He didn't move. This story was his deepest secret, his worst shame. For decades he hadn't shared it with anyone. He might have killed his father. It was abhorrent. He'd hoped Emmy would not judge him; he'd hoped she'd understand. That she'd feel protective of him. His chest sagged into her hug, and he could feel the wetness from her tears against his shoulder;

he heard her steady her breath. His own throat, he realized, had a catch in it too. He breathed in deeply, trying to settle his emotions. Quickly they were welling up: grief, relief, gratitude. He thought he might choke on them. He put his arms around Emmy's waist and pulled her nearer to him. He wanted her close. She couldn't be too close.

He felt her fingers stroking his cheek, and he realized she was clearing his tears. He hadn't even known he was crying. He went to hold her hand in his, and she brought her lips to his knuckles to kiss them.

Then: a knock on the hotel door banged out. *Ram, Ram, Ram!*

They jumped. It was a loud, insistent knock that flattened the room's emotional thickness. Again: *Ram, Ram, Ram!* Emmy sat back, wiping her own cheeks. Her voice was startled; "Are you expecting someone?"

"No." Duncan had already gone through a mental list of the people who might knock on his door; there was no one who would be coming by now. "I won't answer, and they'll go away."

They waited, looking at the door.

"See, they went away," Duncan said, turning to Emmy.

Just then, the door opened, and in walked a woman dressed in the Four Seasons uniform; she was carrying a chocolate milkshake.

Duncan stood up: "Stella?"

"Oh, you're over there," Stella turned toward him. Her jaunty tone cut against the room's sadness. Emmy blinked trying to understand who this woman was. Stella jutted her hip, and in the process, her low-buttoned blouse swung open, revealing her purple leopard print bra underneath. "Usually you're so quick at answering the door."

Usually? Emmy realized: this woman must come to see Duncan frequently.

Duncan's voice was loud: "*What* are you doing here?! You can't just walk in—"

Stella interrupted, "You *said* to come back another night, so that's what I'm doing." Her voice purred. "I wanted to *surprise* you this time."

Another night. This time. Duncan was sleeping with this woman. The knowledge whipped at Emmy like ice water thrown at her face. Emmy took in this Stella. She was like a cheerleader, with her blonde, thick hair in its perky ponytail and her fresh, milky skin. *Oh god.* Emmy stood up; the room slightly swayed. She thought she might fall. "I'm going," she stammered. She didn't want to look at Duncan. Nor at this milkshake girl. She didn't want to see the proof of all she'd misunderstood. The door seemed far away and though she tried to walk straight to her purse, her feet felt uncertain, staggering. She wished to be invisible, gone. She had to *go.* Duncan started to protest; "This isn't what you think."

But Duncan's protests made her cringe even more. *How stupid she'd been. How naïve.* She didn't care she was wearing Duncan's shorts; she didn't want her jacket or jeans. Grabbing her purse, she walked out the door.

Duncan called after her, "Emmy!"

Emmy needed to run. She ran to the staircase entrance and fled down one flight, then another and another. Duncan was yelling after her. Maybe running after her too.

She was choosing to ignore it. She could ignore anything.

SUNDAY, OCTOBER 6:
CLOSE

Duncan left his fourth voicemail message at 6:15 a.m. the next morning. "Emmy, Kallie just texted me your address. She looked it up in some Amherst thing, and if you don't call me back in the next ten minutes, I'll show up at your doorstep." He threw his cellphone on the bed, ran his hands through his hair. His skin could barely contain his agitation.

When Emmy fled from his hotel suite, Duncan had run after her. She'd had a few seconds lead, zipping down several flights of stairs, but Duncan was catching up with her. As he raced down the stairs, he pleaded with her to stop, to let him explain: it wasn't at all what it looked like. But Emmy didn't slow; she didn't respond. It was as though she wasn't hearing him. By the time he rushed into the hotel lobby, he was just ten feet behind her; it would have been so easy to grab her and make her listen. But once he entered the well-lit formality of the Four Seasons lobby, people exclaimed and turned. Emmy was dressed in a man's t-shirt and shorts with her mid-calf boots, and he, the Grier, was chasing after her. Everyone in the lobby stopped to watch. From the corner of his eye, he saw a woman raise her phone to take a picture. That is when he stopped running. He didn't need this moment recorded. He watched Emmy rush out the revolving door into the driving rain. He stood as the door made one, two, three rotations. Walking back to the elevator, he avoided the gleefully curious eyes that followed him.

In his hotel room, Stella was nowhere to be seen, but the chocolate milkshake sat on the coffee table. Without hesitating, he picked up the full glass and threw it hard against the wall. It broke on impact, and milkshake and glass shards scattered everywhere. It was a mess. Duncan didn't care. The last hour had held too many pitched emotions. He couldn't believe Emmy had run. *Why didn't she let him explain?* It didn't make sense. *He hadn't done anything wrong.* There was injustice to the idea that she forgave him his greatest shame but left because of a wrong he hadn't committed.

He called Emmy's cell phone and when she didn't pick up, he left long voicemails explaining how inconsequential the milkshake woman was, how he wanted to see her, how he didn't understand why she wasn't calling him back. He googled Emmy to find her home address, but it wasn't listed under either her or Jack's name. He texted Kallie: "Could you get me Emmy Halperin's home address ASAP. Alumni directory? No commentary. Just address." He waited. That he'd told her everything about his father, that they'd shared that closeness, he kept thinking if she'd stayed, everything could have been right, really right.

Now, pacing through his messy hotel room, he was eager to escape, but had nowhere to go. His phone rang. It was Emmy. He picked it up right away.

"So it's only when I threaten to show up at your doorstep that you call me back?" Duncan did not hide his anger. "Why aren't you letting me explain?"

"I was trying to figure myself out, I'm sorry." Emmy's voice was tired and small.

Hearing her sadness, Duncan softened, "Where are you now?"

"In bed."

"Is Jack there?" The thought made him sick.

"No, of course not. He's away."

Shit, she could have spent the night. "Were you sleeping when I called?"

"No, I can't sleep."

"Me neither. Emmy, it wasn't what you thought."

"It's okay if it was. I'm sure women do those sorts of things for you all the time."

"I didn't do *anything* with her."

"I have no claim on you."

Emmy's statement clipped with its starkness, and Duncan stumbled over its meaning. "What, what if I want you to have a claim?"

Emmy didn't say anything at first, then slowly: "I *want* to have a claim. That's why I feel so stupid. Because I know I can't have a claim."

"Because of Jack?"

"No. That's not even it. It's you. Who you are. What I am."

"Are you disgusted by what I did?"

"By what you did?"

"To my father?"

"Oh, Duncan, no." Emmy rushed to clarify, and her voice was warm again. "No, no, no. What you did was understandable. Even honorable. You were a kid trying to protect his mother. Duncan, I think you are a *good* man."

"You think I'm a good man?"

"A really good man."

"Then I don't understand. Why don't you want to have a claim?" Duncan realized he needed to see Emmy's face to have this conversation. He couldn't understand what she meant. *Claim?* "Emmy, can I come over there so I can talk with you? I have to be back here – shit, I have to be back here soon for a breakfast meeting, but—"

"It's okay; we can just see each other tomorrow."

"Oh. So you'll see me tomorrow?"

"I can come by at the regular time."

"All right. That's good. I think." He thought for a moment, and when he continued, he spoke slowly, "You know, before that stupid misunderstanding happened, it meant a lot to me you heard what happened with my father." He waited to see if she was going to say something. She didn't. "Emmy, I feel… close to you."

"I feel," her voice cracked, "close to you too."

Duncan knew he was missing something. He felt he'd clarified the misunderstanding, but she was still upset. "You're going to see me tomorrow at 11:30?"

"Mmm-hmm."

"All right." He wanted to say something else, but what could he say?

"Bye," Emmy said.

"Okay. Bye."

Monday, October 7:
Stretch marks

It wasn't raining anymore or even drizzling, but it was gray. The rain had stopped Sunday night, like Jack had said it would. Now, Monday morning, the clouds hovered, giving a miserable pall to the sky and ground and all the spaces in between.

Emmy walked the nine blocks from her office to Duncan's set, dodging puddles and kicking occasionally at the soggy brown leaf piles. She was trying to make herself think about her dance. She had her headphones on, and the music was loud and playful, setting a contrast with the thin grayness around her. She meant to be focusing on the section that included a pas de trois, the choreography that she, Sarah, Simon, and Marco had worked on over and over again on Saturday. But she wasn't really thinking about the dance at all.

She was thinking about Duncan, about how much it was going to hurt to see him. She was making herself meet him at his trailer because she knew it was the responsible thing to do. From a therapist's perspective, he had shared something traumatic, and she didn't want to abandon him with those feelings. She had to see him one last time to honor this most basic therapeutic responsibility to him. Her relationship to

Duncan, Emmy had concluded, was solely that of a therapist to her client. This conclusion did not come easily, but
seemed solidly true once she arrived at it. With that lens
in place, she felt foolish to have contemplated any other
picture.

In the moment before Stella had walked through the
suite's door, when she pulled back to wipe the wetness from
Duncan's cheeks, a surge of feeling had come with this simple touch. Perhaps this feeling started in her fingertips, but
it flowed through to all points in her being, becoming, in an
instant, a bodily knowledge specific and overpowering in its
certainty. She loved him. Then, Stella walked in.

After returning home, she listened to Duncan's voice-
mailed explanations; he sounded sincere, even desperate to convince her he hadn't slept with Stella. Maybe he
was telling her the truth, maybe he wasn't. At that point, it
didn't matter. Her upset had grown from the particularity
of Stella's presence to a general awareness of her immense
vulnerability. Emmy drew a bath to warm herself; she peeled
off the shorts and t-shirt soaked from the freezing rain and
sat in the piercingly hot water. Through the bath's suds, she
examined her 42-year old body, the constellation of thin spi-
der veins on her upper left thigh, the shiny stretch marks
around her belly button. She was old; she was a mom; she
was a woman whose own husband barely loved her. *Why had
she thought Duncan Grier would?*

The reality seemed plainly obvious to her now: Duncan
was only attracted to her because she was his therapist. It
was textbook transference, and she'd been a complete idiot
to think otherwise. He might have said those things about
wanting to be two people talking in a trailer, but his attraction had always been motivated by the need to find a safe
way to to tell her about his father. He wanted to confide in

her, be consoled by her. Therapy. Nothing more. *How could she have been so dumb?* Emmy plunged her head under the bath water, coming up only when she was gasping for air.

Now, at 11:30 a.m. Monday, she walked past the security guards who waved her in, through the narrow passageways that the trucks and trailers made in the set's parking lot, following the familiar path to Duncan's trailer. She held some papers she'd printed from the web; she planned to give them to Duncan; they quivered in in her hands. She turned the corner and immediately saw that Ling was sitting on Duncan's trailer steps.

"Hi Emmy," Ling shouted to her with surprising friend-liness. She stood up and rushed to Emmy, speaking as she did. "Filming is going slowly this morning, and Duncan can't get away. He asked me to give you this." Ling handed Emmy a note.

Emmy, I'm sorry, I'm not able to leave the set right now. Would you have dinner with me tonight? Text me, don't give a note to Ling; she'll read it.

Just as Emmy looked up from the note, Ling blurted: "I didn't read it." Emmy gave Ling a weak smile and thanked her for the note. She thought about leaving the papers for Duncan in his trailer, but then decided, no, that was actually a horrible idea. There was nothing to do but go. She said goodbye to Ling. She retraced the labyrinthine path, out from among the trucks and trailers, back to the real world, the world that was gray.

Text message sent from Emmy to Duncan, 11:52 a.m

I'm sorry Duncan. I can't do dinner tonight. I have dance rehearsals.

Text message sent from Duncan to Emmy, 12:23

You don't even know what time I was going to suggest. Are you still dancing at 10?

Text message sent from Emmy to Duncan,12:25

I could see you tomorrow, normal time.

Text message sent from Duncan to Emmy, 12:26

What's the appeal of that time? Filming is hectic this week. I'm not sure the normal time will work. You can't do tonight?

Text message sent from Emmy to Duncan, 1:15

I'll be there tomorrow. Have Ling call if it won't work. Hope filming is going well.

Thursday, October 10:
Smug smile

Duncan was bone tired. The night was settling in, and as he looked out the town car's window from the back seat, cars streaked past, then met them again at stoplights, their brake lights pulsing red bursts into the black. Duncan liked peering into the cars around his. The limo's tinted glass windows made it so he could see out, but no one could see in. He watched kids fighting in the backseat, a business-woman talking sternly on her phone as she drove, a couple kissing at the stoplight. The world was so peopled and varied and vast. He was driven through it.

Tonight the shoot wrapped up early, 8 pm, but the two days before had gone very late, with filming going into the morning hours. All the classroom lecture scenes had to be filmed at Harvard Business School on Tuesday and Wednesday nights, and since they were only given access to the amphitheater lecture hall after 6:30, filming hadn't started until 9:30. Unlike the other scenes they'd shot, these lecture scenes had many actors and extras, and Duncan felt obliged to be on set throughout, being present and friendly. Each night, after the wrap, he did a send-up of the scene they'd filmed. Using different voices from some of his more famous roles, he re-played the lecture scenes alternating the delivery of his lines first in the stoner tones of *Dan the Man*, then with the swagger of Billy from *The Final Frontier* and finally the nebbishy nervousness of Benjamin B. The crew had been in hysterics. It was easy to make jokes when he was the punchline. He did it a lot.

Since the days had been full and demanding, it should have been easy not to brood over Emmy. Yet, she'd slipped into his thoughts all the time. Each day, he hoped he would be able to see her; each day it turned out to be impossible. On Tuesday and Wednesday, his morning shoots were filmed with countless takes, and he'd been forced to ask Ling to call last minute to cancel their meeting. Today, Duncan called himself, but when he reached the beep at the end of Emmy's outgoing message he realized he didn't know how to say what he wanted. He wanted to say he missed her, because he did. But faced with the emptiness of the recorded space, he faltered and instead just reported the facts: today his schedule was messed up again. That was it.

He'd already accepted she was running from him. It was strange to be the person run from, not the person running. Should he concede she was gone? Walk away himself? Chase her? He considered chasing, but he wasn't sure how. The basic mechanics he got: pursue someone who is moving away. But once he caught up, then what? He would say, "Please..." *Please what? Please believe in me? Please be with me?* He'd never asked these things of a woman before. Not really. Not like this, when there were so many reasons she could say no.

As Duncan watched the Charles River whiz by his car window, he wondered for the hundredth time what Emmy believed about the story of his father. He would understand if Emmy did not trust the story. His own mother distrusted it. But he hoped – *god, he hoped* – Emmy believed him. He *thought* she did.

After all, it wasn't the story of his father that made her run. She stayed and comforted him after knowing about that. It was Stella. Stupid, stupid Stella. To him, this was strange. Had he slept with Stella, their sex would have been meaningless. Carefree fun, nothing more. It wouldn't have threatened his feelings for Emmy. Yet, clearly, Emmy saw it differently. Which again was... strange. She was married. Very much attached to another man. Why was it okay for her to return to Jack's bed every night? Wasn't that a betrayal too?

He decided he wanted to see Jack Halperin. Up until that moment, he'd purposefully avoided making Jack too vivid a presence, but now, Duncan pulled his cell phone from his pocket; he typed 'Jack Halperin' into the search engine. The page loaded slowly, but, finally, Jack was there, on the partner page of his architecture firm's website. He was a better-looking man than Duncan had expected and more accomplished too, with degrees, awards, titles – even magazine articles written about his work. He studied Jack's face; there was such confidence to his expression. It'd never occurred to Duncan he wouldn't be substantially more successful than Jack, but now he realized Jack was just a different version of success, one that likely thought little of Duncan's achievements.

The phone vibrated in his hand, and Kallie Stillingard's name flashed on its screen. Duncan thought about not answering; he was tired, it was late; she would annoy him. But she'd called him three times that day. "Hey Kallie."

Right away Kallie had a question: "Did you talk to Chris yet?"

To rebuff Kallie's urgency, Duncan made his response languorous. "Nope. Have not. Noticed he's called, but haven't had a chance to pick up his messages yet." It wasn't unusual for his publicist to call him a couple times a day. "Why, what's going on?"

"You really don't know yet?"

He was impatient with the all drama. "Why don't you tell me? Then I'll know."

"There's a photo going around of you snorting coke."

"What?" His voice blew out. "That's ridiculous. That can't be."

"No, it can be." Kallie was insistent. "It is."

"It's got to be Photoshopped. I don't do coke."

"You look like you're thirteen in the photo. But let's say you're twenty. You did coke then, right? Anyway, I'm not sure why I'm asking you. I *know* the answer; I'm looking at the proof right here: You *did* coke." She paused for a moment. "Here, check your phone, I texted you the photo; I bet it's there now."

His phone sound made the *whupping* sound announcing a text's arrival. "Shit. That *is* me." He held the phone close, trying to examine the background of the photo. "And I vaguely remember that night. But, why would anyone care about this now? It's twenty years ago."

"Well, I'm not sure anyone does care. The guy who had the photo, Brad Follower—"

Duncan interrupted, "Brad Follower? Shit, I haven't heard that name in a long time. He's the one who had the photo?"

"Yeah, I'm guessing he just found it in some old shoebox and– ka-ching! – made himself a pile of cash. I don't know exactly how the photo was passed around, but now TMZ and Smoking Gun have bought it and posted it."

"Posted it? You mean, it's already on the web?" Duncan finally understood the problem.

"Yes."

"Now?"

"It's been up for a couple hours."

"Shit." Duncan ran his hands through his hair. This was awful, embarrassing. *Fuck.*

"Chris wants to talk to you about damage control. He's thinking: set up a profile piece with *The Boston Globe*, have it mostly be about *The Visiting Professor*, how it's filming in Cambridge, blah, blah, blah and then get in a quick quote about how you're clean of the crack."

Duncan didn't say anything. He couldn't believe he was having this conversation.

Kallie interrupted his thoughts. "Were there lots of paparazzi there today?"

"No." Duncan answered distractedly. "They haven't come to the set in weeks."

"Tomorrow they'll be there. In droves."

He couldn't believe his whole carefully-crafted career could potentially be jeopardized by something so trivial. "God, Kallie, is this going to be bad?"

"Nah."

"But you sound worried."

"Well, it's my responsibility to let you know when the world is about to find out you're a cokehead."

"Kallie, I'm not *now*."

"Honey, I know that." Kallie laughed, "God, you don't think I know that? No, this is going to blow over in a week. Ha! Get it? Blow over?"

He didn't say anything. He'd be the punchline to more jokes. He'd have to laugh along, laugh at himself even more.

"Seriously Duncan, don't worry. You'll have a lot of paparazzi trailing you until they realize anew how boring you are. Besides, everyone already assumes you're a bit of a stoner. I mean, Dan the Man is stock photo for pothead."

"But that's..." it made him crazy that he was having to say this, "But that's not me."

"Yeah, well some things stick. Besides, you're a drifter. The stoned thing fits with that."

"You think I'm a *drifter?*"

Kallie's words slowed down, "But not in in a bad way, sweetheart. You're a good drifter. I mean, for actors, it's better to be nomadic. If you were too rooted to a home, you wouldn't want to leave it."

"No, I have no home to root me."

Kallie seemed confused. "D, your home ... is great. I love it; everyone loves it. Who couldn't love it?"

He didn't answer.

"Duncan, *what's* going on? Is this still stuff about Emmy? Is that going okay?"

"It's fine. Everything is fine."

"Are you—"

"It's fine, Kallie. Bloody great."

"Okay. Well, then, you should call Chris. Don't worry, he'll give you a gameplan."

"Yeah, yeah. I'll call. Bye."

Duncan sat there, thinking about how this photo of him bowed over a cookie sheet of coke lines would forever be available to those who wanted to see it. It wouldn't take long, maybe only hours, before the photo became one of the top images associated with his name. He squirmed in his seat and glanced down at his phone, which was still lit up in the night darkness. The screen had reverted to the web page it was on before Kallie's call came in. Jack Halperin's face stared up at him. His smug smile taunted him: *I've never snorted coke.*

Duncan clicked his phone hard to make the photo go away.

Jack walked into his bedroom and saw Emmy in boxers and tank top lying on the floor. Her face was bent down to touch the knee of her right forward-extended leg, her left leg bent behind her, almost straight back. She was stretching, something she did a lot, too much. Jack knew a lot of men found flexibility sexy. He'd never seen the appeal. He mumbled a hello and tried not to look as he walked to the closet to hang up his sports jacket.

This was the first time he'd seen Emmy in at least four days. He'd bumped into her on Sunday, after he'd returned from fishing at the cabin, but other than that brief kitchen encounter, they hadn't been in the same room all week. Like usual, he'd left for work early and returned late, but there weren't any brief bedroom interactions, since she'd been sleeping in the TV room all week. At first, he thought her absence was accidental, that she was merely drifting off while watching a movie or reading a book. But after four days in a row, there was no longer any question: she was avoiding him.

This was a bad sign for their divorce prospects. He'd meant to work harder to take that option off the table, he really had. But after each of his efforts to bring himself closer to his wife, he'd had an overwhelming urge to retreat. He hated the discomfort of begging her not to leave him. *That was what he was doing, wasn't it?* Yes, it was. And it sucked, to acknowledge this weakness. To recognize she might reject his request. He did it only because the alternative – putting his whole life through a shredder – was worse.

Out of his sports jacket now, he emerged from their walk-in closet and came to where she stretched. There was something he needed to ask her about. He tried to use a friendly voice. "Ems, what's the leaf pile doing there in the backyard?"

Emmy sat up from her stretch. "Wow, you could see that in the dark?"

"Well, it is an *enormous* pile." Jack tried to smile to make the situation lighter, but honestly, he didn't think the pile was particularly funny.

Emmy switched the position of her legs. "I asked Renaldo if he would try composting our leaves."

"He's not bagging them?"

Emmy glanced at him briefly before she bent her nose down to the leg extended in front of her. "Nope. The leaves are going to be composted for fertilizer in the spring."

Jack took a big inhale of air, trying to steady a rising sense of irritation. "I don't understand: Why does he think the leaves will stay in that pile? Dead leaves aren't known for staying where you put them."

Emmy sat up all the way. "Jack, there's no need to panic. Renaldo's planning on building some sort of container. The leaves won't blow. Renaldo says this way is, you know, better for the environment. Really, it's going to be fine."

Jack didn't think it sounded fine. *And since when did Emmy become an environmentalist?* She was always forgetting to think first about what was best for the house. "I don't see how an open container is going to keep those leaves from scattering all over the lawn. You don't want leaves all over the lawn, do you?"

"No, of course, I don't," she said, resuming her stretching. There wasn't anything overtly dismissive about the way she spoke; still, he was certain she didn't care about the lawn.

It occurred to him: they were having the exact kind of conversation he'd meant to avoid. *Damn.* He sat on the bed near where she was lying on the ground. He made his voice endearing. "You know, I was just thinking about that big leaf pile that Ben and Marc made when they were, oh, probably nine and eleven. You remember? It was so big they covered Tess completely, even when she was standing up."

Emmy smiled. "I do remember that. They wanted so badly for you to do running jumps into that big pile?"

"I did eventually."

"Yes, eventually, you did. After Marc threw that gigantic fit, you did."

Jack started to laugh, thinking about it. "He said he'd run away from home if I didn't jump in his pile."

Emmy chuckled too. "That he couldn't stand to be in a house with someone who wouldn't honor his creation."

"That boy was always ready to raise hell to get what he wanted." He began to unbutton his shirt.

"Still is. He's like you that way."

Jack looked at Emmy, who still sat on the ground near his feet. He wondered what she meant by that remark, but he didn't ask for the clarification. He peeled back his shirt from his chest. They were being nice to each other now; he didn't want to ruin it. *See, they could do this.*

Emmy leaned toward him. "The kids used to have so much fun in the fall with the leaf piles. It's a shame now that the leaves are nothing but a nuisance."

"I guess." Jack wanted to agree with her, but, honestly, he didn't. "The leaves aren't really that great. They're *deadness*, blowing over everything, getting into everything."

Emmy sat up straight again. "I know, I know. It's just... Don't you think it's sad that phase is over for us?"

Emmy was making it sound like their kids had only recently given up jumping in leaf piles, when he doubted there'd been any fucking pile jumping for the last ten, maybe twelve, years. She was only trying to make his concern for order look petty. "Emmy, everyone envies our yard. There's nothing playful about letting it look like crap."

She swallowed, then stood up. "You know what, never mind. Forget I said anything."

He stood up too. "You must realize I'd prefer Renaldo to bag those leaves and get them out of our yard. You must know that. I'm only going ahead with this whole 'environmental' bullshit because it's what you want. I'm putting your desires ahead of my own."

Her eyebrows skyrocketed. "Wow, Jack. Your desires ahead of mine? About the *leaves?* That's generous of you."

He took a step backward. He *was* being generous. He was trying to take care of their house. *Why couldn't she see that?* "Actually, you never do appreciate my efforts."

She stepped back on her heels. "That's not true. I appreciate what you do."

"Not really." He walked past her to the bathroom, throwing his shirt on the loveseat. Jack expected this exchange to be the end of it. They'd reached an impasse, and with most of their bickering and even their big blowouts, once that impasse point was reached, they each retreated to their own corners. So, when Emmy followed him into the bathroom he was surprised. She stood in the doorway, glowering.

"Are you talking about Jessica again?" Her voice was snide, cutting.

"Jessica? Good grief, no." The thought had never entered his mind. He grabbed his bathrobe and walked out of the bathroom again. "I'm talking about the house. The yard, the leaves."

Emmy followed him again, her head shaking. "You know what? Get the stupid leaves bagged if it means that much to you. I had no idea you cared so much about leaves, but if you do…" Her voice trailed off.

"Good. Then tomorrow, you'll tell Renaldo to bag the leaves."

Her hand pulsed outward. "Why can't you tell him?"

"That's nice. Because you didn't get your way, you won't call Renaldo?"

"And, what's your reason? Because you don't want to?"

They stared at each other. *He hated this. He'd meant for them to get along.* He yanked his robe over his shoulders, tied it in the front. "Emmy, I don't want to fight. Come on." He stretched his arms wide. "This is just about keeping the house nice." He was so tired. *Why did she have to make this so hard?* "To me, this house is a castle. I built a castle. It was an effort. Can't you just be the groundskeeper without complaining?"

He'd expected her to see how petty she was being, but instead her eyes grew more seething. "You built a castle?"

From her tone, he knew this would go somewhere, but he couldn't yet tell where. "Yes, that's what I said."

"Are you *king* of the castle?"

"Sure, I suppose so."

"And *I'm* the—"

Now, he got it. "Oh, spare me." He pushed by her to get his reading glasses off the bedside table.

She followed on his tail. "No, it's telling. You're king; I'm groundskeeper."

"What *bullshit.* What psychobabble *bullshit.*" He couldn't keep the irritation out of his voice any longer. "You want to be queen? Fine, Emmy, you're *queen* of the castle. Make way for her majesty."

"Screw you, Jack."

He put his glasses on, peering at her over the tops. "See, I can't win. Even after I make you queen." He could hear Emmy's heavy breathing, see her cheeks' crimson flaring, feel the rage that steamed the air between them, her impenetrable disappointment. He didn't want to look at her anymore. Sitting hard on the bed, he began to take off his shoes.

Emmy spoke to his downturned head: "Jack." From the word's rising intonation, he knew what she'd say next. The words tumbled forward. "We don't know how to take care of each other; we don't like to do it; we shouldn't be doing this any—"

He had to stop her speaking. "No! No! *No!*" he screamed.

The insistent loudness of the one word bounced off the bedroom walls. Emmy froze, and when he looked up to where she stood, he could tell he'd scared her. Honestly, he'd scared himself. His voice was too desperate.

He cleared his throat to calm himself. "We're talking about the goddamn yard, Emmy. About leaves in the yard. That's all." He righted his shoulders. "If you won't call the gardener, I will. Could you please get me his number?" He held out his hand as though to receive the number. Emmy studied the outstretched palm. He realized it was a ridiculous gesture, and his thoughts flew. *Why am I extending my hand? I know she doesn't have the number with her now. Am I asking her to hold my hand? What do I want her to do?*

Emmy didn't respond. She stood examining his hand, her brows furrowed.

He saw her confusion, but he would not clarify it. He gritted his teeth and held his hand out further. "I need the number."

Emmy's lips started to dip downward, and he could tell her tears couldn't be far behind. "You can find his number," she said in short breath.

He sat on the bed, one foot bare, the other still shoed. "You won't get it for me? You won't do this simple thing I'm asking?" He saw the first tears crest. "No, I won't." And, fast, before they slid down her cheeks, Emmy turned and walked from their room.

Friday, October 11:
Risk

As Duncan walked from the set back to his trailer, he saw, to his surprise, that Emmy was standing outside of it. He hadn't asked Ling to cancel today – Friday – but he also hadn't called or texted to suggest their meeting was on either. After four days of cancellations, he'd expected Emmy wouldn't come. But there she was.

From the end of this block of trucks, he stopped to watch her. Crewmembers ambled past her and stared at her unrestrainedly. To deflect the attention, she pulled her cell phone from her purse and began to busy herself with touching its screen. Despite her self-consciousness, Duncan thought she looked graceful and lovely, even from afar. He'd never known a woman who appeared both soothing and sensual, but he thought Emmy did. He watched her for a minute longer and then started to walk toward her. The closer he came, the more he worked to keep his resolve from slipping away. He tried to remember all he'd decided during the night. All he'd promised himself.

After returning to his hotel room, Duncan had stayed up late checking out gossip sites, message boards and tweets to follow the coverage of his coke snorting. Kallie was right: no one was even slightly upset by the photo. It was regarded as an enormous joke, just another example of the Grier's rakishness. Having studied Jack Halperin's respectable web presence, it was impossible not to note the stark contrast between Jack's image and his own. Whereas Jack gave off old-school credibility and stability, the message boards described Duncan as a teen-like stoner. We wondered if Emmy saw the contrast in that light. Regardless, Jack gave her security. He offered her nothing but risk.

At 1 a.m., Duncan texted Gus to ask if he could accompany him to the New York Film Festival that weekend. He'd known Gus was going; Friday's filming schedule had already been organized to end at 1 p.m. to accommodate Gus' need to be in New York for a reception that night. Despite the late hour, Gus responded right away, saying he'd love Duncan's company. Duncan figured a social weekend would clear his head. He'd see some of the festival's action, go to some parties, have the kind of time that reminded him he was a man who had options and sex and fun. He'd have a great time, a fucking fantastic time.

Earlier, he'd actually believed that was possible. Now, as he walked ever closer to Emmy, he wasn't as sure. Her brown hair was sweeping across her face; she was biting her lip, trying to stay focused on her phone. He came up close to her; he could smell the soap on her skin. He stood beside her.

"Oh!" She looked up at him, startled, "How'd you come up on me so quietly?" She beamed at him. She hadn't intended to smile so broadly; she'd meant to be protective, careful, professional. But there he was, so close, and the happiness surged to the surface; the smile rushed to her lips. The days had been so bleak without him.

He took in her expression but didn't mirror it. "You were concentrating pretty hard."

"I'm about to get hung. See." She held out her phone. A game of hangman was on her screen, the body and face all but complete. Underneath, the incomplete word:

__ H __ I __ E. "What the hell can it be?"

He looked for a second. "Choice."

"Wow, you got that *fast.*" She looked up at him; her eyes sparkled. "Smartypants."

"No one thinks that but you."

"Impossible. It's not like it's hard to discover."

"It's easier to ignore."

"Not for me."

"No, not for you." He looked down for a moment. "We should go inside the trailer."

Emmy examined him more closely. He was different today. She tried to find the reason for it. "There are a lot of photographers at the barricades today. Is that why you want us inside?"

He nodded. "I doubt they have an angle on my trailer from the set's opening, but it's better to play it safe. We should walk into the trailer separately too."

"Really?" She giggled. "That's odd. Why do they care if you're in your trailer with some random woman?"

"I'd hardly call you random." His voice snapped, and he saw Emmy's surprised reaction. He didn't want to be a jerk; he touched her arm. "You head in the trailer first, and I'll grab us coffees."

As Duncan walked off, Emmy headed up the steps and opened the unlocked door. There was nothing inherently nice about the trailer's space – it had a slightly musty smell, the upholstery was mushroom colored, the lighting dim – but Emmy found herself happy to be in it again. She put her phone and purse on the table, took off her coat and pivoted around, taking in its welcome familiarity.

Already, she was aware her thoughts were straying from her original intentions for this meeting. She was supposed to be there for a clear professional purpose. She wanted to give Duncan the papers she'd copied for him, explain what they meant, and then … say goodbye. That had been the plan. But, already, these constraints felt uncomfortably restricting. Seeing him, her body was lightened of the loneliness she'd carried so heavily these last few days. Duncan seemed upset too, and she wanted to find out why, to see if it was because of her. *Would it be so wrong to just talk with him?* She did not see how that could be so bad.

The door to the trailer popped up and Duncan walked in, handing her a paper cup of coffee without saying anything. Emmy leaned against the back of the sofa and pushed back the plastic tab from the coffee's top. Duncan propped against a nearby table and took a sip from his coffee. Facing each other, their toes were almost touching.

Emmy decided to break the silence. "So, can you tell me why so many photographers are outside the set today?"

He doubted there was a way to avoid telling her. "A photo was published showing something stupid I did a long time ago."

"What'd you do?"

Duncan could hear the apprehension in Emmy's voice. He watched to catch the impact of her reaction. "Snorted some coke."

She laughed. "That doesn't seem like a big deal. Doesn't everyone out there do that?"

"No, not everyone 'out there' does. And I don't either. Not for years."

"No?"

"No. Do you believe me?"

"Of course."

"Really?"

"Why wouldn't I?"

"I don't know. I can't keep track of why you trust me with some things but not others." He took a sip from his coffee cup and waited. "It seemed like you expected me to have done something really bad. What'd you think I'd done?"

"Oh, I don't know. The Grier fathers first martian baby. Something like that."

He laughed. "I think you've got your tabloid types mixed up!" He shifted from one foot to the other. "It's interesting your thoughts go to me and fathering children. Now, that's something that scares you."

Emmy studied him. "Your being a father doesn't scare me, not in the slightest. But..." she tilted her head; "I have to be careful here, since the last time I said you'd be a good father, you got mad with me."

"That's because you said were reading about me at the *dentist's office.* Emmy, I don't want you reading about me in some fucking dentist's office."

Emmy tried to determine: What part of that was upsetting? The reading? The dentist? Regardless, she hated the idea as well. "I know," she shook her head. "It's going to suck."

He saw that to her, this outcome – reading about him – was completely inevitable. She had never contemplated their futures could be shared. *Why was it something he considered if she didn't?* "Emmy, do you think I'm a bad risk?"

"A *risk?*" It was an unexpected question. "That word makes me think about investment portfolios or financial planning. All kinds of things I don't care about."

"I'm not talking finances." His voice was still edgy. "I mean do you think I'm safe or risky?"

"Oh." She got it. "Risky." There was no hesitation.
"Why?"

"Because—"

Before Emmy could begin to formulate her answer, the xylophone ring of her cell phone rang out. Both Duncan and Emmy looked to the phone, which was sitting beside Emmy's purse on the table where Duncan stood. As the phone rung, it lit up and showed the caller's name. Duncan saw it; Emmy saw it: Jack Halperin was calling.

Emmy rushed to pick up her phone. "Sorry, I forgot to turn it off."

You should get it." Duncan's tone was insistent. The xylophone ringtone continued its trill.

"No." She looked at the phone sideways to turn the ringer off.

Duncan snatched the phone from her hand. "Really, Emmy; here." He swiped the phone to pick up the call and handed it to her.

She looked at Duncan warily. *Why was he doing this?* He pushed the phone an inch closer to her; she didn't think there was anything to do but take it. "Jack?" she asked weakly.

Jack's voice was quick. "Hey, I'm going by Flour bakery for lunch. Should I pick something up for the brunch tomorrow? You remember Anthony and Francesca are coming over, don't you?"

"I remember." She looked hesitatingly at Duncan who stared back at her.

Jack continued, "So, what should I get? Sticky buns? You like their sticky buns, right?"

This was unusually helpful of Jack. And especially after last night's fight, she was shocked that Jack would offer such kindness. "Ah, sure, sticky buns would be great. Whatever you want, really." She raised her eyebrows to Duncan to show the routine nature of the call.

"Okay, sticky buns." Jack's voice shifted: "I also wanted you to know I talked with Renaldo."

Oh no. Not more of this. Emmy instinctually pivoted her body away from Duncan. "Jack, we can talk about this when I get home."

"No, there's nothing to talk about. Renaldo and I worked it out, and..." He cleared his throat and the pace of his words slowed. 'You know, I'm sorry, about the way we – I – got last night."

He was? Jack never apologized. *Did that mean she had to apologize too?* She wasn't sure she wanted to apologize. On the phone, Jack cleared his throat again, asking for her response. She said it quickly. "I'm sorry too." She glanced at Duncan. His eyebrows twitched at her words, but otherwise he kept his eyes steadfast on her.

Jack continued, "You know, Ems, our house can't mean anything unless we're both in it. It's not a house for one. We both have to be there." Emmy knew he was meaning to be nice, but a thought occurred to her. *Was it possible Jack wanted to save their marriage to keep the house?* She did not have time to consider the question. "I guess that is... true. " It was all she could think to say; it didn't sound like much.

"You guess?" There was a silence. "Emmy, if it wasn't already obvious, I'm calling to try to get us in a better place." Even over the phone, she could tell Jack was picking his words carefully. "I think we have a lot to protect. A lot to honor."

Duncan watched Emmy carefully; he couldn't hear what Jack was saying, but he saw her face flood with confusion.

"Jack, I..." she searched for the right words. What Jack was saying was considerate, she knew that. Still, there was something that irritated her about it too. "I think... it's nice you called to say that. And it's nice you're getting the sticky buns. Thank you." Emmy could tell from the silence that Jack was exasperated with her restrained response. "Right," he said and hung up.

Emmy held the phone out, looking at it to make sure the call had indeed ended. She stepped to her purse and slipped her phone into it. She didn't look at Duncan. She was too busy thinking. Maybe she should have been nicer to Jack. He was trying to be caring. *Should she be trying to be caring too? Maybe she was doing this wrong. Lately, it seemed everything she did was wrong.*

Duncan put down his coffee. He'd watched the conversation carefully; all the words Emmy chose were kind ones, but she'd struggled to put them together. She didn't want to be nice to Jack, Duncan could tell. "So, it sounds like Jack was trying to make up with you. Did you guys fight?"

"Yes." Emmy didn't look at him as she answered.

"But now you've made up?" He knew they hadn't.

"No, I wouldn't say that."

Deliberately, Duncan leaned forward. "So, is Jack risky?"

The unexpected question made her look up at Duncan. Seeing the eagerness on his face, she couldn't help but smile. "I think his risk is actually his security, if that makes any sense."

Duncan shook his head: "It doesn't." He leaned toward her further. "Can you explain it to me? I'm actually quite curious: How am I riskier than Jack?"

"I never said risk*ier.*"

"So, Jack's riskier?"

"You are each risky in completely different ways."

"How? I want to know."

She knew the answer precisely: Jack was risky because she thought she should leave him but worried she would not. Duncan was risky because she thought she would want him to stay and he would leave. But she could not say this. It would reveal all she was aiming to keep securely contained. "Why are you so interested in risk all of a sudden?"

"Well." He shifted his legs again. "You think risk is bad, don't you?

"No, not on its merits. I mean, it depends on what you're risking for what?" She looked at him, trying to determine where he was going with this.

"You think some things are worth risk?"

"Of course." She looked at him jokingly. "Duncan, what's the point of these questions?"

Duncan ignored Emmy's question; he pressed ahead. "What do you think is worth risk?"

"Love." The answer came fast; she said it without thinking; but once the word was out there she realized the charge attached to it.

Duncan's eyes grew wide: "That's an interesting answer."

Emmy tried to play it cool. "Is it? It's not hackneyed? *Risking for love?*" She lowered her head, then quickly raised it again. "What do *you* think is worth risk?"

"I like your answer."

"But is it yours?"

He considered the question for a moment. "It is."

Emmy was the first to look away. She remembered she had come here with a purpose, a professional purpose. It was important. "I have something for you." She went to her purse, "I've been wanting to give you these for days." She pulled out some folded papers and handed them to Duncan.

He unfolded the sheets. "This looks like medical – anatomical – descriptions."

"They are. It's all this stuff I copied from the web. You see..." she paused for a second and took a step closer to Duncan. "I thought a lot about what you told me about your father. And I did some research on the web."

Duncan's face went still, with a look of panic on it. He didn't want to talk about this now, not here, not in the daylight.

Emmy's voice stayed slow and measured. "The way you described gripping your father's neck, you probably placed pressure on these arteries, the carotid arteries." She could have identified the arteries on her own neck but instead she took a step closer and let her finger trace the line along Duncan's outside neck.

Duncan's body braced at her touch.

Emmy continued in a softly explanatory tone, "When you placed pressure here, you blocked blood to your father's brain and this loss of blood caused him to pass out. Only pass out."

Duncan's eyes strained across Emmy's face, trying to understand what she was saying.

"Once the pressure was removed, the bloodflow would have resumed. His consciousness would have been restored. He would have become fine again. You didn't interrupt the blood flow for long enough to cause permanent damage. You stopped when his body began to go limp. And you didn't interfere with his airflow. That could have caused asphyxiation. But that's not what you did. You just temporarily stopped the blood. He didn't die. He fainted."

Duncan still didn't move, though the air in his chest pushed hard up against his throat. Abruptly, he walked away. He sat down on the thin sofa, putting his head in his hands. "How, how do you know this?"

Emmy kept her voice soothing. "I took a couple physiology classes for my degree. Still, I needed to look all this stuff up to be sure." She followed him to the couch and sat down beside him. "I've been waiting all week to tell you this in person."

Duncan turned to her. "So, you don't think I killed him? You don't think I blocked out the memory of taking him away?"

She shook her head. "No, I never believed that. Not for a moment. It's not who you are. The way you told the story you took ownership for what you did. You weren't trying to deny your actions. You weren't seeking to forget. You wanted to be forgiven. Those are different motivations." She put her hand on his arm. "You hadn't done anything wrong. Even if your father had died, even if you'd killed him, you were trying to protect your mother. That is honorable. Not bad."

He stood up and walked back to the table. He crossed his arms, looked at the ground. "You must think I'm really stupid I've never looked into this. I've thought about it. I've thought about it a lot. But I didn't even know what questions to ask or whom to ask them of and then... I wasn't sure... I wasn't sure if I wanted to know the answers."

Emmy followed him to where he stood. "That makes a lot of sense to me."

He still didn't face her. "I wanted to lock the whole thing up. I kept trying to convince myself it didn't matter. But, I have always, always thought about it."

"You were twelve. Your mother said you killed him; she said it over and over again, and she may have believed you did. That is probably how it looked to her. But she was *wrong.*" She took a step closer. "You didn't kill him."

"I didn't kill him." He was trying to take it in.

"You didn't. You didn't do it."

Finally, he brought his gaze up from the floor. There were her deep brown eyes, her plummy lips, the concern she wore so easily on her face. He guessed she would have this power, and there it was: She'd made everything better. The greatest fear of his life, she'd taken it away. The thought in his head came out of his mouth: "Emmy, I wish you'd stayed."

The remark was so honest in its emotion – so bare – that, instinctually, she looked away. Right now, she felt close to him and wanted only to be closer. *Why hadn't she stayed?* She made herself remember; she thought about the purple leopard print bra and all it conveyed. She tried to be glib. "Well, did you like the milkshake?"

"Hah. I threw it against the wall."

"You did?"

"Yeah, they're not thrilled with me at the Four Seasons right now, but I could give a shit." He took the empty coffee cup on the table and crumpled it, then shot it at the garbage can across the room. It went in. *Fuck it; he was going to try one more time.* He faced her straight-on. "Emmy, will you see me this weekend?"

The forcefulness of the question took Emmy by surprise; she didn't know what to say.

Duncan continued, "I'm not sure what happened last weekend, and I don't know if you've decided that Jack is..." He stopped himself; he realized he didn't want to talk about Jack; he started again. "I'd say we should get dinner somewhere, but I've got photographers following me now and I doubt you'd want a photo of us up on a website somewhere. I'm going to be holed up in my hotel – I probably won't even be able to go running – but it'd be nice if you could come by." Of course, he'd made completely different plans for the weekend than the ones he just described, but he wanted to change his plans now, to include Emmy, and this play for her sympathy seemed like a way to get her to agree. "Would you come by?"

Emmy didn't know what to say. "You won't be able to go running?"

He cracked a smile that this would be the piece to which she'd respond. "Yes, that's right, with the paps, I probably won't be able to run."

"You know," Emmy swallowed hard, "you should go to our cabin. It's in New Hampshire; it's remote, no photographers would find you, and there, you could go running."

Duncan studied her. *What was she suggesting?*

Emmy continued. "We call it a cabin but it's not rustic in the slightest. Glass walls, amazing views; it's on this beautiful lake and couldn't be more isolated. Going running up there, it's one of my favorite things in the world. I think you'd like it." Emmy went to her purse on the table and rummaged through it. "Here," she held out a single key on a red tab keychain. Duncan looked at the key dangling. He didn't take it, but instead kept his eyes puzzling on Emmy. His silence made Emmy consider how silly her offer must be; she laughed. "I guess you're not hard up on finding places to stay." She began to lower her hand.

Quick, Duncan grabbed the key. "No, I think it sounds like a great place to get away to." He looked at the key in his hand, turning it over and over. "Would you come join me for a run?"

Emmy thought about this question and the many questions that raced behind it. *Was this why she brought up the cabin? Had she meant to make this plan with him?* Her shoulders slumped. "I'm hosting this stupid brunch party tomorrow."

"But later tomorrow, after the brunch?"

She wanted to go. She tried to remember all her cautionary concerns: that he didn't care about her, that she was just a therapist to him, that his care for her was simply transference. But now these explanations didn't feel compelling. In fact, they seemed contrived. The truth was simpler: she was scared. Her voice grew small. "Duncan, I think I'm too slow for you."

Duncan tried to study her downcast eyes. "Too slow?" He inched closer to her. "Why, why do you say that?"

"Well…" *How could she explain it?* It would be too embarrassing to explain all her insecurities. She shrugged. "How fast is your mile?"

Duncan had not expected this objection. "I don't know, usually six minutes or so."

"See?" Her voice sounded small.

"See what?"

"I'm not fast."

Emmy's bewilderment made him smile. "Emmy, we're not going to race." He leaned toward her. "I'd slow down for you. We'd have fun. You should come."

Emmy tried to find a way to stall as she sought to figure out what to do. "Here, let me write down the address. If you use the google directions, it's really easy. There's a good restaurant in town and a great grocery shop right there too. And the freezer, pantry, wine cellar: all stocked." She handed him the sheet of paper on which she'd written the address.

"That's good about the pantry." He folded the sheet. "But what about the run?" He wanted his question to sound playful, but he cared very much how she answered. "Will you come?"

Her heartbeat quickened. She had been so certain she had to protect herself from this man, so frightened by his worldliness and experience, so aware of her vulnerability. But she didn't feel scared now. She read the wisp of apprehension on Duncan's face as he waited for her response. She smiled. "I bet the leaves will be at peak."

Duncan was unsure what this meant. "Will they?"

Emmy let her smile grow bigger. "And I know the trail we should take."

Duncan wanted to be sure he understood correctly. "You do? On our run?"

"Uh-huh," she said, her smile now rushing out. "I think I can get there by four."

Duncan leaned back, a grin spreading across his face too. "At four, okay. That's good. A late afternoon run, those are fun."

Emmy laughed, and Duncan saw how her eyes danced.

Duncan wanted to stay with the pleasure of this laugh, but he was also keenly aware he'd promised his director only hours earlier a completely different sort of weekend. He looked at his watch. *Shit, he was supposed to be leaving with Gus for the airport in an hour.* He needed to talk to him. "I hate to do this, but if we have this as our plan, I need to run and tell Gus now. Do you mind if we head out?"

"No, no; I should go too." She grabbed her jacket and purse and walked to the trailer door with Duncan a step behind her. He pushed open the door and stood back to let her pass through it first. It was the same tight squeeze they'd been through before. Her body slightly brushed against his and as it did, she looked up to Duncan whose eyes were tight on her. This time, the closeness didn't scare her. Or, even if it did, she wanted to rise above those fears. She raised her head up and brought her lips to his. His kiss tasted warm and chocolate-y bitter from the coffee, and when he tugged at her waist to pull her tighter into him, every part of her wanted to melt there. She pulled back. "The photographers," she whispered, breathlessly giggling, "would love this shot."

Duncan peered over her shoulder, through the thin opening of the trailer door. Pushing the door back further, he looked out to the empty lot before them. "No way they could have had an angle on us." He smiled, and Emmy pecked his lips again before she skipped down the stairs. "I'll see you tomorrow?" Her words trilled with their pleasure.

Duncan nodded. Her taste was still on his lips, and though he knew he should rush to find Gus, he watched as she walked away. Her steps were quick, her hair slightly swinging. His chest was full; she was as happy as he was.

SATURDAY, OCTOBER 12:
FUN

Francesca Trippolli wouldn't stop talking about salad. "I think it was bibb lettuce. I'm surprised I can't remember exactly. It could have been a spring mix, but I think, I think it was bibb."

Emmy smiled weakly, "Oh, it sounds delici—"

Francesca flashed her a disapproving glance. Apparently, she hadn't finished her account. Francesca began again. "A nice mustardy-lemon dressing was on the greens. And the truly lovely thing was that," Francesca paused as though for dramatic effect, "it wasn't too tart nor too mustardy."

Emmy nodded; she tried to put an expression on her face that mimicked interest, but it was hard to conjure. The Saturday morning brunch, which she'd known would be dull, was exceeding her worst apprehensions. It wasn't just that Francesca Tripolli was detailing salad greens nor that it was impossible – *impossible* – to re-direct her into more interesting subjects; no, the real problem was that Emmy wanted to *go*.

Francesca continued, "A subtle dressing is quite hard to get right. When it overpowers, it simply spoils everything. I've always said this and I always will: flavors should be proportionate. The difference between two squirts of lemon or one can be everything in the world."

Emmy had to restrain herself from looking at her watch. Her toe wanted to tap; her fingers wanted to drum. She glanced at her husband. The midday sun was pouring in through the room's abundant windows haloing Jack in a flattering light. Jack and Anthony were sitting across from each other in a pair of armchairs. Their bodies leaned in closely, almost conspiratorially, to one another, and Jack had an unusual grin on his face. He was in animated spirits this morning. Emmy had expected the aftershocks from yesterday's tense phone call would have kept him frosty, but instead, he was making great efforts to be pleasant, as though determined to play the role of a happily married husband not just in front of their brunch audience but even alone with Emmy too. He offered to make coffee that morning and paid Emmy two compliments, one about her egg strata being delicious and the other about how he liked that she was wearing her hair down for the brunch. It should have been pleasing, these unexpected kindnesses. But Emmy was determined to give them no heed. She was tired of riding the seesaw of her feelings about Jack. She would be steadfast, and nothing – not even Jack's unexpected kindness – would deter her from her night ahead with Duncan.

Emmy was trying to feign interest in Francesca's point about pine nuts when she heard the home phone ringing in the kitchen. She sprung upward. "So sorry Francesca, I should get this call." Emmy rushed to the kitchen and picked up the phone: "Hello."

"Emmy!" It was Celia. "Ohmygod! Em-*meeee!*" Her voice blasted in a whispered shriek.

"Celia, what's wrong?" She couldn't tell if her exclamation came from upset or excitement.

"Duncan Grier is in our cabin! *Duncan Grier!* How the *hell* do you know Duncan Grier?"

Emmy froze. *Oh god!* "Celia, wait, you're at the cabin? Why?"

"Hel-*lo*! The bridge project, *remember?*" Her voice hushed again, "Emmy, he's like half-naked in our kitchen. God, he looks so *good.*"

Shit. It'd never occurred to Emmy to check if Celia would be at the cabin. Of course, she'd worried about Jack. On her walk back from the set, she texted her husband to see if he would be using the cabin that weekend, saying that if not, she and Maria might use it for a girl's night together. Jack's response had been quick and typically laconic: "Don't worry. I'll stay away." She never considered that anyone other than Jack would have access to the cabin. *Why oh why was Celia there now?*

Celia's voice interrupted her swirling thoughts. "Stop stalling. I already knew you have a google crush on the man, but how did you *know* him?"

Emmy was puzzling over how to answer that question when she heard her cell phone ringing. "Sorry Celia, can you hold a moment?"

Not waiting for Celia's answer, Emmy dropped the kitchen phone and ran to her purse to get her cell phone. It was Duncan. She walked to the family room to take the call. "Hi."

"Hey." Duncan got straight to the point. "So, your step-daughter just walked in the door."

"I know." Emmy was catching her breath. "She's on the other line with me now. She says you're half-naked in the kitchen."

"Ha. I went for a run and took my shirt off afterward. I wasn't expecting company."

Emmy laughed. She envisioned what that looked like and realized she might have had the same reaction to it as Celia. "Celia gets a little carried away sometimes. She can be ... intense."

"Well, when you explain how I came to be here, do you mind not telling her about the therapy stuff? Maybe say Kallie asked you to loan me your home for the weekend, and you did a favor for your ol' college roommate."

Emmy thought that story sounded as good as any. "Sure, I can say that."

"I'm guessing Celia complicates things a little?"

"Yes." She laughed: "A lot. We can't stay there now."

Duncan smiled at this response, pleased at how freely Emmy talked about their staying together. "So, let's go somewhere else. Where do you want to go?" Duncan was actually glad for this chance to revisit the plan. It was merely an hour he'd been at the cabin but it was long enough to realize this house was the worst place in the world for them to meet.

Duncan had only arrived at the cabin at noon because, at the last minute, he'd decided to go to the New York Film Festival after all. The afternoon before, when he'd sought out Gus on the set, the director had chummily put his arm around Duncan's much taller shoulder and began telling everyone around them how he and Duncan were planning to "storm" the Festival. Duncan realized he couldn't back out; instead, he'd go to New York Friday night and leave for New Hampshire Saturday morning. It'd be no problem; he'd still arrive before Emmy.

The Film Festival turned out to be a more low-key affair than he'd expected. Nevertheless, there were photographers with flashbulbs and reporters who asked inane questions and stragglers who pleaded for autographs. Event organizers told him to "please come this way," and he saw old friends who weren't real friends but everyone pretended. It was what he was used to. The jokes about the coke photo went round and round, and Duncan initiated some of them himself. He kept the conversations lively, asked the right questions, laughed, hugged, kissed cheeks, pretended to drink – all the stuff he was practiced at. Yet, somehow, he felt different. As though he had a place to return. It was a subtle shift, but he liked it.

At the Festival's reception, he saw Celine Varens, a woman he'd dated several years ago. She'd darted across the room to greet him, kissing his cheeks in her French way. When a group of acquaintances gathered to go from the reception to a bar, Celine accompanied them. Later, when this same group moved to a party uptown, Celine came then too. She lingered by his side, looking stylish and svelte. He saw that a lingering kiss to her cigarette smoky lips could turn into a night of good fun. But he didn't linger; he didn't kiss. He said goodnight even when it was morning and returned to his hotel alone. He knew he wouldn't sleep. There was no point in trying. Instead, he showered and changed and drove off at 4 a.m. in the tiny sports car Ling had rented and arranged to have waiting for him in the hotel's garage.

It was a long ride from New York to New Hampshire, but it felt good to be behind the wheel for a change. He kept the radio on, changing the station frequently to find songs that matched his groggy expectancy. Too tired to think analytically, he nonetheless had a vague awareness he was traveling from familiarity to a situation comfortably unknown. The sky lightened behind the treetops and the dawn gave way to morning, then to midday, and with the growing lightness, his apprehensions burned off like fog. He sped through the back roads of New Hampshire singing loudly to radio pop songs.

As soon as he pulled into the cabin's driveway, his mood sunk. The cabin, just as Emmy said, wasn't cabin-like at all. It was a large, impressive contemporary design, and Duncan realized then what should have been glaringly obvious from the beginning: this cabin was Jack's house. It was the wrong place to go, and though the plan had been hastily conceived he wondered how this fundamental point had escaped Emmy's attention.

He used the red tab key to unlock the door and walked into the cabin's entryway. Right away, he recognized the space from one of the photos on Jack's web page. His shoes echoed on the floorboards. The ceilings were high, the rooms expansive and light-filled, the view of the lake everywhere. But what caught Duncan's attention were the pictures – framed family photos – everywhere. What he'd long been curious to see was now on easy display. There were black and white professional shots of the Halperin family looking ridiculously wholesome, like something out of a fucking catalog. Then, there were dozens, maybe hundreds, of casual snapshots framed and scattered around the house. Duncan went from room to room tracing the Halperin family history. There was Emmy exclaiming over a son taking his first steps. Emmy kissing her little girl's cheek as her daughter laughed heartily. Graduation pictures. Shots in front of Christmas trees. Emmy looking at Jack doe-eyed on their wedding day. And there was a series of the Halperin kids as newborns; in each of the three photos, a baby was held in the center with Jack kissing one cheek and Emmy the other. As Duncan looked at these photos, his stomach knotted. These were Emmy's kids; this was Emmy's husband. She had a family. She had a home. He was an interloper in it.

As much as the photos bothered him, he couldn't stop looking at them. Once he scanned the whole house, examining all the photos, he set about to retrace his steps so he could see them again. Emmy as a young woman was radiant, her face rounder, her body more curvy. Her expression was different then: eager and playful; she hadn't grown into her serenity yet. Duncan studied the photos of Jack too. There was Jack smiling, hugging his kids, looking grumpy in some pictures, contented in others, but always coated in self-confidence. Duncan hated Jack's certainty, his preppy wealth, the ease with which he proprietarily put his arm around Emmy. The knot in Duncan's stomach stretched into his fingertips, like a vine that was twisting and swirling inside him. He had to escape that house. He changed and went for a run.

Now, with Emmy on the phone, he was glad to have Celia's arrival as the excuse he needed to convince Emmy they should go someplace else. He said easily. "Name the place you want to go, and I'll meet you there."

"Mmm, okay;" Emmy thought for a second. She was delighted to be talking to him, to be removed from the dullness of the stupid brunch, to think about the fun that awaited her. "There's a few places we could go if we wanted to stay in New Hampshire. Or we could also try someplace along—" Emmy stopped abruptly. She saw Jack was walking toward her, from the kitchen into the family room. His walk was hurried, like he was intent on connecting with her.

He strode into the room. "Ems, I gotta ask you something." He came right up close to her, as though he wanted to say something in confidence.

"Jack, I'm *on the phone*." Emmy didn't try to hide her frustration.

Duncan listened on the other end. Unlike yesterday, when he was only able to hear Emmy's side of the conversation, now he could hear hear Jack too. His rival's voice was deep, fast-talking, snappish. He called Emmy "Ems." Duncan wouldn't have expected that.

Impatient to have Emmy's attention, Jack gestured to her cellphone. "It's Maria, right? She won't mind holding a second. Listen..." He came in even closer to Emmy's space and said in a lowered voice, "I was talking to Anthony about our Italy trip, and he was saying all this stuff about how he'd love to take that trip again. It got me wondering whether we should ask him and Francesca to join us."

"What!? No! That's a horrible idea." The thought of spending more time with Francesca Trippolli's delusions of Julia Child grandeur was too tedious to contemplate. "Jack, *please do* not ask them to come with us. That would be a disaster."

"Okay." Jack studied Emmy for a second. "Well, there wasn't any ambiguity to that answer." He was amused. "It'll stay our trip. It's better that way, you're right."

Emmy thought he was reading meanings into what she'd said that weren't there. "You know," she pushed him to go, "you shouldn't leave our guests so long. Go offer them more coffee." When Jack was finally out of eyesight and hearing range, she held her cellphone back to her cheek. "You still there?" She was eager to plan where they would go together.

Duncan was there, yes, but he was replaying what he'd overheard. "You and Jack are going to Italy together?"

The question took Emmy by surprise. Her responses to Jack had been quickly formed; she hadn't thought how the conversation might sound to Duncan's ears. "No," she laughed easily, trying to clarify the silly misunderstanding. "No, I doubt that trip will ever happen."

"Emmy, I overheard the conversation. You said you wanted to keep the trip to Italy just the two of you."

Had she said that? She didn't think she had. She laughed again, this time less easily. "No, Duncan, that's not it at all." She wanted to soothe Duncan's irritation, but she was also confused: Duncan was leaving in two weeks; why would he care if she went to Italy with Jack? Nonetheless, it should be easy to assure him that Italy was meaningless, because it was. "Italy is just… it's this idea that Jack has, but it's not at all what I want."

"What *do* you want?" Duncan's voice cut.

"I don't understand. What do you mean, what do I want?"

"It's a pretty fucking simple question."

"Is it?" God, it felt like the hardest question in the world to her; she asked it of herself over and over again. "Duncan, this Italy thing is nothing." She tried to soothe him. "I want to come have fun with you."

Fun? His head swam. *"That's* what you want?" He'd misunderstood everything. All of it.

She didn't answer. She was confused. Her heart began to pound; she could tell their plan was falling apart. She wasn't sure what she needed to do to stop it from falling. "Tell me what you want me to say, and I'll—"

Duncan began talking to himself. "What am I doing here? What the *fuck* am I doing?" He shook his head; "I'm your *fun.*" He looked around the room, and there again were the three photos of Jack and Emmy with their newborns. "Emmy I didn't come out here to be a bloody *guest* in your home." He knew this wasn't the clearest way to explain why he was upset, but he didn't care. He'd been so stupid. "You know what, forget it." He touched his phone to end the call, and because that gesture didn't feel satisfying enough he pressed the button to turn the phone off. He couldn't believe how much he'd misunderstood.

Emmy stood looking at her phone. The conversation had unraveled so quickly. She tried to replay the exchange in her head. *What had she said that made him so upset?* She'd explained Italy was meaningless. *Why was he upset she wanted to have fun with him? Why didn't he want to be a guest in her home?* There was an explanation for his reactions, but she didn't trust it. She didn't dare to trust it. She pushed his contact name to dial his number again, but the call went right to voicemail. *Did this mean their weekend would not happen?* But, it had to happen. For the last twenty-four hours, her head had swirled with thoughts of Duncan. Of how badly she wanted to make him happy, of how much she wanted his kiss, his skin against hers. There hadn't been a single minute, even sleeping, when her thoughts hadn't been full of him. Dazed with disappointment, she walked to the kitchen, and there she saw the home phone sitting on the counter. She picked it up. "Celia?

"My god, Emmy, that was one hell of a hold you put me on. What were you doing? I would have hung up long ago if it weren't for this mysterioso of how you know Duncan Grier. So, now, you have to 'fess up. I'm dying to know!"

It was an effort to begin. "I have this old college friend Kallie and..." Her voice sounded far away. "Kallie is Duncan's – Duncan Grier's – manager. Kallie called me up the other day and asked me if I could loan Duncan Grier the house this weekend as a favor. I already told you that he's filming in the area."

"But, have you met him? Do you know Duncan Grier?"

"No." Emmy made herself say the words. "I don't, I don't know him."

Celia was apparently unimpressed with the account. "I thought there would be a *far* juicier story to spill than that. What with your recent midlife hots for him and all." Celia whispered in girly confidence, "Emmy, I have to tell you: he's *way* hotter in person! God, this is going to be a blast!" Abruptly, her voice clipped. "Wait, he's coming. Gotta go."

Emmy started to protest but no real words came out; it was too late anyway. Celia was off the phone. Emmy picked up her cell phone and tried Duncan again. Voicemail. She wanted to throw her phone, but she didn't. She walked into the living room and sat down again across from Francesca Trippolli.

"Would you like a glass of wine?"

The question made him turn in the direction of its asker. Duncan was so fully in his fuming thoughts he'd forgotten about the stepdaughter. There she was, standing against the kitchen's bar-like counter. She faced outward toward the living room, so still, almost posed, holding out a glass of crimson-colored wine like a gift.

Duncan didn't want to deal with her right now. He walked to his open bag and shoved his running clothes into them. "Isn't it a little early for wine?"

Her voice purred. "I just found the keys to our wine cellar. They've been missing *forever,* but today..." she said with glee: "found!" She held the wine to her nose, "I figured it had to be a sign, so I opened this bottle and mmmm, it's very delicious. Here;" she held her glass out again to him.

"Ah," he studied her crafted allure. "Thank you, but actually, I'm heading out."

"Not because of me I hope?"

"No, not because of you." Even in this short interaction, he was aware how this young woman's self-possession was being carefully manufactured for his benefit. "I just have to be going." He continued to arrange the things in his overnight bag; he was almost ready.

Celia let the wine swirl in her glass. "It's a shame you won't have even a sip. I opened this bottle special with you in mind. I think it's like a zillion dollars!"

He shoved his shaving kit inside the bag. "You like expensive wine?"

"Honestly, I can't tell the difference. But my father thinks he can, and me and my stepmother, that's how we get our little revenge."

Duncan looked up from his bag. "You get your *revenge?*"

She saw he had his attention; she giggled. "Ah, yes, we conspire."

Duncan realized he shouldn't let this curious remark delay him, though it would only take a minute to ask. "How do the two of you get your revenge?"

She swirled the wine in her wine glass as she readied herself to explain. "Well. We drink his wine, but tell him we're not. At dinners and stuff, Emmy puts out a bottle of cheapish stuff that's just been bought in town, and then when my father's not looking, she lets me go to the kitchen to fill our glasses with wine that's been pulled from the cellar." She smiled. "As revenge goes, it's pretty minor but somehow it gives us endless pleasure. My stepmother is fabulously giddy when drunk."

"Emmy gets drunk with you?" He wouldn't have expected this. "That's an odd thing for a stepmother to do."

"I egg her on; it's pretty easy to do. She's got this playful side, and my dad," she scrunched her nose in disapproval, "he's not exactly a barrel of laughs."

He took a step closer to her. "Your stepmother and father aren't happy together?"

Celia chuckled. "You sure do ask a lot of questions, Duncan Grier!"

"Do I?" He was serious, though he quickly caught the question's absurdity. He winked to turn the joke on himself.

Celia let her laugh roll like she'd never heard anything so droll. "Here, I think you need to try some of this wine. I guarantee you; it won't disappoint." Celia again held out the full glass to him.

This time, Duncan took it. He saw what Celia was doing; it wasn't hard to get. But what was he doing? He wanted to leave; he hated this place; he was tired, very tired. But there was the question he'd asked. He wanted the answer to that question, and Celia knew it. He held the wine in his hand, cradling the glass by its voluptuous curve. He thought for several seconds. He'd hear about Emmy and Jack, get the information, order his confusion, leave. Knowing the truth would make it easier for him to move on. He raised the glass; it was like taking medicine. A bitter pill. "Cheers," he said, and took a long hard swallow.

MONDAY, OCTOBER 14:
SALTY APPLES

Emmy sat at the kitchen's island sipping her coffee. The morning light was slowly removing the dimness from the nightly world. She was glad at last it was Monday. She could find Duncan today.

All weekend, she called Duncan's cell phone, though he never answered it. There wasn't a landline at the cabin any longer, so she wasn't able to call there. She'd considered driving to New Hampshire but doubted Duncan had stayed, especially with Celia there. She took the T to the Four Seasons, thinking it the most likely place he'd be, though to the extent she was able to wrangle information from the front desk it appeared he wasn't there either. She even called Ling, which was probably a mistake; the young woman had nothing to offer but her curiosity. The whole weekend, Emmy left only one voicemail. It was short but it said all she wanted it to say. Once Duncan heard it, she assumed he would call. He had not.

Her exasperation at this precious lost opportunity was amplified by the displeasure of being stuck in her house. After the Trippollis left, Jack offered to clean the by-then cleaned kitchen so she could go "get girly with Maria." She wearily explained the change in her plans, that she wouldn't go to the cabin after all, that she would instead stay there the whole time. The rest of the weekend, she and Jack shared no further meals, very little conversationally, and Emmy slept in the TV room both nights. Their avoidance of each other was so innate these evasions didn't feel especially strained or hostile. In fact, Jack seemed pleased by the arrangement. He left stacks of family photo albums on the kitchen counter. He picked up her dry cleaning Saturday afternoon. And he called each of their kids Sunday night so they could talk to them together, Jack on one extension, Emmy on the other. When their son Ben complained about the drudgery of his college work, Jack said, "Benj, life isn't always about happiness. Sometimes, it's enough to be satisfied. When you expect too much, it can make you miserable." Emmy understood Jack meant the remark for her.

She took another sip of coffee and looked at how brilliantly yellow the walnut trees were in the morning sun, how the grass sparkled in this first light. *Was Jack right?* She didn't want him to be. She wanted life to hold more than satisfaction, but maybe her yearnings were naïve. Maybe satisfaction and stability should be enough. She wondered, in fact, if this was the reason she'd suggested the cabin, out of an unconscious desire to show Duncan how much she had on the line. "I didn't come to be a bloody guest in your home" was what he'd said. She closed her eyes, thinking how angry he sounded. *It had been so stupid of her to ask him to the cabin.* The offer had spilled out without reflection, and her chest felt darted through when she thought how thoughtless the invitation must have appeared to Duncan.

There was a rustling at the back door. Someone was turning the key in the lock. She stood up: *Could Jack have gone out early and be returning?* "Jack?" she called out expectantly.

But it was Celia who walked into the kitchen. She carried a heavy brown bag that jostled with the sound of glass bottles inside. She held a finger to her lips and whispered. "Oh, most marvelous Emster, I'm so glad you're here!"

Emmy was confused. "Okay, but why are you here? And why are you whispering?"

Celia sat beside her at the island. She pointed to her bag and whispered: "I brought the wine bottles."

"Wine bottles?"

Celia was sheepish; "They're from the cabin."

Emmy didn't understand. "Why didn't you leave them at the cabin?"

"I couldn't leave the evidence behind."

"So you brought the evidence *here*?"

Celia again held her finger to her lips. "Shhh. I'll take the bottles away again, *of course*. But, here;" she opened the bag and showed her the six bottles. "I need you to see what needs to be replaced. We drank enough that I think Dad might notice." Celia looked up at Emmy winsomely, "I know this is a lot to ask, but could you please, please buy some wine – some good wine – for Dad's shelves? I'd do it myself but I could never, ever afford it!"

This was annoying; Celia shouldn't be drinking wine at the cabin anyway. *Ugh, they had talked about this.* Ever since that one time when she, Ben and Celia had gotten tipsy over dinner together, Celia felt she'd been green-lighted access to her father's wine cellar when that wasn't the case at all. Emmy was about to say all this, then decided against it. She didn't have the energy for an admonishment right then, and it was always tricky to rebuke this girl who wasn't her child. "I guess I can take care of it." She looked up from the bag and asked what she really wanted to know. "So, when did Duncan – Duncan Grier – leave the cabin?"

"Oh, he stayed for awhile," Celia said coyly as she stood up and walked toward the sink's counter. "In fact, until *Sunday morning.*"

Emmy's mouth went wide, and she was glad Celia's back was toward her. *He hadn't left? Why hadn't he left? That was odd.* She strained to appear calm. "Well, what did he *do* while he was there? Did he go for walks or…" – *what else could he have possibly done?* – "or drives? Or did he go to town?" Her questions were too eager; she made herself stop speaking.

Celia grabbed a green apple from the fruit bowl and began to rub it shiny. "*Actually,* he just hung out with *me.*" She said it simply, but her pleasure was hardly disguised. "We talked. In fact, we talked a lot about you."

"About me?" None of this made sense. "What did you say about me?"

"Well," Celia took a bite from her apple, "at first I did *not* understand. He kept asking *all* these questions, but" – she swallowed – "finally he explained there's a script he's considering with a character in it – a woman – and he's trying to understand what makes her tick. The character is kinda like you: She's married and middle-aged and sorta sad—"

Emmy interrupted, "Wait. Who described me as a sorta sad?"

Celia froze: "I swear, I said it only in the *most* flattering way." She took another bite. "Trust me. You'd have been blown away by all the nice things I said about you. And Duncan, he was, like, weirdly interested. He looked a lot at your pictures and the house. Said you'd made a beautiful family home. Which is kind of undeniable but, still, nice to have the Grier say that, right?"

Emmy shook her head, not wanting to be distracted when she was trying to figure so much out. "I'm confused.

Did you invite people over? I don't understand how you went through so many wine bottles."

Celia couldn't contain her proud smile. "It was just us."

Emmy teetered as she took in this meaning. "Just the two of you?"

"Yup. Me and Duncan Grier getting drunk together."

"But Duncan doesn't—?"

"Doesn't what?"

Emmy didn't move. Her heartbeat caught, then resumed, its pounding now heavy and hard. She swallowed, but still barely got the breath for the words. "Six bottles?"

"Probably more like five-plus, but who's counting? You know, he got sad drunk, not silly or raucous drunk. Who'd have thought Duncan Grier of all people would be morose? I mean, such a hunk yet still, like, *tormented.*"

Emmy stood looking at her stepdaughter, her headstrong, intensely sexualized stepdaughter. A sick, deadweight cramped her chest; the awful question ricocheting in her head. She made herself find the words. "Celia, did you..." her throat tightened, her breath felt weak, "did you sleep with him?"

Celia smiled mischievously, "Emmy, I've never seen you look so horrified! Jeez, would it be so bad if I slept with Duncan Grier?"

Celia's breeziness felt like a taunt. A sudden anger rushed Emmy's body. "Don't turn this into a joke. Tell me now: Did you sleep with him?"

Celia stepped back. "Good grief, Dr. Prurient. Yes, I had sex with him. There. No reason to have a heart attack. Sex is a natural expression of natural feeling; it's a *good* thing. A very enjoyable, good thing."

Celia's words came like a physical punch. Emmy staggered, hand to chest, then quickly turned away so Celia could not see her face crumble at this news.

"Emmy, *why* are you getting so worked up? It was *fun.* We had a good time. It certainly makes for a great story. I mean, me and a movie star! I can't wait to tell my friends at school, you know?"

Emmy began to walk out of the room.

"Where are you going?" She heard Celia call after her.

"I'm late for work." Emmy barked back.

"Don't forget to get the you-know-what, 'kay?" Celia called after her.

Emmy wished she could forget.

Duncan sat on the floor outside of Emmy's therapy office. He'd been beeped into the general building by one of the other building's tenants, but Emmy and Maria's office door was closed and locked. He guessed one of the two of them would be there soon. The corridor was small enough that with his back against one wall, his fully extended legs almost touched the opposing wall. His legs wouldn't keep still; they twitched and bobbed. He was nervous to see Emmy. He knew he'd screwed up.

In accepting that first glass of wine, his intentions had been innocent. Information retrieval, pure and simple. But Celia was eager to please him and she must have developed an instinctual understanding – perhaps not even on a conscious level – that when she discussed her family, Emmy in particular, this was when Duncan was most interested. So, Celia told story after story about Emmy. She explained Jack's affair with her mother. She described her own mother's hatred of Emmy and itemized all the bad names Jessica used to have for Emmy. "My mother," Celia said, looking with downcast eyes into her wine glass, "is not an easy mother to have ... and when I first met Emmy, I would dream she was my real mom."

Celia picked up a photo of Emmy taken when she was in her twenties. "See, this is Emmy," and she offered the picture to him with such a considerable pride that Duncan wondered if Celia wasn't a bit in love with Emmy herself. "It's funny, Emmy's got such crazy beauty, but she tries to pretend it's not there. I mean, it's actually kinda ... *weird.* As an artist, I'm super aware of how people present their bodies, and most attractive people, well, they own their looks like a prize." She grabbed her wine glass, holding it out extended in her hand. "I asked Emmy once why she didn't do that too, and she was embarrassed. She laughed and said, 'Some things are better left ignored.' Which, you know, was intriguing. She didn't want to talk about it, but I wouldn't let it go, until finally she said something simple; it was like one sentence: 'What beauty gives can't be trusted.'" Celia paused to take a sip of wine, "The way she said it, I had to ask her pointblank: "Do you think my dad would have picked you over my mom if you weren't so beautiful?" Celia paused as she remembered the moment herself.

Duncan waited for Celia to finish the account. "What'd she say?" he finally asked.

Celia was pleased to see her story held his interest. "She said I had a lot to learn about the fine art of ignoring."

These were the kind of stories Celia shared, and Duncan wasn't able to leave while they were being told. Celia kept pouring wine, and Duncan didn't stop himself from drinking it. The warm liquid made the information go down more easily. Into their third bottle, Duncan asked, "Do you think your stepmother loves your father?" He'd already offered a thin excuse as to why he was asking these questions about her family; it was something preposterous about doing research about a married couple for a film. But Celia seemed happy to accept the pretense so she could continue bubbling forth with her accounts. For this particular question, Celia sat up straighter: "Emmy and Jack. Love? Hmmm. Per-haps. Not in an active kind of way. It's a legacy love – for all they made." This remark seemed to jibe with what Emmy herself described as the tension. Celia was proving to be a most reliable reporter.

"Do you think your dad and stepmum will stay together?" Duncan purposefully took a sip of wine to mask his interest in the answer. Celia chuckled, happy to offer more of her insights. "Well, there is some discussion among us siblings on that point. Tess, my half sister, she's convinced there's already a divorce in the works, and they'll announce it at Thanksgiving. Me, I'm not so sure. Honestly, I don't think the one could survive without the other. I mean, what would my dad be as a divorced man? He's already this intensely stoic guy; I think he'd freeze up, turn to ice or rock or whatever. He would never, ever say he needs Emmy, but he does. And Emmy, she can't leave someone in need."

This answer too seemed to have the ring of truth. Duncan took the information in, poured another glass of wine. So it had gone. By 4 p.m., they were both dizzingly drunk. It wasn't sick or silly that Duncan felt, just deeply tired. By then, Celia was becoming sloppy, her poise crumbling and her youthfulness growing ever more obvious. One second she'd be saying something brazenly sexual – "I think I'd like to kiss you, Duncan Grier" – and then moments later, confide there was a boy at school, Rocco, on whom she had the "most delicious crush." "Duncan," she whined drunkenly, "what should I *do* to get him to like me?" Even in his muddy haze, the wrongness of the situation was like a foul smell, he wanted to move away from it. Stumbling, he looked for a bedroom where he could lie down. His plan was to sleep only enough so he could drive away soberly. He anticipated a couple hours snooze was all he needed.

When he woke Sunday morning, it was with a start. His sleep had been enormously deep, and it took him a moment of lying still to remember that he was in a bedroom at Jack Halperin's cabin. Even exerting this slight mental effort made his head pierce with pain. He needed some aspirin and started to get up to search for some. It was then he saw Celia. *Bloody hell.* She was lying next to him, her body wrapped in a sheet. He couldn't be certain she was naked, but it sure seemed she was. He stared and stared at her, his head about to implode. He didn't move; he made no sound. Even in his shock, he knew he didn't want to wake her. Quickly, quietly, he rose, pulled on his jeans and t-shirt from the floor. He walked out the bedroom door, grabbed his shoes, his bag, and noiselessly tiptoed out the cabin's front door. Before he wiped the sleep from his eyes, he was driving his rented sports car, speeding through New Hampshire's rolling mountain roads.

His thoughts were in full-out panic. *What had he done?* He smacked his hands against the steering wheel. *Shit, shit, shit.* He ran through the previous day's events. There were some parts sharply, cleanly clear and others quite muffled. He had no memory of touching Celia. He hadn't even wanted to; *had he?* They'd just talked. *Nothing else.* Yet, as he drove, he realized some items were troubling. He didn't remember taking off his clothes when he'd lain down Saturday afternoon, but he'd woken in his boxer briefs. He also had an alarmingly sharp visual on Celia's naked breasts. These oddities didn't necessarily mean they'd had sex. Maybe he'd undressed himself in the middle of the night to get more comfortable. And he could have easily concocted the image of Celia's breasts. When they were drinking together Saturday afternoon, he'd observed how jiggly her breasts were in her low-cut shirt. This wasn't a lecherous observation, he assured himself; no man wouldn't have noticed them. And, once noticing her fleshy breasts, wasn't it then but a small step to considering how they looked unclothed? Just because he could visualize her nakedness, that was no proof he'd had sex with her. Still. When had he woken up next to a naked woman with whom he'd not had sex? *Fuck.*

He drove with no destination. As someone practiced at the action of fleeing, he knew the point was not to go somewhere but to get away. If he was driving in circles, that didn't matter. What was imperative was to work out what had happened. Uncomfortable flash visuals kept showing up in his thoughts: Celia naked on top of him, Celia kissing him, Celia's face close-up – too close-up. He suspected his imagination was developing these dark and fuzzy images as it tried to find them in his memory bank; they were as likely invented as real. What he knew was that he'd never intended to sleep with Celia; the idea had never occurred to him during the parts of the day he remembered. *Wasn't that enough?* He knew the answer to that question and he didn't like it.

He pulled over to a gas station to fill his car's tank. While the fuel pumped, he pulled out his cell phone and turned it on. There were lots of messages; he guessed most were from people calling to make a joke of the coke photo. He scrolled through the long list of names. There was Emmy's. He hit play. Right away, he could tell she was unsettled, yet her agitation didn't remove the soothing quality in her tone's carriage. "Duncan, I don't know what I said to upset you. Italy, it's nothing. Jack and I, we're not happy. You *know* that. I wish I could find you to explain; I wish I could." There was a slight pause and then she continued, her voice sounding both fragile and strong in that way she had. "Duncan, you make me happy. When I said I wanted to have fun with you, that's what I meant. I mean you make me wonderfully happy. I want to spend all the time we can together." She paused another moment. "Please call me when you get this. I still very much want to see you."

His car's tank was now filled, but, still, he stood there. He wasn't able to tell if he felt better or worse for playing the message. He paid for the gas, bought a coffee and some Advil and returned to the car. He played the message again. Then, once more. Finally, he drove off. He didn't know where he was going. He needed to figure that out.

He considered turning the car around to ask Celia what had happened the night before. That way, he would at least know her version of the night. But, even if Celia were to say they'd had sex, he wouldn't necessarily believe her. She was flighty and young and had, after all, *wanted* to seduce him. No, he felt it was less important to get Celia's account than it was to know his own. Her truth wasn't necessarily his.

It hadn't been lost on him that once again he was in a situation where he was trying to account for a missing block of time. To wonder if he'd done something wrong he couldn't quite remember, this was a reflexive action for him, a looping exercise that had haunted his head for twenty-six years. It was only as he placed these new specifics to the old question's framework that he suddenly realized, *wait,* that earlier missing block of time – *it hadn't ever really gone missing, had it?* For decades, he'd doubted his memory about that night with his father, and now he remembered: he didn't need to doubt it anymore. His father had not died. He had fainted. He had left. It was a relief to remember this new information, to turn it over in his head and feel it sweep away his apprehensions and worries. Emmy gave him that. She gave him this belief in himself. It would be a lot to lose.

As Duncan kept driving, morning eased into afternoon. He hadn't eaten; his stomach was a wreck. He stunk; he needed a shower, clean clothes, a shave. Yet he couldn't get out of the car. Not yet. At one point, when he was stopped at a red light, he glanced at the car beside his. Two young women waved back to him, gleeful to confirm that, yes, it really was Duncan Grier. He knew that for these women seeing him was a story, worthy of telling their friends. They didn't realize: he was just a guy, utterly alone, driving around and around in enormous circles. As soon as the light hit green, he raced off.

Duncan hadn't meant to be taking stock of his life as he drove. His project was supposed to be focused on sorting out if he'd slept with Celia. But in answering this question, there were others to be reviewed. What he believed about himself. What kind of person he was. What kind he wanted to be. Every once in awhile, he grabbed his phone and replayed the part of the message where Emmy said, "You make me wonderfully happy." After a few times, he didn't need to play it anymore; it became something he could hear without the recording. He thought that was better than listening to it.

He made a loose plan. Rather than go back to the Four Seasons, he'd spend the night at a roadside inn. Once settled into the overly-quaint room, he called Gus to explain he'd be late to the set next morning. He set his phone's alarm clock for four, knowing he'd have to wake early to make it to Cambridge before Emmy arrived at her office. And when he drifted off to sleep that night, there was still a lot he didn't understand. But what he did know – and it felt like enough – was that he planned to do everything he could to make things right with Emmy.

As the day had worn on, he'd acknowledged to himself that, yes, it was possible he'd slept with Celia. He decided, however, he'd never share these doubts with Emmy. It wasn't an act of lying, he told himself, but a shift in how to present his conviction. Were he to honestly relay to Emmy his precarious understanding of what happened with Celia, Emmy would assume the worst was true, not just about that night but about him generally. He thought back to her over-reaction with the milkshake girl. If she'd run from that situation, which involved no betrayal, then how would she handle his acknowledgement that he might have slept with her *stepdaughter*. No, complete honesty would ruin everything. By earnestly asserting there was no way he'd slept with Celia, he was choosing to present a version of himself that was, perhaps, more noble than he was. Maybe it was a role he was playing, but he thought this role could be his true self. It was who he wanted to be.

Now, on Monday morning, as he sat on the cold floor of Emmy's office building hallway, he was ready to make a case for his integrity. It was a case he'd never made before.

From below, he heard the building's front door open. Then, a woman's footsteps on the stairs, slow and heavy. Duncan stayed sitting, waiting. The steps plodded upward and then the top of a head crested above the stairwell: it was Emmy.

Only when she reached the landing did her eyes turn to where Duncan sat. He saw right away: she knew.

"What are you doing here?" Her words were sour and stinging. She didn't stop for Duncan's answer. She walked to her office door, unlocked it and stepped in to the waiting room, letting the door swing shut behind her.

Duncan rose to his feet and followed her, pushing the closing door open again. "I wanted to give you your key back, and—"

"Just leave it on the table." Emmy still did not look at him; she quickly unlocked her private office's door and pushed the door so it would close behind her.

"*Emmy.*" Duncan shoved the door back open. Her reaction was what he should have expected, but it jarred him nonetheless to feel her pleasure in him so fully usurped by displeasure. She wouldn't face him. He walked to where she stood and spoke to her back, "Give me a chance; you aren't even giving me a chance to explain."

She whipped around. "*Explain?*" She spit out the word, looking up into Duncan's face. "*Explain?!*" Her eyes swam with tears, but she willed them not to fall. "Duncan, what are you going to say? Sorry, I *fucked* your stepdaughter by accident. Is that what you have to explain?"

"I didn't sleep with Celia. I didn't."

She took a step back, aghast. "You're going to *lie!*" She turned away; she put her hands over her face. She didn't want him to see how dejected she was, how feeble and child-like her sadness made her. "I knew I was going to get hurt. That you would leave, that I'd be sad. But I had so wanted to be happy with you." Her voice trembled, "I never thought you'd *try* to hurt me." Even in her misery, she realized that what Jack had said that weekend was true. When you expect too much from life, it can make you miserable. She shook her head, mumbling to herself. "Jack was right."

"*Jack?*" The very name irritated Duncan. He took two steps toward her and angrily turned her to face him. "Jack's not right. He's *wrong.*" He didn't even know what Emmy was referring to about Jack, but everything about Jack was wrong.

Duncan's hands turning her had been gruff and his voice more insistent than he'd ever sounded before. Now as he stood so close, her heartbeat began to quicken, but it wasn't from fear. Duncan's face was flushed with a strange mixture of indignation and tenderness. He took another step closer into her body. "I didn't do anything with Celia. I would never try to hurt you. Emmy, I... I'm falling in love with you."

She froze, her heart's rapid beating the only movement in her body. She hadn't expected those words or the fear that washed his face as he said them. Her eyes shot over his face. *Was he telling the truth?*

Duncan saw her uncertainty, and he moved to take it away. He kissed her. He leaned in and caught her tear-wet lips – she tasted of salty apples – and her mouth meeting his felt tender and needy and sweet. Emmy knew she should resist, but she could not. She let her chest sink into his, and her lips met his warm mouth, again and again. Duncan gripped her hips to tug her into his body; she let him. The collapse of her will was complete, and the sensation was like falling – a surrender easy and intoxicating since she knew she would be caught, that Duncan would catch her. She wanted to believe him. She wanted his taste and his smell and his skin. She wanted it to be simple. *Why couldn't it be simple?*

It couldn't. When how much Duncan wanted to be forgiven, to be part of her body, to erase their separateness – when all this became insistently clearer, Emmy realized she needed to think. She pulled herself away. Her heart pounding, she tried to steady her breathing. She started to walk toward the window, but it seemed very far away and her legs were wobbly. Everything she wanted was what she shouldn't want. "Did you..." she touched her lips as she made herself articulate the repugnant thought. "Did you *kiss* Celia like that yesterday?"

Duncan came to where Emmy stood; his voice was breathless too. "No. No, of course I didn't." He stepped to her side and tried to catch her eyes. "Emmy, I drank wine with Celia because she was telling me about you. About you and Jack and your family. I wanted to hear. That's all that happened."

This made no sense to Emmy. "You hung up on me. You stopped me from coming to you. Then, you decided to stay at the cabin because ... because Celia was telling *stories* about me." The tears were starting to form in her eyes again, and she shook her head to try to keep them from flowing. "I want it to make sense, but it doesn't; it doesn't."

Duncan took a step closer into her body. "Emmy, there were all those pictures, all those *fucking* pictures – why'd you want me to see those? It was like you were showing me all you had, showing me you weren't going to leave it."

Emmy winced. *She had done that, hadn't she?* Earlier that morning – it felt so long ago – she'd felt guilty about it. Now, her hurt was paramount. "*But you're* leaving *me. You're* the one going in ten days."

Duncan ignored what Emmy said. "Are you going to stay with Jack?"

Emmy blinked at both Duncan's insistent tone and the question itself. "Duncan, you just had *sex* with my stepdaughter."

"I did not."

"Then why'd she say you did? Why would she *say* that?"

Duncan examined Emmy's distrust. "Because it's something to say. She thinks it's cool she got drunk with a movie star and wants to take it to a place where in many cases it could have gone. In this case, it didn't. It didn't."

"But you *anticipated* the allegation. You *knew* it was what she told me."

"That's because…" He ran his hands through his hair; he knew what he said next would not go over well. "After she told me her stories, I was too drunk to drive away and I passed out, I think in one of your son's rooms, and when I woke on Sunday, she was there with me. Lying next to me." He looked to see Emmy flinching at the picture he created. He hadn't said Celia was naked but from Emmy's expression, he guessed she filled in those details. He quickly explained, "All that proves is she wanted to *pretend* something happened."

Emmy scoffed, "Oh, yes, that's all it proves." She walked away from him. She didn't want him to see that as weak as this explanation was, she wanted to believe it. She made herself sound incredulous. "Why would she get in bed with you? She wouldn't do that unless she felt you wanted her there."

"I did *not* want her there. I did not want anything to happen with her, and nothing did. I was too drunk." He paused for a moment, then added: "Really, physically speaking, I don't think it was possible."

Emmy turned to look to see if he was suggesting what she thought he was.

He slightly grinned. "It's not like now."

She couldn't help it; a smile snuck out. She made herself turn away. She was softening, and she wasn't sure she should.

Duncan came up behind her, speaking to her back. "You haven't answered my question about Jack. Are you going to stay with him?"

"This isn't about me."

"Why isn't it?"

She turned to him. "Because... my stepdaughter just told me how great her sex was with you, that's why."

"She's making all of that up." He came in closer, his voice was lower. "Why are all the questions about my sex life anyway? As far as I know, you have sex with Jack every night." He paused. "Do you?"

She walked away from him, toward her desk. She hated that the answer to Duncan's question was one he could trust, that she had the power to reassure him. But Celia's account made all Duncan's reassurance suspect. There was no way for Emmy to be soothed.

Emmy's silence was maddening; Duncan strode to where she stood. "Just say yes or no. Do you still have sex with Jack?"

"No." Though as the petulance of the short word lingered, she recognized she *had* slept with Jack two weeks ago. "I mean, not anymore. I've been sleeping in our TV room this last week."

He stepped so he was facing her directly. "Are you going to leave him?"

She shook her head. "What does it matter if you're *leaving me?*"

"It matters. It matters a lot. How could you think it doesn't matter?"

She didn't say anything.

Duncan waited, but her eyes were on the ground, thinking, thinking. "Emmy, do you think of me like Celia does? Just some *fun* with the movie star."

Her head jerked up, her eyes anguished. "I was going to come to you this weekend; I was going to betray Jack, break all sorts of professional rules. I was going to do that for you." Her voice cracked; "I wanted to be *happy* with you. I wanted that so badly." The tears began to slip from her eyes, and she rushed to wipe them one after the other.

Duncan was relieved to see her tears. If she cried, he could soothe her; that was much easier than what they'd been doing. He took a step even closer into where she stood. Emmy would not look up at him; her breathing staggered and she kept wiping her cheeks from the tears that now peaked and flowed, childlike, down her cheeks. Duncan spoke gently, "I wanted to be happy with you too. Nothing has to have changed."

She shook her head, "No, it's all changed."

He bristled: there was only one reason anything had to have changed. "You believe Celia over me?"

The question was spoken as an accusation. Emmy puzzled to figure out if it was one she meant to make. *What did she think happened? Did Celia make this story up? Would Duncan have done that to her?* She looked over at Duncan whose jaw was set and eyes sharp. Quickly, her thoughts swayed from one position, then to another. "I don't know, I don't know."

Duncan took a step even deeper into Emmy's space, his chest touching hers. She didn't move away; she knew he was coming to persuade her; she wanted to be persuaded. He took her hand and held it in his own. "Believe me."

Emmy looked into his eyes; she felt if she looked hard enough it should be clear whether he was telling the truth. But the answer wasn't there. She stared harder, and Duncan didn't suspend her search into himself; he held his breath waiting to see what she would find.

Then: *Vrrrrr;* the noise came sharp and crackly. It was the sound from the intercom unit behind Emmy's desk. It meant a client was outside waiting to be granted entrance to the building. The electrical sound crackled like the tension that hung thick and full.

"I have to get that." Emmy's body shifted toward the intercom unit but Duncan's grip on her hand tightened.

He had to have her believe him; she'd been so close. "Let me know first." Duncan moved his grip to her wrist. "Don't believe Celia. Don't. Believe me." He looked at her and there was – Emmy saw it – desperation in this request. Her thoughts rushed: *Maybe I should believe him; I want to believe him; why am I not doing what I want?* It would be so easy to simply say: *"I don't believe Celia; I believe you."* She opened her mouth, but no words came out.

The intercom – *Vrrrr* – *buzzed* again, and this time, the intrusion of the unpleasant sound sliced through the moment's tautness. Whispering, she said flatly, "Duncan, I have to let my client in," and she pulled on the hand he held. He let it go. Released, Emmy rushed behind her desk to press the intercom buzzer.

Duncan hated the urgency she gave to pressing this stupid button. She was giving some nameless, faceless person priority over him. *Did she not realize how many people he was making wait for him on set? Did she not see how he was trying to chase her?* As he felt his resentment build, he forced himself to remember he was asking Emmy to believe something he wasn't entirely sure was true. *Was that fair?* Maybe not. Yet, the unvarnished truth wasn't fair either. Not really. What he'd explained was what he'd hoped they could make true. *Maybe it wasn't possible to make a new truth.* Duncan looked around the room, at the door that would soon open with Emmy's client. "I guess I'm going."

Hearing his clipped words, Emmy suddenly worried Duncan meant to be going for good. She rushed to where he stood. "Duncan, I..." It seemed impossible to find a statement she wanted to stand behind. "I care about you," is what she said because even if he'd betrayed her, that was still true. She put her palms on his chest. "And I think..." *What did she think?* She said out loud the only plan she had: "I have to ignore this situation for it to become clearer to me."

The words themselves weren't soothing, but Duncan knew Emmy was meaning to reassure him. Her body leaned into his; he could tell she didn't want him to go. He half-smiled, "You shouldn't practice your fine art of ignoring on me."

Emmy looked up at him: *How did he know about her art of ignoring?*

Duncan didn't clarify the question and instead watched her face as it searched for then found the connection – *oh, Celia.* Even with everything that had happened, he enjoyed watching the thoughts move across her face. He leaned down and kissed her lips. "I'm the one you should trust." He made himself walk out the door.

Tuesday, October 15:
Spilt milk

Emmy lay on the TV room's couch. The digital clock near the TV had a lot of ones on it: 1:11. Sleep would not come. Questions lighted through her brain. It took effort to ignore them, and she was tired; the questions wouldn't go away.

Emmy thought about Duncan referring to her "fine art of ignoring." She wondered in what context this habit of hers could possibly have been discussed. Try as she did, Emmy couldn't remember how she'd come to tell Celia about her practice of ignoring things and regardless, she doubted Celia would have understood what she meant. Emmy called it ignoring, but that wasn't quite accurate terminology. Ignoring would seem to imply a repression of emotions, but as a therapist, she was more emotionally careful than that. *Wasn't she?* Anyway, she tried. And when she set out to ignore her emotions, it was to cope with how overpowering they felt at first.

Emmy knew she emoted too easily. It wasn't merely that her eyes watered over nothing. She was delighted too easily as well. The way light floated through treetops, the way a song's chord hit just so, the way Tess laughed deep from her throat – these little joys sometimes reeled her too. Most people, she knew, didn't give full emotional flower to such trifles, and Emmy thought part of her project as a responsible adult was to manage her sensitivities so she wouldn't either.

This was hardest when she was sad. In her moments of sorrow – they didn't happen often – her body felt as though murky waves roiled inside it, like she was being flooded from the inside. As a teenager, when she'd watched her parents bitterly – sometimes physically – fight each other, she learned these emotional swells were best managed when she refused to ride them, when she simply pretended the waves weren't breaking. By now this coping mechanism was completely instinctual. When something emotionally extreme occurred, she'd try very hard not to think about it at first. The ignoring never completely worked; the feelings would nevertheless seep in, but when they did, they entered her consciousness as slow trickles, not torrents. At this tempered pace, she could hold the emotions, examine them, and turn them in her mind's eye. Ignoring is what she termed it, but the practice was more like stalling. She wanted to give her capacity for reason the time to catch up with her capacity for feeling. It was all pretty sensible, she thought.

That day, she expended great effort to keep her mind from thinking about Duncan and Celia. She met with five clients, went to a dress rehearsal in the evening, and tried hard all the while to keep her thoughts on others, not herself. Yet, despite her efforts, there were moments when her concentration flagged – when she was driving through traffic or watching the others' dance routines. It was then she replayed how Duncan said he was falling in love with her. *Had he meant that?*

She considered how upset he'd been at seeing the family pictures at the cabin, how jealously he'd asked about

Jack. All along, she'd been so determined to recognize their attraction's short-term timeframe. She'd repeated over and over the reasons Duncan wouldn't want anything between them to continue once he left. *But what if she'd been wrong? What if he wanted to be with her in a more meaningful way?* As soon as she realized she was forming these questions, she pushed them away. If she allowed herself to think about Duncan, then the right question, the first question, should be whether he'd slept with Celia. If he'd done that, then, it wouldn't matter how he felt about her. If his 38-year old self had betrayed her trust to sleep with her 19-year old step-daughter, then she shouldn't want his love. Duncan knew that Celia was the product of Jack's betrayal of her, and that, symbolically, sleeping with Celia would carry extra pain. If Duncan could be so cruelly hurtful to her for a one-night romp, then his love was worthless. It should be easy to vanquish him from her thoughts. *Right?*

She did not like this question – or its answer – and that is why all day she tried hard not to ask or answer it. But now, at 1:11 a.m., this call and response knocked and bumped against her brain, like a taunt. She had to get up. Dragging the afghan with her, she stumbled in the dark through the large, cold house to find her laptop case. Once she'd retrieved it, she turned on the kitchen light and set herself down at the island's counter stool with her open laptop in front of her and the afghan around her shoulders. 'Duncan Grier' she typed into Google. She'd looked him up once before, weeks ago, and though she'd read only a little then, she knew there was a lot to see – videos, photos, archived interviews. Now, she set out to see it all.

The first links to come up were gossip articles about the found photo of Duncan snorting coke as a young man. Emmy realized these weren't what she was looking for. She clicked on the Google link for Images, and a flood of snapshots filled the page: paparazzi shots, styled photos, movie stills. In some, Duncan looked at the camera with a straight-on smoldering look Emmy knew from the cover of men's magazines. It made her smile; he didn't look like himself when he did that. There were other photos – especially from when he was younger – where the shots were especially sexualized. She clicked on these.

One photo mesmerized her. In it, a twenty-something Duncan was standing in front of an old-fashioned refrigerator in a farmhouse kitchen; he was shirtless and wearing beltless blue jeans that hung off his hips. The photo, though obviously styled, was meant to feel candid. In the split second caught, Duncan had been drinking milk from an old-fashioned glass bottle when something apparently made him laugh – a big laugh – and as his body lurched with the chortle, the milk spilled, out of his mouth, down his chin. Perhaps most women would not have found it evocative; it was taken in a kitchen; he didn't smolder; it was about spilt milk. Yet, for Emmy, the photo pulsed sex. There were Duncan's rounded shoulders, his bare chest; his blue jeans hanging so low they revealed the arch of his hipbone, a hint of his pubic hair. His expression radiated a rowdy pleasure to it too, and the way the white milk rolled in his mouth and messily fell onto his chin, Emmy's skin grew hot. She ran her finger softly across her lips, back and forth, back and forth. That man had kissed her today. He would have kissed her more if she'd let him.

Eventually, she made herself close the photo. She had a purpose. She couldn't have articulated what it was, but she wanted to make this investigation at least feel methodical. She decided to start at the beginning.

She looked first at the video libraries, sorting them so she could see the earliest ones first. In these first video snippets

– recorded from late night talk shows and a few morning news programs – Duncan looked ridiculously young, no older than her son, Marc, was now. His hair then was shiny, sun-bleached blond, his skin free of its current smile creases and his body lanky. His start-and-stop Australian cadence and his somewhat dazed mannerisms created a mellowness that might have been off-putting were it not for his quick, light-up grin. All together, his personality conveyed an eagerness to please and a lack of pretension that was undeniably charming. Yet, there and again, Emmy thought she saw – it would happen quickly – a look of fleeting fear or confusion pass over his expression. It was hardly the most prominent impression he made; most people would have said he appeared relaxed enough to be stoned. But in rare flashes Emmy could see anxiety that he covered with a joke or a smile.

As he grew into his late twenties and early thirties, Duncan's celebrity became more solid. Now, there were more clips and pieces written about him and everywhere he was referred to as the Grier. The moments of fleeting fear were gone, but Emmy was surprised to see the affected casualness and evasiveness persisted. Every opportunity he had to speak about his work or any research he did for his roles, he instead cracked a joke or made fun of himself. In one daytime television interview, he was asked what he did to prepare for playing the space-cowboy hero in *Final Frontier*, and with a cocked eyebrow and a laugh he responded, "I drove a lot of spaceships." His delivery made it clear he was laughing at his lack of preparation. In fact, with most of his responses, his intent was to establish he didn't take himself too seriously. To Emmy the casualness felt overdone, as though he was trying to mask his complexity, trying to make himself less than who he was. *Did people really believe he was like that?* She had to guess they did.

One red carpet situation stood out. At one of the premieres for *Final Frontier*, a female entertainment reporter exuberantly asked Duncan how he'd felt playing "such an archetypal hero," but her pronunciation of the word archetypal had been off, making the first syllable sound like a nickname for Archie. The mispronunciation registered with Duncan – Emmy saw his eyebrows slightly rise when the reporter said the word – but when he responded, he purposefully chose to say "archetypal" in the same, wrong way. It wasn't meant as a tease or a gotcha; he seemed eager to take the opportunity to misrepresent himself and especially his intelligence. Emmy played the moment several times, and she could see how his eyes sparked as he prepared to respond. He liked cultivating this false impression of himself.

It was a hallmark of Duncan's interviews to be queried about what it was like growing up in Australia, what he'd done there as a kid, etc. After Emmy read and saw enough of these interviews, she recognized this set-up to be the polite prologue to the question the interviewers really wanted to pose: Why did he never go back? His unwillingness to visit Australia was apparently enough of a mystery to give entertainment reporters a pseudo-journalistic pursuit. One MTV interviewer, more persistent than most, arrogantly pressed: "Just what is it that *scares* you in Australia?" Duncan's eyes flared angry for a split second before he stopped himself and said, "It's the koalas, man. I have a phobia of those sleepy critters."

She read two *Vanity Fair* cover pieces, one written when he was a rising star at 26, another right before *Final Frontier* came out when he was 32. Both articles included handfuls of quotes from actors who'd worked with him, all glowing with exaggeratedly generalized compliments – "Duncan is what you'd find if there was an entry for 'great guy' in the dictionary." Emmy rolled her eyes; the remarks sounded like paid endorsements. Nonetheless, a few were intriguing. One director said, "The critics like to think what he does is easy. Not true. Duncan is able to play the non-emoting man in such a way that you nevertheless completely care about him. His reactions are small, but they register big; they have layers. It might not seem such a magic trick, but it is." Another actress said: "Duncan's not a wear-his-heart-on-his-sleeve type of guy. Except when he's with his dog. Then – it's pretty funny to watch – he turns to mush. All the women on set swoon when he plays with his dog."

Both *Vanity Fair* articles were chock-full of references to Duncan's effect on women, and Emmy shifted in her chair as she read these parts. In the article that ran before *Final Frontier*, the writer said Duncan was well known to be a ladies man who "rarely dates actresses, but is also rarely without a date." The writer – a Julia Denigen – seemed herself to be quite smitten with Duncan, and the piece ended with Denigen relaying how she asked Duncan if he ever planned to end his bachelor ways and settle down. She wrote of Duncan's response: "He winked at me and said in that half shy, half sly way he has; 'Maybe tomorrow.'" Emmy read the paragraph five times. She would have bet her therapy license Duncan slept with stupid Julia Denigen. It was the kind of thing he clearly did.

Emmy moved on. After the immense coverage of Duncan's success with *Final Frontier*, Duncan seemed to have fallen out of the limelight. The drop in his press coverage was so considerable Emmy checked to see what movies he'd made in the six years since *Final Frontier* came out. There were a few – eight in total – but only half had seen wide release, and those movie reviews were mediocre. Likewise, of the articles written about him in the last five years, none were profiles and few were about his work. Most were tabloid-ish pieces about his romantic relationships, especially the one he had with Alison Lockyer. To the tabloids, Alison and he had seemed an unlikely couple – she of the British costume drama, he the haphazard good guy. One magazine article referred to them as the Brain and the Brawn, a characterization Emmy found ridiculous since Duncan was lean, not bulky, and probably a lot smarter than Alison too. Regardless, there were whole photo libraries of the two stars together: getting smoothies, walking through an airport together, at a movie premiere.

Emmy found the *Vogue* article about Alison that Duncan had told her about. "Everything with Duncan is fantastically easy. He doesn't ask for much. I pinch myself when I think how I snagged this wonderful man, this love of my life." Emmy read the gossip reports about Duncan and Alison's eventual break-up. Several sources said Alison had wanted to marry, but Duncan balked. "He's not a guy who wants the white picket fence," one of the unnamed friends said. Duncan hadn't described their breakup that way. Emmy wondered which version was true.

In crosschecking all the various windows open on her laptop, she realized that after Duncan and Alison broke up, there wasn't much written about him. In fact, excepting the cocaine coverage, Emmy could only find three items from the last two years. There was a funny photo series for *Men's Health* in which Duncan was all sweaty and muddy from road biking. In the accompanying Q & A, his answer to one question stood out. Asked about his exercise regime, he responded: "I run. I run away from a lot."

The other two short video interviews were conducted at a press junket for a movie she'd never heard of, *The Monkey Chased the Weasel*. In each of the interviews Duncan still joked and grinned, but he seemed tired too, less patient with the enterprise of being interviewed and less careful to camouflage that. In the first interview, Duncan was asked if he ever felt typecast, and he answered: "Yes." The flustered interviewer waited for Duncan to expound, but he did not. "What's your next question?" he asked with a smirk that had more edge than affability. In another interview, a highly made-up celebrity reporter off-handedly referred to Duncan's status as a confirmed bachelor, and he cut her off; "Has that been confirmed? I haven't confirmed it, so I'm curious who confirmed it for you."

Emmy reviewed the various links, but she'd seen them all. She closed her laptop. The night was now slowly surrendering to the morning, with the dawn's light lifting darkness from the kitchen corners. Emmy hadn't slept and she wouldn't have minded her fatigue if she'd found the answer she'd been looking for. She hadn't. She'd hoped to determine if Duncan had told her the truth. About falling in love with her. About not sleeping with Celia. She hadn't figured those questions out.

Of course it was ridiculous to evaluate Duncan's sincerity on these intimate matters by viewing decades worth of movie promotion, paparazzi shots and tabloid coverage. Emmy recognized the disconnect between her research question and its reference material. But the web provided too vast a resource; it called to her. On her laptop screen, she was instantly able to view all that most challenged her trust in Duncan. His fame, the women he'd been with, the attention he received, his celebrity – there it was on display. It was clear Duncan lived in a world where people fawned over him, where few demands were made on his integrity and the only limits to his ego were ones he set himself. He had no commitments. He was evasive about presenting himself authentically. He'd been with many – so many – women. She saw those things. It was not a portrait that recommended trust.

But she also saw Duncan. In the hours that she charted his career chronologically, she'd watched him grow up before her eyes. He captivated her. A glowing smile spread across her face each time she watched his interviews. He was charming and good-natured. Beautiful. Funny. She understood him too. When he was guarded, she knew why; when he didn't want to answer a question, she could guess at the way he would joke his way out of it. His short, evasive answers felt, in their way, rather perfect. She was in love with him – oh, it was pointless to try to deny that.

Was he a man who would have slept with Celia? *Was he that type of man?* Her scattered emotions were very eager to settle on a state of trust or distrust. But they could not. She knew it was a question that had an answer; there was a truth out there. But, how could she ever know it? Celia would always have one report and Duncan another.

She was making herself a coffee when she heard the *whup* sound that meant a text message was received. She searched to find her cell phone in her purse. The text came from Ling.

Don't know what you worked out with Duncan but he's filming at the Harvard Club in Cambridge today. Very hectic. Probably you should reschedule.

Emmy read the message several times, trying to decipher whether Duncan had instructed Ling to send it or if Ling had sent it of her own initiative. She couldn't decide. She turned her phone off. It didn't matter. Either way, she wouldn't see him. She hadn't expected otherwise. Nevertheless, the day ahead grew drearier.

"Duncan, Gus wants you on set in five." Randy, the Assistant Director, stuck his head in the room they were using for make-up and started to duck out again when he seemed to remember something, "Oh, and he doesn't want you talking to Marguerite."

Duncan lightly nodded, choosing not to question this bizarre stipulation. *Why couldn't he talk to the actress he was about to film with?* Duncan was in one of the Harvard Club's overnight rooms, sitting in front of a mirror. Christy, his hairdresser, was fiddling with his hair. She would slick it back with the comb, pouf the left side slightly, then look at Duncan in the mirror and, dissatisfied, repeat the process.

"Do you have any Tylenol?" he asked. His head hadn't stopped throbbing since Sunday morning. It was Tuesday morning now. *Was it possible he was still hung over?* It seemed unlikely. Christy treated the question like an emergency and rushed to see if she could find drugs for Duncan before he had to go on set.

Alone, he sat in the hotel-like room they were using for his make-up; he was trying not to look at the mirror in front of him. He didn't want to see himself right then. There's been no contact from Emmy. He thought she might call last night. She hadn't. And he wouldn't see her today. Ling had already chirpily told him she'd texted Emmy to let her know they couldn't meet.

Today, they were filming what was probably the movie's biggest scene. It was the scene in which Benjamin B meets his mother-in-law – Mrs. Robins – for lunch at the Harvard Club. It was the mother-in-law's only appearance in the story, and the scene that Emmy and he had debated on their walk to his office. *Was Mrs. Robins honestly striving to save Benjamin or trying to ruin him?* After his discussion with Emmy, Duncan had gone back and re-read its ending. He hadn't changed his mind. To him, the book's ending still appeared clear. Here was a weak man about to risk his wife, his life, his home and stability on something that was very obviously pathetic: a preposterous crush on a colleague's daughter. To Duncan, it was abundantly apparent Mrs. Robins was doing Benjamin a favor, preventing his fleeting feelings from ruining every-thing good about his life. To some extent, Duncan thought one of the reasons he liked the book was that Benjamin's midlife crisis seemed like a good sort of crisis to have: he only had to stop messing up the good life he already had. That midlife revelation was far easier than the one where you realize how much you've messed up.

There was a knock on the door, and before Duncan called out a response, Gus walked in. Duncan stood up; his director never came to him when he was in make-up. *Had it already been five minutes?* Duncan apologized, "Gus, I was just getting ready to go—"

"No worries," Gus put his arm on Duncan's shoulder indicating he should sit down again. Gus propped himself against the room's desk, facing Duncan. "Listen, I wanted to talk with you about this next scene. I'm going to try some-thing a little different with it today – nothing to worry about, but I wanted to come and talk with you about what I'm looking for." Duncan nodded and Gus continued, "What you've brought to Benjamin that I like is how you show him struggling with control. You've made it clear Benjamin is that guy – we all relate to it – that yearns for more than he can have. You've done that nicely." He paused and crossed one leg over the other, "But today, I want to see that yearning falter. I want to see if today I can document a man recognizing he has to settle."

Duncan quickly thought about the scene. "Is there a particular line you have in mind?" He didn't understand why Gus was giving him such vague direction.

"You'll feel it when it comes." Gus scratched his chin. "Now I know the other day you had some personal business that needed your attention." Duncan froze; he worried Gus was about to ask for a better explanation for his lateness on set. Duncan opened his mouth, but quickly Gus held up his hands. "I don't know what's going on, don't want to know either. But if you don't mind me saying, I think you like control too. There's a lot more to the Grier than you want to show us, isn't there?"

Duncan could not fathom where Gus was going with this. *Why would he want to discuss these issues now, before this big scene?* Gus continued, almost apologetically, "Listen, I don't mean to disrespect the space you create around yourself. But from a purely professional perspective, I want to see you lose some control today. If you feel like shit, and…" Gus smiled, "you look like you do – let's bring that messiness to today's scene. Don't easy it up for me. Don't take the edge off. Remember the pathos?" He laughed. "This is the scene for the pathos."

Duncan agreed, and together they started to walk to the Harvard Club's dining hall. As they walked, Gus told Duncan he wanted to start rolling right away, no rehearsal, no chit-chat; he wanted to shoot straight off. "Was he okay with that?" Duncan said he was fine, but in truth, all the peculiar stipulations were beginning to make him nervous. The room was, of course, already lit, the extras already in place. Duncan saw that Marguerite, the woman playing Mrs. Robinson, was seated; the crew was already off stage and everything seemed ready to shoot. He was the last remaining piece to fit in the puzzle.

They didn't need to block anything. The scene consisted of Benjamin and Mrs. Robins talking over lunch, and the plan was to film Mrs. Robins' entrance after the meal. Randy directed Duncan to where he was supposed to sit at the table, and that was it. Duncan hadn't seen Marguerite since table readings in L.A. and usually they would have rehearsed the scene a few times or at least talked about how they were going to play it. Duncan remembered what Randy said about not talking with Marguerite, and he kept quiet. As he sat there in the crowded dining room, he closed his eyes to center his attention. He rolled his head and willed Benjamin's nervous energy into his body. He put Dustin Hoffman's nasal-y Benjamin voice in his throat, adjusted his posture and opened his eyes again.

The white clapboard went up. They were filming.

```
INT. HARVARD CLUB DINING ROOM

Mrs. Robins sits opposite from Benjamin at
a table set for lunch.

BENJAMIN
This is an unexpected pleasure.

MRS. ROBINS
Please, Benjamin, you don't have to pretend.
I'm hating this as much as you are.
```

BENJAMIN
Then why did you ask me to this lunch in the
first place?

MRS. ROBINS
I've heard some things about you lately.
(smiling)
And I feel I should help you.

BENJAMIN
Help me? I didn't realize I needed your
help.

MRS. ROBINS
Oh, you do.
(lighting a cigarette)
I know about your young girl, Benjamin. Ah,
don't try to deny it. I know what's true.

BENJAMIN
Do you see the irony in your advising me on
this topic? *You* are going to tell me it's
bad to seduce someone young? Is that your
advice, Mrs. Robins?

MRS. ROBINS
(tersely)
Stop calling me that.

BENJAMIN
What should I call you? *Mom*? Is that what
you want me to call you?

MRS. ROBINS
Good grief, Benjamin. You are difficult.
I'm here because my daughter asked me to
come. El doesn't ask for much these days,
but what she asks, I do. And she wants me
to make you go back.

BENJAMIN
I don't want to go back. I want to go
forward.

Mrs. Robins laughs at Benjamin's expense.

BENJAMIN
Is that funny to you? Why is that funny
to you?

MRS. ROBINS
It's naïve, Benjamin.

BENJAMIN
Is that so?

MRS. ROBINS
You're too old for this. At your age, one
step forward includes two steps back.
It's the science of middle age.

BENJAMIN
I'm not sure what your point is. You
should say what you want to say so we
can get this over with.

MRS. ROBINS
(takes drag from cigarette)
Don't embarrass yourself Benjamin. In a nut-
shell, that's what I hope to pass on to you.

BENJAMIN
There's nothing embarrassing about what I'm
doing. I've found happiness. Love. What's
embarrassing about that? I feel like my
eyes are finally opened, like I'm seeing
what the world has to offer for the first
time. Maggie shows me. I'm not sure I can
see it without her.

MRS. ROBINS
(sarcastically laughing)
And what do you think about my daughter? Is
she supposed to be thrilled you've found
this happiness too, that you can finally
see.

BENJAMIN
(agitated, angry)
El doesn't care. We haven't … we're not …

MRS. ROBINS
You're wrong Benjamin. El does care.
(takes drag on cigarette)
She loves you.

BENJAMIN
Loves me? Hah! And how would you know that?

MRS. ROBINS
Well, how else? From her mouth of course.
Don't you see, Benjamin?

BENJAMIN
No, I don't see. Your information isn't
very accurate. El doesn't love me.

MRS. ROBINS
She does. She said
(takes another drag from her cigarette)
she loves you *very* much.

Duncan was confused: Marguerite had never said this line in table readings as she said it now. Previously, Marguerite made it sound like Mrs. Robins was telling the truth. But here, she made it obvious Mrs. Robins was lying. Duncan almost broke character. There was a beat where he thought of cutting the sequence. Instead, he kept going.

BENJAMIN
Really?

MRS. ROBINS
Of course. She misses you. And don't you
see how your life would miss El? Why, she
positively grounds you. She keeps you who
you are. Benjamin, she is your home. It's
not good to walk away from a home. That
is not easily reconstructed. I … I should
know.

```
BENJAMIN
But I already feel reconstructed. I feel
better than I ever have. New.
```

```
MRS. ROBINS
You aren't. You're forty. That's not new.
Don't fool yourself.
```

The sympathy that Marguerite had previously given Mrs. Robins was gone; Mrs. Robins now sounded curt, not compassionate.

```
BENJAMIN
But it feels … it feels …
```

```
MRS. ROBINS
(interrupting)
Feelings are fleeting Benjamin. Trust what
you have. That is who you are. You have a
company that needs you. A house. (beat)
A wife.
```

Duncan realized that Benjamin's credulity would now sound pathetic; he let it.

```
BENJAMIN
Elaine said she loved me?
```

```
MRS. ROBINS
(stumps out her cigarette)
Yes, Benjamin, yes. You have an enviable life.
All you have to do is not mess it up.
```

BENJAMIN
(suspiciously)
I see what you're doing. You want me to think it's too late to change. You want me to be miserable. Like you.

MRS. ROBINS
(haughty)
That is a very cruel charge. I am trying to teach you what I've learned. You can't run from what you are. When you try it makes things worse.

BENJAMIN
Maybe it's not running; maybe it's changing.

MRS. ROBINS
You can call it what you want. It still won't work.

BENJAMIN
(to himself)
I would not have thought El would say she loves me.

MRS. ROBINS
(smiling)
Benjamin, she wants you to come home to her. She loves you very much. Won't you? Won't you come home?

Duncan saw Marguerite's smile was more self-satisfied, even menacing, than it had ever been in rehearsals. Duncan allowed himself to summon the expression required to take this statement at face value. He let his face show Benjamin's will to believe in that wifely love, in the home to which he could return. His willingness to lie to himself. He used minimal facial movement, but he gave the expression a beginning, middle and end.

"And cut." Gus made the command sound softer than he usually did.

Usually after the "cut" call, there was a rumbling that came from the lifting of the demand for silence, a collection of whispers, sighs, and coughs. This time, however, everyone stayed quiet, as though they sensed the tension had not been severed at all. Marguerite looked over at Duncan as Gus strode to where Duncan sat.

He'd been duped. It wasn't just that the story now had a different meaning than he wanted it to have. It was that he'd been tricked into giving it that meaning. He knew Gus sometimes used unusual techniques to get the performances he wanted. But did Gus think he had to trick this performance out of him? Did he think so poorly of his acting skills?

Gus patted Duncan's shoulder. "My friend, that was brilliant. It was everything I wanted." As Duncan looked up at his director, he couldn't keep the anger out of his eyes; he didn't care if Gus saw it.

Gus leaned in to him to convey an intimacy; he spoke in a lowered voice, "Duncan, this whole movie rises and falls on the moment you just created there. The way I shot today; I know it was unexpected, but I wanted you bare. That look of confusion followed by that willing of credulity, that's what I needed. And, you know…" he shook his head, taking his arms back, giving Duncan more space, "It's a bitch of a story, just a goddamn bitch of a story. You wanted it to be redemptive, but my friend, the cruelty of this story is that it comes so close, so close, but: No. No redemption. Poor Benjamin leaves all his potential to return to a home that has none. It's just a bleak bitch of a story."

Duncan didn't say anything for a second. Leaving aside Gus and his fucked-up method for getting that performance, he was honestly trying to figure out if he agreed with his interpretation of the story. *Did he?* He looked at Gus and realized he would have to say something before he made up his mind. He used his most Grier-like voice, "Yeah, a bitch of a story."

Gus patted Duncan's shoulder and walked back off stage. "I want a few more takes so I have room to play with. Let's take it again, okay?"

Duncan tried to set aside his anger. He tried not to think about what the story meant now, or how stupid he felt in front of this entire crew, or how long Gus' prepared "technique" had been in the making. No, he tried not to think about any of that. He righted his shoulders and tried to remember what Gus was looking for: confusion followed by willed credulity. He could fucking do that.

As Emmy walked from the TV room to the kitchen, she saw the harsh glare of the kitchen's lights bounce off the window's dark night, and she guessed that all twenty-two of the kitchen lights must be on. Jack must be home from work. He was the only one who turned on every single one of the kitchen lights. She squinted as she walked closer.

Jack stood sorting mail at the kitchen's large island. "Have you stopped retrieving the mail from the mailbox?" He threw a catalog onto a stack. "This must be four days worth of mail."

"I might have forgotten today." She didn't want to talk to Jack, not about mail or lawn care or anything. Having not slept the night before, her mind was listless, though somehow still agitated and un-drowsy. She'd come to the kitchen to get a glass of wine in the hopes that the drink would help her unwind.

As she walked toward the wine bottle, Jack looked up from the stack of catalogs before him. "Aren't you cold?" he asked, examining her nightgown.

Emmy touched her hand to a spaghetti strap. This nightgown was more flimsy than what she usually wore to bed. "I was overheated after dance rehearsals." Her tone was drab; she pulled the cork out of the wine bottle.

"Oh." He cast an envelope into the catalog pile. "Is that performance coming up soon?"

"It's tomorrow, Jack."

"Oh, is that right?" Jack gathered all the catalogs into one hefty pile, then hit them against the countertop – *tap, tap, tap.*

Emmy shifted from one leg to the other, waiting to see if he would say anything about his intentions to attend the dance performance. It would be nice to know if he still planned to come. She could ask him, she supposed, but the question might be interpreted as a wish he attend. She had no such wish. She waited quietly to see if he would say anything, and when he didn't, she pulled down a wine glass from the cabinet. She'd get her wine and go.

"That's one hell of a pour." Jack muttered, looking at her filling her glass brim full. "Won't feel good tomorrow."

Emmy guessed he was right, but she took her glass and walked past him. Just as Emmy was about to leave the kitchen, Jack's voice stopped her. "Anthony Trippolli told me to pass along his thanks for the brunch. He said, 'Tell *your wonderful wife* I say thank you.'"

Emmy turned to face Jack. It was unusual for her husband to be complimentary. "That's nice he said that."

"You know, Anthony thinks you're quite something."

Emmy studied her husband; there was something off in the way he made the remark. "Anthony thinks that?"

Jack raised his eyebrows. "Yes, he actually does. He talks about you with such... *admiration.*"

Emmy now understood Jack's tone; Anthony's praise perplexed him. "It's okay if you don't see it Jack."

Jack's head darted forward. "Are you upset because I passed along a *compliment?*"

"In passing it along you made it obvious how you feel. You don't think I'm something; you don't admire me." A question blazed through her head; she let it blurt: "Jack, do you even like me?"

Jack's head jerked forward; "Jesus, Emmy, you're making my head spin. I tell you something nice; you've turned it into something you're pissed about."

She hadn't planned on having this conversation, but she was tired and her carefulness was compromised. It was easier to say what came to mind than to stifle the thought. "I'm trying to understand the way you think, Jack. It confuses me that you want us to stay married when you don't even like me."

Jack's eyes popped wide. "Emmy, how do you even *do* this?! It was a fucking *compliment!*"

"You haven't answered my question."

"That's because I don't want to get dragged into your crap. I'm trying to have us *get along.*"

"But why do you want us to get along? *Why?*"

"Do you hear yourself? Do you hear how hard you're making this?"

She raised her chin. "Jack, do you love me?"

Jack blinked, as though he could see the words flash in the open air. He opened his mouth; "Ems, I—" He stopped, stilled himself, then looked to her: "Did you hear that?"

"God, Jack!" She couldn't believe the lengths he'd travel to evade her questions. "At least have the decency to be honest about—"

Jack forcefully held up his hand to stop her from talking. "No, seriously. Don't you hear that? Someone is trying to get in our home." He craned his head and held it still, as though to listen more carefully.

Emmy had to admit: she did hear something. She didn't want to let Jack off the hook, but it was undeniable there were voices and a key in the lock of their backdoor.

Jack and Emmy stared at each other. It was such a familiar sensation; the sound of someone at the backdoor and the accompanying review of their kids – Marc, Ben, Tess; where they were, when they were expected home, which was the one most likely to come ambling through the door. But tonight this review only reaffirmed what they already knew: Their children had left them; none were expected to come through that door.

The door opened nonetheless. "Hel-lo-o-o." The familiar multi-octave greeting immediately identified the intruder. Celia.

Jack called back, "Ce-ce, is that you?"

"It's me! It's me-e-eee!" Her voice sang out and her feet on the floorboards indicated her approach, "And I've brought a friend." Celia barreled into the kitchen. She went to kiss her father's cheek first and then Emmy's. "Dad, Emmy, I'd like you to meet Duncan Grier."

Emmy's eyes darted to the dark hallway off the kitchen and sure enough, there was Duncan. He walked under the kitchen lights, his eyes squinting as he took in the brightly lit room. He looked at Emmy, but, quick, her eyes shot away.

Her heart was pounding so loudly she worried it could be heard. *Duncan was not supposed to be here.* She couldn't understand why he'd come, and especially why he'd come with Celia. *Were they on a date?*

Celia exuberantly made the introductions. "Duncan, this is my dad Jack. And this is …" her voice built to a purposeful dramatic pause, "Emmy." Still, Emmy would not look up.

Celia bubbled with delight. "Duncan and I were going to go out for dinner, but he worried there would be too many photographers – you know, because of all the coke snorting stuff. That's when I had my brilliant idea – ta-da! – no paparazzi stalking the Brookline Reservoir, right? It was, like, the perfect solution to come here."

Jack turned to Duncan. "You have some coke snorting stuff?"

Emmy peeked to see how Duncan would respond. "I do," was all he said.

Celia nervously tried to change the subject. "I was telling Duncan there were sure to be leftovers in the fridge since Emmy's never really stopped cooking for five." Celia leaned into Duncan's side, "She's, like, the best cook ever."

"Is that right?" Duncan asked, and from the way he said it, Emmy could tell he was looking right at her. She couldn't help look back.

Duncan was glad to finally have made eye contact at least. He was keenly aware that his trip to this house could be disastrous; there were considerably more ways their interactions could go badly than ways they could go well. Emmy was obviously furious; her eyes were fiery, her cheeks crimson. He tried to express with the slightest tilt of his head, the smallest smile that his intentions in coming were good, but Emmy's expression did not soften. Suddenly, he realized: Jack was examining this wordless interaction.

Jack spoke, "I'm trying to figure this out. Duncan, you're the guy in *Last Frontier*, aren't you? But how, how do you know Celia?"

Duncan opened his mouth to answer, but Celia beat him to the response: "Didn't Emmy tell you? God, it was pure madness! When Emmy loaned Duncan the cabin, she didn't know I was heading up then too. And there was this insane moment when I walked into our kitchen and Duncan was standing in it like he lived there himself!"

Emmy felt Jack pivot toward her. "You loaned him *the cabin?*"

Quickly, Emmy mumbled. "I meant to mention that to you."

Celia sputtered on, "Yeah, it's all because of Emmy's friend... Actually, Dad, *I bet* you know her too." She turned to Duncan to explain, "My dad went to Amherst. Wait, what's her name again?"

"Kallie," Emmy said.

Celia continued her explanation. "Yeah, Dad, so Kallie is Duncan's *agent.*"

"Manager, actually," Duncan interjected.

"Oh, is there a difference?" Celia didn't wait for the answer. "Anyway, that's how Emmy found out about Duncan and how Duncan knew about the cabin. Through *Kallie.*"

Jack repeated: "Through Kallie." His repetition of the words only served to highlight how little exuberance he brought to processing this information. "Huh." He looked at Emmy, then at Duncan and Celia. "It was *Kallie* – Kallie from Amherst – who brought you – you three – together."

"Yes, us two. Can you believe it?" Celia beamed.

Jack looked at the three of them skeptically, but before he could respond, the phone rang. *Briiing! Briiing!* High and trilling, the ring cut the tension.

"I'll get it." Jack's voice was gruff, and he took the short step to reach the cordless phone that sat in the back of the counter. "Hello?" He waited. "Tessie?" There was a beat of quiet, then Jack's voice grew worried. "Sweetie, are you okay?" He walked away from where everyone was standing, down the hall toward the TV room. Emmy's eyes followed her husband; she wanted to hear what was happening with Tess. But Jack only walked down the long hallway to the TV room, turned into the room and closed the door.

Emmy was still staring down the hall when Celia rushed to her side. She whispered into her ear, "While Dad's talking to Tess, I'm going to dash to the wine cellar. That's okay, right? Please, please, don't say anything to Dad." She held her finger to her lips, "Shhhh?"

Emmy said nothing, and apparently Celia read Emmy's dazed expression as acquiescence. Celia squeezed her arm; "Thanks Ems." Walking backward, Celia looked at Duncan devilishly, "I'll be right back, 'kay?" Without waiting for a response, Celia rushed down the hallway. The basement door opened, then clicked shut.

As soon as Emmy heard the door snap into its catch, her hands flew to the sides of her head as though to contain its exploding anger. "What are you *doing?* You've come here on a *date?*! How can you—"

In two straight strides, Duncan reached her and grabbed her hands from their outraged position. "I'm not on a *date.* Bloody hell. A date? No, I'm here to see you. Come on, you know that's the truth. Just think."

Emmy could tell he was nervous; his hands were slightly sweaty, his smile awkward. His discomfort was good to feel; it relaxed her.

Duncan started to explain. "Celia showed up on the set at the Harvard Club – she must have found out we were filming there today. She asked to have dinner together, and when I wasn't interested, she suggested coming here, meeting you. She knows the sweet spot. The offer to see you, meet Jack, see your home. I couldn't say No."

Emmy realized Duncan was still holding her hands. She tugged her hands away; she was in her husband's kitchen. "But Celia thinks you're on a date."

"She thinks a lot that's not true."

"That's not very nice to her. You're only using her—"

"She's the one using me. I'm just her good story to tell her mates. Her bragging rights. I'm getting nothing here but a chance to see you."

Emmy had to admit: this version of his motives made more sense than the version in which he came to her house on a date. She wasn't sure what to say.

"That's a nice nightie," Duncan smiled teasingly but then, fast, his smile evaporated. "You put that on to wear to the TV room?"

"Uh-huh." She'd already wished she had a robe. Under the bright light, she felt terribly bare. It wasn't merely that her body was exposed; she knew last night's sleeplessness had to be bringing out all the shadows and creases on her face.

"You're not wearing that for Jack?"

His worry was nice to hear; she shook her head: "No." She pulled one of the counter stools from under the kitchen island. "I stayed up last night reading about you on the web," she said as she sat down.

"Oh?" This was a good sign, he thought. He pulled the stool next to hers and sat beside her. "Why'd you do that?"

She shrugged. "I was trying to see if I understand you."

"From the web?" He thought the web was a strange place to try to figure this out. He arranged himself to face her. "So. Do you?"

She didn't know the answer to his question. "A lot of people write about you and analyze you and think about you. They try to make it sound like they know you."

"They don't."

Emmy noted how certain he was. "I think you purposefully make it hard. You try to confuse people about who you are."

"Maybe. But I've never done that with you."

"That's only because I was your therapist."

"No." The word was sharp. "You know that's not it. Don't *make* yourself doubt me."

She considered whether she was doing that; perhaps she was. Regardless, she didn't want to talk about that stuff now, not here in the kitchen when Jack or Celia might walk in at any moment. "So, you were at the Harvard Club today? Did you film the Mrs. Robins scene?"

Duncan realized Emmy was diverting the conversation, but that was okay. One of the reasons he wanted to see her so badly was to tell her about his miserable day. "We did film that scene today. You were right about the story. I was wrong."

"Why do you say it like that? It's a story, there's no right or wrong about it.'

"Well, Gus disagrees. There's no ambiguity in the way his film will be told. The way the movie is being filmed, Mrs. Robins is lying. So, the story, it's not about being saved from a midlife crisis; it's not about love or how marriage can save you. It's about—" he stopped. "Actually, I'm not sure what it's about anymore."

Emmy could see he was disappointed; she leaned into his side, "I'm sorry. I know you wanted the story to have a happy ending."

"I did." He grimaced, shaking his head. "The way Gus worked everything on set today, god, it was fucked up. He made me feel so stupid." He rubbed the back of his neck; "I hated it."

"I'm sure you didn't look stupid. Gus probably did."

He smiled at her quick protection of her. "You don't think it would have been better if I'd been cynical all along?"

Emmy smiled back. "Cynical's not so great." She pivoted toward him. "You know, I've thought a lot about the story since we talked about it. If Benjamin's wife had loved him, then it would have been the right choice to go back to her."

Duncan found this interesting. "You think El loved Benjamin?"

"No." Emmy frowned; "No, I think El probably didn't. But whether Benjamin's decision is redemptive or bleak, well, it all depends on whether you choose to believe if his wife was telling the truth. Whether she truly loves Benjamin." She looked at him: "Don't you think?"

Duncan thought there had to be another meaning to this exchange, but he wasn't sure how to stack it yet. "I suppose, yes."

"So," she smiled, "there you have it. It's like you said: Love is everything."

He laughed: "I said that?"

"You did. On the first day of therapy with me."

"You remember that?"

"It stuck with me."

He leaned in closer: "Why?"

She shrugged. "It's an unusual thing for a man to say."

"I'm girly?"

Her laugh spilled out. "Hardly."

His tone grew serious. "Do you think I'm right?"

Before Emmy could answer, the basement door creaked from the hallway off the kitchen. As they straightened themselves, Celia walked into the kitchen. When she noticed the hushed stares her entrance received, she merrily held two wine bottles outward like trophies. "Tada!" She springily walked to where Duncan and Emmy sat. "That was *a lot* more complicated than I thought it would be!"

Duncan glanced at Emmy. Seconds ago, her face had been lit with warmth; now, she glowered. Everything was about to fall apart. *Shit.* It had been going so well. He'd come that night to have the very kind of interaction they'd just had, one in which he reminded Emmy that their feelings for each other were real and comfortable and kind. Now, with Celia back again, Duncan tried to make Emmy look back at him, but her eyes stayed fixed on the island's countertop.

Celia positioned herself between the stools where Duncan and Emmy sat, their backs to her. "So, which would you prefer?" she merrily asked Duncan. "White?" she held the bottle forward, "Or red? I seem to remember you being partial to red."

Duncan turned around but he didn't answer; he looked at the bottles like they confused him. There was nothing to do or say that wouldn't make the situation potentially worse.

Under the glaring kitchen lights, Celia noticed Duncan's concerned gaze. "Oh, Duncan," Celia laughed, "You don't have to worry about Emmy. She already knows how we raided the wine cellar." She giggled; "Actually, she knows all about our crazy night. Don't you Emmy?"

Duncan felt his body stiffen. *Our crazy night.* The words couldn't have been worse.

Emmy fastened her eyes on Duncan. "I do. I do know about your *night*. Duncan, how crazy was it?"

"Uh…" Here, Emmy was handing him an opportunity to deny Celia's version of the story, and if he were more certain he hadn't slept with Celia, he would have seized this chance to proclaim how un-crazy the night was, just talk, nothing but talk. *But what if Celia then became insistent about her version?* This young woman wasn't shy. *What would she say?* His breath stuttered; his face went blank. "It wasn't that crazy." He knew right away his response hadn't cut it. Emmy turned away. The credibility of Celia's version of the story had catapulted.

Beside them, Celia's tone was impatient. "I'll open the red first." She pranced to the counter and turned her back to them, rifling through the drawer that held the wine opener.

Emmy had to get out of there. She pushed the counter stool back hard and whirled her body to go. Before she took a step, Duncan lurched forward to grab her arm. He wasn't going to say anything – he couldn't say anything with Celia there – but he wanted Emmy to at least look at him so he could ask her to understand. Her eyes flamed at his, and hard, she jerked her arm out of his grasp. She sprang fully away from the stool, then stopped short.

Jack was there.

At the hallway entrance to the kitchen, fifteen feet away, he stood.

Had he been in the process of walking into the room, Emmy might have entertained the possibility he'd failed to see the brief wordless interaction between her and Duncan. But Jack was like a statue, his legs planted, his face stuck with surprise. He'd seen it.

Emmy swallowed hard, trying to determine what she should do. She gestured to the phone that Jack held in his hand; "Is Tess still on?" she asked, trying to strengthen her wobbly voice.

Jack handed her the phone, his eyes now warily on Duncan. "Your daughter flunked her calculus test. She's upset." He turned to her. "She says she needs you."

Emmy nodded. She didn't understand why Tess would say that; it was not the kind of thing her daughter would say. She held the phone to her chest and without looking back, walked out of the horribly bright room.

There was a hard knocking – *tap, tap, tap* – before Jack pushed open the door. Emmy could tell her husband must have come from the treadmill. He was wearing shorts and a t-shirt darkened with sweat; his breathing still panted. "Are you planning on ever leaving this room?" He stepped across the threshold and pivoted his head around, examining the room as if he hadn't been in it for years.

It was Tess' room, and Emmy had come there to talk on the phone with her daughter. She'd been soothed listening to her daughter confide in her. Her motherly tone effortlessly returned, her voice sounding knowledgeable and reassuring. Their conversation had been over for a half hour, but Emmy hadn't wanted to leave the space. Emmy felt cocooned sitting on her daughter's bed, propped against the numerous pale blue pillows and surrounded by Tess' knick-knacks.

Now, Jack stood in front of her, wiping his brow, clearing his throat. She realized he expected her to assuage the worries the unusual evening had created, and the ready anticipation on his face panicked her. She hadn't worked out what she would say. The truth held no appeal. The mere length of that conversation felt taxing, not to mention the scorn and judgment she'd prefer to avoid.

She picked up the cordless phone as though to indicate a common point of interest. "So, Tess is coming home this weekend. Don't you think that's a good idea?" She continued in a carefree tone. "I'll drive up Thursday afternoon to pick her up and take her back Sunday. Won't that be nice to have her home for a few days?"

"Emmy." Jack took a step closer to the bed.

Emmy rushed to continue. "She sounded a bit down, didn't you think? I guess who can blame her when her roommate is such an inconsiderate nymphomaniac. I mean, how is it that this young woman can—"

Jack cut her off: "Why'd you loan Duncan Grier our cabin?" His voice was hard. He took another step closer to the bed, and his whole posture appeared reprimanding.

Emmy knew his question was reasonable, his anger justifiable. That didn't mean she wanted to answer it. She sat upward in the bed. "Why are you so sweaty?"

"Damn it Emmy! Answer the question."

Jack's body was naturally lean, but the way he stood right then he appeared broad. She stood up. Still, she couldn't bring herself to start the conversation. "I don't want to talk in here," she said and walked out the door.

Jack followed her. "Answer my question!"

"Shhh." She spun around. "They'll hear you downstairs."

"They're gone." Jack's face contorted in scorn. "They left a long time ago."

Emmy wondered if they'd left together. She turned back and continued down the wide hallway, turning the corner to head into her and Jack's bedroom. From her dresser, she pulled out a hooded sweatshirt to put over her flimsy nightgown. The warm cover of the sweatshirt was soothing after hours of being so exposed.

Jack stood by the bed. "Tell me why you loaned him the cabin."

She shifted her weight from one foot to the other. "It's pretty much like Celia said. Kallie called me and said that Duncan – Duncan Grier – needed a place to stay for the weekend because he had a lot of paparazzi following him. I wanted to help Kallie—" She realized there was no more explanation than that. "So, I loaned him the cabin. That's all." She tried to make her face look innocent, but it was a ridiculous story, and with Jack's skeptical eyes on her she was having a hard time pretending she believed it.

Jack snorted in disbelief. "Kallie Stillingard calls you after twenty fucking years requesting a *favor?* Because wealthy-as-shit Duncan Grier has nowhere to go but our *cabin?* What kind of bullshit—? Emmy, why did you let that man use our cabin? That was the weekend you were supposed to go there with Maria." Emmy watched her husband. His face clouded; he looked at his wife with genuine concern. "Emmy, what did you—" He shook his head and didn't let himself finish the sentence.

The remorse hit like a club to her chest. "Duncan Grier was a client of mine." The words tumbled like a confession. "It was Kallie who referred him to me a few weeks ago when he came to town, and he did some therapy with me for a while. On Friday, he needed somewhere to go, and I loaned him the cabin. He was in a tough situation, and it didn't seem like a big deal. But once he went there, it meant Maria and I couldn't go, and that is why we re-scheduled our weekend. There." Emmy was aware this version was at best incomplete, but she owned it like she'd told the whole truth.

Jack thought for a moment, then lifted his wet t-shirt to wipe the sweat that beaded on his forehead and temples. When he let the shirt down again, Emmy could tell he wanted to believe her. "Why'd you lie at first?" he asked.

She stood straight. "Because I'm not supposed to divulge that Duncan is my therapy client. Because Kallie made me sign around seventeen forms saying I would never let anyone know. So I haven't said anything about it to anyone."

Jack was dubious. "I'm sure you told Maria."

"Actually no, I haven't." Emmy felt proud this was real truth.

From the way Jack's face sat loosely confused, Emmy could tell he regarded his newfound suspicion as a nuisance he wanted to discard. It had to be inconceivable that she'd betray him. It had been inconceivable to her only weeks before.

Jack crossed the room to the loveseat and leaned against its back. "You know, your movie star client, he looks at you like he has that thing where he thinks you're his mother or his lover or something."

"You mean transference?"

"Yeah, whatever you call it." He crossed one leg over the other. "What name do you give it when the therapist plays along?"

"I'm not playing along. Jack, there's nothing that has—"

He interrupted her. "Why'd he grab your arm?"

"I don't know," she said with exaggerated innocence. "Maybe he wanted to tell me something." Emmy was surprised at how convincingly her voice sounded guileless.

"But you pulled your arm away?"

"I did."

"You looked like you were angry with him."

Emmy shrugged. "I didn't think it was appropriate for him to grab my arm."

Jack was snide: "Maybe you need to bring that up with him in therapy?"

"Duncan isn't my client anymore."

Jack seemed to find this curious. "Why not?"

"Because..." she hesitated but then decided to explain. "Because he's sleeping with Celia."

Shock registered first, creating a blankness that shortly twisted to revulsion. "He is?"

"He is."

"What a fucking bastard." Waves of disgust and anger washed over his face. Then, Emmy saw a knob in his thinking turn, an idea unlocked. "You said you broke off your therapy relationship *because* he was sleeping with Celia?"

"Yes, that's right. I'm not supposed to mix the professional relationship with a personal one, and this thing with Celia made it... complicated."

Jack studied his wife. "You know, this Grier guy – he left Celia right after you took the call with Tess. As soon as you were gone, he left too."

Emmy shrugged. She wanted it to appear this information was of no interest to her, but actually, she was relieved to learn Duncan hadn't stayed to have dinner with Celia.

"He said he had *an early call.*" He shook his head, disgusted. "Like he has to have some special term for going to work. Celia kept wondering why he hadn't remembered his *early call* before." Jack looked at Emmy directly. "It is curious, isn't it? That he didn't remember until you left the room?"

"I don't know." Emmy arranged her face for innocence. "It doesn't seem that curious to me."

Jack walked toward her. "He came here to see you, didn't he? Not Celia."

He sounded as though he'd worked out a logic puzzle and reached its self-evidentiary conclusion. It took Emmy a moment to recognize she needed to refute his conclusion. "No, Jack." She made her words sound firm: "Duncan was here to see Celia."

"You want to make the truth un-true?"

She was puzzled by the expression. "It is un-true."

Jack scoffed, "Then tell me what you think of this man."

Emmy didn't understand where Jack was going with this. "I don't know. Nothing really."

"Is that so? What do you think about his sleeping with Celia?"

Emmy raised her shoulders. "I don't think anything of it." But her statement wasn't convincing, even to her own ears. Seeing his skeptical reaction, Emmy turned to walk toward the bathroom; she wanted to get away from her husband's questioning.

Jack didn't let her walk away from him; he followed fast behind her. "Really? It doesn't disgust you that this man, who could have *fathered* Celia, is sleeping with her, taking advantage of her. That doesn't make you mad? That he would do that?"

Emmy stopped at the bathroom's threshold; she turned to face her husband. "I haven't thought that much about it. It doesn't concern me."

"Is that so?" Jack was clearly dubious. "I think you looked pretty damn concerned down there in the kitchen. When he grabbed your arm."

"I don't know what you mean." But it was hard to deny that Jack understood a lot.

He shook his head, "Emmy, that man cons his way through life. Women for him are playthings. He dabbles with them, moves on. That man is scum. You have to see that."

Emmy moved back into the bedroom, past Jack and his certainty. "I think you should be saying these things to your daughter. She's the one sleeping with him."

Jack was fast behind her. "Celia is young. This is just play for her. You're not young. You have… We have…" His voice rose, but he stopped himself and started over. "Emmy, that man snorts *cocaine*. He sleeps with girls – not women – *girls*. He does not care about people's feelings. He's selfish. I want you to tell me you realize that."

Emmy stood facing him, silent.

"Say it. Say 'I know he's no good.'"

She did not want to say those words. "I'm not going to make judgments against him, Jack. He was my therapy client."

The remark infuriated Jack. "And I'm your *husband*."

Emmy took a step backward. Since when had Jack claimed this label – husband – so possessively?

"If you loved me, you'd say it."

"If I *loved* you?" Her words were appalled. "I asked you just hours ago, and you wouldn't even answer me. Why do I have to show my love for you when you won't for me?"

Jack appeared unfazed by Emmy's objections. "If I didn't love you, why would I be asking you to say this?" He squared his body toward hers. "I love you Emmy. I love you, and I want you to tell me that you see this man is a selfish, lying bastard. I want you to say that."

He hadn't said the words affectionately, but Emmy was surprised at how the three words nonetheless reverberated in her body. He loved her. Quickly she thought: *Was there any reason not to say what Jack wanted?* Duncan *had* slept with Celia. He *had* lied to her. That truth had just been confirmed in the kitchen. Jack was seeking her allegiance. Why should she rupture her husband's trust to defend a man who had wantonly betrayed her? "Fine, I'll say it: Duncan is lying. He's selfish."

Jack nodded. "That's right." He took a step toward her; he sounded like he was speaking to a child, "He's no good. You see it, right?"

Emmy dipped her chin. "Yes, I see it. He's no good."

Jack came right up close to her; he put his arms around her shoulder. "Trust me, I'm trying to protect you," he said. He kissed her temple.

Emmy realized that in this moment her husband was giving her more emotion than he'd shared in a long time. He said he loved her. He said he wanted to protect her. He kissed her. It was obvious he understood some sort of attraction existed between her and Duncan. She would have assumed her betrayal would have pushed him away. Instead, he drew nearer. His lips were against her skin, his arm pulling her into him. Still, she couldn't relax into the touch.

Jack must have felt her body's stiffness because he made a joke about how he guessed he still needed that shower. He sat down on the bed's edge, took off his shoes, socks and then when he stood up, slipped out of his wet shorts. Emmy was so familiar with his body and all its sweaty smells, his nakedness wasn't revealing. She watched, detached, as he walked to the bathroom.

She knew she didn't want to be in their bedroom once he emerged from the shower. As she plodded down the stairs, she considered how many lies she'd just told Jack. The fabrications fell so easily from her tongue. They were words, just words, and the lying words sounded no different than the true ones. *Was that how Duncan felt when he lied to her?*

The peculiar thing was that when Jack asked her to call Duncan selfish and lying, those words should have been easy to form. Duncan's betrayal was freshly cut, its hurt deep, spilling her body of its new and delicate hope. Still, when she said Duncan was no good, that was the hardest thing she'd said all night.

WEDNESDAY, OCTOBER 16:
PAS DE TROIS

Maria wished she were sitting in front of the TV with Nathan eating a bowl of ice cream. Instead, she was in the concert hall of the Cambridge Multicultural Center waiting to watch a bunch of amateur dance performances. Maria would never have let Emmy know this, but the only reason she came tonight was because she worried no one else would. Jack never attended these performances, and even if he was supposedly "trying" again, Maria still didn't want to bet on Jack's attendance.

That morning, at the office, Maria asked Emmy point blank if the divorce plan was now off. Emmy didn't answer the question directly, but instead mumbled something about how Jack had said he loved her last night. "Oh, that's nice," Maria had said back, trying to hide her shock. As the day went on, Maria spent time contemplating her friend's marriage. If Jack really did love Emmy, if he really was going to try to save their marriage, shouldn't Maria support that project? She didn't dislike Jack after all. He had fine qualities. He was a good father, quite good in fact, and from the way he looked at Emmy sometimes, especially when he'd had too much to drink, Maria bet they still had sex. Maria saw fourteen troubled couples a week; if there was love and sex in Jack and Emmy's marriage, well, that was more than a lot of folks could say. All Maria wanted was for her friend to be happy. True, sometimes Maria grew frustrated with Emmy's indecisiveness and desperately wanted to nudge her toward action, any action. *Propel forward.* She was assertive on this point, she supposed. But, perhaps, Emmy had been right to hold steady, to give her marriage a chance to heal itself. Maybe Maria should stop her pushiness now. Nathan kept telling her to tone her opinions down. She couldn't help it. She kept wishing some piece of information, some event, would crystallize Emmy's decision. She hated stasis. Metamorphosis was so preferable.

In the concert hall, the audience's noise level sharply swelled, and there seemed to be an inclination of people's gaze toward the stairs and then the upper left section of the balcony. It reminded Maria of a Red Sox game, how the crowd would follow a pop foul to see who caught it. The attention focused on a man being seated at the balcony's railing. Maria didn't understand the fuss. It was just a man, now seated and steadfastly studying his program. But as Maria peered closer, she realized: Wait, that man was Duncan Grier. *Holy moly!* That *was* worth the buzz.

Maria seemed to remember Emmy telling her Duncan Grier was shooting a movie in town, but wow, the guy must be one hell of a dance enthusiast! This performance wasn't well advertised, and she'd always assumed the audience to be entirely composed of dancers' friends and family members. Maria began to search for her phone to text Nathan about this – he'd get a kick out of it – but just then, the lights began to dim.

The first dance performance came on; Emmy wasn't in it. The performers danced to the recorded rhythms of African drums, and though Maria was frequently annoyed when white, privileged people tried to take on tribal dances, she decided not to quibble; whatever, it was fine. The second piece was more Martha Graham-y, quite serious and heavy. The dancers were lousy. Maria's attention began to ebb. She had a pretty good angle on Duncan Grier. The lights from the stage spilled onto his section and cast blue-ish shadows across his face. Without his famous smile, he looked weary and more serious than she'd have expected.

Emmy's dance was next. From the very first beats, Maria knew she was going to like it. The music gave off a lively, happy brilliance, with techno rhythms and clapping beats, creating a sense of playfulness. At first, Emmy danced with a group that included two men and one woman, but soon she came to the center of the stage, and her dancing moved in and out of sync with the background dancers.

Maria remembered how much she loved watching her friend dance; a hidden joy pulsed out of her when she moved, always surprising Maria. *Where was that happiness when she wasn't dancing?* Tonight, the movement Emmy particularly employed – a motif Maria guessed – was one that looked like the dancers were unzipping their bodies from the neck down; it happened in a way that was fast and to the beat, yet decidedly sensual, with the dancers' bodies rolling and unrolling as they were "zipped" and "unzipped." The dancers clapped each other's hands at times to punctuate the choreography's sync with the music.

She looked to take in Duncan Grier's reaction. The splash of the theater lights spread across his face, and Maria noticed right away, how differently he watched the stage now. He was leaning against the balcony's railing, and his face radiated an uncontained pleasure. This surprised Maria. There was a distinctive pride to his expression too, almost like a father watching his child. Maria guessed a friend of his must be in the dance troupe, and she looked back and forth at the stage. She swore it looked like he was focused on Emmy.

Maria turned back to watch her friend dance. The two men now joined Emmy dancing in the stage's foreground, and it seemed this pas de trois, like most, was fueled by the tension over which man the woman would choose. Maria always found this dynamic of dance a bit contrived, how the men pulled on the woman's arm like a game a tug of war. *Please.* Emmy hadn't overdone it, yet still the stress of a pending choice was there.

She decided to see what Duncan Grier thought. Well, he wasn't smiling anymore, that was for sure. His face wore a look of intense, almost concerned, interest. Maria didn't want to stare but, gosh, *what was going on?* She fixed her body to give the impression she was focused on the stage, but tilted her head to better watch the Grier. His attention on Emmy remained anxious, until, at one point, he winced with undeniable disappointment. She looked over at the stage: *What had happened? What was wince-worthy?* There was nothing remarkable. Emmy had relegated the male dancers to the background, and everything was merely ending as it began. Maria couldn't understand what would be upsetting about that.

With the song now ended, the stage went dark, and Emmy and the dancers trotted off it. As the audience adjusted themselves in their seats, Maria looked to Duncan Grier again. Without the spill of the stage's lights, it was harder to see him, but she could tell he was leaning forward, resting his head against his hand, his eyes on the ground. Quite suddenly, he sat upright and searched the theater's seating. Maria had to restrain herself from looking around too. His hunt was fast, and it didn't seem as though he found the person he sought. Nonetheless, he stood up abruptly and made his way to the aisle. "Excuse me;" "Sorry;" "Excuse me, thanks." He flew down the stairs. Just as the lights were rising for the next dance number, he walked out the theater door.

The music for the next piece began. Maria turned toward the stage, but she wasn't watching. Her thoughts puzzled: *Was there any other explanation for what she'd seen?* She didn't think there was. Duncan Grier had come to see Emmy. And, it seemed – *it seemed* – that Duncan Grier had left, all upset like that, because of: Emmy. *Holy. Moly.*

Text message sent from Duncan to Emmy, 11:11 p.m.
I snuck into your dance tonight. You were brilliant.

Text message sent from Emmy to Duncan, 11:38 p.m.
I heard you came – everyone was talking about it. Thank you. People said you left in a hurry.

Text message sent from Duncan to Emmy, 11:42 p.m.
I didn't want to get in the way if Jack was there. Thought that could be hard to explain.

Text message sent from Emmy to Duncan, 11:42 p.m.
No Jack or Celia in attendance.

Text message sent from Duncan to Emmy, 11:44 p.m.
I'd try to see you tomorrow, but am headed to Concord. We're doing the Walden Pond scene. Shooting there all day Friday too. Last big scene.

Text message sent from Emmy to Duncan, 11:44 p.m.
Last?

Text message sent from Duncan to Emmy, 11:44 p.m.
Pretty much. Wrapping up next week.

Text message sent from Emmy to Duncan, 11:45 p.m.
When?

Text message sent from Duncan to Emmy, 11:45 p.m.
Wednesday morning.

Text message from Emmy to Duncan, 11:46 p.m.
That's very soon.

Text message from Duncan to Emmy, 11:50 p.m.
It is.

At 11:54 p.m., Emmy sat in the TV room, the ugly afghan wrapped around her; she looked at her phone's screen. When the screen would go black, she'd press the button to look at it some more. She was trying to decide if there was anything more she should say. At 12:07 a.m., she put her phone down, no reply message sent, and tried to make herself go to sleep.

Thursday, October 17: Metamorphosis

Emmy trudged up her office building stairs. She had four clients to see that day, and her first, Louisa Stanton was due in her office in five minutes. At the landing, she took in a deep inhale. She needed to ready herself to focus on other people, to ignore herself for a few hours. Usually, she was good at keeping her focus on her clients during her therapy sessions. If a thought flitted into her head about an argument with Jack or whether to pick up dry cleaning on her way home, she could easily push those distractions aside and return to giving her clients full attention. But this morning, she knew such focus would be hard. Over night, sadness had seeped into her, like ink bleeding into cloth. All she wanted was to see Duncan, to ask him questions so she could order her confusion. This yearning exerted a near constant tug on her thoughts – and she had to keep reminding herself why, rationally, she shouldn't want this. *He slept with Celia.* Her emotions rubbed uncomfortably against her good sense.

She opened the door to her office's waiting room, and flinched. Celia sat on the gray couch, thumbing at her phone. Noticing Emmy, she shot up, her voice springy and energized: "Oh, hello most marvelous Emster!"

Celia's very liveliness grated against Emmy's dull brain. "You keep popping up," she said, her voice drab.

Celia kissed Emmy on both cheeks. "Well, I've come to ask a teeny, tiny favor."

"Why am I not surprised?"

"Don't get nudgy like that. My favor, it's a fun thing!"

Emmy looked at her stepdaughter's expectant face, her overflowing exuberance. In more circumspect moments, Emmy acknowledged it wasn't Celia's fault exactly, whatever had happened with Duncan. But right now she wasn't circumspect and didn't want to be either. "Well, what's the favor? Tell me fast; I have a client coming any minute."

"Okay, okay." She smiled ingratiatingly, "I want to ask if we can have Duncan Grier over for dinner on Saturday night." She lifted her shoulders upward: "Yes?"

Emmy was about to boom out with her "No!" when Maria's door flung wide open. "There you are! Finally." Maria walked into the waiting room right to where Emmy stood. "I've been waiting all morning for you to come in." Her eyes danced as she squeezed Emmy's arm.

Emmy looked at her friend curiously. Since when did Maria bound out of her office when Emmy arrived at work? "You have? Is something wrong?"

"No, no." Maria deliberately eyed Celia, then brought her attention back to Emmy. "Just a few questions I wanted to run by you about your performance and who came to it."

Her performance? Emmy took in her friend's stance, her coy response, her smile that looked like she'd snuck gumdrops. Maria clearly was referring to Duncan. *But why would Maria assume Duncan had come to see her?* He could have been there to see anyone.

Celia lightly cleared her throat. "Well, no offense, Maria, but before you ask Emmy any questions, she has to answer

mine. You see, I want to see if we can invite my friend..."
Celia's voice sweetened with pride, "my friend, *Duncan Grier*
to dinner this Saturday."

Maria's eyes bulged. The three women stood in triangle,
and Maria looked back and forth between Emmy and Celia.
"Celia, you know Duncan Grier too?"

"Too? *Too?!*" Celia faced Maria. "Please. I'm the one who
introduced Duncan to Emmy. Duncan is *my* friend."

Emmy had also caught the implication of the word "too."
So Maria had somehow divined she and Duncan knew each
other. Emmy's skin prickled with a growing unease, and she
tried to think of a way to quickly clamp this conversation. "I
have an appointment that's about to begin," she announced,
but Maria and Celia paid her no attention.

Maria propped herself against the arm of the gray sofa.
"Celia, you have to tell me. How on earth do you know
Duncan Grier?"

Celia was so excited to answer this question, she gave a
small hop. "I swear it was the craziest moment of my life! I
went to the cabin this weekend, you know like I do sometimes. I was walking into the kitchen, all ho-hum, and there
he was, bare-chested, looking through our refrigerator."

"Bare-chested?" Maria sounded like she was drinking
delight. "Duncan Grier sure was making himself at home
at the Halperin family cabin." Maria flew a glance to Emmy,
who looked away fast. "How amazing!" She leaned toward
Celia. " But how on earth did he get there? Was he... coming over to borrow a cup of milk?"

Emmy watched the pleasure pour out of Celia as she
giggled her reply. "No, no! It was all because Duncan's manager is an old friend of Emmy's. This past weekend, the
manager asked Emmy to find Duncan a place to hide from
the paparazzi. So, Emmy came to the rescue! She offered

Duncan the cabin." Celia relayed the story with unblinking faith in it. Nevertheless, the explanation had never sounded more nonsensical. Emmy watched Maria's face as she absorbed the story's odd angles and logical holes.

Maria turned slowly to her friend. "So, Emmy, you were the one to help Duncan Grier find your family cabin."

Celia rushed to clarify. "Well, it wasn't Emmy herself. It was her manager friend. I mean, Emmy, never even spoke to Duncan before I introduced him to her the other night. Right, Ems?"

"Ah, that's right." Emmy didn't want to look at either of them as she spoke. She was now certain Maria had pieced together Duncan had come to the cabin to meet her there, and she worried with eye contact, this awareness would seep into Celia's consciousness too. All she wanted was to go into her office and close the door. "Listen, Celia," Emmy pointed to the waiting room door, "my client is going to walk in any minute. I have to get going."

"But what about dinner on Saturday?" Celia's voice screeched. "Please let's have Duncan over, please, please."

Emmy started to unlock her office door, "I'm sorry, I don't think—"

"Oh, you absolutely have to have Duncan Grier to dinner." It was Maria who interjected, her tone adamant.

Emmy spun around, stunned – What the hell was Maria doing?! She had to remind herself to stay calm, to make her words more measured than they wanted to be. "And why would that be Maria? I thought you'd agree that, actually, it wouldn't be a good idea." She felt the blood rising to her cheeks.

Maria smiled out toward Celia, her voice still playing at the pretense. "Honey, if you went to all that effort to help him last weekend, why not invite him over for a meal?"

Celia clasped her hands together. "Oh, thank you Maria for pointing that out! See, Emmy, *see*. Maria thinks we should do it. Can't we invite him? Please."

Emmy could not believe her friend was putting her in this situation. She twisted the key in the lock and strode into her private office. "I'm sure Duncan Grier has more interesting things to do this Saturday than have dinner at our house. I doubt he'd even come."

Celia followed on her heels. "Oh, he'd come. He actually has this bizarro fascination with you and Dad. He asked me like a zillion questions about you guys."

Maria came to Celia's side. "Is that right?"

This time, Maria's tone had been too suggestive, and with Celia's back now to her, Emmy flashed her eyes at her friend trying to get her to butt the hell out of her business.

Celia turned back to her, and Emmy, fast, stopped her glare. "Emmy, just think: We would be creating a memory. The night that Duncan Grier came to dinner. Come on, how is that not cool? I have his assistant's Lang's number and I can call—"

"Li—" Emmy stopped her correction just in time. She shook her head, trying to clear the muddle from it. "Listen, guys, I'm starting a session in seconds. I don't think this is the best time for this conversation.

Maria walked to where she stood. "You know, Emmy, this dinner could be just the thing to propel forward. A way to leave behind the stasis and metamorphisize."

Emmy could not believe these words were coming out of her friend's mouth. *Her presumptuous, know-it-all friend was daring to tell her what to do when she had no idea what she was talking about!*

Celia was surprised too. "Wow, Maria, you are really getting impassioned about this. Thank you! Listen to what Maria is saying. She is *so right.*"

Emmy had to work to keep her voice from showing its ire. "Certainly, Maria *thinks* she's right, but there are actually a lot of problems with her plan." She faced her friend. "There's Jack, for one. He'd hate this idea."

Celia piped up, "Oh, no, actually he doesn't. I already asked Dad, and he said he'd welcome the opportunity."

"He said that?"

"Yup. He said it could be just the thing. You see, even Dad thinks it would be cool to have a movie star to dinner." Celia leaned her head in beseechingly. "Please."

Emmy turned away from the two women who were watching her too carefully. There were no circumstances under which this dinner was a good idea. If Duncan were to come to dinner, Jack would scrutinize her every move; Celia would make her crazy; she would feel miserable having Duncan near, yet not at all close. It was a horrible, horrible idea. *So, why did she feel herself considering it?*

Maria came from behind her and put her arm on her shoulder, whispering, "All I'm saying is that before you make the safe choice, you should ask yourself if it wouldn't be better to take a risk instead."

Celia watched this interaction from a few feet away. "Wow. This conversation is definitely between two therapists. You guys are going way meta on this dinner invitation."

The sound of the front door squeaking open came from the waiting room. All three women halted and looked at Emmy's open office door as Louisa Stanton rushed in. "Oh, I'm so sorry;" Louisa stopped in her tracks. "Am I interrupting something?"

"No," Emmy said with noticeable firmness. "No, it's fine Louisa, we're just saying our goodbyes."

Celia's whole body deflated. "But Emmy, please. Please, can we?"

It should have been easy to say "No." No other answer made more sense, and it was the response they expected from her. She held her breath, waiting for that word to come to her lips. "Fine," came out instead. She looked up at the three women who faced her so expectantly. "I guess it's okay if we have Duncan to dinner."

Celia threw her arms around Emmy's shoulders. "Oh, thank you! So, so nice of you. I swear you won't regret this decision!"

Emmy wasn't so sure. She shooed off Celia's affection and refused to look at Maria's smug zeal. With a bark-y tone, she told everyone her session needed to start, and like that, Celia bounded out the door, Maria retreated to her office, and Emmy ushered Louisa to sit in their therapy space.

Emmy settled into her rocking chair across from Louisa, and she expected her heart to return to its routine rhythm. It did not. Louisa chattered amiably about the reasons she'd been late. Emmy nodded; she smiled warmly; she appeared to listen. In fact, she heard little. A current of apprehension zipped through her body. She tried to calm it. Louisa Stanton chatted away, and inside her brain, all Emmy heard was the repeating question: *What have I done? What have I done?* She did not know. What she did know, and it puzzled her: she was very excited to find out.

SATURDAY, OCTOBER 19:
GLUE

The doorbell rang out: *Ding Dong! Ding Dong!* Tess looked over at her mother and her eyes grew wide: "Should I get it?" Her voice lilted with excitement.

"Sure, go for it," Emmy said as breezily as she could, then quickly took a sip of red wine. As her nineteen-year old daughter rushed to answer the door, Emmy thought it a good omen that she'd successfully hidden her nerves from Tess. Her daughter was a perceptive young woman; Emmy used to tease that Tess could guess the color of people's underwear by how they walked into a room. But after a whole afternoon of cooking and chatting together, Emmy doubted Tess had any idea that Emmy's pulse was racing like raindrops.

From the hour Emmy had agreed to host the dinner, she'd known she couldn't think about the evening too carefully or she'd call off the plan. Consequently, she actively ignored any conjectures about what could happen that night. Nonetheless, anticipation ratcheted within her, as though she was being cranked slowly up a roller coaster. She tried to reassure herself; she would simply play the role of Calm Hostess. Duncan acted. She would act too. It would be fine.

She'd had some worries about Jack. That morning, when Emmy was unpacking groceries with Tess, he came in and rather pointedly announced he was looking forward to "getting to know the movie star who's so crazy about Celia." Emmy hadn't responded, she'd simply stuffed more food in the refrigerator. *Perhaps Jack was planning some strange confrontation? Nah.* Jack wouldn't seek out unnecessary drama. And he'd never make a scene in front of Tess. *No, no, it would be fine.* Emmy had always hoped Tess and Duncan could meet. Now they would. Nothing would be worse for the wear. She was simply hosting a goodbye party to an experience she still didn't know how to characterize. *That was all.* An evening to mark the closure of an experience. *Right, right.* She took another sip of wine and stirred some melting butter.

Tess called out from the hallway, "It wasn't the Grier, but—" she walked into the kitchen carrying a floral bouquet, "look at the flowers he sent!" The arrangement Tess carried was enormous, and the bouquet was particularly striking for the several branches of autumnal leaves that stood prominently amidst the flowers. "I've never seen an arrangement this big except in fancy hotels."

Emmy smirked. "Maybe he stole it from the Four Seasons."

Tess turned to her mom. "Oh, is that where he's staying?"

Perhaps this was information Emmy wasn't expected to know. "Hmm, I thought Celia said so. Anyway, what does the card say?"

Tess reported, "It says, 'Thank you for your invitation tonight.' Wow, who knew movie stars were so gallant? It's such a pretty arrangement too. Do you think he was the one to suggest all these red and yellow leaves, or was it the florist's idea?"

Emmy began to break a chocolate bar along the divided squares. "Probably just the florist."

Tess smelled the flowers. "You know, in my biology class, my professor gave a lecture about how scientifically anomalous it is that leaves get so pretty in the fall."

Emmy feigned interest as she readied to chop some the chocolate squares. "Oh, what'd he say?"

"Well, *she, she* said," Tess corrected her mother's assumption of the professor's gender, "that from an evolutionary perspective it's nonsensical that leaves get more brilliant in the fall. Of course, it makes sense they're pretty in the spring, with flowers and such. They need to attract the bees and birds to move their seeds around then. But, from biology's perspective, once an organism has procreated and safely seen its offspring off, it's basically dying. It doesn't need to look good." Tess suddenly looked over at her mom: "No offense."

Emmy smiled as she chopped the chocolate. "None taken."

Tess snuck a chocolate piece from the bowl Emmy was stirring. "But, you know, it could be leaves are happiest when they're at the end of their life. They're finally freed from all life's obligations. Maybe that's when living is sweetest."

Emmy glanced at her daughter's wry expression. "Are you trying to spin it for me so I don't feel so bad?"

Tess laughed. "A little, yes," She ran her finger around the bouquet's card again, and her voice grew dreamy. "You know, what if Duncan Grier is really falling for Celia? She's young for him, but those movie star types do that a lot." Tess' eyes lit up. "What if Duncan Grier became my brother-in-law. And your son-in law!"

Emmy feigned a smile; "Coo-coo-ca-choo Mrs. Robinson."

"What? Did you just pretend sneeze?"

Emmy was glad the allusion was lost on her young daughter. "No, no. It's nothing."

The doorbell rang out again: *Ding, Dong!*

Emmy knew it would be Duncan this time. She grabbed her wine glass. Her head started to pound. *Who had she been kidding?* She had no composure. She couldn't act.

"I'll get it." Tess called, and she ran to get the door.

Duncan was certain: "No."

"Not even once?" Tess asked earnestly.

"Nope. Never." Duncan confirmed.

"Hah! Another one." Celia sounded triumphant.

Duncan sat sandwiched between Tess and Celia, and they were playing a game to see if they could name celebrities he had *not* met. So far, they'd come up with quite a lot. He didn't travel in the same circles as the young crop of actors the two women cared about. The game had been Celia's idea. To him, it made no sense. Wouldn't it be more fun to play a game where they found out all the famous people he *did* know? There were a lot after all. But that wasn't what appealed to Celia, and so they were playing this game, the point of which as near as he could tell was to establish that he was old and un-cool. Whatever. He played in a half-engaged way. His attention was elsewhere.

He was watching Emmy at the counter, making her chocolate cakes. The smell in the kitchen was amazing – rich and deep – and even though he tried not to be obvious about it, he watched everything she did. She sipped her wine, mixed ingredients, opened the refrigerator when needed, stirred things on the stove – but she never once conversed with

Duncan and her daughters, who sat only twelve feet from her. He guessed that after their initial disastrous hello, she had decided it was best not to interact with him.

When Tess brought him into the kitchen an hour ago, Emmy appeared to be waiting for him. She walked to him, poised and serene; said a warm hello. He thought she looked especially beautiful. Her hair was down, and she was wearing a long, thin cardigan over a silky camisole; her cheeks were flushed and her eyes liquidy and luminous. At first, he stumbled over whether a handshake, a hug, or a kiss to the cheek was the most appropriate greeting for their pretended circumstances. He decided to kiss her. He leaned toward her, but as he did, he became altogether too aware of the scent on her hair, the loose neckline of her camisole, how her hand rested against his chest as she received his light peck. For a brief moment, his chest was hit with an awareness of what he was losing. He loved her. He would lose her. He wanted things to change; it had felt like they were going to; it had been so close. But, no, nothing would change. Everything would end as it began.

When he pulled back from this polite cheek kiss, it was then that Emmy's poise disintegrated. An unusual, almost zany, smile filled her face and her whole posture went slack, like she'd received the most heartfelt gift. With Tess an active audience to the moment, Duncan didn't know what to do or say. Eventually, Emmy tried to erase the smile and say normal things, but it didn't quite come off. She blushed and fumbled and then stared at Tess guiltily. Tess appeared mortified: "Mom, are you oka—" But, before Tess could even finish the question, Emmy announced: "So sorry, but I have to return to my cakes." Emmy didn't wait for either Tess or Duncan to respond. She turned and made her way to her mixing bowl.

When Ling had first told him of Celia's invitation on the drive back from Concord, his first instinct had been to say No. *Why would he return to the Halperin house after the last time had been so bloody awful?* However, as Ling was busy updating him on various other items, she received a text from Celia that made her laugh. She handed her phone to Duncan so he could read it. "I forgot to mention, please tell DG it was Emmy who asked him to come. Please don't forget to say that explicitly." Even though he recognized the text was motivated by Celia's self-interests, he doubted she was lying either. Emmy had to have endorsed the plan or the invitation would not have been extended. He told Ling to RSVP "Yes."

He figured tonight would be his last try. So far, he'd surprised himself with how easily he'd taken to the chase. Accompanying Celia to the Halperin house. Attending Emmy's dance performance. These were the kind of effortful overtures he was usually disinclined to make. Yet, in each instance – and tonight as well – he'd figured he had nothing to lose. What else would he be doing? Having dinner with Gus? Returning his calls to Kallie? Ordering a milkshake? All those options were considerably more depressing to him now than they'd been a month ago. Emmy was finally someone who understood him. A person with whom he wanted to share himself. And he was just arrogant enough to believe Emmy still might choose him in the end. He was the Grier. *Wasn't he?* This was the kind of self-important thought he'd entertain for a few moments before it would smack against another, far more vulnerable one. In the end, he was less lonely making the effort than not making it.

Now, as he stole glances at Emmy's back, the discomfort he felt reminded him of the sick feeling he experienced during very long runs. Inevitably, there would come that time when his whole body would want to stop, and the discomfort would feel pressingly urgent. His stomach, his legs, his lungs – all would unite in sending a message to his brain: Stop. But he wouldn't stop; he'd continue to clock the time or the distance he wanted. Right now, sitting in this big, open kitchen, he felt similarly. Every part of his body was telling him to get the hell out of there. But he was making himself stay still. He got the irony: everything he knew about staying he learned from running.

He wished she'd just look at him. He felt confident if Emmy simply turned around, she would at least observe the complete and utter lack of chemistry between Celia and him. In fact, earlier in the evening, when Tess made a passing reference to her understanding of him as Celia's date, his face had gone slack with surprise. His thoughts had been so exclusively about Emmy's motivation for inviting him that he had all but forgotten the stated reason for his invitation was as Celia's friend. The idea was completely preposterous and, frankly, insulting. *Why would he be the date of this silly 19-year old girl?* It was absurd. To Celia, he was a novelty act. That was all. She had no interest in who he was, only what he was. Even now, despite her apparent eagerness to have him come to dinner, her focus was divided between quizzing him about celebrities and checking her cell phone. All night, there'd been a constant dinging and whizzing as she sent and received text messages, and whatever the content of these back-and-forths, it made her extremely pleased.

In between her texting, she'd turn back to Duncan and Tess, her manic energy upsetting their easy conversation. Her flirting was outrageous and purposeful, as though she had an aim to achieve. She leaned in too close when speaking to him; she put her hand on his knee. Duncan leaned back; he removed her hand, but the presumptuousness of her behavior and its very nervous quality were tough to respond to politely. At one point, after Celia picked up a text message, she leaned over Duncan to ask Tess if she'd like to join a group of her friends later at a dance club. She whispered: "Rocco will be there." Tess looked at Duncan, unsure as to why Celia would be announcing her interest in another man in front of him. Tess mumbled that she had to study after dinner, to which Celia responded: "Oh, Tess, how grim."

The only positive to this so-far dismal evening was that Duncan was increasingly certain he hadn't slept with Celia. Some considerable doubts on this point had crept into his thoughts over the last couple days, but tonight, he was bloody fucking sure nothing had happened. In his experience, even with the most meaningless of hook-ups, there was usually some lingering sense of rapport, a fondness born from the fun physicality of sharing sex. There was none of that with Celia. No familiarity, no rapport, no fondness. He found her ridiculous, and he was having a hard time hiding his frustration with her inanity. Up until now, he'd tried to be kind to Celia, aware his possible actions at the cabin should summon his best behavior. However, as she sat beside him now, thumbing at her phone, making sassy observations one moment and outrageously flirtatious gestures the next, he could barely muster tolerance. And with the easing of his guilt came a growth in his anger. It was Celia who singularly ruined everything; it was she who stole into his bed; it was she who lied to Emmy about what happened between them. All the misery of the last week, everything that had been ruined: it was all Celia's fault. As she sat beside him now, he could barely tolerate her.

He was grateful at least that Tess was there. In this miserable last hour, he and she had eased into a relaxed camaraderie. When Celia was occupied with her cell phone, Tess and he sat chatting, splitting pistachios. This young woman had many of her mother's features without quite capturing her mother's beauty. She was smart and shy and fully uncontrived. As young as Tess was, there was a soothing perceptivity to her that was like Emmy's.

Since Celia had turned back to write another text, Duncan and Tess were released from the stupid celebrity game Celia had devised. He started to tell Tess about how his film was loosely related to a movie made thirty-five years ago. "Did you ever see that movie, *The Graduate*?" he asked her.

Tess' response was reluctant. "I hope this doesn't offend you, but I never liked that movie."

"It's kind of slow for your generation, isn't it?"

Tess shook her head, "That's not it. I like slow movies. But that movie is a trick, the way the story's told. The movie gives all the trappings of a love story, but it's not one at all."

Duncan was impressed with this insight. "I don't think most people realize that. It really is a desperation story more than a love one."

Tess smiled. "Yes, that's what I thought too. The two of them come together out of desperation, not love. You see it at the end. When they're on that bus. They sit there, and at first they seem thrilled, but it doesn't take long before they look a little horrified."

Duncan smiled back. "That's a good way to put it. They've escaped, but they have nowhere to go."

"They take this big risk, they've really burned a path behind them to get on that bus. But as they sit there, they're detached from the other and you realize: they don't love each other. And... without the love, they have – like you said – nowhere to go."

Duncan purposefully watched Emmy as he spoke. "I guess what they say is true: Love is everything." From across the kitchen, Emmy's back stiffened. She grabbed her red wine and took a long drink.

Celia put her phone aside and leaned toward the two of them. "Are you guys talking about that really old movie? About the guy who graduates from college and constantly swims around his parents' pool?"

Duncan nodded at this interesting description.

"If you ask me, that movie's super weird. The way the guy has to choose between the daughter and the mom – *yuck-o.*"

Duncan's eyes darted to Emmy. She froze and then, again, took a sip of wine.

Celia continued, "But I liked the soundtrack to the movie. It's those folksy guys that sing the songs—"

"You mean Simon and Garfunkel?" Duncan asked eagerly, hoping to pivot the direction of the conversation.

"Yeah, the one that's all *Coo-coo-ca-choo Mrs. Robinson.*"

Tess' head darted toward her sister: "Wait, what did you say?"

Celia's excitement was too peaked to answer. "And there's that super great line!" She sprung from the stool and put her hands on her hips. She wet her lips and looked at Duncan: "Would you like me to seduce you? Is that what you're trying to say?" The preposterous question hung in the air. Duncan stared at Celia and Celia stared back, nodding slightly to suggest Duncan should now respond. Duncan tried to remember he should be pleasant. "That was a nice imitation," Duncan said, his words dry and flat. He turned away from her and began to open another pistachio.

"Did you like it?" Celia shimmied her hips again and put her arms around his neck. She started her imitation again, this time making her voice more sultry: "Would you like me to—"

There was no way he could listen to Celia deliver this line again. This stupid, stupid girl was so self-involved, so insipid. He couldn't stand her, and it was beyond time to make that clear. "No!" His voice was loud and insistent, "No, Celia, I don't bloody want you—"

"*Duncan!*"

The name tore into the air. It stopped Duncan in his tracks. It was Emmy who'd called him. He turned fast to where she stood in the kitchen. Tess and Celia looked there too. Emmy's back still faced them; she was taking a long sip from her wine. Then, slowly, she turned around.

The urgency with which she'd said his name made Duncan apprehensive; he guessed his yelling at Celia must have pissed her off. But, when Emmy faced him, he saw instead: she was about to crack up. Her face looked sunburn flushed, and her eyes ripped with the merriment of trying hard not to laugh. Duncan stared at her, and when his eyes met hers, that's when it happened.

She burst out laughing, the wine flying. Crimson liquid spewed onto the counter, the floor, Duncan, Celia.

Tess was horrified: "Mom!"

Duncan thought Emmy couldn't have even heard Tess' exclamation. She was laughing too hard. She turned from facing the three of them – it was as though the sight was too funny to bear. She kept her arm braced against the counter and stood doubled over, laughing uncontrollably. Her body shook; her face was beet red. Just watching her, Duncan laughed too. He didn't understand what was happening, but it was hard to watch someone laugh this hard and not join them.

Tess walked to where her mother stood and leaned down to speak to her mother's bent frame. "Mom, are you okay?"

Emmy nodded, slowly trying to calm herself. It took a few false starts – she stopped, breathed deeply, then began giggling again. Eventually, she was able to speak. "I'm sorry, Tessie," she said breathlessly. "It's just the way you three looked at me. It was like a Renaissance painting – a story in stillness. I'd thought it would make me feel one way, but instead, it was... oh god," she tried hard not to begin laughing again, "*so funny.*" Emmy wiped the tears from her cheeks as she spoke.

Duncan could tell Tess was working to piece together what had happened before the outburst. "But you said 'Duncan!' Remember? You called *Duncan's* name before you turned around?"

"Yes." Emmy was smiling, as though recollecting the joke. "Yes, that's right, I wanted to ask for his help."

This surprised Duncan. "You want my help?"

"Yes, with the ramekins." Emmy turned to him, matter-of-factly.

"The *ramekins?*" The word sounded strange in his mouth.

"Yes, they're up there." She pointed to a cabinet above the stove. "I'm not tall enough to reach them. Could you help me?"

Emmy's request for his help rolled forth like a natural thing. The girls both looked at their mother, then at each other, trying to communicate their complete befuddlement with what was happening.

Duncan decided it would be best for the room's dynamics to keep everything moving forward. He stood up, "I can help you." He was glad to have the excuse of the ramekins, whatever the hell those were. He walked to where Emmy stood. "What do you want me to do?"

Duncan handed Emmy the last ramekin. Even if Emmy hadn't spit wine across the kitchen moments ago, he would have known she was drunk by her eyes' glassiness and her slow, slightly uneven movements. He couldn't fathom why she'd let herself become inebriated on this of all nights. But he didn't mind seeing her this way. The bitterness of the other night was gone; her protective cloak had slipped off. He realized: this might be their last chance to talk. He couldn't be relegated back to the kiddie table. "Is there something else I can do?"

Emmy smiled and handed Duncan the yellow bowl of chocolate cake batter. "Here, you can pour this cake mixture," she pushed the eight small ramekin pots over to his side of the counter, "into these."

Duncan had no experience in a kitchen. He arranged a ramekin on the counter and stood over it, tipping the mixing bowl so the chocolate poured out of it. "Up to there? Like this?"

"Perfect." The word was blanketed in reassurance.

"Perfect?" Duncan looked up skeptically. She'd gone from ignoring him to extolling him.

She nodded and smiled. "Perfect."

Emmy recognized Duncan was perplexed. It made sense; she'd acted very strangely. It was his light peck on her cheek that had un-done her plans for perfect composure. The kiss itself had been appropriately cordial, but when Duncan pulled back from kissing her, Emmy saw his famous smile lines were downturned in a wince. His expression telegraphed sadness, until, with a shake of his head, he reset himself. She'd been looking for the answer everywhere, and right then she saw it. Duncan had been telling the truth: he was in love with her.

The pleasure this insight exploded was not easy to contain. Since Tess was there, observing everything, Emmy retreated to her corner. She made herself go through the list of sensible cautions. If Duncan loved her, it shouldn't necessarily matter. He'd slept with Celia. He was leaving in four days. Nevertheless, the pleasure slipped into her sensation of herself and with it, her nervousness about the night morphed into a more expansive uneasiness. It was a sensation that reminded her of when she danced in performances – of the queasy moment when the music started and she had to will her body to move with it. She drank wine to dampen this feeling that felt like nerves. Yet, her nervousness never receded; it became part of the pleasure itself.

As she mixed her chocolate cake batter, she listened to the conversations at the kitchen island. From the banter's stop and go, the tones used, the words said, it was easy to recognize: Duncan and Tess got along; Celia and Duncan did not. Had Emmy faced the room, she doubted these dynamics could have been more crystalline. For instance, it was baldly apparent to her what was happening with Celia. Rocco, the boy for whom Celia had pined for months, had tonight asked her out dancing. This small event changed everything in her young stepdaughter's world. The interest in Duncan that yesterday burst with excitement, now was challenged by a desire longer-held and easier to make real. Celia wanted an answer: *Was Duncan interested or not?* Because if not, Celia had somewhere else she needed to be.

What Emmy recognized too was that every word Celia uttered and every gesture she made irritated Duncan deeply. She didn't have to see Duncan's face to know this. The knowledge traveled to her in the sounds, in the silences, in the ether of the room. Emmy knew it in the same way she knew Duncan was watching every move she made, every trip to the refrigerator, every stir of the bowl, every lick of chocolate stolen from the spoon. She sipped her wine, stirred the chocolate and thought about how this famous, fawned-over man sat in her kitchen sandwiched between her daughter and stepdaughter. She knew he was miserable to his marrow. He was there only for her. When she spit the wine everywhere, it was because what was sad was absurd too. Laughing was so much better than crying.

Now, Duncan was here at the counter. His body, tall and strong, stood only a foot from her. "So, I filled the *ramekins*," Duncan said as he straightened himself. He put down the empty yellow bowl on the counter. "Now what do we do?"

Emmy looked at the eight ramekins spread across the counter now filled with the thick, fragrant chocolate. "We..." she started to respond, but she liked how the word sat on her lips. "We..." She scanned the rows of ramekins and then looked up to see Duncan's cocked eyebrow staring back at her. "We have to put the raspberries in." And before Duncan could respond, Emmy leaned over the counter and pulled forward a pint of red bulby berries. She took four perfect raspberries out of the pint and held them out. "You see," she whispered; "you take a few raspberries and push them into the chocolate pots and then," Emmy demonstrated the process she had just explained, "when you've done that, sprinkle the top with just a smidge of sugar from here." She took a pinch of sugar from a bowl. "Like this." And Emmy sprinkled the sugar on top of the small chocolate pot.

"Your fingers get pretty messy," Duncan said looking at the chocolatey and sugary tips to Emmy's fingers. "Do you get to lick them?"

Emmy had expected Duncan's question to be flirtatious but when she looked up at him, there wasn't a trace of jokeyness. She couldn't help giggling. "Only at the end."

She was drunk, she knew. *Were Tess and Celia watching her?* She glanced behind her back to see. Tess was seated at the island counter but was pivoted toward Celia with her back against Emmy and Duncan. Celia, on the other hand, sat facing Tess. If Celia wished, she could easily see Duncan and Emmy; they were standing in her field of view. However, Celia appeared uninterested. She was rolled tightly into Tess' space, whispering feverishly to her sister.

Emmy turned back to face the cakes, to face Duncan. She would have to talk softly so the girls would not hear; she would have to make sure to keep her body language of the sort that a host and guest would use. She could do these things. She took a few raspberries from the pint and began to push them silently into her first chocolate pot.

"I liked meeting Tess." Duncan spoke in a whisper without looking up from his cake. "She's a lovely young woman."

"Is that what you think?"

The jesting in Emmy's voice confused him; he didn't see what was funny about this observation. "I do," he said. "She has a lot of your qualities."

"Well, that daughter," Emmy leaned across the ramekins to bring her wine-soaked whisper closer to Duncan, "*that* daughter you can't sleep with."

Duncan's eyes popped wide. "Wow." He hadn't expected that. "You really are drunk."

"A little," she admitted.

"A lot." Duncan stood for a moment assessing Emmy's joke. It wasn't the kind of crack he'd have expected Emmy to make, and it hadn't escaped his attention what lay behind the punch line. The joke rather pissed him off. "You still believe I slept with Celia?"

Duncan's voice, even in its whisper, was angry, and Emmy saw his eyes had a hardness that matched. She wondered for the hundredth time if she should reconsider her understanding about Duncan and Celia's interlude. A huge part of her wanted to disregard the matter altogether, to say that it simply didn't matter one way or another. *Yet, how foolish would she be to disregard such a transgression?* And there was little doubt in her mind that if Duncan hadn't slept with Celia, he would have clarified the matter the last time he sat in this kitchen. Emmy's tone was apologetic. "I wish I believed you."

"But you don't?"

"No."

Duncan stood, angrily considering how powerless he was to change her conclusion. "I'm certain I didn't do anything. Now I know it didn't happen."

Even in her intoxicated state, the phrasing of this statement struck Emmy; Duncan was meaning to persuade her of his strong convictions, but his words acknowledged that, previously, he'd been uncertain. Emmy opened her mouth to point this out, then realized, no, she did not want to talk about Celia or truth or betrayal; she did not.

Duncan sprinkled sugar. He knew his statement had begged a follow-up, that Emmy had opted instead for silence. He decided to ask the question he'd thought about all week. "Do you now also think that I—" He stopped; he didn't know how to ask what he wanted without using a word he rarely let himself say. "Have you reconsidered what you think happened with my—"

"No." Emmy knew what he was asking, and she made her response to his question firm and undoubting. She looked directly at Duncan as she whispered, "What happened with your father, it's entirely different. I know the truth there. I would never, ever reconsider it."

Duncan studied her face; she looked at him reassuringly and spoke with such certainty. He used a dishtowel to wipe the cake batter from his fingers. "I can't understand how you know that truth and not the other. Emmy," he tossed the towel on the counter, "why did you invite me here?"

Emmy didn't respond; she sprinkled sugar on her cake. "Is Jack going to be here?"

She took some raspberries from the pint and looked at them in her hand. "He said he'd come down later."

Her unwillingness to look at him made him lean toward her. "What are you trying to do? Twist the knife?"

Her face looked to his. "Twist the knife? What knife?"

"That you aren't leaving Jack."

"No." The idea had never occurred to her. "That's not at all why I wanted you to come here."

"Then why?"

She took the berries and smashed them into the small chocolate cake. "I can't explain it in any way that's rational."

"Try the irrational."

"I'm..." Emmy stopped; she held out her chocolate-tipped fingers. "I'm..." She didn't know if she should say it, but there was no other explanation to offer. "I'm going to miss you so much."

It wasn't the words that most surprised Duncan, though they did. It was how quickly Emmy's face lost its protectiveness. In that moment she appeared childlike with her befuddled confession and her messy fingers outstretched. "You're going to miss me?"

"Yes."

He raised his eyebrows skeptically. "That's why you want me to have dinner with your husband?"

Emmy smiled. "It doesn't make much sense, does it?"

"No. Not a lot." Despite his curt words, Duncan was not unhappy with Emmy's explanation for the invitation. "*I'm going to miss you so much.*" The words gave a pleasure they then took away. They would miss each other; they wouldn't be with each other. He had to make himself remember this last point. He pointed to Emmy's four ramekins. "Have you finally finished?" he asked.

"Finally?"

"You were quite a slowpoke, I noticed."

Emmy evaluated Duncan's expression. It had taken her a while, but she was finally letting herself feel how disappointed he was with her. It didn't feel good. "Duncan," her voice was tentative; "you think I'm going to mess everything up tonight, don't you?"

He wondered what she meant by messing up. Did she mean Tess would learn too much? Or that her marriage with Jack would be ruined? He thought he might *want* everything messed up. "It depends on what you want to make true."

The words had a challenge to them, and she couldn't figure how to respond to it. She pulled a water-filled pan from the back of the counter and started to place the chocolate pots in the pan one by one. "It's a water bath," Emmy mumbled as though Duncan had asked for an explanation. "It's so the chocolate won't burn when it cooks." She placed the last ramekin in the water, but before she moved, she stood looking at the cakes in the pan, arranged in rows of two. The wine, Duncan's words, the creeping sadness of the evening's coming ending, it was all pouring down on her. She whispered, "Will you help me figure it out?"

Duncan didn't understand. "Figure what out? How not to mess up? Or what you want to keep true?"

Her eyes went wide. "Aren't they the same thing?"

He decided not to answer the question. "I'll help you," he said. He tried to make it seem like it wasn't hard to say, like he knew what he was agreeing to. He didn't know. It was hard.

"Thank you." There was an awkward stillness between them, and she pushed the yellow bowl toward him to break it. "Did you ever take a lick?"

Dutifully, he stuck his finger in the yellow cake bowl that was now before him on the counter and took a taste. The deep chocolate flavor flooded his mouth with pleasure. "*Shit,*" he said his mouth still full; "it's *really* good."

Emmy skimmed the side of her thumb against the bowl and sucked the cake batter off it. Duncan watched with a cocked eyebrow.

"You should be careful how you do that."

"Do what?"

Duncan couldn't tell if Emmy was truly unaware or merely playing at it. "Lick your thumb like that. You might give me the wrong impression."

She grinned. "I'm not sure what impression you're getting. I like the cakes we made, that's all."

"*We* didn't make the cakes; you did."

"Not true." Emmy smacked her lips on the last bit of chocolate. "They're our cakes."

He found this silly assertion left him confused with how to respond, and Emmy beamed as she whispered: "You are a cake maker!" She liked how flummoxed he seemed by this new identity. Before he could protest it, she picked up the pan heavy with the ramekins and water bath. "Would you open the bottom oven door for me?"

He stepped ahead of Emmy and opened the lower oven door. She walked slowly toward him, carrying the heavy tray, then bent sharply at her waist to place the cakes onto the lower oven racks. This posture allowed her to lean forward to wipe the chocolate off the lips of the ramekin tops and space the dishes evenly in the water. But he wasn't thinking about the baking as he observed her round ass jutting toward his body, first moving slightly forward, then up toward his belt buckle, then down again. His head tipped as he took it in.

When the oven door closed tight – *thump!* – Emmy righted her bent stance, and Duncan was suddenly aware how he'd not disguised his gaze. He pivoted to the kitchen behind him to see if the girls had noticed. But it wasn't Tess or even Celia who'd been watching him.

It was Jack.

Jack stood at the entranceway between hallway and kitchen. He was leaning against the door jam, and Duncan remembered it was the same spot from which he'd watched Duncan grab Emmy's arm four nights before. *Had Jack planned this surveillance?* The question flashed through his head as he turned to face him. Their eyes locked, and Jack tipped his head to mimic Duncan's stance. His nostrils flared.

Duncan considered: He could try to make this a joke; he could look away; he could somehow express contrition. This was, after all, Jack's house, Jack's wife, Jack's wife's ass. Duncan was a guest. But he didn't feel apologetic in the slightest. Duncan squared his shoulders; he glared back. No words were said, but it was a specific communication nonetheless.

Jack smiled, not kindly; it was a smirk that asked Duncan to watch what he would do next. With confidence, he sauntered across the kitchen. He walked past Duncan, past the ovens, past the girls sitting at the island counter. He stopped right behind where Emmy stood.

Emmy hadn't heard her husband's footsteps until he was directly behind her. She turned with a start, and when she saw Jack so close, reflexively, leaned backward. Jack ignored Emmy's retraction from him; casually, he leaned across the counter to dip his finger into the chocolate bowls she'd been stacking. "Mmm," he said, appreciatively, licking his finger. "Thanks for making my favorite cake. You know how much I love it." Then quickly, like it was a natural thing for him to do, he leaned in to kiss Emmy' lips.

Duncan stood only feet away. There was no option but to watch this kiss happen, to see what Jack wanted him to see. It wasn't a long kiss, and Emmy hadn't expected it. Still, it was undeniable: she kissed him back. Maybe it was reflexive, this return of her husband's kiss, but then, perhaps that was Jack's point. It was instinctual for Emmy to kiss her husband. Jack never doubted she would.

A collective stillness settled in the kitchen as Jack pulled away. Celia and Tess stopped their hushed conversation, and as Jack strode across the room to the refrigerator, their eyes followed him. "Are we eating soon?" Jack asked, as he yanked open the refrigerator and pulled a beer from it.

Emmy turned outward to face the refrigerator, and the room slightly spun. To steady herself, she braced her back against the counter. She glanced at Duncan; he looked away. Her heart beat faster; she traced a finger along her lips where Jack's territorializing kiss had left its imprint. She tried to think, to think fast: *What did she want to make true?* It was the question she had to answer. Everyone looked at her as the silence grew and grew.

"Emmy, how many minutes before we eat?" Jack asked again, frustrated with her lack of response.

The answer to her own question was close, but just out of reach. For now, all she could say was: "Dinner is ready."

❧   ❧   ❧

Tess was trying to put her finger on what was amiss. She wasn't sure what she'd expected, having never had dinner with a movie star before. Perhaps it was only that no one knew how to make the right conversation for the situation. Tess looked around the long table; she supposed that could be it.

The food had already been passed. The lamb first, then the risotto cakes followed by the spinach gratin and the walnut, endive, apple salad. Everyone had dutifully made a remark or two about the deliciousness of some dish or other. Celia had spiritedly explained why the wine pairing for the meal should include both a white and red wine and had implored everyone to pour a glass of each to accompany the meal.

But after Celia's boisterous advice, a silence fell onto the dining room.

Tess scanned the candlelit table. Duncan was seated across from her, Celia to her right, her father at the head of the table, and Emmy at the foot. There was a fire in the fireplace – the first of the season – and the dimmed lighting and thick Persian carpet should have created a cozy atmosphere for the meal. Instead, the room's air was stiff.

There were only the sounds of forks hitting plates and wine being swallowed. Tess looked at her mom, hoping if she caught her eye, she'd say something. Her mother, however, seemed wholly absorbed by the task of eating her risotto cake. She was acting strangely tonight. Usually Tess loved it when her mom got tipsy; it made her playful in a way Tess adored. Tonight, though, Emmy's tipsiness was drunkenness. *She'd spit her wine out, for crying out loud.*

Earlier, Tess thought it was Duncan Grier's celebrity that was making her mom nervous and her nerves were what were motivating her to drink so much red wine. However, this explanation didn't seem right anymore. She hadn't seen much of what transpired when Duncan helped her mom with the ramekins, but from what she caught, her mom appeared comfortable in his presence. The thought had even occurred to Tess that her mom knew Duncan from some other situation. The idea was far-fetched of course. First, where could they have met? Her mom didn't exactly frequent celebrity circles. Second, why then not simply come out and say, "Yes, we've met before"? *Why would they pretend?* Well, they wouldn't of course. It made no sense; Tess gave up the notion.

Tess looked over at her half-sister thinking that perhaps Celia would step up to fill the room's swelling silence. But no, Celia had snuck her phone into the dining room with her. It was on her lap, and Celia was surreptitiously reading a text message. Tess rolled her eyes; she couldn't believe how little effort Celia was extending to make the evening comfortable for Duncan. He was her date. Remarkably, Celia seemed to have forgotten that. Now, she was all about Rocco, Rocco, Rocco. It was hard for Tess to watch. She found her half-sister pathetic in her moments of boy mania, her neediness horribly compulsive and dysfunctional. It was their father's fault, or at least that's what Tess believed. Because of what he'd done – his big mistake that hung over everything – Celia grew up knowing hers was the family not chosen, she the kid not selected. Now, Celia was always desperate to prove she could be the one.

Tess glanced across the table at the movie star who sat across from her. She'd avoided looking at him until then, too embarrassed by the awkward reception her family was providing. Yet, Duncan Grier didn't appear ruffled by the room's cacophonous quiet. His face had the same sad resignation as when he'd first walked into the house. He'd been such a good sport so far. He didn't seem to mind when her mom was rude to him in the beginning of the evening or when she spit wine on him. Still, his patience had to be wearing thin. Tess wondered why he'd come. It couldn't be because of Celia. It was obvious she drove him crazy. *So, why?* It was a puzzle. Poor guy; she had to guess he was used to being the center of attention, and here, her family was all but ignoring his existence.

Tess tried to think of a question she could ask. *Oh, she had something.* She hurried to swallow her bite so she could ask Duncan about superhero movies, but before she was able to begin her question, she heard her father clear his throat and his gravely sound bounced off the walls.

"Duncan, it's nice you made space in your busy schedule to have dinner with us tonight. From the way I understand it, you are working very hard right now."

It was a stiff way to begin a conversation, but still better than silence. "Well, thank you for having me here." Duncan's tone matched the cordiality. "It's been awhile since I've had home cooking."

Her father held his fork outward. "And here I thought all you people have chefs specially concocting things for you? Food with no carbs, no fat, no anything good."

Duncan smiled weakly. "Not all *us people* have that. I actually was told to gain ten pounds for the role I'm playing now."

"Is that right?"

"Yes. It's nice for a change, to indulge when I want."

"Ah, I would have thought you indulged all the time."

Tess looked up the table at her Dad, trying to alert his clueless self that this last remark hadn't sounded nice. *God, Dad was daft.* But her father had moved on. "What about when you and Celia were at the cabin?" Her father turned to

Celia, "Cece, did you cook for Duncan when you guys were up there together?"

It took Celia a second to respond, and Tess guessed it was their father's overly-friendly tone that was disorienting her. "Um, no. We didn't have time for cooking."

"What?" Her dad was too surprised. "You didn't make Duncan your egg scramble surprise? I thought you'd have made him a nice breakfast in bed."

The word "bed" made everyone look up. Tess could not imagine why her father would allude to Celia and Duncan being in bed together. Tess saw Duncan assess her father carefully. He spoke firmly: "There was no egg scramble surprise."

"Oh, that's too bad. Maybe next time, right?"

Tess flipped to look at her mom, hoping that she would interject. Her mom held her fork up like an explanation point, but there were no words, only stupefaction.

From the other end of the table, Jack boomed again, "Perhaps the two of you can get away again. You guys are welcome to use the cabin if you'd like."

"No, Jack." It was obvious this line of questioning was irritating Duncan, and Tess saw him work to collect a more courteous response. "I'm going back to L.A. early next week."

"Really? That soon? Emmy told me – she told me a lot about you – that you had another week in Boston."

Duncan began to turn to her mom, but, noticeably, he stopped himself. "The schedule changed. I will leave on Wednesday."

"Wednesday? That's only four days from now. And L.A. is so far." He paused, then his face sprung as though he'd just had an idea. "Cece, you should visit Duncan in L.A. Maybe you could go out for a weekend of fun there."

Tess could tell Celia was confounded by her father's persistence on this subject. "Daddy, I'm not going to L.A. It's not like that. Really, it's just that Duncan came to dinner tonight. That's all. Why are you asking these kinds of questions? It's really weird. You should stop. I mean, talk about something else. Really."

Jack chuckled; he lifted his hands to show his blamelessness. "Just trying to make conversation." He gave the table a look of exaggerated befuddlement before taking a drink from his wine glass.

What the hell was her Dad doing? The questions weren't rude exactly. In fact, they were too chipper. The cheerfulness was itself odd, but what was more perplexing was how *purposeful* it was. Her father wasn't naturally inclined to act this way, and he'd intentionally ignored both Duncan and Celia's discomfort to ask these awkward questions. *Why would he do that?*

From Tess' left, her mom's voice hurried to change the subject, "Duncan, are you looking forward to going home?"

This would seem like an easy question, but Tess swore she saw Duncan flinch. He cut a bite of lamb. "Home? No, there's no home. I have a house." His words had an edge Tess wouldn't have expected. "I'm not eager to get back to it either." He took his bite.

Celia perked up, "I bet it's a nice house. Is it in Beverly Hills?"

With the bite on one side of his mouth Duncan answered: "No. Pacific Palisades. In the hills."

"Does it have a pool?" Celia asked enthusiastically.

"Yes." He swallowed. "A nice pool. By any objective standards, it's a great house."

Emmy asked, "You don't feel it's a home?"

"No, it's just a place." Duncan looked at Emmy, then away. He took a sip of water.

Despite Duncan's curtness, her mother seemed to take his remark to heart. She repeated his words, "Just a place. It's funny you say that because I've been thinking about houses and spaces lately. Trying to figure out why some feel cozy, others not. It's hard to pinpoint. I hadn't thought of it with those words before: house versus home. Maybe that's it. Maybe that's what I've been noticing too."

Tess could see that Duncan was aware of how drunk Emmy was. He seemed to want to help her. "It's probably just that a house needs to be shared for it to feel like a home. If someone is in your house, then it probably feels like a home."

"No." Emmy smiled, shaking her head. "No, I don't think that's it. A place can feel horribly lonely even when it's shared. Even scary." Her mother took another sip of wine.

"Are you talking about *this* house?" The question flew from down the table.

Emmy finished swallowing her wine with a gulp. "I guess I am. This house has so many memories in it. But sometimes, it feels empty without our children in it. I mean, don't you sometimes feel something's *missing* here? Don't you feel that ever?"

"No. No, I don't feel that. Ever." Tess noticed her father's voice had none of his forced cheerfulness when speaking to her mother. He was as openly irritated with her as usual. "What could you possibly think is missing in this house? And *scary*? What the hell is scary here?"

"Okay, guys," Celia held her palms outward; "please don't do this now. No freakouts in front of Duncan. Besides, the little mysterioso you're arguing over, it's not so complex. *Love* makes a house a home. Ta-da! I'd like to take some credit for this profundity, but the insight's been embroidered on, like, a zillion pincushions."

Tess saw her father's face register displeasure when Celia said the word "love," but he quickly resumed his forced geniality, making himself chuckle slightly. "So, Duncan, a zillion pincushions think it's love that makes a home. Is that what's missing at your house? Is it the love?"

Tess winced. *Oh god. Why would her father ask that?* She looked to see how Duncan would respond. He chuckled too, and his laugh felt as stiff and fake as her father's, almost mimicry. "Probably Jack. Probably." He put his hands on the table. "What about your house Jack? Is that what's missing in your house too? The *love?*"

Tess' mouth swung open. That was an incredibly hostile exchange. She looked back and forth at the two men, who sat glaring at one another, their fake smiles now vanished. Her mind spun: *Why would her father and Duncan dislike each other? They didn't even know each other!* She had no time to consider the possibilities. What she had to do – what felt like a reflex – was to keep her father from answering. "Duncan," her voice creaked as she rushed to speak for the first time since dinner began, "have you ever," she swallowed, "played a superhero?"

"Yes, yes," Emmy rushed to add. "That's just what I... what I was wondering too."

From across the table, Duncan blinked at the sudden shift in conversational subject and tone. Tess felt a blush prickle her cheeks. Earlier, when she'd tried to come up with a conversation starter, this had been her question, and now, in her desire to shift the subject, it was all she could think to say.

"A superhero?" Duncan paused. "No, I've never played a superhero." He smiled across the table to her; he could tell she was trying to help the situation out. "I do like superhero movies though. Do you like them?"

"I do," Tess answered, and was striving to consider what more she could say on the topic when Celia's voice rung out from beside her.

"Please tell me you're kidding. Superheroes are the worst."

Duncan arched one eyebrow. "What don't you like about superheroes, Celia? I thought they were, by definition, super."

"Well." Just from this one word, Tess could tell Celia was about to deliver one of her wackadoodle theories. "We were just talking about superheroes in my class on the constructs of contemporary symbolism, and you know, the symbolism behind superheroes is actually horribly demoralizing and, ironically, quite harmful to children. In my class, some students said they thought it was time for superheroes to be outlawed."

"Outlawed?" Duncan was trying not to laugh. "They want to make superheroes *against the law?*"

"Well, at least for children. I mean, they're so bad for kids. Superheroes run around, showing off their superbodies and are all like: 'Look at me; my body is *impervious;* it can deflect bullets; it can *fly!*' But how do you think kids feel when they hear that?"

"Like arresting them?"

Celia didn't laugh, but Tess couldn't keep from giggling. This was good, she thought, maybe they'd make it through dinner by simply steering the conversation away from her father. *They could talk about superheroes all night.* Tess pivoted to her sister beside her. "You do realize that superheroes don't really exist?"

"Well, of course, they don't. Please. But on TV and movies, they're everywhere." Celia was huffy. "You guys can laugh at me, but while the poor, poor children are watching super-duper man, what message are they internalizing? Shame. Shame that their sweet little bodies aren't impervious too. It's just awful."

Tess thought that even by Celia's standards, she was laying it on a bit thick. "The *poor, poor children?* You don't really believe that, do you?"

"Hmm." Celia took a quick sip of wine. "I think I do."

Duncan smiled at Tess. "Celia, don't you think it's possible superhero stories are actually stories about regular-ness? I mean, isn't it pretty normal for people to want to believe in their better selves? That's what superhero movies are really about, right? The desire to make a better version of yourself."

Tess realized she must have been looking admiringly at Duncan as he spoke because he winked at her. That was cool, she thought. Duncan Grier and she were on the same side of the argument, just like they'd been when they were talking about *The Graduate.* He was smart, Tess thought. She was thinking these things and waiting for Celia to swallow and continue her pontifications when she heard her father laugh.

Duncan pivoted toward him. "Is something funny, Jack?"

Tess felt her whole body stiffen as she watched her father gather himself to respond. "Superhero movies are about selling sugary soda and crappy plastic toys. They don't have grand meanings."

Duncan had a forkful of salad but he put it down. "Just because a movie sells a soda, that doesn't negate its story. The story is still told; it still has meaning."

"And you think these movies' meanings are that people can transform themselves?"

Tess could tell that Duncan was trying to stay pleasant. "Sure, at least part of the meaning. That's why people love those stories. They like seeing that a regular guy can be transformed into something so much better."

"But people don't transform, do they? Those movies just tell lies."

Duncan's face registered an exaggerated surprise: "Lies? Do you really think *lies*? People can't fly, but they do change. Or do you believe people are incapable of making themselves better?"

Her father leaned forward in his chair. "Well, Duncan. People might make small changes – they can quit smoking or lose weight, stuff like that. But transform? Adults? No, I don't think there's a lot of transformation happening for fully-grown people. We are who we are." He pointed his knife at Duncan. "Think about a man who's, say, a *slacker*. Does he suddenly become reliable? A man who's untrustworthy his whole life, can he become honorable overnight?" Jack waved the knife back and forth. "No. At our age, our lives are made; we aren't making them. Any 40-year old who believes he can morph into something else," Jack smiled a fake smile, "is deluding himself."

Duncan was fast: "You think you're as good as you'll get?"

Her father's eyes flared. "I don't pretend otherwise."

"No, you're not one for pretending."

From Tess' other side, her mom spoke out: "Would anyone like more salad?"

But silence was the only response. Tess could feel her pulse pounding in her temples. *What the hell was going on?* Her dad and Duncan glowered at each other when they spoke. Their words had staccato pointedness. They said each other's names too frequently and with snide disparagement. *What could possibly make them dislike each other so greatly?* Her father was supportive of Celia and Duncan's trip to the cabin, so Celia wasn't the source of their animosity. Tess couldn't understand. She was scared to move. Her father leaned toward Duncan again. *Oh, no.*

"You, on the other hand, Duncan, you *do* like pretending. Pretending is your job, isn't it?"

"My job is storytelling, yes, and part of that is pretending, if you want to call it that."

"In that space movie of yours, I remember how you zoomed around in your space suit and *blasted* those bad guys, and then fought with those ugly, ugly space aliens." Her father's smile was close to a sneer. "Tell me: did you feel brave when you pretend killed them?"

Tess gasped. She searched for a way to intervene when her mother spoke up.

"I loved that movie," Emmy said. Everyone turned to look her. "At the end of *Final Frontier*, when Duncan killed that horrible, disgusting alien, that was such a fantastic moment. Everyone loved it. I did."

Usually her mom knew how to right conversational awkwardness, but just now, it hadn't worked. Her praise was too enthusiastic, not neutral enough. *Shit, she wished her mother wasn't drunk.*

"I'm glad you liked the movie." Duncan said. From the speed with which he spoke, Tess could tell he was also trying to distract from Emmy's freeness. "It feels like a long time ago that the movie was—"

"And I think you're a good storyteller," Emmy interrupted, smiling broadly. Her tone was almost flirtatious. Tess wished her mother would *stop*.

"Well, thank you," Duncan said warily.

"Stories are very important, or at least that's what I think. It doesn't matter if they're about superheroes or space aliens or Shakespeare, they're... essential."

"Is that right Emmy?" Jack's voice did not try to disguise his scorn for her idea. "Stories about space aliens are essential? Why, I'm just curious, why would that be?"

"Well." Her mother looked directly at her father, then paused as though she was readying to say something substantial. In this brief conversational stillness, Tess made a fervent wish her mom wouldn't say something stupid. *Please, please.* Emmy started slowly: "I think stories about space aliens – just like any story – they provide a trip. And with any trip, you learn a lot."

"So, you're saying space aliens teach you things?"

Emmy nodded, and Tess thought she could see her mother sobering up right in front of her eyes. "Most knowledge comes to you from the outside in. You're handed facts; you learn them. But with stories, the learning happens the other way around. You feel it in your body first. It's emotional before it's mental. It's a different way of knowing something; it's a different truth. But just as real." Emmy regarded her husband from down the table. "Do you see what I mean, Jack?"

Jack met her gaze, then demonstratively, he began to slowly clap his hands. *Clap. Clap. Clap.* The sound and the insult it meant to give bounced off the dining room walls. "That was very moving. Actually I'm surprised you aren't already crying over your poignant profundity."

"Dad!" Tess hated it when her father was mean like that.

"It's okay, Tessie." Her father exaggerated his abashment, "I'm just impressed your mom has thought so much about this topic. I hadn't known she put such effort into thinking about *stories*."

Emmy sat up straighter. "Now you know."

He leaned into the table. "I'm just curious: why are you thinking about stories? Because you want to defend playing pretend for a living?" Tess wasn't sure what her dad was asking, but her mom seemed to know; she answered quickly.

"No, Jack. That's unnecessary to defend. It's because my work has to do with stories."

"Your work?"

"Yes, of course." Her mother smiled tightly. "There's storytelling in therapy too. In fact, some people talk about therapy as the process of organizing the stories of yourself. They say therapy is about deciding which stories to move front and center and which ones to push back."

"Is that right?"

"Yes," Emmy tried to laugh. "It's an interesting process."

"Is that what you thought Duncan?" Jack's words clipped.

"Excuse me?" Duncan looked at Jack, confused.

"In therapy? Did you do storytelling?"

Tess saw Duncan's eyes flash. "I'm not sure I understand," he said with purposeful restraint.

"Really?" Her father shook his head; "I thought you would." Quickly, Jack turned to face her mom, his voice growing noticeably louder. "Emmy, here's what you seem to have missed about stories. Not all make-believe is good. Storytelling can also be *lying*." Her father leaned his head to the side to indicate Duncan. "When a man tells you he's one thing, but that's not who he is, that man is not a storyteller. That man is a *liar*."

Tess' eyes darted from her father to her mother to Duncan. *What was her father talking about? Why did he want her mom to think Duncan was lying?* It didn't make any sense, unless... It had to be that her dad thought her mom knew Duncan. *Yes, they had to know each other. None of this made sense unless they knew each other.* Her dad had asked Duncan about therapy. *Had Duncan done therapy with her mother?* That must be it. The pieces of information popped inside her head, like kernels on a hot pan.

Celia nervously laughed. "God, this conversation is really, really weird. Please, let's talk about religion or politics or favorite sex positions. Anything would be better than whatever it is you guys are talking about now!"

Tess wondered: *Did Celia see it too? Was she starting to understand too?* She studied her half-sister. No. No, Celia didn't look shocked, only annoyed. Tess noticed something else too: the cellphone that Celia had hidden on her lap throughout dinner was now lit up. Tess guessed Celia had just checked a text message or sent one. Maybe this was why Celia wasn't connecting the dots. Right away, Tess realized it would be better if it stayed that way.

Beside her, Emmy spoke stiffly, "Celia is right. There have to be more fun topics of conversation." She set her eyes directly on Duncan, and her voice had a crafted composure to it. "Duncan, do you have any interesting projects coming up?"

Before Duncan could respond, Celia exclaimed: "Oh, I know. You should tell them about the film you were describing to me when we were at the cabin. The one where you're, like, having to research the tensions in contemporary marriage. You should explain—" Celia stopped abruptly. Her phone began to vibrate on her lap. It wasn't a loud sound but its distinctively digital quality nonetheless stood out in the candlelit quiet of the dining room.

Jack's voice snapped: "Celia, did you bring your phone into the dining room?"

Celia didn't answer his perturbed question; she was more concerned with looking to see who was calling. "Don't hate me," she hurriedly pushed her chair from the table, "but I have to take this call!" She made a face of exaggerated contrition first to her father and then Emmy. "So, so sorry!"

Before her father had a chance to protest further, Celia was gone from the room, her retreating voice betraying the urgent matter she had to address. "Hello? Rocco? Hi! No, no, it's fine, no worries." Celia's voice slowly retreated with her footsteps, "Yes, I was thinking that too. The Downtown Crossing T is probably the one to meet at and then we can go..."

As Celia's voice gradually trailed off, Tess looked around at the people who still sat at the table. It was only a small adjustment to the table that Celia's departure provided; there had been five, now four. Nevertheless, there was a palpable increase in the tension of the current configuration. Tess didn't think she was the only one to feel it. Each person sat as though scared to move.

Tess picked her napkin from her lap and laid it atop her mostly empty plate. *What reason was there to stay? Shouldn't they all want to go?* She turned to her mother, "Mom, thank you for this—"

Her father's voice broke into hers and stampeded ahead: "Duncan, I want to hear about this research you're doing. Celia said it was research into the *tensions of contemporary marriage.*"

Duncan lifted his head as though he'd been challenged. "Yes, that's right." Tess studied the two men. They wanted to see this out; they wanted to *fight.*

"Have you ever been married Duncan?"

"No, Jack I have not." His eyes went straight to her father's.

"And so your 'research' is asking people like Celia to help you understand it?"

"She had interesting things to say about some marriages she knows. Your marriage, in fact."

"Oh, was that your pillow talk? Asking her about Emmy and me? You sleep with girls, then ask them about their parents' marriages. That's some research method you got there."

A look of disgust washed Duncan's face; his words hissed, "You *know* I didn't sleep with Celia."

Tess's eyes bugged at this remark. *Really?* Hadn't it been established that he had? *Was Duncan lying?* He didn't seem like he was.

Her father laughed haughtily. "Is that the story you tell? I notice it's conveniently told when Celia is no longer in the room. Did you notice that too Emmy, or were you too wrapped up in the rhapsody of Duncan's storytelling?"

"Please stop, Jack." Her mother sounded anguished, "This is making everything worse."

"*I'm* making it worse?" Jack fumed, "Oh, that's rich. You see the irony there, don't you?" Jack faced Duncan, his tone no longer disguising its anger. "What did Celia tell you, Duncan? Did she tell you things about me and Emmy?"

Tess cringed; she didn't see how this question could be answered without exploding the situation. She held her breath; she waited for Duncan to answer, but to her surprise, he said nothing. With his eyebrows knitted and his gaze downturned, he looked to be considering his response. When Duncan lifted his head, his voice was much calmer than it had been moments before. "Celia told me some things, yes. But you're right; she's never been married, and she's young. Celia isn't the right person to ask about marriage. You are though. You're an expert."

Tess didn't understand; the argument had been about to burst from all the pretenses that boxed it in all night. Yet, Duncan's latest question only shoved the tension back in the box.

Her father picked up his wine glass but didn't take a drink. "Is that your thinking now? That I'm an expert?"

"Yes. You're a married man, and it's clear you have opinions. Obviously, you're the man I should ask, the man who can give me insights for this film's role. So, tell me, if you could, what's the secret to your marriage's *success?*"

Tess looked at Duncan closely. His sarcasm was clear, but his intentions less so. *What was he trying to do?*

She'd expected a speedy insult from her father, but to her surprise, Jack also let the question sit. He put his wine glass neatly next to his plate; he pushed his chair back slightly. "The thing you need to know about marriage is that it endures."

"It endures?"

"Yes."

"Life's little obstacles – those annoying irritations that show up unexpectedly – marriage endures through those."

"And what is the objective of this endurance?"

Jack chuckled snidely. "Endurance *is* the objective."

"There's no other?" Duncan waited. "What about love?"

Jack scoffed, shaking his head. "I can see what you're trying to do here. You want me to look bad because I'm not getting all pretty and poetic, because I won't read from your fairy tale. I've been married twenty-two years; marriage isn't a lofty story to me. I won't apologize for that. You see, Duncan, marriage isn't lyrical. It's practical. It's glue. Marriage holds everything together. All the decisions. All the stuff of life, the logistics, the memories, the pieces of yourself. Marriage holds those in place."

Jack shifted in his seat and continued. "You have your stories, Duncan, but I have my principles. When Emmy came to me when I was twenty-two, marriage wasn't what I wanted for my life right then, I'm not going to lie. I married her anyway. We made our family safe and strong. That's what principles are. Doing what you have to do, what you should do. A principle, it isn't slippery like your stories." Jack's voice lowered. "If it's a principle you do it even when you don't want to." He paused. "You stick it out, stick like glue."

Tess noticed Duncan kept his face blank as her father spoke. Even when it was clear her father was done, Duncan still didn't respond. Instead, he turned to Emmy; he looked at her. Emmy would not look back. Tess felt sure her mom had to be aware of how carefully Duncan was regarding her, but her eyes stuck to her plate.

Duncan leaned in toward Emmy. He bent so deeply his chest touched the table and he stretched his arm so his hand grazed Emmy's hand. Tess felt her eyes go wide as she realized what he was about to do. "Emmy," Duncan's voice was low and serious. "What do you think? What do you think of what Jack said?"

Tess felt her heart thud, thud, thud against her chest. *Why was Duncan asking the question like that?*

Her father responded fast, before her mom had a chance. "Emmy thinks what I think, that's what she thinks. Emmy, explain that to Duncan."

There was quiet. Duncan's question, her father's imploration, they required a response. Emmy sat, pushing a few stray pieces of risotto rice along the side of her now empty plate, and the silence ached with the heaviness of its load. "Marriage is a glue, yes Jack. But I think—" her voice creaked, "I think sometimes it keeps us stuck."

Tess saw the pinch of disappointment register in her father's eyes. "Marriage attaches you is what Emmy is saying. It gives you a sense of security is what she means."

Duncan snapped back: "That's not what Emmy's saying."

Tess gaped at the man across from her. It wasn't the words alone; it was the proprietary tone in which Duncan spoke them. Suddenly, all the other explanations were used up. There was only one left, and it didn't make sense exactly, but that didn't mean it wasn't true. Her father and Duncan Grier were fighting over her mother. Duncan wanted to take her mother from her father.

The inescapable meaning of Duncan's words was not lost on Jack either. He pushed back his chair, bolting up. His storm clouds thundered down. "You don't know Emmy! You don't know *anything!*" His face contorted with disgust: "You snort coke; you sleep with—" he spit, "*girls*. You have no principles. You are a worthless man."

Duncan stood too, shouting back: "You're wrong, Jack. You have no idea who I am! I am a good man, better than you."

"You think you're better than me?" Her father jerked his hand and pointed to the dining room's opening. "Get out of my house!"

Emmy stood now too. "Jack, you can't do that."

Jack faced her. "I can't? I can! It's my house! I want him out of here. And you do too. You know he lies. You said it yourself." Jack whipped himself toward Duncan. "Three days ago Emmy told me she thought you were a no good liar. Selfish. A jerk. That's what she said."

Duncan turned to face Emmy. Tess was sure Duncan could tell: her father wasn't lying. Emmy had said those things about Duncan.

"You think you have everyone fooled, but Emmy sees." Jack faced Emmy again: "Just say to him now what you told me then!" His voice boomed: "*Just say it to his face!*"

"No." Her mother's word came short and hard.

Jack shouted, appalled: "*No?*"

Her mother kept her head level, her voice clear. "I don't believe it Jack. I don't believe it, and I can't say it."

"You believed it a few days ago."

Her mother shook her head, and now her face began to crumple. "I didn't. I didn't believe it then. I only said it because I was confused. Duncan's not bad or selfish. He's a good man."

"Emmy, I am your husband, and I want you to say to Duncan what you said before." Her dad was meaning to be imploring, but he sounded frightened too.

The tears started to fall from her mother's eyes: "No."

Tess realized that no one seemed to remember she was seeing all of this. And as intimately as the action before her affected her life, she also watched it with some detachment. She noticed, for instance, that Duncan was standing square in between her parents. She kept wishing her father would move closer to her mother, who was now crying openly. *Walk to her,* Tess found herself urging her father in her head. But she knew he wouldn't. He only made his voice more imploring. "If you say what I ask, nothing has to change."

Emmy wiped her cheeks and looked at her husband directly: "I won't say it."

Her father leaned toward her mother. "You can't take this decision back. Do you see that? Do you see what you're doing right now?"

Her eyes spilled big teardrops down her cheeks; her voice wailed: "I do. I do."

Jack looked around the table in disbelief. His hand went to his forehead, then slowly, he began to walk out of the room. At the door, he turned back, and when Tess saw the fury on his face, she braced for the verbal slap she knew was coming. His eyes fixed on Emmy; his tone sliced the air: "I never wanted you. You know that, don't you? Never." He roared: "*Never!*" The word hovered in the air as Jack stormed out of the room.

Though Tess sat solidly on her chair, the room spun. She pushed her chair back from the table. She had to leave.

Her mother turned to her. "Tess, I'm so sorry." Her words were thick with tears, "Let me explain it to you." She began to walk to where Tess was seated.

Tess held her hand up to halt her; she shook her head back and forth. "Not now." Tess didn't want to hear an explanation. No explanation would matter. She didn't care who was right or wrong. She didn't care how Duncan was involved or why it had started. She didn't care that her throat was tight or that her lip trembled. No, what mattered was it was over.

It was all over.

Duncan's body felt as though he'd emerged from a physical fight. The t-shirt underneath his sweater was wet with sweat and stuck clammily to his skin; his arms were lank, his knees weak. Standing, he leaned forward against his chair's back for support. The candles in the table's center had burned to their nubs; their light danced skittishly.

Emmy and he were the only people left in the dining room. She stood only five feet from him, so close he could touch her. He didn't. He waited. Her tear-wet face seemed to be studying the stain-spotted tablecloth, the dirty dishes. Slowly, she began to move around the table, picking up plates. First, Tess's plate, then Celia's, then Jack's. She wasn't crying anymore; her face was dazed. As she approached his spot, she stopped. From the stilled expression on her face, he guessed she was replaying the fight in her head. Maybe she could still hear the echo of the voices bouncing off the walls. Though the flickering candles washed her face in shadowy pulses, her eyes did not flutter; they were wide and worried as though the more Emmy thought, the more scared she became. He waited for her to look at him. It seemed there would be a lot to say.

In her stillness, Emmy could sense Duncan's relief, even exultation, over what had happened. Those weren't her feelings. Her head was full of fire; her body drilled with alarm. Her marriage had ended. She'd ended it. She needed to be alone in her thoughts. They were muddled. Lost. *She was lost. What had she just lost?* She tried to catalog it. Her husband. Her intact family. Her house. Her name. Everything had changed. She'd wanted things to be different, she reminded herself. She'd wanted to end her marriage. She knew that, she did. But what she'd just let loose was a lot. Everything. Her history. Herself.

There was such hostility still in the air. She'd always assumed that if she and Jack ended their marriage, they'd do it carefully, with a composed respect for all they'd shared. Instead, what had occurred in this dining room was messy and mean. Awful. She'd made it happen this way. Maria's talk of "metamorphosis" had allowed her to pretend it was reasonable to see this situation play out. It wasn't reasonable. She'd hurt her husband. Her daughter. Probably Duncan too.

She looked to where he stood. "You acted like our therapist." Her voice was breathy and wobbly. "The way you asked Jack first about marriage, then me. It was like you were counseling us."

He studied her. Her eyes were coming out of her daze. "You asked for my help; I wanted to give it."

Putting down the stack of plates, she took the step to where he stood and took his hands in hers. "You did help me, Duncan. Thank you for doing that." She squeezed his hands tight, and her face stretched with emotion. "But I think... I think you should go now."

He blinked; it wasn't what he'd expected her to say. "Okay. Right. I can leave."

"I'm sorry." She wanted to explain more, but she knew Duncan wouldn't want to hear her explanation. She wanted to find Jack. She had to have him understand she'd never meant to hurt him or humiliate him. There had to be a different ending to their marriage than the one that had just transpired here. There had to be.

Duncan wouldn't comprehend her worry. After all, Jack had said he'd never wanted her. *Why rush to apologize to a man who said that?* That's what Duncan would ask. But, Emmy knew her husband. His cutting words hadn't traumatized her – or not so very much. In that moment, Jack wished he'd never wanted her. He wished he could be saved from the humiliation and grief and grave disappointment Emmy was handing him. She didn't wish for different things.

Duncan was waiting for Emmy to say more, and when she didn't, he realized there was nothing to do but go. "I... I left my jacket in the kitchen." He stumbled slightly as he made his way out of the dining room, down the carpeted, quiet hall and into the bright whiteness of the kitchen. Emmy's footsteps stayed just behind him, not beside him, and as they entered the kitchen, there on the island, scattered amongst pistachio shells, sat the tray of ramekins with the un-eaten chocolate cakes. He guessed Tess was the one who'd saved the cakes from burning, and the whole kitchen was thick with the smell of baked chocolate. Duncan wondered who would eat the cakes now. *Would Jack?* Duncan's suede jacket hung on the back of the bar stool; he put it on. Emmy shifted on her feet, her usually

serene energy usurped by a fidgety anxiety. "I don't mean
to be keeping you," he said, as he pushed his arm through
the sleeve.

"You're not. Not at all." Yet, she doubted her words
disguised her impatience. She had such discomfort in her
chest, and it reminded her of a night, long ago, when she
and Jack tried to sleep train Marc, then just eight months
old. Marc had screamed and screamed, but Jack had insisted
Emmy couldn't go to him. Now, it was Jack she wanted to
rush to soothe, and though her husband was hardly infan-
tile, she knew she'd wounded him, that it was her fault that
he was in pain. He had to know – *she had to tell him* – that she
never wanted their family, their beautiful, wonderful family,
to fall apart like this.

Duncan took a few short steps toward the hallway, then
stopped. He had the sensation he was leaving something
behind. He patted his jacket. *No, he had everything he'd come
with.*

Emmy grabbed his arm, leaning into him. "Duncan, I'll
talk with you about all of this, I will, but right now—"

"You have to go to Jack."

She nodded. "I can call or text you tomorr—"

"Sure; fine." He made himself configure a smile, though
he guessed the effect conveyed effort rather than ease. "You
should go." He waved his hand toward the opening on the
other side of the kitchen.

"I can walk you to the door—"

"No, don't."

Emmy heard how Duncan's voice curdled, but right
then her need to console Jack was too great to attend to
Duncan's hurt too. She leaned to kiss Duncan's cheek, her
cheek's warmth touching lightly against his. "Thank you,"
she whispered.

This small peck on his cheek reminded him of the night's earlier kiss, and suddenly he wondered whether anything had changed. "Goodnight Emmy." His words were stiff, but before they fully thinned into the air, she was walking fast down the hall. He heard her turn a corner, her pace quickening. By the time her footsteps were overhead on the staircase, she was in a full-out run.

He plodded out of the kitchen, trying to remember the way out. Just as his hand touched the front door's knob, a voice came from behind him. "How do you know my mother?"

He turned; there was Tess standing in her socks at the edge of the living room.

Given everything that had happened that night, her tone was remarkable for its lack of rancor, and this made it impossible for him not to answer her. "She was my therapist," Duncan said, hoping this would explain enough.

"She's not supposed to be involved with her patients."

Duncan shrugged. "Well, she's not really."

"That's not the truth." The statement wasn't accusatory, only certain.

Duncan wasn't sure what to say. "Nothing inappropriate happened Tess."

"Did you fall in love with her? Did she fall in love with you?"

The questions were uncomfortably direct, like a finger pushing on a bruise. "I don't know." He couldn't decide whether it should be his role to offer honesty or reassurance. "Everything will be all right with your parents. Your mother's upstairs now, talking with your dad. Maybe they'll… make up." He stammered on these last words as he wondered if that could happen. Tess' head tipped, and Duncan recognized the gesture as one of Emmy's. He couldn't help himself: "What are you thinking?"

She spoke slowly, "I'm trying to decide if you believe what you just said. I don't. My parents won't make up."

"It doesn't really make any difference what I believe. What matters is what's true."

Tess blinked. "You *know* it makes a difference what you believe." She stepped closer to him, her eyelashes fluttering. "That's what you were trying to prove all night. Wasn't it?"

He wasn't sure he understood her question. Or, maybe he did. But right now he couldn't answer it. Her chestnut brown eyes looked so much like her mother's it was making his head hurt. He should go. He opened the front door. "Thank you..." but he quit the sentence; it was ridiculous to thank her for this night. It had been a shitty night for her too.

Quick, before he knew what was happening, Tess leaned in and put her arms around him. "Goodnight, Duncan Grier," she whispered. "I hope you'll be okay."

"Goodnight, Tess," he whispered back. "I hope you will be too." He walked into the dark night.

It would mean the house.

Jack walked to the bedroom window and looked out into the blackness. It was hard to see much, but he could make out the outline of the walnut trees that spread their spidery limbs over the brick driveway. Those trees, Jack remembered, were the first to turn in the fall, their disc-like yellow leaves scattering across the yard. His yard. The yard he would have to sell to someone else.

It was not the material aspects of his house he would miss. Hell, he was hardly there these days anyway. But, this house had held his life. It was an impressive structure. Solid. His kids loved it. He felt good calling it his home. Now, he would lose that grounding. He couldn't live in this huge house alone. And he'd never let Emmy keep it.

She wouldn't want it anyway.

She hadn't wanted it for a while, had she?

Jack heard the front door close, and he pressed his head against the window to see who was leaving the house. Duncan Grier. Well, that was fast. He would have thought he and Emmy would be downstairs together gloating in their sick triumph. But no, the man was leaving. The man who came to dinner and ruined his life.

Emmy would regret this decision. Jack was certain of that. What was there about this aimless, make-believe guy she could rely on? Nothing. She was going to embarrass herself. And in the process embarrass the whole family. That's all he meant to show at the dinner. That no one should trust the easy, pretty things this pampered man said. Though Jack knew he was right, he also had a dull discomfort that in their argument, Duncan had come across as the more circumspect adult. Everyone at the table tonight – Emmy, Tess, Celia – they all thought it was he who had acted unnecessarily provocative and mean, a jerk. No one understood how he was trying to do the best for his wife and family. No one gave him that credit. He wanted to believe it didn't matter what other people thought; he knew his actions were respectable. But, honestly, it pissed him off that no one appreciated his efforts. Sure, he was harsh. He was also right. *Why didn't anyone see that too?*

The tiredness was coming onto him, heavy and thick, like his body was being draped with an x-ray blanket. Times likes this when he let his anger blow, these times left him weary afterward. He had tried so hard. It hadn't worked. Not at all.

He felt Emmy's presence before he heard it. When he turned, it was his impression she'd been standing there awhile. Her face was a wreck, her eyes bloodshot, her cheeks blotchy. Emmy cried all the fucking time, but usually only quiet cries. On the rare occasions when there was the chest-heaving and that horrible breath-catching, it unhinged him, frightening him, if he was to be honest about it. Right now, however, he was gratified she was so discombobulated.

Emmy walked to where Jack stood by the windows. She stood four feet from him, as though ready to make a presentation. "Jack. I'm sorry." That was all she said. He could tell she tried hard not to cry as she said it, but it hadn't fully worked.

He didn't say anything. He wondered for which part she was apologizing. There were a lot of things to apologize for as far as he was concerned. Regardless, he didn't want her this near. He strode past where she stood, toward their bed. He didn't want her to see his face when he asked this next question; even the words were humiliating. "Did you lie before?"

"About?"

"Sleeping with him?"

"No. I didn't sleep with him."

Jack thought she was qualifying her answer. "You've kissed him though, haven't you?"

He turned to see the confusion register on her face.

"Shit, you've kissed him." Somehow this revolted him almost as much as the thought of them in bed. "He's going to chew you up and spit you out. You see that, don't you?"

Emmy started as though she was going to protest this point, but instead took a deep breath. "He's leaving this week. *He's* not what this is about."

"You honestly think we'd be having this conversation if that bastard hadn't come into the picture?"

"Yes, some version of this conversation; yes, we would." Emmy's protest was firm. "Jack, we were supposed to start our divorce two months ago. That had been our plan. Don't try to pretend that plan didn't exist."

"I remember our plan. But our plan would have changed, and you know it." He was making his voice just as firm as hers. "If that man hadn't showed up, you and I would be planning our trip to Italy next summer. We'd be debating whether to have Thanksgiving here or at the cabin." His voice abruptly rose: "Tell me that's not true!"

Emmy stood staring back at him, her cheek twitching. "We've been unhappy for such a long time. We don't have to stay so unhappy."

The ease of her conclusion infuriated him. "Really? Is that right?" He walked toward her. "Now that you don't want the commitment anymore, you've decided it's no big deal to give it up? But how did we get to where we are now? How Emmy? Because when I look back it seems like we did everything the way you wanted it. You created an obligation; I honored it. You asked for commitment; I gave you commitment. Happy? There was no talk of *happy*."

Her mouth flew open. "Is that the way you think of us?"

He shouted his answer: "It's the way we *are!* I did exactly what you wanted me to do! Our problem – *you* made it!"

"God, Jack..."

Jack watched as Emmy stood there, and slowly, very slowly her face collapsed into her sorrow. She walked to the bed and sat on its edge; her posture slumped, her face crumpled.

Jack stood and waited. This was the way their big fights usually went. They would shout and spar until Emmy started to cry. Then – it happened every time – the tone of the fight would change. It was as though Emmy's crying marked the pivot point that shifted their fights from explosion to reflection.

After several minutes, Emmy looked over at Jack standing above her. "You know, I never wanted your obligation, your stupid commitment." Her words were thick with tears; she sounded pouty, like a child objecting to her parent's admonishment. "I guess that's the way it seemed to you, but it's not what I meant to be asking for." She paused, like she was trying to decide if she could continue. "After Jessica, when I made you stay, what I had wanted was..." her voice cracked, "your *love*."

She looked away from him, shaking her head, "It was pretty pathetic. I knew it even then. I knew I would be a stronger woman if I wanted to renounce you or hurt you or leave you. I didn't want to do those things. I used to lie in bed and watch you sleep and just wish..." she sounded like she was wringing the words out of her throat, "that you would feel for me again what you felt in the beginning. My chest would be heavy with this... *longing* for you." She wiped her tears. "I worked very hard to think about us differently. I got there eventually. But, for so, so long I wanted you to love me." She swallowed. "And you didn't."

Watching Emmy's sadness, Jack felt his anger soften; he didn't want it to. He said tersely, "The other day I told you I loved you."

Emmy's mouth was full of tears: "But you don't. If you did, everything would be different. It would have been different all along. But..." she wiped her cheeks from her streaming tears, "you don't love me, Jack."

He was not unmoved by the certainty in her voice. In fact, his first impulse was to protest, to say the stupid three words. But, no, it was too late for that now.

Emmy spoke into the silence he left. "I want you to know…" she grabbed a bit of the bedspread and began to knead it, "when I asked you to choose me so long ago, I didn't mean to be asking you to pick unhappiness. It all happened so quickly, but to me… it was like Jessica took our happy family and threw us into the air. All I wanted was to catch everything fast before we smashed apart. That's all I was trying to do. But maybe…" she clenched her eyes shut and more tears seeped out, "I should have let us fall." She looked up at Jack, and he thought the sadness etched on her face had to be mirrored in his own. "I didn't mean to take your happiness, Jack. I only wanted everything to stay the way it was."

He flinched. That was what he wanted now too: to have everything stay the same. He wasn't going to say that, but somehow the observation made him realize he didn't want to stand anymore. He sat down on the edge of the bed beside his wife. They faced outward to the room, like they were passengers on a train.

Emmy's voice was thick and breathy. "It's so long ago, but I wonder if you still think about your decision. Do you?" When he didn't respond, Emmy continued; "Do you wish I'd let you go?"

He let there be a long silence, but then he cleared his throat: "Are you asking this now because you want me to let you go?"

"No." The word came fast, but then she turned to look at him as though she was evaluating his calmer tone, his softer question. "Maybe. I don't know actually."

Jack pierced his lips; he had a retort ready and if he slung it, he knew it would hurt. However, he was too tired for it. His body was so close to Emmy's, and sadness filled the space between them. He decided to answer her question; it surprised him that he wanted to. "I used to think about my decision a lot. All the time. There was no point in talking with you about it, because... there was nothing I could say. But yes, I used to wonder whether I made the right choice."

Emmy waited a long time, but finally, she asked, "What did you decide?"

He shook his head. "I decided not to ask the question anymore. There wasn't going to be a re-do. And with Jessica..." he sighed, "she and I would have been miserable no matter what. She was mad at me for what I did, but I think she would have been mad at me even if I'd done it differently. She's an angry person."

"Do you still love her?" Jack was surprised to hear how nervous Emmy was in asking the question.

Jack said it easily: "No." He ran his hands over his face. "It's such a long time ago now. I don't think about this stuff at all anymore. I haven't for years. Do you really still think about it?"

Her lip quivered: "All the time."

"But *why?*"

"Because you've been angry at me for so long. I always trace it back to that. Everything comes back to what I made you give up. And, as mad as you make me," she smiled through her tears, "and you do make me really, really mad, I also feel responsible for your unhappiness."

"I haven't been *that* unhappy."

"Jack, there's no reason to lie now."

"Well, I don't blame you for it."

"Just ten minutes ago, you said over and over again that you did."

He thought for a moment. He'd said that; he'd felt that, and in fact he knew he would feel it again. He took a deep breath. "I guess what I don't say is that I blame myself too. I knew..." He stopped; his voice felt suddenly unsteady. He tried again: "I knew I'd messed it all up. We were so young. God, do you realize I was only as old as Marc is now? We were such *babies.*" He thought, then continued, his voice very solemn. "Emmy, I hadn't meant to hurt you." His voice was weakening but he plowed ahead: "I kept trying to fix what I ruined. I tried, but it never… it never came off."

"I know you tried." Emmy said it soothingly.

"You do?"

She nodded.

They sat there quietly beside each other for a long time. Jack hadn't expected to say what he had. It was the tiredness that allowed him to say it. He was wearied by the night, its loudness, its anger. Maybe it was something else too, a bigger tired, a longer exhaustion.

Emmy wiped one cheek, then the other. The tears were slower now, but they still streaked her cheeks until she wiped them away. Jack tried to remember the last time the two of them sat so closely, so communed in thought. It was strange to think this was the closest he'd felt to Emmy in a long, long time.

Emmy's voice wobbled when she finally spoke, "We did make wonderful kids. They were happier, don't you think? With us together?"

Jack nodded. "We did good by them." He could feel his throat growing tighter; it was harder to keep his voice from wavering. "We gave them stability and this beautiful house."

Emmy smiled; he didn't turn to see it, but he heard it in her voice. "It *is* a beautiful house."

There was a long silence. They sat there on the bed on which they'd slept night after night for twenty-two years. He thought they both knew what had to come next. They were still beside each other, waiting for it.

It was Emmy who broke the weighty quiet, and her voice caught with the heaviness of the words, "But I think we will make better futures without each other."

The statement was too simple. For all that had come before it, he was incredulous that their ending could be condensed to so few words. He went to speak, but his voice caught in his throat, "Is it really just that? All these years and that's..." he tried to keep his eyes from welling with tears, but he could not, "that's it?"

Emmy leaned her wet cheek against his shoulder. She gulped for air through her tears; "I think it is."

SUNDAY, OCTOBER 20:
RIGHT

Text message sent from Emmy to Duncan, 9:11 pm
I'm staying at Maria's house. Jack and I decided last night to divorce. Thank you for helping me when I needed a friend.

Text message from Duncan to Emmy, 9:11 pm
Was wondering all day how you were doing. Is Maria's really where you want to be?

Text message from Emmy to Duncan, 9:12 pm
For now, Maria's works. I'll start apartment hunting tomorrow. Are you around tomorrow? Or Tuesday?

Text message from Duncan to Emmy, 9:18 pm
Filming tomorrow.

Text message from Emmy to Duncan, 9:18 pm
Okay, Tuesday. I want to see you before you go.

Text message from Duncan to Emmy, 9:48 pm
Right.

Text message from Emmy to Duncan, 9:30 pm
Will you text me when we get closer to figure out when
and where we can see each other?

Text message from Duncan to Emmy, 9:31
Right.

Text message from Emmy to Duncan, 9:31
Okay. See you Tuesday.

TUESDAY, OCTOBER 22:
BENDING TOGETHER

Duncan was still dozing when he heard his cell phone's vibration. Usually, he turned his phone off when he went to sleep, but the last few nights he'd not. He didn't let himself dwell on why he'd made this small change in his usual habits. It was an absence of an action, so it was easy to pretend it was an accident. Duncan groped at his bedside table trying to locate the phone's vibratory buzz. He pulled the phone to his face. It was Kallie. *Shit.* There was a quick impulse – it hit like a heartbeat – to throw the phone. But he didn't. He sat up a little more in bed, ran his hands through his hair and let the phone ring a few more seconds. He knew he would get it eventually.

It had been a miserable few days. On Saturday night, he'd returned to his hotel room and stayed up late channel surfing. Sunday, the hours passed heavily, and Duncan was unsure how to fill them. He returned phone calls and read two scripts, but he couldn't convince himself he wasn't waiting for something to happen. It was only when night's chill descended that Duncan let himself acknowledge: he'd expected Emmy at least to call. *That she hadn't even called...* It confounded him. He told her he was falling in love with her. He tried to chase her, to protect her. He stayed there through that awful, awful dinner trying to help her. And now she hadn't even called him to tell him what happened. *Could he have been wrong that she cared about him?* He wore a path in his brain with how many times he walked between Yes and No.

Then he received her text. She and Jack were divorcing, that was good. But Emmy had turned to Maria, not to him. She wanted to see him, sure, but not urgently. Tomorrow or Tuesday sounded like they'd work equally as well. Just so long as it was before he left. Probably all she wanted was to say good-bye.

Just good-bye.

That night, he called Gus to ask if there was any way to fit all the remaining shots in on Monday. There were only four scenes left to shoot – all of them quite short and all of them on the set of Benjamin's apartment. Gus disliked night shoots and he'd set the schedule to film two scenes on Monday and two for Tuesday afternoon. But Duncan realized: he wanted to be gone by Tuesday night. He couldn't stand waiting in limbo any longer. Duncan made up an explanation, something about needing to take a meeting in L.A. early Wednesday, and though he suspected Gus knew this thin excuse was a lie, Gus only took a second to consider the request. Yes, he said, they would find a way to swing it. Next, Duncan called Ling to arrange his flight out of Boston for Tuesday late afternoon. Maybe he and Emmy would see each other, maybe they wouldn't. Regardless, he was leaving Boston by dinnertime. He felt more in control knowing he'd made a plan. Now, at 8:37 Tuesday morning, he held his phone to his face. He didn't want to talk with Kallie, but there was a piece of news he had to give her, so he swiped his phone on. His voice, even its grogginess, had an exasperated edge. "You're up early."

"I think I had a dream with you in it. That's how hard I work for you honey, you're even in my sleep." There was a sipping sound, and Duncan realized Kallie must be drinking coffee. "So, did you wrap last night?" she asked after her swallow.

"There's still the California parts to do in the next couple weeks," Duncan stretched his back as he answered, "but yeah, after last night, no more Boston."

"Gus told me everything is…" she mimicked his intonation, "'*exceeding his expectations.*'"

"Only because his expectations were so fucking low."

"Honey, don't say that. Gus thought you were one thing; now he sees you're more." She took another coffee slurp. "You know, on the phone the other day, he said *Oscar*."

"What horseshit." His hostility was surprising even to himself.

"Wow. Why do you say that? I mean, I've seen some video. It looks good; you look good."

"No, I don't." He ran his hands over his face, "Kallie, you were right about this whole project. This role, it's not right for me. I'm too tall; I'm Dan the Man; I'm not the guy to play Benjamin B."

"Your delivery is fantastic; you sound just like Dustin Hoffman. You walk like him too."

"But it's like you said, that stuff won't matter. The audience will never get beyond who they expect me to be. It was a mistake. I should have listened to you."

"Well, you should always listen to me. But in this instance, you're being too hard on yourself."

Kallie's voice was schoolteacher-y, and Duncan was thankful she wasn't gloating. Regardless, he didn't want to talk about it anymore. "Anyway, that's not the reason I picked up your call."

"Hold on a sec, are you saying there are times you *don't* pick up my call? I'm shocked!"

Duncan obligatorily chuckled, but he wanted to get this over with. "Listen, I want you to tell Ned I'll do *Black Attack.*"

"What? Why? You said *Black Attack* was dumb."

Duncan got up out of bed. "Well, I've decided to stick with what I know."

There was a silence. "Duncan, what's going on?"

Kallie's concern was comforting. He rather wanted some petting. But, as he felt this impulse to lower his defenses, he purposefully made himself remember: Kallie was doing her job. He walked to the window and pulled the curtain back to look out. "Nothing is going on." He watched the busy street below. "Absolutely nothing."

"Oh," Kallie said with a dawning certainty; "This is still about Emmy."

"No." The word had too much bluster. He let the curtain sweep closed again; he walked away from the windows. "I'm saying yes to *Black Attack* because I've thought more about how my horse left the barn. Remember when you said that? And so, just like you told me to, I'm trying to be happy with what I have, who I am." Duncan walked from one room of his suite to the other.

Kallie's tone was stern: "You should not do *Black Attack.*"

"Last week you got mad at me for not taking *Black Attack!*" He imitated her voice: "'*So many actors would be happy to have what you have.*' Remember, you said that?" He paused, then said the thing he knew would most piss her off. "It's fine, I can call Ned myself."

Kallie's voice was fast on the other end of the phone: "Dammit Duncan, you *do* make it hard sometimes. Stop pouting and listen." She paused, and Duncan knew she was trying to determine how best to make her point. "I've actually thought quite a bit about our conversation last week. And…" she stopped herself.

"Yes?"

"I do want you to have a safe and solid career – I'm not going to apologize for that – but more than that I want you to be contented with it. That's what I want. You never seem to believe me when I say this…" she stopped herself again. "Honestly, I don't know why I bother…"

"Just say it, Kallie."

She took a quick inhale of breath, "I care about you. There. I've said it for the five millionth time. It's my job to take care of your career, but I also think of you as a friend. To me, that means I try to take care of you too. If you do *Black Attack* you'll be miserable. I want you to be *happy*. So, there it is. I've changed my mind. I don't want you to do that stupid movie."

"Your new advice is no to *Black Attack?*"

"Yes, that's my new advice. That, and go see Emmy." There was a slurp from her coffee.

Duncan knew Kallie was trying to be nice. "Kallie, thank you, but you don't know what happened; how can you tell me to—"

Kallie interrupted, "Because I know you. A baby could have grown to adulthood in the time I've known you. I can hear it in your voice…" Her voice softened, "I know disappointment; it's my good friend actually. So, when I say go see Emmy, I say this from experience. Go find her and tell her thank you. Whether it's for what you shared or learned. 'Thank you' really helps put a resolution on disappointment. Otherwise, it… festers."

Like so many of his conversations with Kallie, Duncan thought she'd probably given him sound advice, yet he felt compelled to question it first. "How do you know there isn't already a resolution? That we haven't already said goodbye?"

Kallie was certain. "You haven't."

There was a long silence.

Finally, Kallie asked, "Are you going to tell me if I'm right?"

"No."

"But I am, aren't I?"

"Yes." He stopped his pacing of his hotel suite and briefly held his phone down to see what time it gave. He put the phone back to his cheek. There was enough time to see Emmy before his 4 pm flight. "Okay, I'll stop by her office."

"Thata boy. I think you'll feel better for it." Kallie's voice was warm.

He was aware Kallie was doing more than she needed to, and for once he didn't undermine this observation. Kallie gained nothing from caring about how he said goodbye to Emmy. In fact, it was more of a risk for her to express her opinion than to withhold it. She always said she cared about him. Maybe it wasn't just her job she worried after, maybe it was him too. There weren't many people in his life he could say that about.

Kallie's voice interrupted his thoughts, "And I won't call Ned on *Black Attack*. Right?"

"Right." He was about to say goodbye when he realized he needed to say something else. "Kallie!"

"Uh-huh?" She sounded puzzled, and Duncan knew it was because he'd called her name urgently.

He ran his hand across the back of his neck; his face contorted with the effort of the words he knew he was going to say. "Uh, thank you. Thank you for what you said, and I want you to know – I've never said it all these years but... I do, I do love you." The words hung there, slightly stunned themselves. "I know I can be a shit sometimes, I do know that. But your friendship is important to me, and I wanted to tell you that."

There was a full second of silence. "Wow, you really are a wreck." Kallie's flippancy did not, however, disguise her pleasure. Duncan heard the happiness in her voice as she strained to sound casual, "I love you too D and don't forget to call me when you're home. 'Kay?"

"It's small." Maria's tone did not disguise her disapproval.

"It's cozy small," Emmy said, correcting the implicit criticism. They strolled down the center of Riedesel Street, a narrow residential street near Harvard Square with large Victorian homes packed in small lots. Big oaks lined the curbs, and the trees' limbs soared outward over the street creating a canopy under which Emmy and Maria now walked. As the branches swayed gently in the breeze, the midday sun flickered between the yellow and orange leaves, a mix of shadow and light dancing around them.

"Come on, look at how quaint this street is." Emmy leaned into her friend, nudging her to agree. Maria was clearly un-enthused by the apartment they'd seen, and Emmy wanted her friend to at least acknowledge its obvious fine qualities.

"Well, sure, it's quaint," Maria looked over at her friend with concern, "but I don't like that side entrance. Won't you feel like you're squatting in someone else's home?"

"It will be nice to have neighbors. They'll have their big space and I'll have my little one. I'll feel less lonely knowing other bodies are in the house with me. And that fireplace is so pretty, and look," she held her arms wide in front of her, "*look* at how easy it will be to walk to work!"

Maria glanced sideways at her. "Sweetheart, you don't have to make this decision now. There's no rush. You can stay with me and Nathan as long as you want."

Emmy smiled mischievously. "I already signed the lease."

"What? When?"

"When you were out examining the parking space." Emmy leaned in toward Maria; "What were you doing out there anyway? Taking measurements?"

Maria scoffed, "That space did not look like it could fit a normal car!"

The friends walked several more paces in unison, before Maria turned to her. "Are you *sure* you want to leave your house? It's not an easy decision to un-do, and Jack, he has no more claim to that house than you. Maybe it feels good now to move ahead so quickly, but you're used to a really big, spectacular house, and that apartment, there's nothing spectacular about it."

"I know." Emmy didn't hesitate. "I don't care. It's what I want."

Maria shook her head in disbelief. "You sound so *certain*."

Emmy laughed. "I actually *feel* certain."

Since Saturday night, Emmy had experienced a wide seesawing of emotions, but she hadn't wavered – even slightly – on the rightness of her decision. Sunday morning, Jack and she had tersely worked out the details of the near-term changes. They agreed they would wait to tell their children their news in person, and they picked the weekend two weeks hence as the one when they would assemble the family. They decided that other than Maria and Nathan, no one should know about their divorce decision until their children were told. Finally, they concluded that they would stop living together immediately. It was Emmy who was most insistent on this point. Jack suggested they could live in separate parts of the house, but Emmy was clear: she wanted to go. For the last two years, her marriage to Jack consisted chiefly of their arrangement of shared space. Now, to demarcate the changeover, Emmy wanted a separate roof, separate walls. Jack's house could not be hers anymore.

That afternoon, while Jack drove Tess back to Amherst, Emmy packed three suitcases and readied herself to go to Maria and Nathan's house. When she walked out of the house she had lived in for sixteen years and locked the door behind her, the door's lock clicked in the latch, reverberating in her fingertips. Her eyes did not even slightly water, and she walked with purpose to the car.

Over the rest of that day and Monday too, her steps remained strong and forward-moving. All the years that she had weighed the pros and cons of divorcing Jack, she had worried her equivocation would remain even after the decision. It had not. Her body felt physically lighter for discarding the weight of her decision-making.

Washes of loss nonetheless came on fast, like summer storms that had the power to soak her to her bones. On Monday morning, when she waited in line at the bank, her mind flitted to her son, Ben. He'd tried so hard over the years to smooth out the frictions between Jack and her. After fights or tension-filled exchanges, Ben would frequently seek Emmy out. "Daddy loves you," he'd say to her, his head burying into her chest when he was younger or towering over her in a bear hug when he was older. Thinking how disappointed her Benji would be, her chest clamped so tightly she had to leave the bank line.

The surges of grief came in waves, but they went out again. All along, she'd expected her separation from Jack to capsize her, sinking her into a murky whirlpool. Instead, to her surprise, she felt lifted, as though she was emerging from a tunnel and could finally see the horizon in front of her. She planned the trips she would take to visit each of her children and the fun they would have with each other one-on-one. She thought of decorating her own home in the kind of cluttered, hodge-podgy way she liked and dancing as she cooked with the music really, really loud.

She thought about Duncan. She re-lived how on Saturday night he'd looked at her when he pulled back from kissing her hello. How he'd grinned when he licked the chocolate bowl and solemnly agreed to help her figure out what was true. Her thoughts swung back to him over and over again, and as they did, the memories began to twist into fantasies. She let herself consider how good it would be to touch her lips to his skin, to ease herself against his body, to be warmed inside his hold.

She thought about calling Duncan, to explain further what had happened and to see how he was doing. However, she never did. She rationalized this reluctance by saying she wanted their next conversation to be in-person, not on the phone. Besides, she was so busy. On Sunday, there'd been the rush to clean up the dinner party dishes and pack her suitcases before Jack returned from his drive to Amherst. That night, at Maria's, her friend had walked out a long parade of questions. And on Monday, Emmy had seen three clients, met with her real estate agent, looked at four apartments, had a long meeting with a divorce attorney, visited the bank and ordered a mattress. But her busyness wasn't the reason she wasn't calling.

She simply wasn't sure what to say. What she felt was straightforward. She loved him. She wanted to be with him. Yet, this certainty rested in a heart just barely seamed together, and Emmy worried her stitches could easily flit apart. Duncan lived thousands of miles away. His world was bright and fast and nothing like hers. And, he'd slept with her stepdaughter. This last point was the objection that had always loomed largest in the past. Now, she had to keep reminding herself to care. He didn't have feelings for Celia, that was clear. And if he'd slept with Celia – and she still thought he had – he clearly wished he hadn't. Emmy was no longer sure how to weigh the matter. *Did that night identify him as a reckless person who would break her heart? Or, was the situation instead inconsequential to Duncan's trustworthiness?* She asked the questions over and over without an answer.

Regardless of the question's answer, she still wanted to tell him how dear his friendship was to her, how terribly she would miss him. She couldn't have him leave town without saying at least that much, and since he was leaving tomorrow, time was running out for this last meeting. Her plan had been to drop off her lease at the office, then walk to his Allston set. He hadn't texted her with what time would work best, but since she had no other appointments today, she was planning to wait on his trailer stairs until he was free. As her and Maria's heeled steps clomped steadily on the sidewalk in unison, her nerves zipped up and down inside her.

"Have you figured out what you're going to say?" Maria asked, as they approached their office building.

Emmy lifted her shoulders, trying to sound more nonchalant than she felt. "Not really. There's a lot of things I'd like to say, but I guess I will mostly say goodbye." She could feel her stomach flip saying the word. They began to trod up the outside flight of stairs.

"You know, goodbye isn't a very good proxy for saying other things. Goodbye ends a conversation, so if you want to, say, continue or start a conversation, then goodbye is not the thing to say."

Emmy held the outside door open for her friend. "True." Her pulse quickened.

"Honey, you know, it's okay if you make it up as you go along."

She began to climb the indoor flight of stairs. "Make it up?"

"I always remind my clients they're the ones making up their own stories."

Emmy tried to sound calm, though her words were wispy. "That's a nice way to put it. I'll have to remember that one." As she climbed the last stairs, she slowed her ascent to search her purse for her office key. That key was always lodged in the bottom of her purse's interior pocket, and she had to really dig for it.

Only when she reached the top stair did she pull her head up out of her purse. There was Duncan, waiting in front of her office door.

Emmy was surprised at how quickly Maria made herself scarce. She didn't ask to be introduced, barely said "hello," and quickly closed her squeaky office door behind her. Though the distractions were several in those first few seconds – doors unlocked, jackets taken off, lights turned on – very soon, it was Duncan and Emmy standing in the empty office waiting room.

Emmy was able to tell even before she unlocked the door that Duncan had his guard up. He'd been waiting for her, true, but when he responded to her greeting, his eyes weren't warm, his hello curt. He seemed to be there from some grudging sense of obligation, not because he wanted to be. She wasn't sure what to make of it. But immediately, his uneasiness made her own nervousness retreat.

Duncan was finding it disorienting to be in Emmy's physical presence again. He'd expended a lot of energy these last couple days building his frustration toward her; yet, when Emmy emerged from the stairwell and found him standing there, her face flashed surprise, then: Pleasure. This warmth dislodged his anger, and now, as he stood before her, he tried to reset it. It required some effort.

"It's nice to see you." She stepped closer to him.

"You too." He put his hands in his jeans pockets.

"You look tired, though." She raised her hand to his cheek and ran it against the stubble there. "Your beard has gray in it;" her voice conveyed her surprise.

Duncan tried hard not to lean into her hand. "I'm old." He said it brusquely, then tried to smile to make it a joke. It didn't come off.

Emmy took a step back; she tipped her head slightly in the direction of her office door. "Do you want to talk in my office?"

"No, that's okay." He didn't want this to feel like a therapy session. "I just stopped by."

"It's funny you're here because I was about to walk to your trailer."

Duncan quickly reviewed the information conveyed, not just the words but her smile and the playful intonation of her words. He shook his head. "I wouldn't have been there. I'm leaving. I'll be on a plane in a few hours."

This news hit Emmy's body before it made it to her brain. Before she could stop it, her eyes prickled. "I thought you weren't going until…" her voice cracked, "tomorrow."

Duncan heard Emmy's voice; he saw her eyes fill. His anger slipped further away. "No. Today." He waited a moment then took a step closer to her. "So. Why were you coming to the set?"

Emmy began to dab at her eyes, embarrassed that, even when she meant to be strong, her tears always betrayed her. "I wanted to say... goodbye." Maria had told her not to use that word, but she hadn't come up with anything else to say.

"Oh." His tone was flat. "Goodbye," he repeated.

"Why did you come by?" She sat down, so she could better collect herself.

He swallowed. "I wanted to say thank you."

"Thank you? But, for what?"

Duncan sat down beside her. This was after all what he'd come to say. "For helping me."

"You mean with therapy?"

"No," he shook his head, "not with therapy." He paused; it was hard to find the right words. "For understanding me and..." He glanced down at his hands. "Yeah, for that." He looked up at her.

"I want to thank you too." Her voice dipped; suddenly, felt shy. "You took such good care of me Saturday night and you gave me the strength to make this change. I'm not sure I could have done it without you."

Oh? This was the kind of thing he'd wanted her to say these last two days. He sat up straighter; he ran his hand across the back of his neck. "And you were coming to the set to say *goodbye?*"

"Well." She looked down, then into his eyes. "I was coming to the set to say *something.*"

"What did you *want* to say?"

The question sat anxiously on his lips, and in that moment, Emmy could see Duncan's heart was stitched together too. She kissed him. There was his earthiness and warmth and sadness. She wanted all of it. As his lips met hers again, then again and again, Emmy could feel his desire for her. It was real. She couldn't name it or see it, but it was a truth. He could fall into her, she thought. She would catch him. She edged her body closer to his; she slipped her hands under his shirt. His skin was smooth and warm. She wanted all his skin against her body.

Duncan gripped his hands snugly around her hips and brought her body atop his. She slid so easily onto him; her head dipped down to kiss his; she smelled like honey. He wished they were not in the waiting room of her office; he wanted to peel off her clothes, to feel her nakedness, to have no space between them. He kissed her neck and tasted its salty sweetness and his mind raced with pleasure and relief and hope. This was the beginning. Jack was gone. There did not have to be a stop.

Then, abruptly, the office door creaked open.

There was a beginning, middle and end to the door's creak. It played out like a song. At its first note, Duncan and Emmy sprang away from each other, and by the time the door hit its full extension, the highest pitch of the squeak, Emmy was already sitting upright and Duncan standing. The waiting room couch was to the right of the entrance, and Duncan and Emmy could not see the visitor until she stepped ahead of the door.

It was Celia.

"*Fuck*," the whispered word slipped out of Duncan's mouth.

Beside him, the same word came to Emmy's lips, but she stopped its entrance to the air. "Oh hi Celia!" she chirped too cheerfully.

Celia jumped, "Oh, wow! Hi!" She laughed, nervous with the surprise. "I've never walked in here before and found anyone in this room. It's always... empty." Her smile faded. Her eyes darted back and forth between Duncan and Emmy before settling on Duncan. "Why are *you* here?"

Duncan worked hard to keep his face from expressing the befuddlement this question provoked. "I wanted..." He realized he needed to adjust his voice to meet Celia's upbeat, light tone. "I wanted to come and... thank Emmy for dinner the other night."

"*Really?*" Celia's head shot back. "Thank her? That dinner was, like, the worst ever!" Celia began to laugh, "I guess my dad doesn't like superheroes, huh?" She chuckled at her own joke, then stopped. Emmy and Duncan had forgotten to laugh, and Celia examined them with renewed curiosity.

Quick, Emmy turned the attention back to Celia. "So, why are *you* here?"

"Well, my sweet Emmy..." Celia leaned her head in, "I wanted to see if I could borrow the keys to the cabin."

Duncan froze. *Was she fucking kidding?* Celia was here to talk about the *bloody fucking cabin!* He looked at Emmy, whose expression was similarly stunned.

For Emmy, the word "cabin" was like a flooded room's door opening, and the dank, dirty water spilling outward. Realizing that Celia was watching her reaction, she moved her face out of its stunned position, seeking words to fill the silence that had now lasted a half-second too long. "Oh. Okay. I can give you my keys to... the cabin." Dazed, she began to walk to her purse, but before she had even made it a few steps, she halted. Her lips still tingled from the brush of Duncan's stubble against them. Her abdomen still ached from the longing lodged there. Quick, Emmy turned around. "Duncan, it was very nice of you to stop by," she said in a take-charge voice. She saw his eyes squint, but Emmy said nothing, even visually, to him, nor did she check to see

Celia's reaction. She leaned to where Duncan's jacket sat on a nearby chair, picked it up and handed it to him. "I really hope you have a good trip back."

Duncan wasn't sure he understood Emmy's intent, but he sought to follow her lead. "Yes, it was nice seeing you too." He took his jacket from her and was about to say good-bye, when Celia's voice rung out.

"Your trip back? Are you going back to L.A. already?"

"Yes," Duncan distractedly responded. He had to hope Emmy knew he'd return after Celia left. Since there was no way of conveying that hope to her, he started to walk toward the door. His head was filled with a low hum, like an over-loaded electric circuit board. He was trying to make sense of these last sixty seconds. *Shit, could this possibly be falling apart again? No. Maybe. Fuck.* He felt how sweaty his palms were on the office doorknob as he twisted it to open. He was about to leave when Celia's petulant voice stopped him in his tracks. "God, Duncan! I can't believe you aren't even going to hug me goodbye!"

Honestly, he would have preferred to tell Celia to go to hell, but instead he turned around and put his arms around this young woman in a loose, light hug. Emmy stood right there, and again, Duncan tried to catch her eye. Very fixedly she looked at the coffee table. He guessed it made sense she wouldn't watch him embracing Celia.

Celia pulled away from the hug, all smiles. "You know, Duncan, I'm so glad we had that wonderfully special time together at the cabin. I will *always, always* treasure it."

Duncan felt a sharp shiver run though his body. He visibly shuddered.

Celia giggled. "Are you cold?"

"No." He looked at Emmy, but, again, no go; she turned away. "Yes, well. Ladies, take care."

Emmy looked over at him. "Bye, Duncan." Her voice was clear and casual, like this was no big deal. There was little time to evaluate her expression as he passed through the office door. She looked determined. But he did not know of what.

The sound of the door closing was squeaky and horrible. Emmy walked toward her purse that was sitting on the coffee table. Her head throbbed, and all she knew was that Celia had to leave quickly. She wanted Celia and all the annoying, flooding questions neatly locked up. *Should she want that? Was that irresponsible?* All the questions she'd asked and re-asked had literally come to her doorstep with Celia.

"Oh my god, was that *awk-ward!*" Celia propped herself atop the arm of the waiting room couch. "Do you think I handled it okay?"

"Sure, I guess." Emmy rummaged through her purse for the key.

Celia grabbed one of the couch's throw pillows and began to play with its fringe. "At the cabin, when I first saw Duncan standing there shirtless," Celia paused as though reliving the moment, "I swear, it was like a Santa sighting. Like seeing a mythical man with my own eyes."

"Is that right?" Emmy shot back. "Well, Duncan's not Santa. Not mythical. Real." She held out the key. "Here."

"Oh, thanks." She twirled the key on its chain. "You're right, not mythical, but the man does have a damn nice kiss."

Emmy worked hard to keep the waves of revulsion from showing on her face. "Is that right?"

Celia twisted her lips. "Yeah, for being so sleepy, Duncan Grier was still super hot. Of course, now I far prefer Rocco's kiss. I mean, Rocco is a Greek god!" Celia groaned slightly for emphasis. "That's why I've got to get him to the cabin."

Emmy took in this information. "You're taking *Rocco* to the cabin? *That's* why you need the keys?"

Celia nodded.

"My, but you *do* move fast."

"Oh, Emster, don't say it like that."

"Like what?" Emmy asked, though she knew exactly how disapproving she'd sounded.

"You're making me sound like a hussy. I may enjoy life's sensual pleasures, but I'm not *cavalier*. I have an honor code after all."

Emmy evaluated her stepdaughter. "You have an *honor code?*"

"Well, of course."

Emmy puzzled to understand Celia's exact meaning. If Celia was suggesting she was more sexually constrained than she typically implied, a very specific follow-up begged to be asked. "And with your particular honor code, how do you decide which sensual experiences to indulge and which to deny?"

"Well, by how much pleasure is involved." Celia smiled wryly, as though she'd told a great joke. "You see, it's quite a pleasure-driven honor code."

Emmy tried to muster a slight laugh. "And with Duncan, *which was it?*"

Celia's body noticeably stiffened. "Well, you know, it's not like I asked Duncan to come to the cabin. He was just there."

Emmy didn't say anything; she didn't breathe. Her pulse throbbed in her temples; she waited for her stepdaughter to continue.

Celia shrugged. "And it wasn't that big a deal."

"No?"

"Not really."

Emmy stared at Celia. She took in Celia's wide-eyed look of innocence, the way she folded her arms across her chest, the way she leaned slightly back. The stance was defensive, but Emmy was unsure which portrayal of herself Celia meant to protect. The possibilities popped in her head: *Maybe Celia had never slept with Duncan after all. Maybe Celia would finally acknowledge that. Maybe Duncan had never lied.* The door to all Emmy's worries could be locked shut. "Celia, did you and Duncan really have—" But, abruptly, she quit the question.

The unspoken word hung in the silence, and Emmy let it disperse into the waiting room air. She didn't need Celia to answer this question. It would clarify nothing. Emmy knew what she believed. Not necessarily about that night, but about Duncan. He loved her. He wanted to be true to her. He wanted to take care of her. That night was only one element of their story. She could risk her uncertainty about that one element – she could – because she believed in the rest of the story.

Celia giggled at the awkwardness with which the question had halted. "Emmy, I thought you were going to ask me a question."

Emmy shook her head. "No."

Celia was skeptical: "Really? Because it sounded like you were about to ask me if—"

"No." Emmy quickly cut her off. "No, I wasn't going to ask you that."

"I would be happy to tell you. I don't want to kiss and tell, but if you want to—"

"No!" The forcefulness of the one word response surprised Celia, and Emmy had to come up with something quick to lighten the situation. "What I mean is that it's none of my business. I don't want to know."

"Oh. Okay."

The two women stood there facing each other, and Emmy could tell Celia was bewildered. Her stepdaughter tried so hard to be clever but she was still ridiculously young. And as though there was a cause and effect between this observation and her conclusion, Emmy decided she would never again worry about Celia and Duncan's night at the cabin. She would not merely ignore the night's existence or lock it behind a mental door; no, instead, she would – now, this instant – nullify the night's relevance. Just like Maria had said, Emmy was the one who made up her story. She could turn the page on that night, and with that page turned, she would be free to write many, many more. *All along, that had been the trick: To pick the story she wanted to tell.* She'd picked. She smiled at her stepdaughter; it was a genuine smile. "You should go have a good time with Rocco."

Emmy put her arm around her stepdaughter protectively. "Now, when you're at the cabin..." her voice of stepmotherly counsel was returning with surprising ease, "please promise me you'll be careful. I don't want you to go getting yourself hur—"

Celia interrupted her with an embarrassed laugh, "Oh, I'm *always* careful!" Her stepdaughter leaned into her and kissed her on the cheek. "Thanks for the key," she said with extra sweetness. She started to walk toward the door, but then turned back. "I do love you, Emmy."

"And I love you." Emmy said it easily. She meant it, after all.

⚜ ⚜ ⚜

Duncan leaned against a lamppost; he waited. He was on Mt. Auburn Street, across the street and down the block from Emmy's office building. It was a winding street clogged with sluggishly-moving buses and a near constant stream of pedestrians hurrying their way to Harvard Square. Duncan's idleness contrasted with the surrounding hustle; he did not have many tasks or places to be. He was singly preoccupied with what was happening in Emmy's waiting room office.

He tried to think what Celia and Emmy could be talking about for so long. He'd like to think that whatever it was, Emmy would put it in proper perspective. He hated that Celia had talked about the "wonderfully special time" they'd spent together. *Shit, maybe he had slept with her.* He paced.

Looking back at the building, finally, someone was opening the front door, and right away, he could tell it was Emmy. She flew down her office building's porch stairs, her brown hair breezing behind her. Duncan had to wait for one car, then another to pass before he made it across the street.

"I'm glad you didn't leave." She rushed to him on the sidewalk.

"I wouldn't leave." He evaluated her face trying to learn what had happened in the waiting room. "I was waiting for Celia to go, then I was planning to come back to you."

"She's gone." Emmy said, still breathy from her rush to get to him.

"You were running after me," Duncan said with admiration.

She laughed. "I was." She paused. "Just so you know, I can run *a lot* faster than that."

There was happiness in her eyes; she wasn't mad at him. Perhaps Celia hadn't ruined everything. Perhaps he could make it work. He'd already planned what he would say. He took a step nearer to her. "You know, I don't have to be back in L.A. until next Monday. If you want, we could go somewhere together for the next few days." He took one of Emmy's hands. "Would you come with me somewhere? Come and be happy with me?"

The question unleashed such pleasure that merely saying, "Yes," didn't seem enough. Her arms flung around Duncan's neck. She kissed him and was ready to kiss him again when she felt his face go slack.

"Bloody hell," he mumbled.

Her first thought was that Celia was there, behind her. *Not again. No way.* She turned fast; but no one was there. "What? What's 'bloody hell'?"

"That man," he pointed across the street, "is videotaping us."

"What man?" But before the question was out, she saw him. He was short, heavy-set and held a large digital video camera on his shoulder that was pointed right at them.

"Shit, I didn't think there were paps on me anymore." Duncan began to walk backwards from Emmy. He couldn't believe there was yet another hitch. *Were toads going to fall next? Hail? Would Jack Halperin bike by?* Duncan knew they needed to move off the street right away, but he couldn't see a restaurant or store to which they could retreat. "Should we go to your office?" He had to shout this question because a city bus loudly lumbered and exhaled its stop at the corner where Emmy was standing.

"No, not my office," she shouted back. She didn't want to go there; it felt like going backwards.

"Well, where then?" Duncan stopped his retreating walk to hear the plan better.

"The bus?" She pointed to the 73 Waverly whose doors were separating down the middle only a few feet from her.

412

The bus? This was not the sort of escape he had in mind. "Why the bus?"

But Emmy was already stepping toward the 73 Waverly's doors. After a departing passenger made her way down, Emmy climbed the big stairs of the bus's entrance and looked back at him. "Come on!"

There wasn't time for Duncan to persuade her of a different option. He rushed to catch up with her, and by the time he climbed up the two tall stairs, Emmy was already slipping dollar bills into the fare machine. The bus lurched forward, and they steadied themselves, walking slowly down the narrow aisle.

Duncan couldn't remember the last time he'd been on a bus, yet the lolling, lethargic roll of the bus's engines felt familiar. The bus wasn't half full, and its few passengers, mostly senior citizens and students, barely glanced at them as they passed. There were empty seats in back, but Emmy grabbed a pole by the back entrance, and Duncan stood next to her grasping the horizontal rail overhead. He looked out the bus's big windows at the bustle of Harvard Square. "Do you even know where this bus is going?"

Emmy smiled. "No idea."

Duncan could see Emmy was amused by the situation. He was not as sure. "I can't believe we're on a *bus*."

"You have something against public transportation?" Emmy teased.

"No, that's not it." He glanced at the back of the bus. "It's just that, being on a bus, it's similar to the..." He stopped, realizing it would be better not to explain. It was a peculiar connection he was making, and once explained, he would have to detail why it bothered him, and that explanation would be convoluted indeed.

Emmy studied his confusion, and it took only a second to guess what he was worried about. The night of the dinner party, she'd overheard Tess and him talking about the last scene in *The Graduate*. "They've escaped, but they have nowhere to go." That's what Duncan had said about the characters on the bus. Holding to the pole, she leaned into Duncan and tiptoed to reach his ear. "We have somewhere to go," she whispered.

Duncan stared at her. It was as though she'd responded to his specific, quite obscure concern. Still, he wanted to be sure. "Are you saying you'll go away with me this week?"

"For starters."

"For starters?"

She nodded, smiling broadly. "I think there are lots of places to go."

He was certain now she knew exactly what he'd been thinking about. "Could we go together to those places?"

Emmy beamed with a pleasure so strong it throbbed under her skin. "We could."

Duncan held the moment. There was a rushing in his chest; he guessed it was joy. He used his free arm to pull her into him, kissing her plummy lips. Emmy laughed as she kissed him back, wrapping her arms so she could cling to him instead of the pole. The vehicle lurched and squeaked with its ancient brakes, turning broadly and braking hard. They leaned into each other, bracing and bending together as the bus drove toward its unknown destination.

ACKNOWLEDGMENTS

There are a lot of people who fostered this story into being. My agent, Jennifer Unter, took a chance on me, and I'm so glad she did. I thank her for working so hard to shepherd my novel to its audience.

Deanne Urmy, Adrienne Brodeur, and Justine Cook gave me fantastic professional guidance and editorial support. These wonderful women received no particular gain for helping me, but they did it anyway, and I'm endlessly grateful for their kindness.

My wonderful family and friends took time out of their busy lives to read my rough draft manuscripts. Anne Bernheimer, Richard Bernheimer, Doris Caro, Cheryl Edelman, Neal Grossman, Manon Hatvany, Laura Gabel-Hartman, Karen Kraut, Sarah Lewis, John Moschandreas, Carol Moschandreas, Demetrios Moschandreas, Susan Olsen, and Stephanie Poon. Each person's insights were different from the other, and all of it was discerning and sensitive. My story is endlessly better for their collective inspirations. I thank my lucky stars for having such fascinating, wonderful people in my life.

Joanne Nerenberg was always happy to chat with me about Duncan, Emmy, and Jack as though they were real people, and I can't thank her enough for these fun conversations, her careful feedback, and her wise, ebullient encouragement at every single step of this long process. She is the best friend a woman could have.

Drew Fitzgerald is gifted with an amazing design eye and a big heart. He made the dynamics of cover design come alive for me. I am forever grateful.

Several friends were wonderful in providing feedback with the book's design elements. Beth Frankl, Krystyn Van Vliet, Alice Mark, Jenny Berz, Rachel Kalvert, and Kate Dautrich Rubin. I thank them heartily for helping me with hard decisions.

Elaine Lui of Lainey Gossip is someone I've never met and probably never will, but reading her fantastic celebrity gossip blog allowed me to understand that crazy world more than I ever could have without her.

Boston's Grub Street was the best learning environment a writer could hope for. A special thank you to Sophie Powell for her excellent teaching and enthusiastic feedback.

My groovy kids – Justin, Sophia, and Lara – were so patient with me. They understood that Mommy's work was quirky, that it involved long trips to the library, and produced a story about "adult stuff" they weren't supposed to read. I thank them for being such caring and curious kids that they snuck access to the manuscript anyway! They are my treasures.

My husband, Jeff Grossman, read this book a gazillion times and always had whip-smart feedback, whether on character development, pacing, or typos. I thank him for believing in my writing even when I wasn't sure I did. Most of all, I thank him for bringing the best sorts of happiness into my life. He is my life's jackpot.